Born in Dublin, **Oisín McGann** spent his childhood there and in Drogheda, County Louth. He studied at Ballyfermot Art College and the Dún Laoghaire School of Art and Design, and then worked in advertising, design and film animation. He now lives in Drogheda and works as a freelance illustrator and artist. He is the author of *The Gods and Their Machines* and *The Harvest Tide Project* (Volume I in *The Archisan Tales*).

Under Fragile Stone

Stone

THE ARCHISAN TALES

Oisín McGann

THE O'BRIEN PRESS
DUBLIN

First published 2005 by The O'Brien Press Ltd,
20 Victoria Road, Dublin 6, Ireland.
Tel: +353 1 4923333; Fax: +353 1 4922777
E-mail: books@obrien.ie
Website: www.obrien.ie

ISBN: 0-86278-835-8

British Library Cataloguing-in-Publication Data
McGann, Oisin
Under fragile stone. - (the Archisan tales ; v. 2)
1.Fantasy fiction 2.Young adult fiction
I.Title
823.9'2[J]

The O'Brien Press receives
assistance from

1 2 3 4 5 6 7 8
05 06 07 08 09

Editing, typesetting and design: The O'Brien Press Ltd
Printing: Nørhaven Paperback A/S, Denmark

For my little sister, Kunak; the big sister I never had.

Acknowledgements

As ever, I'd like to thank my family for their insightful critiques of the first draft of this story, as well as all those who offered input and advice while I was working on the book, including everyone at the O'Brien Press for their hard work and enterprise. Particular gratitude goes to my editor, Susan Houlden, for her guiding hand during the painful trimming-down process; every wordaholic needs a counsellor. I'm grateful to Joe and Kunak, for their hospitality in giving me a base in Dublin whenever I needed it; it's really meant a lot to me. And finally, a special thank you to my brother, Marek, for all his work on the website (www.oisinmcgann.com); his substantial brain remains an invaluable resource.

Thanks to all of you.

Oisín

CONTENTS

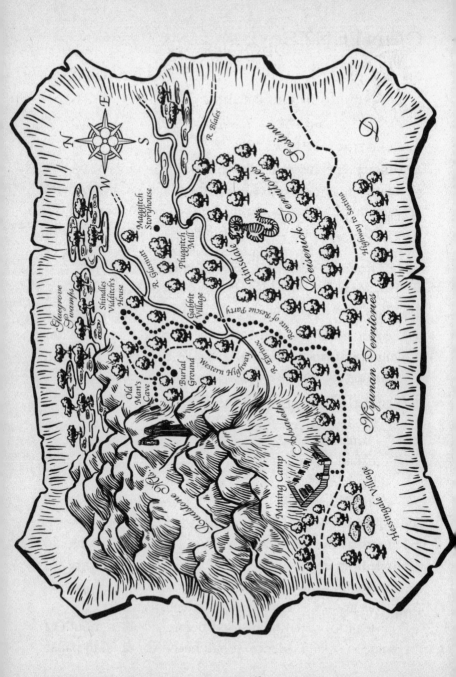

PROLOGUE

The mountain, known as Absaleth, was haunted. The miners had laughed at the stories when they had first heard them months before. Most of the men tasked with extracting the iron ore from this rock were seasoned veterans, with years in the pits behind them. Haunted mines were the kinds of stories that they used to scare their children to bed.

But two months after starting work on this mountain, they had three tunnels on the go; each had got no further than twenty or thirty paces in before it hit problems. Not your average problems either, not unstable ceilings or flooding, no; this dig had thrown up a whole new set of obstacles. Whenever they tried to bore into the rock, the drill bit would make a noise like a child screaming – a sound none of the miners could bear.

There had been cases where workers swore that after managing to open a crack in the walls, the fissure would reseal itself, almost as if it were healing. Sometimes they would sense vibrations in the ore; a low tone would reach their ears, as if from some huge tuning fork, and they would stumble from the mine suffering headaches and toothaches.

The strangest thing, though, was the way the tools rusted. That was just the damnedest thing.

The team of seven men stood before the dark mouth of the mine in solemn silence. It had become a ritual to pause before entering the tunnel, like a stand-off, warriors taking the measure of an opponent. A few of them gazed up at the rock face above the mine, their expressions bitter, but determined. Paternasse, the oldest of the group, regarded the shiny new head of his pickaxe. It was his fifteenth since starting the dig. The others had rusted into powder. In the thirty-six years he'd been digging metal and minerals from the ground, he'd never heard of anything like it.

'Right, let's get started,' Paternasse grunted. 'That pit won't dig itself.'

They marched inside, armed with brand new tools: pickaxes, spades, hammers and wedges and the other trappings of the mining trade. Along with their digging equipment, they each had a helmet with a headlamp, to bolster the glow of their lanterns. One man pushed the cart that carried their heavier gear and the timber supports and would later be hauled up the rails to the surface by a winch, carrying their spoils back out of the tunnel. That was if they managed to get any work done that day.

Paternasse spat on his hands, rubbed the saliva into them to get his palms soft enough for a good grip, then studied the face of the rock for the chink in the mountain's armour that his pick could get its point into.

This cursed hill was still the richest source of iron ore he had ever seen, and he was damned if it was going to get the better of him. Soon they would break its spirit and then they'd really get to work …. He found a thin crack in the rock and swung his pickaxe back over his shoulder. Just as he did, two eyes appeared in the stone and the crack opened into a mouth and screamed. Paternasse gasped and stumbled back, tripping over a water bucket behind him and landing flat on his back. Further down the tunnel, someone else was shouting. A piece of the mine-face the size and shape of a child peeled itself from the rock, dropped to the floor and ran towards the tunnel entrance. Moments later, another one sprinted up from the back of the mine, jumped over him and followed the first. The sounds of giddy, high-pitched laughter reached his ears.

Noogan, the youngest of the miners, ran up and knelt down by his side.

'Jussek?' he asked the older man, concern in his voice. 'You all right?'

Paternasse lay there for a while longer to let his heart calm down. It was beating like the hooves of a racehorse. He was short of breath too; the years of mining had taken their toll on his lungs.

'Just got a fright, lad,' he muttered, sitting up. 'Those blasted Myunans have gone too far this time – too far by half. If they can't keep a leash on their young 'uns, one of those little whelps is going to get hurt down here. I could've killed that one if I'd hit it. Little animal.'

He coughed up some long-lost dust from his lungs, hawked and spat at the rock face.

Noogan looked at the square of light at the end of the tunnel.

'They're not natural, those Myunans,' he said, bitterly. 'The way they can carve themselves into shapes like that.'

'Oh, they're natural all right,' Paternasse sat up and clambered to his feet. 'Natural-born scoundrels. Still, the Noranians'll see to them. If there's one thing Noranians are good for, it's putting people in their place.'

+ + + +

Taya Archisan stifled another giggle as she ran, dodging behind one of the dirt-encrusted wagons that served the mine and ducking underneath it, slipping behind one of its six steel-rimmed wheels to hide. From this vantage point, they could see a long stretch of the palisade fence and the gate that opened onto the road. Lorkrin skidded in behind her, a giddy grin on his face.

'Did you see the look on that old lad's face?' he whispered. 'He nearly jumped right out of his skin!'

The misshapen, stony effect of his flesh receded as he crouched there, the colours of his skin returning to normal and his impish facial features reasserting themselves. Their disguises had been meticulous. Mimicking a mine wall well enough to fool a miner was no easy feat, but they had done it. Sculpting, or 'amorphing', the texture into their skins had taken all their skill and every tool they had, but the effect had been worth it.

The two children were brother and sister, both clad in the garb of their tribe, tunics with cloth belts, Taya in leggings and Lorkrin in trousers. Their clothes and skin had swirling markings, Lorkrin's more angular in blues, greens and greys, Taya's in reds, oranges and browns, and it was difficult to see where their skin ended and their clothes began. Taya's hair was light brown, long and tied back in a braided ponytail, while Lorkrin's was blonde and cropped short. They were both in their early teens, but it would not have been clear to an observer which of them was older, although Taya was a little taller. She was also the one who liked to be in charge, and so was already working out their next move.

They had to get out of the compound, and that meant crossing a wide stretch of open ground to the fence and the trees beyond.

Taya saw the old man Lorkrin had scared walking across to the building that served as offices for the Noranians. He looked serious. She had almost been caught when she jumped out at the group of men who had passed her, but they had been too shocked to grab her. Seeing the expression on the old man's face, she realised how lucky she had been.

'I think we might have gone a bit too far,' she said softly to her brother.

'Nah,' he replied. 'They're not supposed to be here anyway; you know what the elders are always saying. If this lot won't leave by themselves, they have to be made to leave. We're just doing our bit.'

Taya nodded. This was all for good cause. Self-consciously brushing the mine-dust from her hair with her fingers, she cast her gaze around the compound. To their left were the newly constructed buildings, with four trucks lined up outside. Beyond the yellow-brick offices and living quarters, there was the gate, guarded by two Noranian soldiers standing in the wooden tower. More wandered around inside the fence and these were the main problem. The Noranians believed in security and they were good at it. The fence was a wooden palisade twice the height of a man and each pale was sharpened to an evil point at the top. Lorkrin had his tools out and was using a whittler to craft his fingers and toes into hooked claws that would give him a grip on the smooth wood.

Taya was about to do the same when a pair of legs

approached and clambered up onto the wagon. Another pair of legs strode up and around the front, a pair of hands fitted a crank handle into the engine's crankshaft and turned it until the engine coughed and caught. The driver revved the motor while he waited for his passenger to get on board before settling it into a rumbling idle. There was the gnash of worn gears and the smell of burnt bule oil and greasy smoke wafted over them. The two Myunans exchanged glances. Their hiding place was about to drive away.

'They're opening the gates!' Lorkrin hissed. 'We can go with the truck!'

They reached up and caught hold of the steel chassis, lifting themselves off the ground. The truck lurched and started to roll forward, bouncing across the rough surface of the compound and through the open gates to the road. The truck was old, and slow enough for Lorkrin and Taya to drop safely to the ground and scamper into the bushes once they were out of sight of the gates. High with the thrill of their escape, they ran weaving through the trees to the path that would take them back to their village.

1 SOMETHING IN THE GROUND

Marnelius Cotch-Baumen pinched the bridge of his nose and winced. He was getting a beastly headache. The climate of Sestina did not agree with him. It was not as cold as Noran, but it was definitely wetter, and the damp caused terrible clogging in his sinuses. The fact that he had to live in one of the hovels Sestinians called 'manor houses' did not help either. The sooner his new keep was built, the better. As Provinchus of this area, he was entitled to a decent standard of living and his poor health demanded it. He gazed dourly at the woman who stood before his desk. Dressed in unadorned travelling clothes, she was crude and unladylike, with the ever-present Myunan tool roll slung over her back and the unsightly coloured markings arcing across her otherwise attractive face – even running through her long, dark hair in pale streaks. He despised Myunans.

'I'm sure you can understand the dangers of mixing mining and children,' he said to her. 'They are like white wine and red meat: incompatible, and hazardous to the constitution. Out of concern for your youngsters, I would ask that you exercise proper control over them.'

'Our children were not in danger until you started mining in our territory,' the woman replied. 'I would ask that you exercise proper control over your forces … and leave.'

'We have gone over this time and again,' Cotch-Baumen sniffed, dabbing his nose with a handkerchief. 'You hold no title to this land; you have no right to it under law. Indeed, you wouldn't know what to do with land if you did own it. You Myunans wander like a herd of cattle, making no attempt to civilise yourselves. If you want land, apply in writing for a grant of land, like any civilised person.'

'We didn't need *titles* until you concocted them and all the laws are yours! Our people have *always* lived here ...'

'Yes, as I have said, we have gone over this time and again. Your protests have been duly noted. But on the matter at hand, I have asked politely. Now I must insist. Keep your children away from our operations at the mountain or your tribe will be held accountable. You may go now.'

Nayalla Archisan stared down at the Provinchus, struggling to maintain her composure. This thin string of a man had insulted her and dismissed her as if she were a lowly servant rather than an elder of the powerful Hessingale tribe. He was already reading from a report on his desk, paying no more attention to her. She closed her eyes and willed the colours of her face to change. Her flesh paled to whiteness, shadows deepened and in moments, her face bore an uncanny likeness to a human skull. She leaned in close to the Provinchus and her eyes flicked open in their sunken sockets. Cotch-Baumen looked up and gave a start, taken aback by the sight.

'Do you think that planting your flag in our territories will make this land yours?' she hissed. 'Listen to what we are saying. This land delivers dire retribution upon those who abuse it. Do not make enemies of the Myunans.'

Cotch-Baumen sat bolt upright.

'Such theatrics,' he said, flustered. 'Really!'

Nayalla turned and walked out, the skull vanishing from her face. She was done with the Noranian. Now it was time to have a few words with her children.

+ + + +

The episode with the Myunan children had served to release some of the tension the miners were feeling and the rest of the morning had passed without any further mishap. The mines were still so shallow that the miners could come out for lunch to soak up some sunlight and spare their spirits the gloomy darkness while they ate. Noogan decided to stay and work on for a while, encouraged by the progress he had made that morning and eager to chip away more of the slab of hard, grey stone he had uncovered. He was only seventeen, with dark hair, and a face that bore a perpetual gormless expression. He was tall, but still had a boy's build and he was struggling to earn the respect of his workmates. A farmer's son, he had turned to mining when his brothers took over the family plot. Like any young lad, he had made the usual cock-ups as he learnt the ropes and the older men weren't letting him forget them. Working under this mountain made him nervous, and that was causing him to make even more mistakes. Mistakes were not easily forgiven by men who worked in fear of cave-ins and gas poisoning.

A sound made him stop and turn around. He could see nothing in the light of his headlamp, so he picked up the bule-oil lantern and held it out in front of him. The noise was grainy, like sand being poured from a bucket. He ground his teeth together. He knew the rest of the team were up at the mouth of the mine. But there was definitely someone down here with him. The Myunans again. Bloody whelps, he thought as he cast the light of the lantern around. He'd spank them black and blue if he caught them.

A movement on the floor of the tunnel caught his eye and he knelt down. Some of the dust from the ore they had dug out was cascading down the pile of rock and shifting along the floor. Noogan frowned. He hadn't noticed any draught. He wet his finger in his mouth and held it down near the floor, expecting the side facing the draught to turn cold. It didn't. He put his cheek down near the shifting dust. Definitely no breeze. He stood up and shone the lantern on the ground further down the tunnel. The dust and some of the smaller lumps were moving along the ground, like a column of ants. He laughed nervously and thought of going up to fetch some of the others, but his curiosity got the better of him and he followed the trail of iron ore to see where it was going.

It led him to a pit that Balkrelt, one of the other miners, had been working in that morning. It was waist deep and twice as wide. Balkrelt had found a rich deposit there and had been crowing about how he had cleaned it out as he walked up the slope for his lunch. There was another sound coming from the bottom of the pit. Noogan peered in, but the light was still poor and he could not see the bottom properly. The trail of ore fragments was pouring into the hole as if it were trying to refill it. He climbed down into the pit and was astounded at what he found.

The ground was moving beneath his boots, tickling the soles of his feet. It was boiling like water in a pot, but there was no heat coming off it. He put his hand down to touch it and felt it pull at his fingers. He jerked upright, intending to step out of the pit until he knew what he was dealing with, but his feet would not move. He was ankle deep in the ground, his feet stuck as if in a marsh, but this was dry earth. Fear started to rise in his chest. He dropped the lantern, which smashed and went out as he grabbed for the edge of the pit. The earth around his feet was folding in on itself, pulling his feet with it.

'Help!' he screamed. 'Somebody help me! Please …'

He had his elbows on the edge of the hole and it took all his strength to hold himself up. More debris slipped down from the pile of ore and skated along the ground towards him, flowing over his arms and shoulders and into the pit. He shrieked again and heard boots running down the tunnel. His right elbow slipped over the brink and he reached back up and dug his fingertips into the tunnel floor. As more of the ore filled the hole, he could feel the grip lessen on his feet, but now he was buried up to the knees and something was still tugging at his boots.

'Jussek … Balkrelt! Somebody, help!' His other elbow was slipping and the fingertips of his right hand were sliding back. A light appeared and then another, the headlamps of his workmates. Moments later, strong hands were seizing his arms and pulling at him, but at first it seemed the ground's hold was too strong. Then he felt something give and he was hauled out of the hole. He thrashed out, knocking away their hands and backed up against the wall, shivering and close to tears.

'What was it, Noogan?' Balkrelt asked. 'What had a hold of you?'

Noogan's chest was too tight to speak. He knew if he tried to say anything he would start to cry and that would be too much, so he just shook his head and pulled his knees up to his chest. He stared down at his socks and ground his teeth to stop a sob escaping. The earth had taken the ankle-high boots right off his feet.

'I'm going to have to dig all that out again,' Balkrelt moaned. 'What were you up to?'

'Leave it,' Paternasse told him.

'What are you talking about? We've got quotas to make.'

'Fill it in. Put it all back in. Whatever's in there can bloody stay in there. The lad didn't bury himself. Fill the hole in.'

They stood around the small pit, staring down into it in bewilderment and unease. Then they grabbed their shovels and dumped the ore back where it had come from.

+ + + +

Mirkrin Archisan was returning to his village from a market in a local town when he came across a triangle scraped into the clay of the track ahead of him. Glancing around, he frowned, and then rubbed the mark out with his foot. As he wandered back into the glen where their tribe, the Hessin-gales, spent part of the mild Sestinian summers, he spotted his Taya and Lorkrin coming out of the trees nearby. He sighed and beckoned to them.

'You're late for your lessons,' he chided them. 'Where were you? If I find out you were up at the miners' camp …'

'We weren't, Pa!' Taya answered, automatically.

'… I'm going to be very annoyed,' he continued, ignoring her. 'You know you're not supposed to be wandering out of the village with all those Noranian thugs hanging about. They're a bad crowd, and I don't want to see you …'

His voice drifted off as he caught sight of his wife, Nayalla.

She was striding towards the elders' lodge when she saw them. She spun on her heel and marched straight at them, her face a mask of fury. If looks could kill, Taya and Lorkrin's remains would have been spread over a wide area.

'By the gods,' Mirkrin muttered, looking at his wife's expression and turning to his children. 'What did you do?'

Nayalla stopped in front of them and went to say something, but took a breath first. She was almost too angry to speak. Lorkrin and Taya both turned pale.

'You two are …' she started, then took another breath. 'It is going to take you a long, long time to make this right.'

Mirkrin's face darkened.

'What is it?' he asked.

'It has taken us three weeks to get a meeting with the Provinchus,' she growled at the two children. 'It is the first chance I've had to talk to him without having to hold a mob back at the same time. The tribe was counting on me to make him understand the damage he is doing to Absaleth, to our land. I walk in there and have to wait for him to finish being shaved and perfumed by his barber, then wait again as he reads some … some … I don't know – some periodical. Then, when I finally have his attention, he turns around and tells me my *children* have been scaring the living daylights out of some of his miners. This, as far as he is concerned, is all that we need to talk about. I am there to try and stop our land being desecrated and end up getting told off for not keeping control of my children!'

'Ma, it wasn't us …' Lorkrin began.

'Don't even try it!' Nayalla snapped at him. 'Don't even open your mouth! Your class is starting, hurry up over there

21

or you'll be late again. I need to talk to your father.'

Lorkrin and Taya trudged on towards the communal lodge that stood in the centre of the glen. The village was made up of domed lodges; each one roofed with sods of grass and dug in so that part of it lay below the level of the ground. For the children, it was the least interesting place in the world. Mirkrin watched them walk away, and then put a hand on his wife's shoulder.

'They were down in the mines?'

She nodded.

'He said they were hidden against the wall of a tunnel. One of the men almost hit Lorkrin with a pickaxe.'

Mirkrin grimaced and shook his head. He was a burly man, with a mop of dark hair and a strong, square face. He was of a mellow disposition, in stark contrast to his wife, but even he had limits.

'We're going to have to do something serious this time,' he muttered. 'They have to learn. I thought that disaster in Noran would have taught them some sense, but they're as bad as ever. I don't know where they get it from.'

'They get it from us,' Nayalla smiled tiredly. 'Not that they can ever know that, of course. When I think of the stuff we got up to … But they have a habit of getting into trouble with the wrong people. I mean, the Noranians for goodness sake.'

Like their mouldable flesh, Myunan children had very impressionable natures. It would be all too easy for them to pick up bad habits from their new neighbours – particularly Lorkrin, who was developing an unhealthy interest in swords and all manner of other dangerous weapons.

'Oh, I nearly forgot,' Mirkrin looked at her. 'Emos is here. He left his mark on the track for me.'

'I wonder what he wants. It's not like him to leave the farm so close to Harvest Tide.'

'Well, we'd better go and find out; it can't be good, whatever it is.'

'Before or after we punish the brats?'

'Oh, before,' Mirkrin nodded solemnly. 'Best to let them stew for while. Nothing like a bit of anticipation to put a lively fear into them.'

+ + + +

Emos Harprag was Nayalla's brother. He was an outcast, exiled from his tribe and forbidden to have any contact with Myunans after he had mysteriously survived an epidemic that had killed his wife. They feared that he might still be infectious; even if the disease had not killed him he might still be a danger to others. It was believed that he had survived by practising the black art of transmorphing – manipulating lifeless materials like metal or wood as if they were his own malleable flesh – a crime punishable by exile. Transmorphing was considered an assault on nature itself. Nayalla and Mirkrin had kept in contact with him – discretely, so as not to embarrass their tribe – and they knew there was no danger of infection. They had helped him recover from his wife's death and his exile, and he was always there for them when they needed him.

Emos had become something of an enigma. He still practised the transmorphing and he had travelled to more strange lands than any Myunan alive. He had eventually settled down on a farm in Braskhia, giving up the nomadic Myunan lifestyle, but he still went wandering when the mood took him. It could not be a coincidence that he was here now, when the Myunans were facing an invasion of their territory.

Mirkrin and Nayalla walked until they were well out of sight of the village and sat down to wait on one of the fallen monoliths that had once marked the boundaries of their ancestors' territory. They knew Emos would be watching the village and they only needed to wait and he would find them. While they waited, Nayalla told her husband about her audience with the Provinchus.

'By the gods, it was embarrassing,' she sighed. 'I lost the rag in the end. I had to give up or just scream at him. He had no interest in listening to us. We're just cattle to him.'

'It was only going to be a matter of time before they started settling here.' Mirkrin lay back on the stone. 'They've filled every land around them. We don't have the Braskhiams' technology or the Karthars' strength, so the Noranians were bound to turn on us eventually, once they got over their superstitions about us. There's some who're starting to think a fight is the only way to go.'

Nayalla looked up sharply: 'I know that you're not one of them, right?'

Mirkrin shrugged and avoided his wife's gaze.

'How much territory do we let them take, Nayalla? They're destroying the birthplace of our culture – the place that's made us what we are. What will be next? The smelt pools? The birthing glens? How long do we stand for it? '

Nayalla scowled. Beyond the occasional fight between tribes over territory, the Myunans were a relatively peaceful race. She was not averse to a stick-fight every now and then – it kept everyone on their toes – but a fight with the Noranians would be for keeps. And the Noranians were experts in war. The Sestinians had fought for decades against their northern neighbours and the wars had crippled their country. Now they were little more than a Noranian province. The Myunans could not win a war against Noran.

She was spared further brooding by the appearance of her brother over the edge of the trees in the shape of an eagle. He glided down, landing lightly and then slunched, letting his malleable muscles relax to regain his normal form. A lean man with grey, shoulder-length hair and a face marked with a blue, triangular tattoo, he always had the air of someone who knew more than he wanted about the world. Walking over to them with a rare smile on his face, he hugged his sister and then grasped Mirkrin's hand. He stood back after greeting them and hesitated. Emos had been looking after Taya and Lorkrin the previous summer, when they had run away and got involved with an attempt to rescue a gardener from the Noranians. The two children had nearly been killed several times as a result and Emos winced with shame every time he thought of it. Now, he had come bearing more grim news.

'Kalayal Harsq is coming to Absaleth,' he told them, his face even more grave than usual.

'The exorcist from Braskhia?' Nayalla frowned. 'Why is he coming here?'

'The Noranians have contracted him to purge the mountain of its soul,' Emos grunted bitterly. 'It seems they believe in ghosts when profits are at stake.'

'When is he coming?' Mirkrin asked.

'He could arrive at any time. He left Braskhia with his followers two days ago, before I heard the news,' Emos replied. 'I flew out here as fast as I could. He and his people are coming in trucks. He is supposed to pick up a Noranian escort along the way.'

'I've only heard stories about him,' Mirkrin looked out towards the horizon. 'They say he can wipe the life from a land. Fields that he has blessed bear crops with no taste or goodness; lakes and rivers with the purest water carry no fish. Makes me wonder why anybody would want him around.'

'Because forests had to be felled where those fields were planted, and dams had to be built in front of those rivers,' Emos said. 'And for that, part of the land's spirit had to be broken. Going up against nature takes good judgement and a sense of balance. With a man like Harsq, you need neither. And the Noranians are bringing him to Absaleth.'

All three were silent. Nayalla could sense the anger in the two men and it scared her, because she knew that the rest of her tribe were feeling the same. Absaleth was of huge spiritual importance to the Myunans, and the mountain was considered the anchor of this land's soul. That the Noranians were defiling the mountain with their mines was bad enough – she was having trouble keeping the peace as it was. But an exorcism! The men of the tribe would kill anyone who tried such a thing. And the Noranians would know that. They would be prepared.

She looked wearily out towards the tall mountain and wondered how she could prevent her tribe from starting a bloody battle that they could not win.

✦ ✦ ✦ ✦

Taya and Lorkrin sat quietly through their class. Ceeanna, the matriarch of their tribe, was teaching them texturing. She had set them the laborious task of mimicking the bark of the oak tree. Lorkrin worked on his arm listlessly with his routing skewer, pressing ridges into his flesh. By slunching his muscles – relaxing them to make them malleable – he could mould the soft flesh into shape with his tools. The art of amorphing. His tools were a novice set, made eight generations before; he could name all of the previous owners. As with all Myunan tools, the amorite used to make them had come from the open veins in the streams high up on Absaleth. Legend had it that the great prophet Amarrin had come down from the mountain, after weeks of fasting and praying, with the very first set of amorphing tools – tools bestowed upon him by the mountain's spirit.

Lorkrin thought it was a load of rubbish, but would never have said it to anyone but his sister. He crefted his reformed muscles, tensing them so that they held their new shape. It was a half-hearted job; bark was boring, and he just wasn't in the mood.

'I said "oak", Taya,' he heard their teacher say. 'That's more like chestnut – and mouldy chestnut at that. Try paying a bit more attention.'

The two youngsters didn't know what was going to happen to them, but they knew it would be bad. Myunans beating their children was not unheard of, but children soon learnt that they could take a lot of the pain out of a slap by letting their flesh go soft to absorb the blow. Like all skills motivated by the avoidance of pain, it was learned quickly and as early as possible, with the result that slapping Myunan children was considered somewhat futile. Unwilling to raise the levels of pain on their beloved offspring, Myunan parents became more inventive in their punishments instead. Lorkrin and Taya's parents had a wide range of options open to them.

They dragged their feet on the way back to their lodge after class. Mirkrin and Nayalla were sitting facing the entrance as they walked in. The lodge was a low, domed timber construction, covered with a canvas tarpaulin and sods of earth and grass. Inside, earthen steps led to the floor, which was below ground level to help keep the warmth in and a section of canvas hung down over one part of the large room to partition off their parents' bed. This was home. Apart from a single low table, a simple stove, cooking implements and some bits and pieces their mother had picked up on her travels, the room boasted nothing but warmth and a raw animal comfort. Their father, who was the tribe's toolsmith, worked outside for the most part and kept his tools tucked carefully away near his small forge, which he could dismantle when the tribe moved the village. Myunans did not care for collecting things and it showed in the way they lived.

Taya and Lorkrin stood sullenly in front of the hide flap of the door. One look at their parents' faces told them this was going to be bad, that excuses would just draw it out and that they should just fall on their swords and be done with it.

'I'm sorry,' Taya mumbled, looking at her feet.

'I'm sorry too,' Lorkrin mumbled too, staring sideways at the wall.

'Give me your tools,' said Mirkrin.

Lorkrin gaped.

'Which ones?'

'Now don't get smart with me, boy. All of them.'

The two children were stunned. A Myunan without tools was half a Myunan. They would be unable to assume anything but the most basic shapes. They would not be able to play with their friends. In fact, they would not even be able to show their faces in front of their friends. They would only have their colours to hide them when they were away from the village. There were so many places they would not be able to go and things they would not be able to do. It would be like wearing chains.

'You can't!' Taya whined, close to tears.

'You have got to learn,' their mother said, softly. 'You can't go on behaving the way you do.'

'You're not having my tools!' Lorkrin yelled. 'I earned them! You don't have the right!'

'Mind your tone!' Mirkrin warned him. 'Now, hand them over. We won't have any more argument about it. Do as you're told, young lad.'

Lorkrin pulled the straps of his tool roll from his shoulders and threw the pack at his parents' feet. Mirkrin jumped up, but Nayalla grabbed his wrist.

'I hate you!' Lorkrin bellowed, then whipped the heavy hide flap aside and ran out before they could see that he was ready to cry.

Taya slung her pack from her back, stepped forward and dropped it in front of her father, her face frozen as she cast her eyes over her parents.

'I don't hate you,' she said. 'I just think we're *your* fault. So why are *we* always the ones getting punished?'

She turned and walked out after her brother. Mirkrin sighed, shaking his head and flopping down to put his arm around his wife's shoulders.

'Why do I always end up feeling that we come out of these things in worse shape than they do?'

2 A RING OF SKACKS

Evening fell early because of an overcast sky, the sullen, grey clouds blocking out the last light of dusk. This suited the four Myunans of the Hessingale tribe who stood near the top of a bank that overlooked a flat, straight stretch of road. Their skin and clothes reduced to muted earth colours of greys, greens and browns, they waited invisible, watching out for the first sight of Kalayal Harsq. The mumble of distant engines reached their ears and all eyes turned east. There, coming around the side of a hill on the horizon, they saw the twin oil lamps that lit the way for an oncoming vehicle. These were joined by another pair, and another. There was a long column of vehicles rolling down into the valley.

Mirkrin and Nayalla watched the approaching lights with Ceeanna. The matriarch's colours were starting to fade with age, but she had lost none of her strength, or sternness. Standing a little further from the others, the fourth figure was Westram, a tall, commanding man, and the tribe's border chief. Now that the elders had agreed that Harsq had to be stopped, there only remained the question of how. Westram was in favour of attacking the convoy and killing Harsq before he reached the mining compound.

'There are a lot of them,' Ceeanna observed. 'I count a dozen trucks. Why would he need so many?'

'They've sent an entire battlegroup with him,' Mirkrin

sighed. 'Infantry, armoured wagons, even a crossbow turret.'

'So you say Draegar told you about this?' Ceeanna enquired, referring to an old friend of the couple. 'Why didn't he come down to the village? Not worried about being saddled with your little terrors again this summer, is he?'

Nayalla shot a glance at her husband. The tribe were not supposed to know that Taya and Lorkrin stayed with Emos – she always told them that the children spent part of the summer with Draegar. She knew Ceeanna suspected otherwise.

'He was in a hurry towards Brodfan,' Nayalla shrugged. 'Once he'd told us, he had to head on.'

Ceeanna clucked her tongue as she regarded the approaching convoy, and then glanced at Westram. He kept his eyes on the oncoming convoy. Mirkrin spat and said what they were all thinking.

'We can't take on those kinds of odds. They'd slaughter us.'

'What other choice do we have?' Westram responded.

But there was doubt in his eyes. He knew the stakes were too high.

'We'd lose this,' Nayalla shook her head. 'People are going to get killed for nothing.'

'Harsq has a machine,' Mirkrin spoke up. 'He used to rely on blessings alone, but they were too arbitrary. Now he uses science too. He uses one of the engines that make lightning. If we could destroy that, I think it would hold him up … until he got another one, at least.'

'We'd need to find a way in through all those extra guards,' Westram nodded towards the approaching battlegroup.

'I say we don't wait for them to get there,' Mirkrin said.

'We go in now, set ourselves up in hiding before they even arrive. Wait for the machine to be brought in and then destroy it tonight.'

'It would be dangerous, but smarter than fighting them head on,' Ceeanna nodded. 'I am in favour, but we need to act now. Inform the other elders. We must have a decision immediately.'

+   +   +   +

In the trees atop another hill, not far away, two other men took in the scene before them. One was Emos Harprag, his solemn face showing nothing of the feelings that boiled inside him, seeing his tribe before him in dire need and being unable to join them. The other figure was a Parsinor. Taller than his Myunan friend by a head and shoulders and twice as wide across, Draegar hailed from a race of desert-dwellers and it showed in his appearance. His face was broad, his nose and ears small and his wide mouth lined with yellow, crooked teeth. Braided hair swept back and down off his massive skull.

But it was his body that was striking. He had a hinged shell that protected his back. His legs and feet were extraordinary; two legs extended from each hip, joining again at the bottom to a single, long foot on either side. Knobbly armour shielded his shoulders, forearms and thighs and the tops of his feet. If his physique was fearsome, it only reflected his character, for Draegar was a map-maker and he travelled the wildest, most dangerous lands to plot and record them. He was Emos's closest friend and he was here now to help the Myunan outcast in any way that he could.

'That's a lot of soldiers,' his voice grated. 'It's going to take more than brute force to better that lot.'

'They need to destroy the machine,' Emos said quietly. 'They'll see that. But the Noranians will too. This night will be a reckoning. If Harsq isn't stopped tonight, we will have lost Absaleth. I have to help them any way I can. Let's go and stir up some trouble.'

+ + + +

Marnelius Cotch-Baumen watched from the window of the minemaster's office as the vehicles pulled into the compound. He glanced towards the open gate, but the soldiers had things well in hand. The men in the tall, wooden watchtower were his best, and even with the poor facilities of the camp, he was confident that with the extra forces, he could keep a tight rein on things. Checking his appearance in a full-length, gold-framed mirror that travelled with him wherever he stayed overnight, he walked out the door and down the steps to greet his guest.

A small, gaunt-faced man swung down from the lead wagon as it ground to a halt. He was dressed in the blue robes of an eshtran, a Braskhiam priest, and his long black hair was tied in a ponytail. He drew a small canister with a mouthpiece from inside his robe and took a long breath as he gazed up at the mountain. His eyes were wide and bloodshot and had an intensity about them that could have been religious fervour or just plain madness. Cotch-Baumen strode over to him.

'Eshtran Harsq, I am Provinchus Cotch-Baumen. It is a pleasure to meet you, sir.'

Harsq took his hand and nodded.

'That's one cursed hill of rock you have there, sir,' the

priest intoned. 'But we shall remedy that by and by. Brask, the good Lord of the esh, has just the answer for such evil promontories.'

'Excellent, excellent.' Cotch-Baumen clasped his hands together. 'I look forward to seeing you work. I have read all your essays on the spiritual effects of electrical projection and must say that I find them fascinating. I am something of an amateur scientist myself, you see ...'

'Science is only a *lever*, sir, onto which I apply my Master's blessed will. But it is heartening to hear that you are a man of education, for it is only through knowledge and enlightenment that we will subdue the rebellious spirits of the land.'

'Yes, of course,' the Provinchus smiled uncertainly. 'Rebellious indeed. I think you will find our situation an interesting challenge ...'

'I do not seek personal gratification beyond the service of my Lord's will, sir. Rest assured, however, that your great lump of uncooperative rock and iron here will be pacified by this time tomorrow.'

'Excellent, excellent. Would you like to come up to the office and we can discuss the terms of your payment?'

Cotch-Baumen waved the eshtran ahead of him and sighed in disappointment. He had hoped to enjoy some intellectual conversation with a like mind, but it seemed this particular mind was of a slightly distracted nature. When they reached the office, he gestured to the other man to take a seat and he himself sat down behind the minemaster's desk, a rather ramshackle, tradesman's affair, but unfortunately the only one available.

'As an educated man, I'm sure you're aware of the importance of my generator in this operation,' Harsq said, leaning towards him. 'You realise those ungodly Myunans will make every effort to get in here and destroy it.'

'I do,' the Provinchus replied. 'In fact, I would be surprised if there were not one or two already in the compound somewhere. They are sly demons and terribly difficult to find when they have a mind to conceal themselves. However, I have taken measures to ensure the safety of your wonderful device. I can assure you that it will be quite safe.'

He stood up and walked to the window, inviting the eshtran to join him. There, in the compound below them, a van was reversing up to the large generator truck that formed the centre of Harsq's ceremony. Stakes with metal rings had been hammered into the ground around the truck. Unnerving howls and screeches rose up from the back of the van as two soldiers with thick leather gloves and heavy wooden clubs opened the rear door. The animal they pulled from the vehicle was a skack. It took both of them holding onto its two leashes to hold it still. One of the men turned and beat back a second beast which was trying to clamber out. Then they led the first creature to one of the stakes and attached its chain to the metal ring.

The skack was a native of the volcanic region of Guthoque. A mottled purple and grey in colour, it was roughly the size of a large man, but living in one of the most dangerous regions in the Noranian Empire had honed the skack's evolution to a fine point of savagery. Powerful arms hung from its muscled shoulders. Its forearms each ended in a long, curved and serrated claw, which folded down along the forearms when the skack wanted to run on all fours. Its hind legs were short; its back was hunched and covered in spines. Because of the poisonous gases of Guthoque, eyes would have been useless to a skack. Instead, it had a deeply ridged forehead that could detect the reverberations of its high-pitched screeches – much like a bat – and this sense guided it with deadly accuracy. Heavy jaws dominated its short, blunt snout, bearing poisonous, razor-sharp teeth.

Far craftier than most animals, it had lightning-quick reflexes and could track prey better than any dog. Their bloodthirsty instincts made them virtually untameable. The two handlers led one beast after another out to the stakes, until eight skacks formed a perimeter of snarling, screeching death around Harsq's generator truck.

'Praise be to Brask,' said the exorcist.

+ + + +

'Look, skacks!' Lorkrin said excitedly.

He and his sister were ensconced in the branches of a tree on a hill overlooking the compound. They were supposed to be back at home, helping to pack up and move the village in case the Noranians came looking for the tribe after the ambush; but the temptation to see the action had been too great. From the road, they had trailed their parents and the others here, but had lost them when the grown-ups had dispersed into the darkness around the mining camp. They wondered why the adults had let Harsq reach the safety of the compound. Now, there were skacks out in the yard, and the situation looked worse still. Lorkrin had a young boy's fascination with fierce creatures, but Taya just hated them. She could not forget the night they had been chased by these predators the year before and it still gave her nightmares.

'Why have they been spread around that truck?' she wondered out loud.

'To guard against us,' Lorkrin guessed. 'It must be important. I wish we could help.'

He had been making brave noises like this all evening. He couldn't help it. Whenever he shrugged his shoulders to straighten the straps he knew should be there, he noticed they were missing and he became conscious of the space on his back where his pack should be. It was unsettling to remember how helpless he was. To his surprise, the other children had not laughed when they heard. They all agreed that losing your tools was not a laughing matter.

Taya did not reply to his remark. She knew how he felt, even if she didn't feel the need to hide it with bravado. But she did want to do something to help the tribe. In some ways, she and Lorkrin knew more about the Noranians than a lot of the grown-ups. After all, they had nearly been killed by their soldiers several times.

'Do you think they'll stop him?' Lorkrin asked her.

'How should I know?' she snapped back, wishing he would shut up.

Even the soldiers were nervous about the skacks, she noticed, despite the fact that they were chained to posts. Everyone was nervous about skacks. She wondered what the elders were planning to do.

+ + + +

Cotch-Baumen had been mistaken when he had guessed that there were one or two Myunans already in the compound. There were no less than thirteen of the shape-shifters hidden around the mining camp. Some had flattened themselves out against banks of stone or earth, some hung underneath trucks disguised as part of the iron chassis, or as spare wheels. Others were concealed in the shadows of the heavy plant, the cranes, winches and mechanical scoops that threw criss-crossing shadows over areas behind them. Dozens of bule-oil lanterns lit the great yard. But even with the thirty guards patrolling it, there were any number of hiding places for a well-camouflaged Myunan.

Nayalla was hidden in the corner of the yard, her shape melding with a pile of gravel. Her eyes carefully shielded, she watched the skacks being led out and cursed under her breath. The plan had been to wait until the early hours of the morning, when the guards would be less alert and slow to react, then to strike. They had thought causing damage to the truck itself would be the main problem; the generator was a massive, cylindrical device mounted in a steel frame, there was very little about it that would burn, so slinging burning missiles at it had been ruled out. Braskhiam technology was second to none, and they built things to last. Instead, it had been decided that those in the compound would create a diversion, while the main attack would start from above, from the top of the mountain itself. But they had not counted on skacks. She breathed out through her teeth and resigned herself to wait; they would have to deal with the animals when the time came. In the meantime, she stayed perfectly still, watching the Noranian defences unfold.

The signal to begin was the appearance of the harvest star, the brightest star in the east. No sooner had it lifted itself over the horizon, then a fire broke out in the guards' quarters. Men and women came running out, struggling into their armour, some trying to fight the flames, others casting around for an enemy to fight. Another fire flared up in the offices, and by this time some of the miners were up and out. They immediately began filling buckets of water and started a chain up the stairs to the burning room. The soldiers were slower to tackle their fire, being more intent on finding the arsonists. Cotch-Baumen arose from his bed in the mine-master's quarters to find the mining camp in complete confusion. With no time to see to his uniform, he shoved his feet into his slippers and pulled on his dressing gown before marching out, bitterly cursing the Myunans for forcing him to appear before the soldiers in such a state of undress.

'Whipholder Mellev!' he roared.

'Yes, sir, Provinchus!' The burly commanding officer ran up.

'Get your troops in order. Stop wasting time looking for the Myunans. Ensure the safety of the eshtran and the generator truck, and assign a detail to deal with the fire in the guards' quarters! The remaining troops will secure the palisade. Have them stick a spear into anything moving that isn't Noranian. If we can't stop them getting in, we'll bloody well stop them getting out.'

'Yes, sir!'

Even as the officer answered, he noticed fire start to climb several sections of the palisade. The Myunans were attacking from the outside as well. Suddenly hot flames burst from the door of the minemaster's quarters.

'Not my clothes!' Cotch-Baumen shrieked.

Miners rushed to fight the blaze, but it was already raging out of control. The Myunans were determined to burn every building in the compound to the ground.

The soldiers in the watchtower at the gate kept their heads, loading their crossbows and seeking out their first targets. But with their attention drawn into the camp by the fires, they failed to see the Parsinor at the foot of the tower. The desert-dweller was up the ladder and among them before they knew it, swinging sword and battleaxe and bellowing his tribal battle cry as he waded into them. All around the perimeter of the mining camp, soldiers found themselves fighting shadows – camouflaged Myunans attacking from the dark, their faces sculpted into fearsome battle-masks.

In the midst of the chaos, no one in the compound heard the rush of air over wide wings, and only the skacks looked up in time to see three figures dropping towards the top of the generator truck. Mirkrin, Westram and Ceeanna had shaped their arms, chests and backs into wings and their feet into powerful claws. Westram carried a large bottle of the volcan acid that Mirkrin used in his toolsmithing. He dropped onto the top of the machine and slunched into his normal form as the other two swung away to distract the skacks.

Westram threw the raging animals a wary glance, trying to block out their constant screeches as he strode forward to find the controls for the machine at the end of the truck. Pulling a sturdy brace from his tool roll, he leaned down and prised off the cover panel to expose the bare mechanical workings underneath. A skack leapt at him, causing him to jerk back, but Ceeanna dived in and kicked it in the head, knocking it away. Westram plunged the brace into the workings, breaking up what he could. Then he uncorked the bottle and poured acid over the whole mess, watching it dissolve into metal sludge.

Ceeanna and Mirkrin were struggling to keep the skacks back. Their chains were long enough to allow them to reach the top of the machine and it would only be a matter of time before one of them managed it. A crossbow bolt struck the metal near Westram's shoulder and he rolled away in alarm, spilling some of the acid on his hand. He cried out and wiped the burning hand on his tool roll. Another of the arrows buzzed past his face. He turned to see a soldier about sixty paces away, her foot holding down the nose of the crossbow as she pulled back the cord to reload it. Ceeanna wheeled around and swept down towards her.

'Ceeanna, no!' Mirkrin called after her, jinking to one side to draw off the snapping jaws of a skack.

The soldier saw the ageing Myunan coming and smoothly finished loading her crossbow. Then she raised it and fired the bolt straight into Ceeanna's chest. The Myunan's momentum carried her on towards the soldier and she crashed to the ground, her limp body sliding up against the woman's feet. Two of the skacks raced forward to try and seize the easy meat, but their chains pulled them up short.

The soldier reloaded and took aim at Mirkrin. But before she could take her shot, a nightmarish winged creature suddenly crashed down on her, throwing her backwards and seizing her crossbow with four writhing tentacles. It was a jankbat, another native of Guthoque, and it had a triangular brand on its bony, spine-laden face. It pulled the weapon apart and swept on to attack other soldiers who tried to take aim at the saboteurs.

Mirkrin wanted desperately to go to Ceeanna's aid, but he was now on his own against the skacks. Turning his back on his friend, he flew circles above the animals, dodging left and right, infuriating them, his shoulders aching, his back and chest ready to cramp.

Westram was satisfied with his damage of the controls, but

there was still the generator's engine. He could see the fuel tank down on the side of the vehicle. If he could reach the cap … He pulled a tinderbox from his pack. He heard the metal slap of a chain and turned to see a skack advancing along the top of the truck towards him. He hurled the last of the acid at it, and then threw the bottle, making it stumble backwards off the roof. Another vaulted up to take its place. With Ceeanna gone, Mirkrin was losing ground to the beasts. He swooped in and delivered a kick to the skack's ribs. It staggered sideways and, finding nothing on the smooth metal to grip, slipped down the curved side of the generator to the ground below.

Westram turned his attention back to the fuel cap of the engine. He could just reach it. His fingertips touched the knurled disc. A serrated claw slammed into his forearm and dragged it downwards. He slipped off the top of the generator and into the clutches of a snarling skack. Mirkrin caught his foot and hauled upwards, but the skack had the better grip and was not about to let go. Westram screamed and thrashed wildly as the animal's jaws bit into his shoulder and held on. With his teeth clenched and every muscle straining to its limits, Mirkrin heaved his friend upwards.

Another skack leapt at them and got a grip on the first one's leg, and Mirkrin was lost. The weight dragged them all to the ground and he kicked desperately at the animals that came at him. Two more skacks piled on top of Westram, tearing in with claws and teeth and his screams rose to a piercing pitch and then went quiet. Mirkrin could not get to his feet while he was kicking out at his attackers and so was unable to fly. He dragged himself backwards to get out of reach of the animals' chains, but his wings made him slow and clumsy. A skack was making straight for him, but was suddenly shoved aside by another winged Myunan. Nayalla banked around and grabbed Mirkrin's shoulders, driving down hard with her wings to get enough lift to pull him from the ground. More soldiers were becoming aware of the fight over the generator and crossbow bolts started shooting past them.

The jankbat dived down at the soldiers, scratching and clawing at their faces with tentacles lined with claws. Other Myunans joined in the fray, attacking the soldiers in a range of winged shapes. Nayalla hauled her husband upwards into the dark sky, sweeping out over the trees to lose their silhouette against the hills so that they could no longer be seen. She released her grip and followed him as he glided wearily to the ground. They watched from the hillside as the tattooed jankbat made a pass over the remains of Westram's corpse, and then flew down and seized Ceeanna's body, picking it from the ground and carrying it out over the palisade.

Whistles sounded: the signal for the Myunans to fall back. All over the compound, flickers of movement could be seen as some of the camouflaged figures slipped over the palisades or through the burnt gaps; others scaled the steep face of the mountainside and the rest took to the sky. The Noranians turned their defences outwards, rushing to shore up the holes in the fence and make ready the perimeter in case another attack should come at them from out in the darkness.

3 ELECTRICAL EXORCISM

Once the skacks had been safely reined in, Harsq surveyed the damage to his machine, shining a lantern over the ruined control mechanisms.

'Well?' Cotch-Baumen demanded impatiently. 'Can you fix it?'

The eshtran's brow furrowed and he grimaced.

'I could patch together some of it, Brask willing. I have a few of the parts. But I need copper wire, a forge and something with which to make moulds, and a drill with a bit that can bore through steel.'

The Provinchus looked to the minemaster, who nodded.

'Yessir, we have it all but the copper. There's not much of that hereabouts.'

'How about gold?' Harsq asked. 'That'd be even better.'

'The frame of my mirror was gold.' Cotch-Baumen snapped his fingers at the minemaster. 'It is ruined, useless to me now. You may melt down the remains and make the wire.'

'Then I can fix it,' the eshtran said.

'Have it functioning by this evening,' the Provinchus insisted, and then raised his gaze to the whipholder, who stood to attention nearby. 'Are the fences fixed?'

'Just about, sir,' the officer replied. 'We're making the last repairs now.'

'When they are, release the skacks outside the compound. They have a taste for Myunan meat now. Let's see if they can find some more. The curs will have left spies to see whether or not they have succeeded. It is imperative that they do not make another attempt to impede us before the ceremony. Leave the skacks outside until the exorcism is complete.'

'Yes, sir.'

'At dawn, I want you to take the skack-keepers with two of their animals, along with some troops, and find the Myunan village. We shall return their compliment by burning it to the ground.'

'Yes, sir.'

Cotch-Baumen looked distastefully at his dressing gown, now blackened and grubby. With his wardrobe burned, he would be reduced to wearing one of the whipholder's ill-fitting uniforms. It was unpardonable.

'And Whipholder?'

'Yes, sir?'

'Ensure the rabble burn with it.'

'Yes, sir.'

+ + + +

Taya and Lorkrin were perfectly still up in the boughs of a tree that overlooked the yard. They had moved closer during the night to get a better view of the attack and were only a stone's throw from a section of fence that had been set on fire. Now soldiers were moving around the gap with lanterns, replacing or reinforcing the burnt pales. The two children could not leave their hiding place for fear of being seen by them. Dawn was approaching and with no tools to disguise themselves, they would only be able to rely on their colour camouflage in the light of day, an unsettling situation for a hunted Myunan.

'How long does it take to fix a jaggin' fence?' Lorkrin muttered.

'They're almost finished. Can you see what they're doing over at that truck?'

'They're all standing around talking. One of them looks like he's havin' a go at fixing it.'

'That can't be good.'

'No.'

They had seen Ceeanna and Westram die, and the shock of it was still sinking in. Part of each of them still believed they would be back in class that afternoon, learning texturing from Ceeanna, or birdcalls from Westram. It didn't seem real that they were gone.

Neither of the youngsters knew why the truck was so important, but if the damage Westram had done could be fixed, then the tribe needed to know. And Lorkrin and Taya would tell them, as soon as they could get out of their tree.

'Did you see that jankbat?' Taya whispered.

'Yeah, it was Uncle Emos, wasn't it? And I'm sure that was Draegar beating up the guards in the tower.'

'What're they doing here?'

'Same thing everyone else is, I suppose.'

Just as the soldiers were finishing, another came jogging up and said something to the men on the outside of the fence. The group hurriedly packed up their tools and made their way back to the gate. Lorkrin heaved a sigh of relief and began to climb down, but Taya stopped him. She could see the gateway from her vantage point and she saw the skacks' van reverse up and manoeuvre the rear door into the gap between the two sturdy wooden gates. Six of the eight skacks were pushed out by their handlers, each one sniffing the terrain and then bounding off into the trees in a different direction.

Then the gates were closed and barred.

'Aw, bowels!' said Lorkrin. 'There's no way I'm getting down now.'

'How do they get the things to come back?' Taya thought aloud. 'It's not like they can be *trained*, is it? Are they just going to let them loose for good?'

'Hajam weed,' Lorkrin told her. 'They put it in their food. The skacks get addicted to it. If they don't come back, they get sick.'

Taya stared dejectedly at how her smooth skin stood out against the rough texture of the bark. For a Myunan, being unable to fit into their environment wasn't just a survival issue; poor camouflage was considered uncouth and ugly.

'I wonder how long it takes them to get sick?' she muttered.

'We may have to find out.'

+ + + +

One by one, the Myunans appeared in the weak light of dawn. The sheltered clearing had been the agreed meeting place for everyone to gather after the attack on the mining camp. Some were injured, most blackened with soot and smoke. Not everyone had heard about Westram and Ceeanna, and as word spread, the mourning began.

Nayalla and Mirkrin heard that three others had also been killed, cut down as they started the fires at the palisade. Everyone was exhausted and Mirkrin, in particular, was devastated by what had happened. He kept playing the events of the night back in his head to see if there could have been some way he could have prevented the deaths of his friends. If only he had been quicker to pick up Westram, or stopped Ceeanna flying straight at that soldier … there must have been something that he could have done. Nayalla leaned her head against his shoulder. She had tried to comfort him, but words could only sound hollow at a time like this.

Once everyone had been accounted for, they set out to catch up with the rest of their tribe, which was already making for the mountain refuge of Garrain. The Noranians would be out for blood, and the children and the elderly had to be taken to safety. They had left lookouts to watch the compound in case the generator was repaired, but they could not continue the fight for their mountain until the weakest in their tribe were out of reach of their enemies. It would be a long time before this land saw peace again.

It was mid-morning by the time they had found the tribe, the horses and carts loaded with the dismantled lodges and the villagers' other belongings. One of the elders, Tennu, saw Mirkrin and Nayalla coming and hurried over.

'Taya and Lorkrin are missing,' she told them, her face drawn with worry. 'Some of the other children said they heard about the ambush and followed you. I'm so sorry. We only noticed when we started to pack up, we … we should have been watching them more closely. We've sent out some people to look for them.'

Nayalla put a hand to her mouth and turned to look back along the trail. Mirkrin just closed his eyes and had to sit down.

'The Noranians have let the skacks out,' Nayalla said almost to herself. 'There will be soldiers out hunting us now too. How are we going to find them in time?'

'They have no tools,' Mirkrin rasped.

Tennu was taken aback.

'Why not?'

'We took their tools off them,' Nayalla told her, her voice cracking as she spoke, 'as punishment for going into the mines. And we thought it would make them stay put.'

'We have to go back and find them.' Mirkrin got to his feet. 'Nayalla and I will go alone. You take the others on to the hills. We'll see you back at the meeting point when the tribe is safe.'

'Bring them home safe.' Tennu hugged them both. 'We'll be praying for you.'

The two parents took some things from their cart and packed them into bags that they slung onto their backs, and then they headed off back towards the soldiers, the skacks and their sacred mountain.

+ + + +

The skack had found a scent. It snuffled around the dead leaves and undergrowth, trying to find out which way the prey had gone. It was definitely prey. There were only two kinds of animals in the world according to the skack's mind: prey and not prey. It had tasted some of this kind of prey already this morning and the taste had been strange, not like normal meat. But meat all the same. The meat from earlier had thrown something in the skack's face, something that burned but wasn't hot and now it could not smell very well and its face itched and stung. Not being able to track the new prey was starting to aggravate it. It felt around with its sound, but could sense only trees. There was little prey in the ground and the bushes around it, but it was not hungry enough to bother with that yet. It wanted the bigger, strange new meat.

✦ ✦ ✦ ✦

Lorkrin barely dared breathe. The skack was right below them, sniffing the ground and rubbing its face with its arms as if it had an itchy nose that wouldn't go away. The creature lifted its head and screeched into the forest. Taya hung onto the trunk behind her brother, pressing herself into it as tightly as she could. Their camouflage colours were useless against the skack – it did not see anything; it felt out things with its shrill cries. It aimed a string of high-pitched clicks up into the trees and then froze. It made the noise again, and this time Lorkrin was certain he felt the pulses of sound hit him. The skack edged towards the tree, sniffing. It was raising its claws to start climbing when something distracted it. It turned its head to the side and then ducked suddenly into some bushes and went quiet.

A stooping figure came into view among the trees. It was a lean Myunan with grey hair and a triangular tattoo on his face – their Uncle Emos. He had found their trail and was tracking them. Lorkrin and Taya nearly called out, but then realised the skack could scale their tree in moments if it heard them. They stayed silent, not knowing what to do. If they shouted out, the beast would get them. If they didn't warn their uncle, their trail would lead him right up to where the predator was hiding. Then Lorkrin had an idea. He concentrated for a moment and turned bright red from head to foot. Taya smiled and changed to a brilliant orange hue.

The bright colours caught Emos's eye and he spotted them up in their hiding place, but he stayed where he was, reading the sign for danger. He reached behind him and drew out a knife, searching warily for the threat. Putting a hand to his mouth, he gave a sound like a birdcall, as if warning someone nearby. Taya willed a rough spearhead to appear on her back in yellow, its point aiming in the direction of the skack. Emos's eyes found the bush, but dropped away and he straightened up and strode off in another direction.

+ + + +

More prey. The skack stayed crouching in the bush, unable to decide whether to follow this one, which moved like it was hunting and might put up a fight, or see what was in the tree. It slunk out of the bush and crept after the moving prey. It felt ahead with its sound, using its highest pitch so the prey could not hear. Hunting pitch.

The prey had got further away, but the skack was not worried. It could feel the meat clearly in the trees ahead. It crawled faster, keeping low to the ground as it closed on its victim. Its face itched worse than ever, but it ignored the irritation. It was about to make a kill – the only thing that mattered was the prey. It got close enough to make the final sprint, squatting in readiness to dash the last few paces for the kill …

+ + + +

Emos was amazed at how little sound the skack made behind him. If the children had not warned him, it could have caught him off guard. It was close now. He knew its sound vibrations would be measuring the distance to him. It was now or never. He stopped and turned around, knife out before him, feet planted in a fighting stance.

Just as the skack was about to pounce, it stopped, spinning instead to avoid a battleaxe that flew at it from behind. The axe caught it in the shoulder rather than the back, but still sent it sprawling. Draegar launched himself out of his hiding place behind a rotten, fallen tree, falling on the creature before it could get up. He swung his short sword at the animal's neck, but the skack deflected it with one of its long claws. Emos wrenched the axe from its shoulder and as it turned to lash out at him, Draegar lopped its head off with a backhand swing of his blade. The lifeless body slumped to the ground.

'Damn it all, they're quick!' the Parsinor breathed.

'There's more of them around and they'll smell the blood,' Emos said, wiping off the axe. 'Taya and Lorkrin are back there. Let's get them and leave before we run into any more of these things.'

✦ ✦ ✦ ✦

Paternasse stood with the other miners behind the cordon of soldiers, watching as Kalayal Harsq and his fawning, sycophantic disciples set up his machine. The circle of Noranian troops kept everyone back from the Braskhiam truck and its feverish group of priests. Up in the watch-tower, the Provinchus and some of his officers sat drinking wine and watching through spyglasses as if this were some kind of theatre. There was something unholy about all this, the old man thought to himself. He had been a miner all his life, like his father before him, like all the men in their family, and it had given him a healthy respect for the land they worked under. This mountain had proved to be the hardest, most unforgiving mound of rock it had ever been his misfortune to dig into, and it had beaten them down ... but that was mining. Some places gave up their loads easily; others held onto them like grim death. It was just the way of things, that was all. But what this Braskhiam was doing now, this disturbed Paternasse more than he liked.

They had bored holes in the walls of number two tunnel, the middle one, and now cables were being run from terminals on the machine to pins driven into the holes. The eshtran had spent all day repairing the damage the Myunans had caused, but now the 'dynamo', as the priest called it, was ready and he could perform his ceremony. Paternasse had seen into the machine while Harsq had been working on it. The body contained a drum wound thousands of times around with copper wire. He had seen one of the eshtran's tools flip out of his hand at one point and stick to a part inside the drum; the thing used magnets too.

Now, the eshtran put the machine into gear and the heavy steel body vibrated as the drum inside began to turn, slowly at first, then faster and faster. As the rumble of the mechanism increased, Paternasse and the others sensed a fuzz in the air, like the atmosphere before a thunderstorm, and some of them looked up into the darkening evening sky, but saw few clouds.

The disciples stood around the machine, hands raised in the air, eyes fixed on their master, mouths chanting praises to Brask. The exorcist himself, dressed in extravagant ceremonial robes, stood out in front, between the truck and the mouth of the mine. His face was alive with religious fervour, his body tensed with passion. As the tumult grew, a combination of the chugging engine, chanting voices, crackling static and the spinning hum of the dynamo, Harsq stopped reciting prayers and instead called directly to his god.

'Lord Brask, give these hands the power to smite the evil from this cursed mountain, that these good men may dig in peace!'

'Help them Lord!' the chorus sang. 'Help them dig in peace!'

Harsq reached up and his fingers curled as if he were clutching something invisible in the air.

'Give me the power, Master!' he roared. 'Make me the instrument of Your will!'

With each cry that burst from him, the chorus answered. The eshtran led his followers in an escalating fever, his bellowing growing more and more intense.

'I feel Your power in my veins, Master!' he cried. 'I feel Your strength in my bones!'

'He feels the power,' the disciples sang. 'Praise be to Brask in the Esh!'

Harsq fell to his knees, planting his hands on the ground before him. His eyes closed, he intoned a string of arcane, guttural words, repeating them over and over again. The disciples fell silent, one of them moving to stand by the patched-up controls of the generator. Harsq dug his fingertips into the clay, his voice rising, his face expressionless as if he were in a trance. Then he lifted his hands up again and thrust them in the direction of the mine.

'In the name of the Lord Brask of the Esh, I drive the evil from this rock!'

The priest at the controls threw the lever and there was a crackling of power. Paternasse felt the hairs along his arms and neck stand up; the air was charged with energy. The generator hummed, then whined and sparks spat from the mouth of the mine where the pins entered the walls. At every joint of every cable, electricity arced out, lighting up the evening sky. A deep bass sound began under their feet and even the soldiers looked down in consternation. The sound grew louder and a shudder ran through the land.

Paternasse could feel it in his bones; it made him feel dizzy and sick with its deep vibrations. Two of the men behind him fell over, disorientated.

Harsq lifted his hands once more and the priest at the controls threw the lever back to cut off the power. Another priest took the engine out of gear and the drum began to slow. As the noise of the machine faded, no other sound intruded. There was complete silence in the compound once the engine was shut down. Harsq, utterly exhausted, was about to get to his feet, when he hesitated. A hairline crack in the ground split its way from the mouth of the cave and stopped between his knees. He stared down at it and frowned. The eshtran looked tired and disturbed. One of his disciples came forward, threw a blanket over his shoulders and took his arm to support him as they walked away.

'What was all that?' Noogan wondered weakly. 'Is that it? Is the mountain safe now?'

'He's done something to that bloody hill, lad,' Paternasse replied, shaking his head. 'But I'll be damned if I know what it was.'

✦   ✦   ✦   ✦

Nayalla fell forward and vomited. Mirkrin was already on his hands and knees, retching. The last whines of the dynamo died down and left an eerie silence hanging over the valley.

'By the gods, he did it,' Mirkrin gasped, wiping his mouth.

Nayalla couldn't speak for fear of throwing up again. The surge of the mountain's deep, bass moan had sent a wave of nausea through them, and now she shivered as she suddenly turned cold. Mirkrin crawled up and collapsed beside her.

They were high up on the side of the mountain, overlooking the mining camp. They had watched in horror as they realised that their attack the night before had failed.

'They have Absaleth,' Nayalla said at last. 'What do we do now?'

Mirkrin felt empty, drained of any will to fight.

'Let's just find Lorkrin and Taya and go home.'

+ + + +

Emos sat with his head in his hands, not saying a word. Taya and Lorkrin exchanged looks. They sensed that what they had just witnessed was bad, but could not say why. They had camped out in the shelter of some ancient cairns on a hilltop. The hill was high enough to allow a partial view of the valley they had spent all day walking away from. Flashes of what looked like lightning had caught their eyes and a low, moaning sound had set their teeth on edge. Draegar had sworn softly to himself, but Emos was visibly shaken.

Their uncle eventually lifted his head and stood up, pulling some food from his pack. He started tearing up some pieces of bread and buttering them, acting normally once more, but his face was still pale. They had a simple meal of bread, smoked meat and cheese. There was very little talk, even from Draegar, who would normally have had a story to tell the children. They lit no fire, wary that the light might attract attention, but Taya and Lorkrin soon fell fast asleep despite the chill, exhausted after the events of the night.

'What are you going to do?' Draegar asked, once he was sure they had nodded off.

Emos shrugged. Tribal law demanded the death of Harsq and anyone else responsible for the sacrilege that had just been committed. It was a crime that struck at the heart of Myunan culture. But he was no longer part of the Hessingale tribe, or its culture.

'I'm going to see the children get home,' he said finally.

4 WEAKENED STONE

Something moved in the pile of rusted tools. Along with the blades of shovels and the heads of pickaxes, there was any number of other objects that had been ruined by the mountain's decay. There were also bits and pieces of scrap that had been thrown there as the pile grew and became a garbage dump. Now the heap was even bigger because all the debris from the fire had been dumped here too. In amongst all this junk, something moved. It was a length of baling wire. It wriggled slowly like a worm through the red-brown building site of its world, every movement strained, as if the rigid wire were resisting its own motion.

The piece of wire nosed up against the blade of a trowel and painstakingly wrapped itself around the haft. Once it was satisfied with its grip, it crawled on, dragging the trowel with it. It crossed the path of another wriggling piece of wire, carrying a rusty bolt. They both continued on their courses. At one point, the trowel clanged against the burnt frame of a mine cart. The wire froze. Gradually, it slithered on, collecting more items – tools, nuts and bolts, hinges, brackets – criss-crossing over other snaking wires intent on their own searches.

+ + + +

The remaining miners' hut was the only habitable building

left in the mining camp, so it had become the home for the officers. The miners and their possessions had been distributed between soldiers' tents, the stores sheds, the workshops and the backs of two of the trucks. They had learned long ago not to complain about being second-class citizens – most of them were Sestinian, and it came with the territory.

Paternasse woke up on the hard, lumpy floor of a tent and stretched, rubbing his hands through his shock of grey hair. He groaned as his old body accused him of betrayal, weighing him down with all the aches and stiffness it could muster. He rolled over, looking blearily at the crack of light at the edge of the tent flap, seeing the familiar yellow-grey glow of dawn. His bunch always got to work at dawn, but with all the faffing about with the soldiers and that twisted priest of theirs, he knew they'd be making a late start. Besides, he had no heart for it today, so he stayed under the blankets, shifting his rolled-up coat to a more comfortable position under his head.

Halerus Jube, a miner who led one of the other teams, was sleeping next to him. He stirred, opened his crusty eyes and yawned through his beard.

'I can't be havin' with this sleepin' on the floor nonsense,' his voice slurred.

'Tem dah ta ah gug lawg's and massas,' Paternasse grunted back.

'Put your damned teeth in, Jussek, I can't understand a blessed word you're sayin'.'

Paternasse reached over to a tin cup of water near his head, took a sip, swilling the water around his mouth to moisten his gums, then stuck his fingers in the cup and took out the false teeth, carved from bexemot bone. He put them in his mouth and worried them into place. His round, worn face had a terrible sunken look without them.

'I *said*, "tell that to our good lords and masters", dolt.'

'Can't be havin' with them, neither.'

'Oh, you're a mornin' person and no doubt.'

They both lay beneath their blankets, uncomfortable on the hard floor, but reluctant to face the chill morning. A foot-soldier lay on the far side of Jube, snoring unevenly.

'Can't take much more of that snorin',' Paternasse groaned. 'Might go and clear my bowels.'

'There was absolutely no need to tell me that.'

+ + + +

Nayalla and Mirkrin had spent the night searching around the camp, using all their stealth to avoid being spotted by the soldiers inside the compound or the wandering skacks outside. In the early hours of the morning, they found where Lorkrin and Taya had sneaked in a few days earlier, the children's footprints still visible near a hole dug under the fence. The tracks were definitely old, but the two parents could not take the chance that the children had not found their way into the compound again. They decided to search inside. Once in, they lost the trail, but kept looking anyway.

In the first light of sunrise, they found tracks again outside the entrance to the middle tunnel, the one where the exorcism had been performed. Again, the tracks were old, but there were dozens of sets of footprints going in and out of the tunnel and finding a single trail would have been next to impossible.

'It's getting too light,' Mirkrin said softly. 'We can't stay here.'

'Just a quick look,' Nayalla urged him. 'Just to the end of the tunnel. It won't take long.'

'We can't even use a light,' Mirkrin argued. 'They're not here.'

'If you were them – out on your own – where would you be after what's happened?'

Mirkrin shoulders heaved in surrender. She was right. They'd want to see how Absaleth had been conquered.

+ + + +

Paternasse's team gathered in front of the mouth of the mine, gazing up at the mountain and then down into the black depths of the tunnel. The hole did not have the same menace that it had exuded the day before. Something had changed, but it was not for the good. Today, the hole had the air of a grave about it.

They marched down the tunnel, Paternasse running his fingers along the stone, brushing over the timbers that shored up the walls and ceiling. It felt wrong, this ground. It felt dead. They've driven the soul from it, he thought to himself.

The air in the tunnel was chilly and damp, and water dripped down the walls. The further in they went, the colder it got. Their headlamps and lanterns shone on the gleaming, dull, grey stone, but did little to lift the gloom about the place. Above the sound of their footsteps and the cart's wheels on the rails, Noogan started whistling.

Paternasse hawked and spat out some of his lung's store of dust, lifting his hand to the wall again. The place gave him the shivers now. His hand brushed across a warm, dry section of stone. He stopped, looked at where his fingers were touching the wall and up into a pair of eyes. He slammed his elbow into the rock at chest height and a figure grunted and leaned out from the wall.

'Myunans!' he bellowed, grabbing hold of the shape-shifter.

Mirkrin got one hand free and landed a blow across the older man's face, knocking his helmet off, but the miner held on. Nayalla got an arm around Paternasse's neck and pulled him backwards, all three of them toppling over. The other miners were around them now, some laying in with kicks and punches on the Myunans, the rest just hurling abuse.

Nobody noticed the first tremor.

The second one was bigger and dust fell from the roof of the tunnel. The miners froze. Paternasse pushed Mirkrin away. A third shudder ran through the ground and suddenly every miner was pushing past the fight and running up the tunnel. Mirkrin grabbed Nayalla's hand and they took off after them. The Myunans were light on their feet, faster than the Sestinians and had overtaken half the pack when there was a bone-shaking crack and the wooden supports ahead of them gave way. The roof collapsed in a cloud of stone shards and dust. One of the miners was caught under the falling rock, his scream cut off almost instantly.

'Back!' Paternasse yelled. 'Get back down the tunnel!'

They all turned and started running, coughing and gagging in the dust-filled air. Another section of roof came crashing down behind them and two more men were swallowed beneath it. The noise was horrendous. Mirkrin pushed Nayalla ahead of him, his eyes darting up to the wooden beams above him, trying to gauge their strength in the bouncing, jerky light of the remaining miners' head-lamps. He heard wood splitting, the air pressure changed and with a desperate cry, he shoved his wife forward as the roof crashed down around him. He was trapped; in a final effort, he slunched and shut his mind to the pain as his world crushed in on him.

+ + + +

The men started digging as soon as they were sure the trem-ors had stopped. They waved Nayalla back, telling her this was best left to them. She was sobbing, distraught at the sight of the mound of rubble that had buried her husband. Another of the miners had been caught too, leaving three to dig desperately, in the slim hope that some of their friends might still be alive. They had pulled neckerchiefs over their noses and mouths to protect against the dust and Nayalla pulled a cloth from her pack and did the same. The air was thick with it, making the thin light from the two headlamps and the single lantern seem even weaker still.

Paternasse and Noogan hoisted a slab of stone aside, and then Paternasse called through a small gap between two more chunks of rock.

'Shout if you can hear us! Can anybody hear us?'

There was no reply. Nayalla slumped to the ground in despair.

'Can anybody hear us?' Paternasse yelled again, his voice cracking. 'It's Jussek! Shout out if you can hear this!'

He stopped and put his ear to the gap to listen.

'I can hear something,' he told them. 'I can hear breathing. Help me move this.'

Noogan got on the other side of the piece of stone that

Paternasse was gripping and they hauled it aside. Sticking out from under the slab behind it were four fingertips. Nay-alla gasped.

'Mirkrin!'

'He can't be alive under that,' Paternasse stared aghast at the massive boulder that lay on top of the Myunan.

'I can hear him breathing, Jussek,' Noogan said.

'We need something to lever it up,' Dalegin, the third man, spoke up. 'He's not going to be breathing much longer with that sittin' on top of 'im.'

+ + + +

Mirkrin was barely conscious. He tried to open his eyes, but he couldn't. He tried moving, but he couldn't do that either. He could breathe in thin, tight gasps of air, but it was as if something was holding his lungs closed. The memory of what had happened came slowly back to him. He had been caught under a cave-in. The reason he wasn't dead was because he was Myunan. His body had been squashed by the rocks, but he could not be broken or crushed nearly as easily as a human could. There had been enough space under and between the lumps of debris that fell on him to let his malleable body make space for his brain and his lungs and the other, more vulnerable bits of him that could not be flattened out quite so much as the rest of his body.

Along with the memory came the pain. Every inch of him was under unbearable pressure. He felt it most in his head and his chest – the terrifying, helpless feeling of being trapped, knowing most of his body had been reduced to a thin skin, the hard edges of the rocks piercing right through in places. He tried to scream the pain away, but he could barely breathe. Myunans could go some time without air, but he was buried beneath a mountain of rock. Nayalla was probably nearby, suffering the same fate. Nobody was coming to get them out. He tried to scream again; his thoughts faded away from him and he surrendered to unconsciousness.

+ + + +

They used the split end of a broken support timber to prise the slab a hand's width off the ground, and then wedged it with other rocks. Sliding the shore further under, all three men got their shoulders under the other end of their lever and roared as they heaved it upwards. Nayalla crawled in under the precariously raised boulder and carefully peeled her husband from the ground, quickly checking to see if any part of him had been torn away, relieved to find that it hadn't. She dragged him out and clear of the three miners. The strain showing on their faces, they eased the boulder to the ground again.

Then they stood back in shock at the sight of Mirkrin's body. Apart from the odd lump here and there, he was flattened beyond recognition. There were bloody holes in some places where his flesh had been pierced under the irresistible pressure of the rocks and when he was laid flat, he covered the floor of the tunnel from one side to the other.

'We were too late,' Noogan shook his head and sat down shakily.

Nayalla stroked the mat of hair that had been her husband's head.

'Mirkrin? Can you hear me, my love? You're free, I know you're alive – please Mirkrin, tell me you can hear me.'

There came a ragged gasp of air and the fingers of his right hand twitched. The miners stared in amazement as the crushed Myunan started to contract, hauling the over-stretched muscles of his body into their normal form. Mirkrin's head and chest expanded first. He drew in a gasp of air and screamed. His body continued to regain its shape, but it was going to take time. He was injured and in pain, his elasticity damaged by the pressure of the rock. Nayalla stayed kneeling by his side, murmuring words of comfort and encouragement.

The miners stepped around him and got to work again, pulling aside the moveable stones and digging dust and debris out with their picks and shovels. But they soon hit more of the larger boulders and had to give up. They were going to have to wait for the rescue teams to dig through from the other side with heavy lifting gear. Noogan and Dalegin sat down to watch Mirkrin's recovery, and grieve for the friends they had lost. Paternasse picked up the lantern and took stock of the situation.

They had enough oil to last them into the night, and meth-ylated spirit for the lamps on their helmets. Walking down the tunnel to check their supplies, his heart sank as he found another pile of rubble down near the end. The cart lay some-where underneath. He sat down and pulled the neckerchief from his mouth, rubbing the dust off his face and wiping his running nose. He hawked and spat a knot of phlegm from his throat. Then he pressed a finger against one side of his nose and snorted a lump of snot from one nostril, and then changed sides to clear the other. Their first problem was air. If the top end of the tunnel was completely closed off, they would be dead in two or three days. If they had enough air, then their next problem was water. The cave-in had filled at least forty paces of tunnel, probably more. That could be a few days' digging for the rescue teams, more if there were a lot of those big slabs to move and he knew that those lads would be working flat out. But he and the others would be suffering the first real effects of thirst long before they were freed.

But these were not his biggest worries. Paternasse had been buried three times in his life, and had been on the other side of cave-ins more times than he wanted to count. His biggest worry was the tremors. Because tremors never travelled alone; they always brought company. There could be more and that meant that they could still get buried and that the rescue teams would be in danger too. The shakes bothered him for another reason. Earthquakes happened in certain areas. Places just didn't start getting them all of a sudden, and this land had no history of them. What did that mean? He shook his head, it didn't matter now. All that mattered was that another one could bring the mountain down on them.

Cave-ins too, created their own instability. If a section of rock fell downwards, it changed the structure of the ground above it and around it – one cave-in could cause more. This mine had turned into a death-trap. Cotch-Baumen would be considering all this, and the loss of potential time and profits. And Paternasse could not escape the conclusion that if he were in the Provinchus's place, he would write this tunnel off, and them with it.

He spat again, getting to his feet and stretching his aching back. They would have to salvage what they could from the cart, dig out anything useful that might have survived. He stood motionless for a moment. There was the faintest hint of a different smell in the air. Picking up the lantern, he held it up towards the pile of rubble at the end of the tunnel. He climbed up and found a small gap between the top of the debris and the ceiling, just large enough to squeeze through.

Pushing the light in first, he scraped his head and shoulders through and discovered a crawlspace over the top of the pile. The scent was a little stronger here. He shuffled along it and saw that the wall at the end of the tunnel had split. There was a crack running down from the roof and there was empty space on the other side. It was too narrow to get the lantern through, but the light told him enough. There was a cave through there, and there was a faint smell of cool, stale air coming in from that cave. They might have another way out.

Noogan's voice carried down to him, calling him and he wriggled backwards out into the tunnel again.

'It's the lads!' Noogan said to him as he walked up towards them. 'Jube and the other lads are diggin' in from the other side, I can hear 'em. We're going to be all right!'

'Jussek!' a faint voice called. 'You there?'

'Aye!' Paternasse shouted back through a crack in the rubble. 'You've a beautiful voice, Jube, never appreciated it before!'

'Well hold on in there, old man. You'll see I've got a face to match!'

'I'm desperate, lad, not *blind*!' Paternasse roared back joyously.

'Who's alive in there?'

'Me and Noogan and Dalegin. And two Myunans too!'

'Myunans?' the distant voice called back. 'What are they doin' in there?'

Paternasse frowned and looked back at the shape-shifters. The question hadn't even occurred to him.

'We were looking for our children,' Nayalla supplied, quietly.

'Lookin' for their young 'uns!' Paternasse called out. 'Get their people down here. They might be of some use an' all. Listen, Jube, I found a cave at the end of the tunnel. There might be another way in!'

'We'll have a look. Hang in there, you old fart. We'll get you out of there!'

In the quiet that followed, they heard the distant bite of steel against stone, and if they had ever heard a more wonderful sound, none of them could recall it.

✦ ✦ ✦ ✦

Emos led the small group across a verdant meadow, Taya and Lorkrin listening to Draegar as he told them one of his dramatic stories with typical modesty.

'... so I took on the four of them single-handed, armed with nothing but a monoclid's jawbone and my wits! Those jankbats were fierce, with razor-sharp wings twice the width of my outspread arms, their tongues lined with teeth and their tentacles bristling with claws, and me trapped on the side of an erupting volcano! It was a close thing, but ...'

Draegar halted in mid-sentence. The rumble from the direction of the mining camp made them all look up. They could not see it from where they stood, but there was no mistaking the source of the sound.

'What now?' Emos muttered.

After waiting for a while to see if there would be any more developments, they continued walking and Draegar took up where he left off.

'Those jankbats almost had me, but I managed to smack one of them over the side of the head with the jawbone and it crashed to the ground. I cut it a bit with its own claws, rubbing its blood over me, and then I hauled it onto my back and walked around holding its wings out and flapping them. That confused the other jankbats. It was as if I had disappeared. Their eyesight is poor, and the blood was telling their sense of smell that I was one of them. They flew off, thinking their prey had escaped and was further down the side of the volcano ...'

'Someone's coming,' Emos interrupted.

Draegar paused impatiently. They were walking downhill towards a road. They were in plain view and Emos considered moving into cover, but the vehicle growling along the road was a mining truck, with only two men in the cab. They seemed to be in a rush.

'Let's see what's going on,' Lorkrin suggested.

Against his better judgement, Emos nodded. He was curious too.

They hailed the truck, half expecting the miners to ignore them, because of their Myunan markings. But the vehicle skidded to a halt.

'What's happened at the mine?' Emos asked. 'Sounded like a cave-in.'

'Aye,' one of the men said. 'A bad one. We're making for Ungreth. They've got guides there who know the land. We can still talk to the fellows trapped down the mine. They say they found a cave, might be another way into the mine. What about you? Do you know of any entrances to caves on Absaleth?'

Emos knew the area as well as anybody. He looked at Draegar. The Parsinor shrugged. The miners had dug their own hole. Let them lie in it. The guides in Ungreth might help, but there was no way the Noranians would allow a Myunan to get involved.

'There are no cave mouths on Absaleth,' he told them. 'But there is a system of caves that stretches in from the other side of the mountain range, on Reisenick territory. There's a chance they might reach in as far as the mountain. It's a two-to three-day journey to the entrance, but there are people in Ungreth who can help you find it. It's blocked off. You'll need to move a massive stone to get in.'

'You know the way?' the driver asked. 'Will you show us?'

'I don't think so,' Emos waved him on.

'Shouldn't you help them?' Taya asked quietly. Lorkrin nodded in agreement.

'Look, there's two of your kind trapped down there as well,' the driver pleaded.

'A likely story,' Draegar snorted.

'There is! A couple – names're Murkin and Nalla or some-thin' like that. They were lookin' for their young 'uns down there. Said they were missing.'

Emos stared at him, Lorkrin and Taya's faces dropped. A sudden sense of dread came over them, and they looked up at Emos in desperation. His face did not give them much hope.

'Make room up on that contraption,' Draegar barked at the men. 'And get it turned around. We're wasting time standing here!'

+ + + +

Forward-Batterer Cullum was stout, some would even say big-boned. No one would actually say he was fat unless he was out of earshot, as Cullum was also a prize-fighter of some renown. His success in this particular field came largely from the false sense of security his protruding belly offered his opponents, shortly before his quick, hard, meaty fists pummelled them into unconsciousness.

His language skills were somewhat less developed. So when a pair of Gabbit women approached the gate of the compound with a donkey pulling a cart full of rubbish and shouted some gibberish up at him, he instinctively looked around for someone else to do the talking. The other two soldiers on watch at the gate were equally bewildered and just shrugged at him.

'Gutt ye eny uld lumps fur dumpin', hardhide?' the taller of the women called up again.

Cullum stood staring down helplessly at the pair. Known as dog-people by those who avoided or ignored them, Gabbits were itinerants. Moving from place to place in small communities, they salvaged the rubbish of towns and cities and made use of it for their own purposes. The two women had mottled pink and yellow skin, and were shorter and thinner than the average human. They had tiny heads, half the size of a normal skull. Their clothes were patchwork affairs, held together with buttons for easy rearrangement. They had their own singsong language that few could understand.

'Does anybody here speak dog-tongue?!' Cullum roared at a group of miners in the yard.

Halerus Jube came up the steps into the watchtower. He peered down at the two women, who were standing hands on hips, waiting for a sign of comprehension.

'They're here for the scrap,' Jube told the soldiers. 'They're Gabbits, lads – what did you think they wanted?'

He leaned over the rail.

'Goofurnuffin' stuff seek ye?'

'Aye,' the taller woman replied. 'Takin out for makin' back to mother. Hardhide here typically nearside of thickendom, not hawkin' the talk.'

Jube laughed and waved them in.

'What was she saying?' Cullum asked suspiciously.

'Just sayin' she wanted to take the junk away and make use of it – and she complimented you on your gentlemanly manner.'

'Really?'

'No.'

The two women had been to the camp before, so they made their way straight over to the pile of scrap with their donkey and cart. Despite the rusted junk, there were plenty of rich pickings for an inventive Gabbit; but when the two women tried to pull the choice bits out, they found the heap of metal waste was impossibly tangled with baling wire.

'Unweavin' be work for busy-handed scamps,' the tall one said impatiently. 'Pack back to the village this all, and set the pets on it.'

The short one nodded; better to bring the whole lot with them back to the village and let the children untangle it, leaving their mothers to more important work. With some struggle, they dragged the mess of rusted and discarded scrap up onto the back of the cart. It did not seem to want to go, but eventually they managed it. Then they sifted through the rest of the heap and took some other bits and pieces of clothes, wood and glass and anything else they could use. With the cart full, they led the donkey back to the gate – ignoring the dark looks from the fat guard – and left the compound, taking the road west towards the hills where their tribe had set up their village.

5 THE HOLY MAN'S VISIONS

Mirkrin had recovered his shape, but it would be some time before he was back to normal. There were dents here and there in his flesh and bruises covered most of his body. He lay off to one side, with his head on his wife's lap, fast asleep, exhausted by his experience. Noogan was puzzled by the fact that the man's clothes seemed to have bruised too. He failed to put two and two together.

'How come your clothes are bruised?' he asked.

'We don't actually wear clothes,' Nayalla told him gently, her eyes never leaving her husband's face.

'But you've got … oh.' Realisation dawned.

'Centuries ago, when other races first started trading with Myunans, they considered us savages because we didn't wear clothes,' Nayalla told him. 'We had no reason to; we're not as vulnerable to the elements as humans. And we couldn't start wearing them, because we needed to be able to sculpt ourselves without layers of cloth getting in the way. You see, even our hair is really made up of the same flesh as the rest of our bodies. But being naked put us at a disadvantage, so we started shaping our flesh into garments to keep up appearances whenever we met other tribes. Now, we do it anyway; it's become part of life for us.'

Dalegin was looking slightly disgusted. Noogan was

determined not to seem too taken aback by the revelation, but it raised all sorts of questions that he just did not want to ask.

'Put your headlamps out, lads,' Paternasse said. 'You're wastin' fuel.'

Noogan and Dalegin took off their helmets, opened the lenses and pinched out the little flames. The pool of light from the lantern seemed all the more paltry now. The scratching and tapping sounds of the distant digging carried through to them, reassuring and frustrating them in equal measure. There was nothing to do but wait.

'Anybody got any jokes?' Dalegin asked, his thin, moustached face barely visible in the shadows.

'For pity's sake, Dal,' Noogan said. 'Balkrelt and the other lads are dead!'

'And we could still follow them – I need a bloody laugh, man!'

Paternasse could hear the tension in Dalegin's voice and knew he was close to cracking. The old miner had been there and felt sympathy for the younger miner.

'Here, how many Noranians does it take to boil an egg?'

'Dunno.'

'Ten. One to heat the water, the other nine to do the paperwork!'

'Ha! Good one!' Noogan's laugh was forced, but it was still good to hear. 'I've got one for you: what's the difference between a Noranian and a skack?'

'Dunno.'

'The skack has a mother who loves it.'

'Ha, ha, haaaa!'

'Ah, we're too hard on them,' Paternasse chortled. 'Wish

the Provinchus was here now. I'd be heartbroken if I died before I got to tell 'im how fetchin' he looked in that nightshirt.'

The strained, but rowdy laughter helped to release some of the tension.

'How do you stop a Myunan from drownin'?' Dalegin asked.

'Dal, don't,' Noogan muttered.

'Take your foot off his head.'

Nayalla was sitting outside the light of the lantern, but Noogan still avoided looking in her direction. He was embarrassed for the shape-changers and thought Paternasse might come out with something to make it right, but the old miner said nothing. Noogan opened his mouth to speak, but did not know what to say. Myunans had always made his skin crawl, but they were all stuck in this hole, and making jokes about them didn't seem right now.

Paternasse cocked his head and listened. He put the flat of his hand against the floor, and then stood up suddenly. The tremor started slowly and rose in strength. Dust fell from the ceiling and the lantern started bouncing along the ground.

'Noogan! Pick up the light!' Paternasse snapped.

The young miner swept the lantern off the floor and held it up, anxiously watching the ceiling. Mirkrin woke, felt the shuddering and curled up into a ball, moaning. Nayalla hugged him, leaning over him protectively.

'It's going to hold!' Paternasse told them. 'The supports are holding.'

There was a muffled rumble and the tremor eased off. They all waited stock still for something else to happen, but nothing did. Paternasse walked over to the crack in the pile of rubble.

'Jube!' he yelled. 'You all right, up there?'

There was no answer.

'Jube, can you hear me? Can anybody hear me?'

There wasn't a sound. Paternasse hung his head.

'What does this mean?' Nayalla asked him. 'Are they still coming for us?'

'I don't know,' the old man replied. 'I don't know any more.'

+ + + +

The miners had guaranteed the three Myunans and the Parsinor safe passage into and out of the camp. Emos decided Taya and Lorkrin would be as well off with him as they would be if he left them outside, so they came in with the two men. There was some arguing between the miners and the guards at the gate, but eventually the truck was let through. A crowd of miners gathered around as they dismounted from the truck. The Provinchus came out of the officers' quarters, dressed in a poorly fitting whipholder's uniform and flanked by six burly soldiers. He did not look pleased to see the new arrivals.

'Forward-Batterer Cullum, arrest these Myunans,' he snapped at the soldier in charge of the gate. 'What do you mean by letting them enter the camp?'

'They're here to help our mates,' the driver of the truck told him. 'You leave them be.'

'You will hold your tongue or you will join them,' Cotch-Baumen warned. 'Forward-Batterer, you have been given an order!'

There were angry shouts from the crowd of miners and some of them placed themselves in front of the soldiers.

'We're not ones to shirk work, sir,' a stocky, middle-aged man with a black beard spoke up. 'But you won't get one more crumb from that mine until we know there's help on the way for our boys.'

There was a murmur of agreement from the others.

'If these people can find these caves then we need them,' he went on, turning to Emos. 'We've just had another cave-in, nearly lost another team trying to get to the first one. There's no way we'll reach them in time, even if we could dig and that's lookin' just too damned dangerous now. We can't even be sure that they made it either, but we're not giving up until we've given it our all. If there is a cave back there, it's their only way out. But they're down there in the dark, running out of light and water. So, can you find a way in?'

'There are no cave entrances on Absaleth,' Emos told him. 'But I can lead you to an entrance in Ainslidge Woods, on the far side of the hills that could take us underneath it. It's about two days' travel by engined wagon. I don't know if it's a way in, but it's the only cave system in the area. My family is down there with your friends and I think it's their best hope. They'll know about the entrance, though they might not be able to find it. I can find my way round down there, but I need help. The entrance is blocked by a huge stone.'

The man nodded.

'That's good enough for me. Every man here'll come along if needs be.'

'Splendid,' Cotch-Baumen clapped his hands together. 'However, I fear that might deplete our workforce some- what. And might I remind you who is in authority here?'

But the Provinchus was weighing up the situation; he

could not afford a revolt now. Production was already well behind schedule and he had learned from experience the desperate lengths the lower classes would go to when their brethren were in danger. They all wanted to be sure that others would do the same for them if the situation were reversed. It would be better to let a few of their number make their rescue attempt and get the rest back to work as quickly as possible.

'Three will go: a miner and two footsoldiers, for security.'

'No soldiers,' the lead miner said. 'And we need more men.'

'It's enough,' Emos said. 'We'll be travelling through Reisenick territory and they would not take kindly to a large party of strangers anyway. Three it is.'

There was a clamour of volunteers, but the stocky man told them he was going himself and would brook no argument.

'My name is Halerus Jube,' the miner said to Emos, as the crowd began to disperse.

'Emos Harprag, and these are Taya, Lorkrin and Draegar.'

'Come with me. Let's talk about what we'll need.'

Taya and Lorkrin watched their uncle walk away with the miner. They looked over to the mouth of the mine tunnel; broken rubble was just visible in its shadows.

'They were in there looking for us,' Taya said shakily.

Lorkrin did not say anything. He had a knot in his chest that would not go away.

'It doesn't matter.' Draegar put a hand on each of their shoulders. 'None of that matters. Do you understand? You're not to blame. This is down to a mix of things that nobody could have foreseen. Blame serves no purpose.'

'We're going with you,' Lorkrin told him.

'It's not a good idea, Lorkrin. It might be dangerous. The Reisenicks can be a hostile lot.'

'How are you going to stop us?' The boy looked up into his eyes and Draegar was struck by the intensity in the lad's stare.

'We'll follow you.' Taya's voice was as serious as her brother's gaze. 'It doesn't matter what you do. We'll follow you. You know we will.'

Draegar looked at them. He had seen how wilful they could be, even when they were merely up to mischief. But he also saw a new resolve in their eyes. Now their parents' lives were hanging in the balance. He reminded himself that they had already been through far more than most children their age. He nodded to them.

'It's your uncle's decision. Let's see what he has to say.'

+ + + +

Emos was helping to load supplies onto one of the trucks. They were to take two of the six-wheeled machines. They would need one just to carry the massive hoist that would be needed to clear the cave entrance. Jube came over with the whipholder; the officer was being trailed by two soldiers.

'They're insisting we take two of their lot rather than some of the lads,' Jube told the Myunan.

Emos nodded. It did not matter to him. He just needed enough strong hands to unblock the cave. Otherwise he would have flown there alone. He had to will himself to be patient, aggravated at how long all this preparation was taking. Nayalla and Mirkrin could be injured, or already lost in the caves. He was not ready to consider the possibility that they were dead. He lashed a barrel of water in place to the side of the flatbed and jumped down.

'These are two of my best,' the whipholder said, 'Forward-Batterer Cullum and Crossbower Khassiel. They will ensure your safety on this mission.'

Emos – in no mood for pleasantries – was about to walk past when he recognised one of them. Khassiel was the woman who had shot Ceeanna. Her stance and the grey-and-black ornacrid's shell that formed her armour were unmistakable. The other one did not look any friendlier. Emos swallowed his hate; grudges would only get in the way of his task.

'Get aboard,' he told them, and then strode past the soldiers to help load part of the hoist.

+ + + +

On the far side of the compound, Kalayal Harsq sat on the chassis of his generator truck, glaring at the mouth of the mine. He couldn't take his eyes off it. The dark circles of skin around his eyes spoke of two nights without sleep, a warning to his disciples to stay out of his way. Harsq had a violent temper when he was on edge.

He took the canister from inside his robe and pressed the mouthpiece against his face, inhaling the purified air. It had a metallic taste to it. He tossed it aside in disgust. The taste of metal had not left his mouth since the exorcism; even his stores of blessed air seemed tainted. And he had been having visions. Not like his normal ones, not revelations from his master, but disturbing ones. Visions of being swallowed up by the ground.

Harsq had once been a traditional eshtran, serving his flock out on the esh-boats. The vast ocean of gas that lay off the coast of Braskhia had been his home. But he had almost died when the ship he was serving on was wrecked in a storm and most of the crew killed. He and some of the others had survived by hanging onto a flotation bag. They had hung there for three days, with nothing but the pale yellow gas beneath them. On the third day, they discovered that the bag was slowly deflating. They were already very low in the esh. Panic set in and a fight broke out. Two men fell to their deaths, disappearing into the bottomless fog. The remaining five were able to stay afloat for another day, when a Noranian frigatch pulled them out. Harsq had been unable to go out to esh again, terrified of being suspended above the misty depths. And an eshtran who could not go to esh was no eshtran at all.

So he had taken to wandering instead, exorcising spirits from the land, eventually perfecting the electrical projection method that had made him famous. But his work had resulted in his being exiled from Braskhia. Now, frightened of the esh, driven from his homeland, and under sentence of death from the Myunans, he discovered the land itself was threatening him. Well, he knew enough about the spirit world to understand the nature of his enemy. He would rise to the challenge.

'Get the trucks started,' he rasped at the nearest disciple. 'Inform the Provinchus we are ready to take our leave.'

'Yes, Kalayal,' the young woman answered. 'Have we been called on to purge another evil spirit?'

'No. We're not done with this one yet.'

+ + + +

'Uncle Emos?' Taya's voice made the Myunan turn around to see her standing with Lorkrin and Draegar.

She was about to say something else, but hesitated when she saw the expression on his face. He noticed how the two children were standing with feet stubbornly planted and how Draegar waited supportively behind them.

'You'll need tools,' he said to his niece and nephew. 'Find yourself some steel. I'll make them along the way. And get yourselves some backpacks too. We might be doing some walking.'

He turned away without another word and went back to work. Taya and Lorkrin shared a triumphant look and ran off to find some scrap pieces of steel.

Draegar, who spent his life being ready to travel, saw that Emos and the miners had the loading well in hand, so he took a roll of vellum from a tube in one of his satchels and spread it out on the flatbed of the passenger truck. From the satchel on his right, he took out a bottle of ink and a quill. Then he dipped the nib in the ink and drew a little compass marking north, south, east and west on the top right-hand corner of the calfskin. It was how he always started a new map. He had never been to the Reisenick area that Emos would lead them through. His quill scratched over the sheet, drawing in the mining camp, the mountain and the road to Sestina. The rest of the map was yet to come.

6 THE UNDERGROUND WINDOW

The two Gabbits were having problems with their donkey. It kept pulling at its rope and twisting to the left and right, as if it were trying to escape from the cart. At first they thought it was just bothered by the ever-present insects in the air; the gnats swarmed around it constantly. The two women tried soothing it, then coaxing it, then cursed it when it kept up its pesky behaviour. The donkey brayed back at them, nipping at their hands and craning its neck forward. Curious, the two women fell back to the cart and examined their load, just in case they might have picked up a spidersnake or some fire-mites. But there was nothing alive among the rubbish.

It was late afternoon and they were still a good walk from the thick and tangled woods where their tribe had taken up temporary residence. There were some farms and a story-house to visit along the way and the donkey was going to wear itself out if it didn't settle down. Once it stopped walking, there would be nothing the women could do to get it to start again until it had rested, and they wanted to get as far along that forest road as they could before dark. The Reisenicks were tolerant of the Gabbits, but some of them were nasty for the sake of it and the two women did not want to take the chance of bumping into them after nightfall.

They slapped the donkey's flanks and urged it onwards,

pulling at its halter impatiently. They would give the farms and the storyhouse a miss. The cart was fully laden anyway. They would come back in the morning. The other people's garbage wasn't going anywhere, after all.

+ + + +

Paternasse had decided that help was not coming. Whatever hope there had been of rescue had disappeared with the last earth tremor. The crawlspace through to the end of the tunnel was still there, as was the smell of the cave air. While Paternasse was pondering on how to chip away at the crack in the tunnel wall in such a tightly confined space, Nayalla slipped in first and pulled herself up to the end of the narrow channel. Slunching her shoulders, she stuck her head through the crack, and then one arm. Bracing herself on the wall on the other side, she hauled herself through. Mirkrin followed her a moment later.

'Stone me,' Paternasse grunted, seeing the Myunan's feet disappear through the crack – a gap too narrow for a grown man's head.

'Hand us through the pickaxes,' Nayalla called. 'There's room to swing them on this side.'

It took some time, but the two shape-changers managed to widen the crack enough for the other three men to squeeze through. They brought with them everything they could salvage from the cart, including a spare bottle of oil for the lamp, some of the men's packed lunches, and their canteens of water. Each man still had his satchel and tools and Noogan and Dalegin had their headlamps lit again. Even so, the group was ill-equipped for exploring caves.

They took in the scene around them. There had been

room to swing the picks, but not much more. The walls on either side leaned in oppressively, rising to meet at a point out of sight above their heads. The air was damp and the grey and orange-streaked walls glistened with moisture; the sound of slow dripping water could be heard nearby.

'We have water, then,' Dalegin muttered. 'That's something at least.'

'Can take a long time to collect a cupful of dripping water, and our canteens are almost full anyway,' Paternasse told him. 'We can't hang about. This only goes one way. So let's get crackin'.'

The rugged corridor twisted away downhill. Paternasse led the way with the lantern, his feet finding their way carefully on the slippery stone. Their breathing was loud in the narrow space and any word spoken had an eerie resonance.

Mirkrin and Nayalla were in the middle of the group, with the other two miners taking up the rear. She noticed that Mirkrin had a tight grip on her hand and was keeping his eyes on the floor, not looking up. His breathing, too, sounded controlled, as if he were willing himself to relax. She knew then that the cave-in had damaged more than her husband's body.

'What the blazes ...?' Paternasse exclaimed.

They jumped down a high step and followed the old miner's gaze.

The flickering yellow light illuminated a bizarre sight. Off to their left was a large, stained-glass window. They crowded up to it, examining it in disbelief. Stained glass was a mark of luxury; few buildings outside Noran could boast such a thing, and here was one in the middle of a mountain. It was coloured mostly in reds, yellows and greens. The

pattern was traced in lead, strange flowers over a back-
ground of leaves. The top was arched, the frame made of
what looked like oak, stained with damp and dark with age.
The bottom of the window was at waist height, the top out
of reach above their heads.

'Who would put a window in a cave?' Noogan wondered
out loud.

'Somebody who wanted to believe they could see outside,' Nayalla said, looking at a metal plate that sat in a shallow alcove in the wall facing the window. 'Something
burned on this plate to create light, it shone through that
window to make it seem like sunlight shining in.'

'So, what's on the other side of the window?' Dalegin
asked quietly.

'One way to find out,' Paternasse raised his pick to the
dirty glass.

'Don't!' Mirkrin stopped him. 'There'll be a way in.'

They walked to the end of the passage and came upon a
door. It was wooden, the iron hasps rusted through, the
wood soft with rot. Paternasse put his hand against it and
shoved; the door pulled free of its hinges, but stayed stuck to
the frame. Another push sent it crashing to the ground. They
walked into the room beyond. And it was a room, not a
cave. About fifteen paces square, but quite a bit taller, it
could not have been a greater contrast to the tunnel they had
just left. The lower walls were flat, carved with intricate
images of flowers, trees and other illustrations of the world
outside. The upper walls curved into arches that formed the
ceiling. Lumps of crumbled wood could have been the
remains of furniture, and the doorframe and other features
of the room were inlaid with a greenish metal that must

once have been brass. Cobwebs hung like thin, sticky curtains.

Noogan jumped when he saw an animal in the far corner, but then he saw it was covered in dust. It was a lifelike sculpture of a dog, a wolfhound sitting on its haunches looking expectantly at its master.

'This place is old,' Paternasse breathed. 'Must be hundreds of years old.'

'There's another door,' Noogan said, staring at the other side of the room.

'Let's go through it, then.' Mirkrin walked across the room, noting that the floor too was rotten oak. He grabbed the latch of the door. It was made to open in, but the handle came off in his hand. The miners' picks made short work of the decayed wood and they broke through into a much bigger, more impressive version of the first room.

It was octagonal, with steps down to a sunken section in the middle. There were windows in four of the walls; one of them was broken and behind it was an alcove holding a metal plate like the first one they had found. Here too, there were sculptures of animals, all in materials that mimicked their natural colours. Two cats, one in pitchstone, with its back arched, one in striped sandstone, curled up as if asleep. There was another dog too, a shepherd's collie, made of marble and quartz, lying on its side, sleepy eyes regarding the room. Around the middle of the room, rusted wrought-iron columns extended into the roof. Paternasse went closer to study one.

'Odd,' he grunted. 'Some of the carving at the top looks like stone, some like metal; can't see where one starts and the other ends. Like they're growing into one another.'

'It's just the rust,' Dalegin shrugged. 'Makes it look that way.'

'Don't know, looks odd to me,' the older miner frowned.

There were two more doors.

'One of these has got to lead out,' Paternasse lifted his chin towards them. 'People lived here once upon a time. They had to have a way out somewhere.'

'You would think,' Noogan said, raising his pick. 'Makes me wonder though; if there were people about hundreds of years ago who could make stuff like this, where are they now?'

+ + + +

Taya and Lorkrin sat with their feet dangling off the tailgate of the wagon. It chugged along at a little faster than walking pace, belching oily smoke and making a sound not unlike an enormous cat coughing up a hairball. They were on the road, off to find a way into the caves that might lead them to their parents. And despite the fear for their mother and father that gnawed at their insides, they were flushed with excitement. Behind their truck, the second vehicle carrying all the equipment brought up the rear, driven by the soldier, Cullum.

'The smoke smells a bit like fried food,' Lorkrin commented.

'It's the bule oil,' Taya told him. 'Reminds you of Ma using it for cooking.'

The thought of their mother caused them to lapse into silence again.

'What if we don't get them out?' Lorkrin said, after another while.

'Don't, Lorkrin. I can't ...' Taya's voice cracked and she stopped talking, snuffling instead and wiping her nose on her arm.

Lorkrin gazed morosely at the dry mud road passing by under his feet.

'Uncle Emos and Draegar will find them,' he reassured her.

Taya nodded. She wanted to believe it; she wanted to believe that she and Lorkrin would help the men pull back the stone and descend into the caves to bring their parents out safely. She imagined the celebrations and the pride of their mother and father on seeing how their children had helped rescue them. She even smiled a bit at the thought. Then she remembered the last words that she and her brother had thrown at their parents and she despaired at the thought that it might be the last time they would ever see them alive.

Lorkrin looked sideways at his sister's face and knew what she was thinking. He nudged her with his shoulder and she leaned against him and they both watched the road unwinding achingly slowly beneath them.

Emos spared a glance at his niece and nephew before bringing his mind back to his work. He had still to make their tools, but there was a more urgent task to perform first. He had picked up a piece of quartz and had asked Jube to find him some brass and the miner had obliged by bringing him the melted remnants of two chest handles. Emos did not ask whom the chest had belonged to, but brass handles suggested someone of importance, perhaps someone who travelled with a lot of clothes.

He was using the brass to make a chain. Mouthing words

as he worked, his fingers pressed, squeezed and tore at the metal as if it were putty. It seemed to anyone who watched that he had massive strength, but it was an illusion. This was transmorphing, the mental ability of a Myunan to transfer the qualities of their flesh onto other materials. A dark and forbidden art in Myunan culture, he had started practising it in a desperate attempt to save his wife from a terrible disease. He had failed, but that had only driven him on and now he was a master of the craft, and he worked the brass as skilfully as a sculptor used modelling clay.

The bouncing and jolting of the truck prevented him from doing any fine shaping, so once he had the rough cut of a pendant done, he put it in his pack and sat back to relax. His eyes fell on Jube, who was peering back through the small window in the rear of the cab in a mixture of horror and amazement. The miner blessed himself with one hand, wiping it down his face and flicking it as if he were throwing away the 'ungodliness'. Emos did not normally allow anyone to watch him work, but they had no time to spare and he needed to finish this before they reached the border of the Reisenicks' territory.

They travelled on into the evening, the shadows behind the trucks lengthening and growing fainter as the sun dropped below the hills. Emos called a halt for a while so that the drivers could survey the land ahead one last time before dark and he could finish the pendant. The children watched as he fashioned each chain link into a snake swallowing its own tail and then joined them all together. The quartz itself he shaped into a wide, rectangular ornament with cut-out symbols.

The children had spent enough time with their uncle to

recognise that the symbols were letters of some kind, but could not place them.

'What does it say?' Taya asked.

'It's Reisenicken, it says "Ludditch".'

'What's a ludditch?'

'He is the chieftain of the land we're going to be travelling through. This is a gift for him to show our good will.'

Taya regarded the hefty piece of jewellery with a critical eye.

'It's a bit … *chunky*, isn't it?'

'He is not a man of refined tastes,' Emos said, winking at her.

The trucks moved off again. From where they sat, Lorkrin and Taya could see into the cab and noticed that Jube had a necklace of his own, made of small acorns. He fiddled with it any time he glanced back at Emos.

'He is a worshipper of Everness,' Draegar muttered to them. 'A Sestinian god. The Noranians don't like religions much, so worshippers have to be quiet about it. Sestinians are superstitious about Myunans and a transmorpher would make them doubly suspicious.'

'They look for protection from acorns,' Lorkrin sniffed. 'And they think *we're* strange.'

It was dark when Emos stood up in the flatbed, looked out ahead of them and slapped the roof of the cab. With a squeal of worn brakes, the truck came to a halt. Taya and Lorkrin, who had been half asleep, sat up drowsily and took in their surroundings.

They were at the edge of a wilderness. Thick, thorny bushes on either side gave way ahead to the heavy foliage of cobrush trees. With their wide, tangled limbs, the web-like expanse of trees formed a mass of tendril leaves and branches, broken only by the road itself. Vines wound from tree to tree to increase the sense of a woven fabric gone badly wrong. Totems made from painted animal bones stood around the entrance to the jungle, holding a variety of coloured glass chimes that clinked in the gentle breeze. From the dark mess of the trees, birds awoke and called out in hoarse, high-pitched voices.

'We wait here,' Emos told the group. Then to the soldiers, 'You two keep to the back, Noranians aren't too welcome in here.'

'Why not go on in?' Forward-Batterer Cullum demanded. 'If they want to stop us, they can catch up. Why waste our time sitting around here?'

'Hear the birds?' Emos cocked his head. 'They're carkhams – trained to warn of intruders. The Reisenicks already know we're here. If we enter their territory without being invited, they'll come down on us like a landslide. We wait for per-mission.'

'Permission, my foot,' Cullum snorted to himself. 'Should've brought some more troops and just marched right in there.'

'You would need an awful lot of troops,' Draegar informed him. 'And some luck besides. The Reisenicks are no strangers to battle.'

Silence settled on the group as they waited. Emos carried out some finer work on the tools he had started, and talked softly with Draegar, who was adding to his new map. The lamps on the fronts of the wagons lit up the road ahead, but cast little light into the trees. There could have been an army watching from in there and they would not have been able to see them. Eventually, there came a clicking noise. It was irregular, but had a certain rhythm to it. Out of the darkness along the road came a strangely unbalanced figure. Dressed in rawhide, with a fur hat, he leaned on a stick and seemed to walk with a different kind of limp in each leg. The clicking sound came from his joints, which were swollen and stuck out at odd angles. He was stooped and could have been mistaken for an old man, if not for his face, which was that of a young man, even if the features were slightly askew.

Lorkrin and Taya looked at each other. They had seen Reisenicks before, but only those who came to trade with the Myunans. Their father had once told them that Reisenick families did not mix with outsiders much, being wary of other races. Centuries of mating within their small tribes had made their blood so pure that it had concentrated and exaggerated all the Reisenick traits. This particular man was obviously more concentrated than most.

'Whaddaya want?' he croaked, raising his misshapen face to glare at them.

'We would like permission to travel through your clan's land,' Emos told him respectfully, walking forward so that the man did not have to squint against the lights to see him. 'We bring a gift for your chieftain.'

He held up the pendant. The man's eyes widened, clearly impressed as he took the chain. He grasped the quartz in his fingers and raised it up to the light.

'Good workmanship,' he nodded. 'Bit on the dainty side, but good nonetheless.'

He clucked his tongue several times and a large crow-like bird, dark blue and green, swooped in and landed on his shoulder. Dropping the pendant in a little drawstring bag, he held it up for the bird, which took off, grabbed the bundle and disappeared over the trees.

'Where would ya be wantin' ta go?' the border guard asked.

'To Old Man's Cave.'

The ugly man shuffled over to the trucks, noting the lifting gear on the back of the second one.

'Gonna try and get in, are ya?'

'Some of our friends are trapped down there. They got in another way, but there was a cave-in.'

The guard shrugged and handed Emos a pebble, etched with the Reisenick symbol for 'visitor'.

'Ludditch'll like the tribute. You can head on in, I reckon.'

Emos thanked him and swung back up onto the flatbed. Draegar cranked the engine up while Jube took the wheel, and they rumbled on up the road. Taya and Lorkrin watched the border guard fade back into the trees, and then turned to gaze up the dark road.

'Why is it called Old Man's Cave?' Lorkrin asked to relieve the boredom.

'Because an old man lived there for many years,' Emos replied. 'They don't believe in over-complicated names for things around here. In fact he had lived there for as long as anyone could remember. His name was Caftelous. He was a grouchy old hermit, but he had a great knowledge of alchemy. He helped me in my study of transmorphing after your aunt died. He couldn't do it himself of course; he wasn't a Myunan, but he was as skilled an alchemist as I've ever met and he taught me a thing or two about the nature of materials. A few years ago, I went back to see him, but the entrance to the cave was blocked by a massive stone slab. No one knew where he had gone. Some said he was dead, others that he was alive, but that he had wandered into the forest and disappeared. I tried to trans a hole through the slab, but it was made of something that I couldn't affect. I've never seen its like. To this day, I've never found out what happened to the old man.'

'Do you think he put the slab there?' Taya asked.

'It's almost certain, he would know how to create something that couldn't be transmorphed, and transing through the side of a mountain would take weeks, if it could be done at all, especially if the mountain's spirit is strong. It's likely that he didn't want the cave disturbed after he was gone, which makes me think he's still alive somewhere, or at least he was when it was sealed up.'

'Maybe somebody sealed him inside,' Lorkrin murmured, earning a sound thump from his sister. He scowled at her, but did not retaliate.

They still had at least two days' travel before they reached the cave, two days that their parents would spend beneath a soulless mountain. The Myunans silently urged the vehicles on, desperate for the wheels to eat up the long stretch of road ahead of them.

+ + + +

The dratted donkey had seized up. The two Gabbit women pulled at its halter and pushed it and shouted and cursed, but it would not budge. At first it had tried turning itself to face the cart, but had only ended up walking around in circles. Now it just stood there shivering, its eyes wide, staring back at its load. It was starting to frighten the short woman and she gazed around at the trees that lined either side of the road and made a roof over their heads. This forest was an eerie place to be at night with a terrified donkey.

A metallic rustle caught their attention, some kind of movement in the back of the cart. The two women circled it warily holding their lantern aloft, sure that they had picked up some crawling creature or other. Quite a big one, by the sounds of it. The mass of scrap quivered and the women jumped back, clutching each other. They both picked up sticks and started batting the mess of wire and metal bits and pieces, hoping to scare the creature out of hiding.

Suddenly the rusted mesh of scrap started to move, dragging itself towards the tailgate of the cart. The latches on the tailgate flipped open all by themselves, and the scrap heaved itself off the end of the cart, dragging most of the garbage with it. The women screamed and hugged their panic-stricken donkey. Covering its eyes as well as their own to stop this strange evil from entering their heads, they cowered, unable to move.

When they dared open their eyes again, the scrap was gone, lost in the darkness of the trees, although they could still hear it, dragging itself along the ground, snaring bushes and catching on undergrowth. The donkey decided it had had enough. It brayed hysterically, shook itself free of the women and bolted, galloping up the dark road towards the village, hauling the cart after it. The remains of the rubbish spilled out of the back, but the women didn't care; they sprinted after their cart, intent on getting home even before the donkey did.

+ + + +

The lantern was going out. Paternasse shook it gently to listen to the oil; it was almost gone. In the light from

Noogan's headlamp, he turned down the wick until the flame went out, used a cloth to lift off the hot glass and then unscrewed the body to check the length of the wick. It lay there like a coiled worm; there was plenty left. He refilled the reservoir from the tin of oil he had in his satchel and put the stock and glass back on. They had enough for one last refill after that. The methylated spirit in the headlamps was low and they had one tin bottle between them, but that would last them less than half a day.

They had found more rooms, smashing down each door they came upon, only to find that each of the twenty-three rooms joined up with another, forming a network of chambers, corridors and stairways – none of which led outside. They had discovered three wells, but the water in each was stagnant and would have to be filtered and boiled before it could be drunk. All the rooms had the same style of decoration, carvings of flowers and leaves and trees and disturbingly lifelike animals, all suggesting a yearning for the outside world. There were false windows in every room. It was downright peculiar.

'I've found something,' Dalegin called.

He had been searching some of the alcoves and storage areas and came into the large octagonal room now with a glass jar full of silver powder.

'We haven't seen any candles or lamps, right?' he said, once he had their attention. 'But they had to have light. I found bits of this powder in the plates behind the windows, and just on a hunch, I flicked a match over it.'

The powder in the jar had solidified, so he jammed a chisel down into it to loosen some and tipped a small pile of the grains onto the stone tiles. Then he took out a box of matches and struck one, touching it to the silvery grains. The powder ignited, burning with a brilliant blue-white light.

'It's beautiful,' Nayalla said softly, as they all leaned in for a closer look.

'You haven't seen the half of it,' Dalegin chuckled.

He reached down and rubbed his finger in the still burning powder, then lifted it out. Part of the flame flickered on his fingertip. They all gaped.

'It has no heat,' he said. 'This stuff burns cold.'

They each found a piece of wood or rusted metal that could be used as a handle and coated the end in the powder which they set alight, equipping themselves with torches brighter than any lantern.

'Right,' Nayalla said. 'Let's search this place again, from top to bottom. We have to have missed something. What about the passage we first came in through?'

'I checked it,' Noogan told her. 'There's nothing.'

'Okay, but we can assume that there are other passages like it around, bits of what must have been the original cave this place was built inside.'

Mirkrin had stepped down into the sunken section in the middle of the room, examining the broken metal remains that lay there. His attention was attracted by a joint he saw among the rusted pieces, his craftsman's eye spotting something the others had missed.

'These were once stairs,' he said to himself.

Lifting his torch, he stared upwards. The light revealed a shaft that went straight up, the top out of sight in the darkness above.

'Anybody up for a climb?' he asked.

The ceiling was the height of three men above the ground.

The miners had some rope, but nothing with which to make a grappling hook. Instead, Mirkrin and Nayalla took out their tools and extended the length of their bodies, Mirkrin wincing as he crafted his bruised flesh. Then, Nayalla climbed up onto his shoulders with the rope coiled over one shoulder and balanced there as she looked for handholds. Her head level with the lip of the shaft, she cast her eyes around her, holding her torch up for light. She threw the torch up onto a surface above her, found a grip with both hands and hoisted herself up, her lanky legs dangling for a moment before slithering up into the darkness. The end of the rope dropped down into the waiting hands of her husband.

One by one, they hauled themselves up and found themselves on an entirely different floor of the strange system of rooms. The steady burning of their powdered torches revealed a round chamber with more rusting columns, and what looked like small trees growing around the edges of the room. Noogan spotted something off to one side and went to take a look. He knelt down to examine a pile of dusty rags on the floor and gasped. It was a skeleton, or at least what looked like one.

'By the gods!' he yelped, jumping back. 'What's this?'

They all crowded in to see.

'Skeleton,' Paternasse observed. 'But it's not human. Don't look like anything I've seen before.'

Its eyes were huge, as was its head. It had two arms, but the forearms branched to end in two opposable hands. The hands were long and delicate. It had quite short legs, half the normal length, and its feet were small and quite dainty. The disintegrating rags were all that were left of what must have been fine robes.

'I think we're looking at one of the owners,' Mirkrin said quietly.

'I've seen drawings of people like this before,' Nayalla told them, her brow creased in an effort to remember. 'In some scrolls my brother has. I thought the stories were myths.'

'What stories?' Paternasse enquired.

7 ANYTHING THAT DOESN'T BELONG

Learup Ludditch III sat in a rocking chair on the porch of his wood-and-hide house. In the light of the lantern hanging on the post above him, he was admiring the brass necklace that had arrived by carkham earlier.

'Harprag. I'd know 'is work anywhere,' he chortled, draping the chain around his neck, adding it to the collection of heavy jewellery on his broad chest. 'So the Myunan's come callin', 'as he? Whaddaya think o' that, Pappy? That a fine piece o' ornamentation, or what?'

'Don't trust them Myunans,' coughed his father, who was sitting in another chair to his right, a sour-smelling pipe between the last of his teeth. 'Yer eyes don't tell ya nuthin' about them.'

Ludditch III nodded sagely, but wished that his pappy would agree with him just for once. His father was no longer the great chieftain he had once been. The bone-rot had got him good, his elbows, wrists, knees and ankles so swollen and painful that he could no longer walk on his own, reduced to looking out over his land from the porch of the house at the top of their hill. He still tried to play the twangoe, but his arthritic fingers could barely pluck the four concentric rings of strings on the wooden bowl. It was sad to watch, and worse to listen to. It broke Ludditch's heart to see his pappy like this.

Ludditch now, he was a different matter, he was in his prime. Powerful arms and shoulders carried arms with bunches of corded muscle; his slightly hunched back was still strong. There were no signs yet of the bone-rot that plagued all the Reisenick clans. His flat, wide skull and bulging features came from his father, as did his wily cunning. He had all but taken over the running of the clan from Learup Senior and he was determined to make his patronage of the land one that would be talked about around the supper tables for centuries. The Noranians, for instance, had been making eyes at his territory for years and he wasn't having that. They were already at Absaleth by all accounts. They might get away with pushing the Myunans about, but they would get a lesson in manners if they tried marching into Ainslidge Woods. The Reisenicks would die before giving up their lands to the northerners.

'Learup?' a voice interrupted his thoughts.

'Yup?' he and his father said in unison. Ludditch Junior scowled. He was supposed to be in charge now. He added: 'What is it?'

Spiroe, one of the Cruddip boys, stood at the foot of the steps, hat in hand. His knees were bent backwards in that Cruddip way and his words cut up by teeth that were too large for his small mouth. The sinewy woodsman was a mite green-skinned for a Reisenick, but Ludditch was sure the rumours about Spiroe's grandmother and the Traxen were just malicious gossip. Spiroe was pure-bred.

'There's a priest on the border, wants ta see ya.'

'A priest ya say? What about?' Ludditch Senior asked gruffly, much to the annoyance of his eldest.

'Won't say,' Spiroe replied. 'Kalayal Harsq's his name. Ornery type, only wants to speak to the chieftain.'

He was careful to direct his remarks to both Ludditches. Senior still demanded respect, but Junior was head of the clan now and everyone who knew what was good for them knew it.

'Bring 'im up,' Junior jutted his goateed chin out. 'Let's see what the boy has to say.'

Two trucks had drawn up on the road at the foot of Lud-ditch Hill. The eshtran was led up the steep steps to the house. Harsq took a breath of purified air from his canister as he took in his surroundings. Among the cobrush trees, a single-storey house made of tanned animal hides over-looked the misty valley. Small crude windows glowed with a warm light. On the porch sat two more Reisenicks, one a clenched-up skeleton of a man clutching a twangoe, the other a tall, powerful-looking young man in rawhide jerkin and trousers, with a marrowshanks pelt draped over his wide shoulders. Harsq immediately saw that the clan's power rested with the younger man and after a cursory greeting to the father, addressed the rest of his remarks to the son.

'My compliments to you and your clan, sirs. I am a humble pilgrim on a holy mission to cleanse this land of a wicked bane. I would like to a make a proposition to you, one that would benefit both our causes in the fullness of time.'

'What's this bane?' Ludditch III asked. 'And why have you come on our land to find it?'

'I'm talking about a malevolent ghost, sir. A shade of pure evil that will rest at nothing until it has returned to the seat of its power.'

'And where might that seat be?'

'Absaleth, the cursed mountain,' Harsq clenched his raised fists. 'Cursed no more, since I drove the ghost from its depths, but that spirit has a will like I've never seen. It has found new ground in which to root its evil and it will not relinquish its grip until I deal it a final blow.'

Ludditch's eyes widened.

'You did an exorcism on *Absaleth*? And it *worked*?'

'I freed it from its curse. But I was merely an instrument of Brask's will.'

Junior caught a sharp look from his father. If this was true, it could only mean that the priest did not understand what he had done. Or what he meant to do still.

'And you think the mountain's soul's moved out here?' Ludditch pressed the eshtran.

'I have no doubt,' Harsq nodded. 'Somehow it evaded me and has now infected this land. I can feel its presence in this forest. And that is why I need your help. It could have run to ground anywhere. I can't find it in this wilderness, but you can. And I can make it worth your while to do so.'

Ludditch snorted, suppressing a laugh. The priest had no idea what he was saying. If his claims were genuine, then it would be a dream come true for the Reisenick clans. The fact that they might get paid into the bargain was sugar on the pie.

'What you offerin'?' he asked, eyeing the priest's fancy clothes.

'A down-payment of five hundred drokes.' The eshtran folded his arms. 'And another five hundred when you find it.'

'Any man who'll pay a thousand drokes to catch a ghost'll pay two thousand,' Ludditch stuck his chin out and took his pipe from his pocket.

'This thing will haunt your land as it has haunted Absaleth …
one thousand two hundred.'

'Seems to me that this is personal.' Ludditch took a pinch
of tobacco from a pouch and tamped it down into the bowl
of the pipe. 'If we needed your services, we'd ask for 'em.
One thousand seven fifty.'

'One thousand five hundred.' The eshtran raised his bid.

'I see desperation in your eyes, Mr Harsq. And desperate
men pay. One thousand seven hundred.'

The eshtran's lip curled.

'All right, one thousand seven hundred. May Brask have
mercy on your soul. Seven hundred in advance, one thousand on delivery.'

Ludditch nodded, took the stem in his mouth, struck a
match against the wooden post of the porch and cupped the
other hand around the bowl of the pipe as he lit the tobacco.
He shook the match out and tossed it in the darkness.

'And what are we lookin' for, just out of interest?'

'I'm not sure, but there will be signs of its presence that
can be read by the enlightened eye. Wherever it has taken
refuge, there will be an unholy, unnatural aura. I will have to
see it with my own eyes to identify it, but tell your people to
bring me word of anything they find in the forest that is
strange or out of the ordinary.'

'Forest is full of strange things – not least some of our
people.'

Harsq gave him a dry look.

'Then bring me news of anything that doesn't belong.'

Ludditch sucked on the stem of his pipe and blew a
smoke ring.

'Now, that we can do.'

+ + + +

Nayalla frowned as she tried to recall the details of the legend she had seen narrated on the scrolls in Emos's workshop.

'Long before the Myunans walked this land, there was another race which lived here, a race of alchemists, called the Tuderem, I think. They came here many centuries ago and found a country that was rich and fertile, but suffering from some kind of curse. They somehow used their ability to change elements to release the land of its bane and made their home here. But the peace did not last. They had been here for decades, living in prosperity and contentment, when the Barian hordes came to the area. They laid waste to the alchemists' towns and villages, killing and torturing thousands.

'This was in the time of Gorskin Rax, the Brain Eater, when the Barian Empire was at its peak. It covered everywhere south of Guthoque and west of the esh. The Tuderem who survived the slaughter were facing an existence in cruel slavery, like so many other races that had fallen to the Barians. They had wandered ever eastwards to stay clear of the hordes, but now there was nowhere to run. North of what is now the Reisenick territory lay the Gluegrove Swamps, a death-trap to anyone who did not know the paths, and beyond that marshland, the Barians ruled. All the plains to the south and east, and the mountains in the west, were also under their heel; the alchemists had nowhere to go.

'Except for Absaleth. In their day, there was a cave entrance at the foot of Absaleth; it led into a network of caverns and it was the last Tuderem outpost. Faced with slavery or death at the hands of the Barians, they decided to take one last desperate step … and sealed themselves into the caves. They blocked up the entrance, using their sciences to form a seal even the Barians could not break through, and that was the last that was ever heard from them.'

'By the gods,' Noogan breathed. 'Is that true?'

'I had always thought it was a legend,' Nayalla said. 'There are so many about Absaleth. It has always inspired stories. But Myunan writing is different from yours. We use pictograms. In Myunian, this is the symbol for Tuderem.'

She drew a simple figure in the dust with her finger. It had a large head, short legs and a pair of hands at the end of each arm.

'Begs the question …' Paternasse put in. 'If your story's true, did they ever get out?'

'If they did,' Nayalla looked at him. 'It's a part of the legend that I haven't heard.'

'Of course they got out!' Dalegin exclaimed, his voice a little too high and a little too loud in the stone room. 'What kind of lunatics would seal themselves up forever?'

'You're right, Dal,' Paternasse reassured him, concerned about the hint of hysteria in the younger man's voice. 'They were smart. They'd have made sure there was a way out.'

Dalegin stood up and waved his torch around. The light caught the branched shapes around the edge of the room.

'They had trees! How did they grow trees in a cave?'

They all turned their lights on the trees. Mirkrin was the only one who did not approach them, one look at them told him they were artificial and he preferred to stay in the open space in the centre of the room. There were no doorways in this room. He held up his light to peer further up the stairwell.

Paternasse touched a bough on one of the trees and the decrepit limb dropped off, shattering into powder as it hit the floor.

'It's wood,' he said. 'But it's not a tree. It has no grain. It's uncanny though. It doesn't look like it was carved.'

'It was moulded,' Nayalla told him. 'Cast and put together as if it were metal. It's beautifully done. Even a Myunan transmorpher couldn't manage this – create wood that has no grain. Some of them still have what look like leaves on them. These have been transmuted, made in one material and then changed into another.'

'They made trees.' Noogan shook his head in wonder. 'It's like they knew they were never going to see them again.'

'Well, we are,' Mirkrin's voice said, tightly. 'There's nothing for us on this floor. Let's keep moving.'

'Bloody right,' Dalegin joined him at the foot of the shaft. 'Who gives a damn about some old fossils? They're dead, and I don't mean to join 'em.'

The ceiling was lower in this room, and Nayalla was able to reach the rim of the next floor by putting her foot in Mirkrin's cupped hands and hoisting herself up. She found more columns, tied the rope to the base of one and dropped it over the edge. While the others climbed up, she took a look around. It was another round room, but this one had doorways leading off it. Six doorways, all with stone doors, all standing open. She held her light up into the shaft above them. There were at least three more floors.

Paternasse was the last to come up the rope. As he lifted his elbows up onto the edge of the floor, a shudder ran through the room and then grew in intensity. The room echoed with a deep rumble. Paternasse lost his grip on the edge and dangled precariously from the one hand that clutched the rope. He got his other hand on it, but the shaking was bouncing him around and he slid downwards. Noogan dived forwards, grabbing hold of the old man's wrist. Dalegin and Nayalla caught hold of Noogan and between them, they hauled Paternasse up. The room was shaking violently and Mirkrin was crouching on the ground, holding onto one of the rusted columns, his face tense with fear. A section of wall fell away to reveal bare rock behind and cracks appeared across the ceiling.

'Get in the doorways!' Paternasse roared over the chaotic noise.

They rushed for the reinforced frames of the doorways, Nayalla pulling Mirkrin's arms from the column and dragging him with her. More chunks of stone fell from the wall and dust burst from some of the fissures appearing across the ceiling. The air filled with the stone powder, choking them and getting in their eyes. The shaking died down and they moved cautiously out from the doorways, coughing and wiping the dust from their faces. Nayalla stayed close to Mirkrin. She could feel him trembling, holding tight to the doorpost. Her knees were shivering too, from the adrenaline, but she knew that the tremor had terrified her husband, even more than the rest of them. He was reliving the time he spent crushed beneath the rock of the mine tunnel. She coughed and put her arm around him.

'It's over – come on, it's over.'

He prised his fingers from the stone and opened his eyes.

'Never knew I had such affection for architecture,' he sniffed self-consciously.

He stood up straighter, ashamed of his fear, but the miners

were busy studying the damage to the room.

'Haven't seen anything like this in the other rooms,' Paternasse was saying. 'Apart from things that have fallen apart from rot and rust, the place has had no structural damage at all. And now this. I think these quakes are a new thing, something the mountain hasn't seen before.'

'We don't get earthquakes in this area,' Nayalla told him. 'I don't know what these are, but they only started after the exorcism.'

Paternasse nodded gravely. He put his hand on the wall, his eyes raised to the ceiling above them. In his mind's eye, he pictured the damage being done in the rock above them. Stress fractures would be weakening the structure of the stone, causing it to settle under its own weight. This would cause pressure below, pressure that the rock would try to release in any way it could. The caves were an inherent weakness in the mountain and all this space offered a means of releasing the pressure through the walls and ceilings. If weakened enough, the rock could keep collapsing in on itself until it had settled as far down as it could go.

'The place is weak, without its soul,' he muttered. 'We need to get out from under it. This whole mountain could come down around our ears.'

With no idea which door to take, they replenished the powder on their torches and split up, each trying a different way. Three of the doorways soon turned out to be dead ends, leading into smaller rooms. One went through to another well, a waist-high rectangular wall containing a black pool of water. Two others led to corridors that ended in closed doors, their silvery white metal curiously free of corrosion. Noogan and Dalegin attacked one and then the other with their pickaxes, but the metal was barely scratched.

'Try some wedges lads,' Paternasse said as they battled with the second door.

The gap between the jamb and the door was too thin, but a few blows of a pickaxe made enough of a hole to get a wedge in. Dalegin drove the wedge in harder with a lump-hammer, but the door did not budge. Nor could he get the wedge out. They tried hammering in two more, but with the same results.

Paternasse stepped forward and ran his finger down the door, sticking the tip of it in his mouth and swilling the taste around.

'It's metal, but not a type I know.' The old miner hawked and spat. 'Harder, denser too, strong like steel, but it's not steel. I can taste rutile or ilmenite. These doors are barricades, made to keep something in … or something out. They'll take some shiftin'.'

'We have to break through,' Dalegin snarled. 'We have to.'

'It'll take days to get through this door.' Paternasse shook his head. 'Even then, I'm not sure we could do it. Let's see what else is around.'

'I'm starvin',' Noogan said abruptly and as soon as he said it, they all realised how hungry they were. And cold too. The search for a way out had distracted them from their bodies' demands, but the events of the day were catching up on them.

They sat down where they were, propping up their torches, and took out all the food they were carrying. The miners had their packed lunches, pasties and biscuit and some apples; the Myunans had bread, cheese and a spicy pork paste. They all looked glumly at the collection of food.

'We could stretch this out for a day, maybe two,' Mirkrin said. 'But that's it. And we need to check the water in that well – my canteen's almost empty.'

It was true for all of them. They had all been sipping at their water since the first cave-in, but their thirst was growing and their water supply dwindling. Thirst would kill them long before hunger broke them down, but the water in the well could deal out death even faster if it were contaminated.

Nayalla clutched her empty belly. She should have been making dinner for her family around now; she thought anxiously of her children, and one look at her husband told her he was sharing her concerns. With all that had happened, she had had little time to worry about them. She felt a rising dread at the thought that they might have fallen foul of the Noranians, or the skacks. Mirkrin squeezed her hand and shook his head. There was nothing they could do for them now but hope.

'There are no cave openings on Absaleth,' Nayalla told them. 'The nearest caves that I know of are up north. This place may connect up to them somewhere. We should try to head in that direction if we can.'

Mirkrin took his compass out, but the needle spun lazily, failing to point in any one direction.

'Too much iron,' Paternasse told him. 'That'll be no good down here. I think I can keep us pointed the right way, but that's assuming we can find a route that'll take us out.'

They pooled the food, and Paternasse rationed it out, keeping two thirds of it for later. The paltry pieces of sandwich were downed in seconds, and then they all felt even more miserable than before. Nothing was worse than feeding a hunger with too little food.

'What was that?' Nayalla said suddenly.

They all froze, listening intently. There was a skittering sound and then a wet, gulping noise. All five of them jumped to their feet and rushed back up the corridor. Casting their lights around, they spread out. Paternasse and Dalegin crept into the room with the well. They could see nothing moving. They were about to leave and continue their search, when Dalegin tugged Paternasse's sleeve.

'Jussek, look!'

There, within the well's stone walls, ripples disturbed the inky waters of the pool.

+ + + +

The mist had grown so thick over the road that Jube had slowed the lead wagon down to a crawl. Taya and Lorkrin were fast asleep on top of some sacks near the front of the flatbed and Draegar was dozing in his usual sleeping position, curled up into an armoured dome that offered both shelter and protection.

'Can't see a thing out there,' Jube muttered. 'It's like looking into the esh.'

Emos nodded. He was weary but couldn't sleep, his mind haunted by thoughts of Nayalla and Mirkrin. He put down the wood chisel that he was shaping into an amorphing tool for Lorkrin and shook his head in exhaustion.

'We need to pull over for a while,' Jube called back to him. 'Let the engines cool down and refuel. I probably need to top up the oil too.'

'We could do with some hot food and drink, too,' Emos

assented. 'I'll take a turn driving when we get going again. I won't sleep tonight.'

Jube found a flat stretch of grass under the trees and pulled the truck off the road. Khassiel brought the second wagon to a halt behind them, cutting the engine and jumping from the cab to stretch her stiff limbs.

The sudden silence woke up the sleepers. Taya and Lorkrin blinked and looked groggily over the side of the flat-bed. Draegar uncurled and sat up.

'What's all the rubbish on the road?' Lorkrin asked.

There were pieces of clothing, tin cans and other bits and pieces strewn down the road.

'Looks like your side of the room after your friends have been over,' Taya murmured.

'At least my friends keep the mess on my side of the room.'

'Let's get a fire going,' Jube said. 'That's a damp mist. It'll put a chill on you if you let it. Fetch me a pot down, Taya, lass. I've a hankerin' for some tea.'

'I'll get some wood,' Lorkrin piped up, jumping over the side of the wagon.

'No, you won't!' Emos said sternly. 'I'm not having you wandering off into these woods in a fog. I'll go. You and Taya stay here.'

Lorkrin folded his arms, looking out into the trees with a sour expression.

'We're not babies, y'know,' he sniffed.

'I'll do it,' Cullum grunted, grabbing a lantern. 'I need to stretch my legs anyway.'

He had fallen asleep with one leg tucked under the other and was now pacing about woodenly, trying to rub the pins and needles from his unresponsive limb. He picked up his weapon, a battle-hammer with a flat head on one side and a sharp spike on the other, and made his way off into the woods.

'You work on their tools,' Draegar told his friend. 'We'll get the firewood.'

He lit a candle and followed Cullum into the grey darkness. Emos shrugged and sat down to finish the finer work on the tools he had started. Jube picked up kindling from under the trees nearby and got a small blaze going. Cullum came back with an armful of wood and Jube soon had the food heating over the fire. The Noranian headed back into the trees to get more and that was when they felt the ground start to shake.

The carefully stacked wood of the fire collapsed; the pots clattered to the rhythm of the trembling ground and the wagons bounced on their suspension. Taya and Lorkrin deliberately stood up and tried keeping their balance, but tumbled to the ground, giggling. They stopped abruptly when they saw Emos's anxious face and they remembered where their parents were and what this tremor would mean for them. Even as this thought occurred to them, the earthquake quickly faded into stillness. Somewhere out of sight of them in the forest, there was a sharp crack and they heard Cullum bellow. Khassiel seized her crossbow and another lantern and charged into the woods. Emos leapt to his feet.

'Stay here!' he barked at the two children. Then he bounded into the fog after the soldier.

Jube got up and followed their uncle. The two Myunans stood sullenly, looking into the trees.

'Make a sound and we'll make mince of yuh,' a voice

whispered abruptly behind them.

They turned to see two men holding broad-bladed knives at the ready. Out of the mist came more Reisenicks. Some dropped down from the trees, others materialised out of the fog. All of them wore the distinctive clothes of rawhide and fur, all with long knives or blowpipes held ready. There was the sound of clicking joints as they moved and the exaggerated features of their faces were stony and hostile.

'Oh, right,' Lorkrin snorted. 'This is what we get for doing what we're told!'

The leader held up his knife, then raised a finger to his lips. Lorkrin stood up, using his body to hide Taya as she quickly gathered the tools their uncle had been working on and stuffed them into her backpack. She stood up beside him, anxiously eyeing the clansmen's sharp blades.

'Does this mean Mr Ludditch didn't like the pendant?' she asked.

+ + + +

Cullum had a thin wooden stake through his left leg, just above the ankle. He had triggered a trap intended for a much smaller animal, set by the trunk of a tree. He lay with both hands clutching his leg, roaring defiance at the offending spike for its assault.

Khassiel reached him first, with Emos close behind.

'By the gods!' Khassiel scoffed. 'I thought you were being disembowelled, or something, Cullum. Stop being such a baby.'

'Lie still,' Emos ordered the Forward-Batterer. 'It's gone clean through. I don't think it's hit anything important.'

'It hit my bloody leg! Is that not important enough?'

'You walked right into a skunkrin spike. Weren't you trained to avoid booby traps?'

'I was watching out for man-sized traps. Nobody said anything about any damned skunkrin spikes.'

Khassiel raised her crossbow. Someone else was coming. Draegar crashed through the brush. He stopped and sighed when he saw what had happened.

'I thought somebody was in danger,' he chided the injured man. 'Is that little thing what all the noise was about?'

'That little thing is my *leg* ...'

'You're lucky,' Emos told him. 'They don't poison these kinds of traps.'

'Lucky, my arse! Lucky would be stepping on a bag of gold. There's a bloody *spike* through my leg.'

Jube trotted up.

'What's all the fuss?' he asked.

'Cullum's pricked 'imself,' Khassiel cocked her head in the direction of her comrade.

'That's right!' the Forward-Batterer fumed. 'Have a laugh at a man's misfortune! I won't be able to walk on this ...'

'It's not a trivial wound,' Emos agreed. 'Let's get you back to the fire where we can have a proper look at it.'

He drew his knife and cut the spine free of the branch that held it, then he and Jube helped Cullum hop back towards the road. They found the pots of food boiling over, the camp deserted. Emos jumped onto the back of the lead truck to look around. There was no sign of the children.

'Reisenicks,' Draegar growled, reading the tracks on the ground. 'A hunting party.'

'Get in the cabs!' Emos told them. 'Now, everyone in the cabs!'

A dart struck Cullum in the arm.

'Hey!' he yelped, and slumped against Jube, knocked out cold.

The miner dragged him to the cab of the lead truck and hauled him in. More darts struck the windscreen. Khassiel jumped into the other cab, quickly followed by Emos.

Draegar, who would struggle to fit in the cab of a wagon anyway, grabbed a crank handle from the side of Jube's truck, and Jube threw the starter switch as the Parsinor twisted the engine into life. Darts zipped through the air, bouncing off his armour and sticking uselessly in his tough hide. It would take a lot of darts to bring down a Parsinor. He fitted the handle into the socket on the front of Khassiel's truck. As he cranked the second motor up, he looked through the glass into Emos's eyes.

'Get out of here!' he bellowed to his friend. 'I'll find them! You know I will! Now go!'

Stones started to smack off the sides of the trucks, one finding the windscreen of Jube's truck, smashing a white cobweb of cracks across the pane.

'Go!' Draegar roared. Then he turned around and plunged into the forest.

They had no choice. Outnumbered and under attack from an enemy they could not see, the rescue party were forced to gun the engines of their vehicles and flee. Driving recklessly through the thick fog, they soon outran their attackers, but Emos could not take his eyes off the back window. Somewhere back there were his niece and nephew, and he had deserted them. The Reisenicks had turned on the group. He did not know why, but the rescue party's chances of escaping them and getting out of Ainslidge Woods were slim, if there were any chance at all. He knew Draegar was right. He had to carry on and reach the caves or Nayalla, Mirkrin and the trapped miners had no hope. But even though he had absolute trust in his friend, his heart was wrenched at his own failure to help the children.

+ + + +

Taya closed her eyes as she was flung through the air. The Reisenicks were following a path through the cobrush jungle, but in many places the track ran up fallen tree trunks or over ravines and rather than wait for their bound captives to stumble across the obstacles, the Reisenicks carried them along, tossing them over any break in the path. Strong, bony hands caught her as she flailed over to the other side of the stream and their tight grip made her cry out. Lorkrin came flying over behind her. The Reisenicks moved quickly, accustomed to the difficult terrain and seeming to know their way through the woods even in the misty darkness.

She was scared. The clansmen were putting more and more distance between them and the road, and soon after they had headed into the forest, another one had shown up behind them to announce that the rest of her 'gang' had got away. Got away? Where could they be going? They were supposed to be coming after her and her brother. Where were they getting away to?

Lorkrin had attempted to bite through the hard cords that bound his wrists, but a Reisenick just laughed and slapped him across the head. He looked closer at his bonds in the gloom and gagged. The 'cords' were nothing of the kind; his wrists were bound by a long, thin spidersnake. Invertebrate constrictors, these creatures would wrap themselves around their prey and sink their fangs into it. This one had not bitten him and he realised the Reisenicks had pulled its fangs, but the reflex to constrict made it a perfect means of binding Myunans. He had tried slunching, to slip his hands out, but the spidersnake constricted with his flesh; the Reisenicks had dealt with shape-shifters before. He was forced to creft his flesh to stop the creature from squeezing his wrists down to nothing. They were now half their normal thickness and hurt more than ever.

They travelled into the night, the Myunans sore and uncomfortable from being carried over the bony shoulders of the clansmen. As they got further into the forest, the Reisenicks started to chat among themselves. Some of it aimed deliberately at terrifying their captives.

'We gonna have us some Myunan roast tonight, boys!'

'What the hell are you boy, some kind o' savage? Myunans gotta be *stewed*!'

The one carrying Taya pinched her arm and she swore at him.

'This one's got spirit, but not much eatin' on 'er.'

'Nah, Myunans is stringy, but they got no bones to speak of! Plenty of eatin' on her, just got to stew 'er for a day, add some onions, some earthfruit, bit o' ginger … Our mama got the best recipe in the clans for Myunan.'

Taya clenched her eyes shut. She was not going to give them the satisfaction of seeing her cry. She had heard that Reisenicks ate other races, but Uncle Emos had assured her that it wasn't true.

Sensing light on her eyelids, Taya opened them to see that the hunting party had arrived at a Reisenick village. She had never seen one before and it was something to behold.

The smells of old fur, spices and boiling fat filled her nostrils. All of the structures were built of wood frames covered in animal hides, all with drawings marked out on them, depicting hunting scenes, battles, marriages and important deaths.

The place seemed to be asleep, although lanterns burned on posts along the main road through the village. Everywhere, metal and wooden wind chimes tinkled, crafted into arcane shapes to ward off evil spirits. Freshly skinned hides hung out to dry. The bones too were put to use, for each doorway had its totem of skull and bones to keep the malevolent ghosts of the forest at bay.

Lorkrin shivered. It was not a place that welcomed strangers. The gleam of painted metal further down the street caught his eye and there he saw two wagons parked up next to a large building. One of the wagons was the Braskhiam generator truck. He clicked his tongue at Taya and pointed with his head. She twisted around to look over her bearer's shoulder. A dark look passed over her face. This could not bode well for them.

They were carried up the muddy street to the meeting-house and brought inside. The smells of old leather and animal fur were stronger inside. The place was a large rectangular hall, with an open central area in which a fire blazed. Lorkrin and Taya had not realised how cold they were until they felt its blazing heat. The damp night and the fear had taken a toll on them.

'What you got there?' came a voice, and their eyes turned towards the top of the hall. Sitting in a hefty, carved wooden chair was a big Reisenick with piercing eyes. The children immediately recognised one of the brass chains that hung on his chest. It was Ludditch.

Beside him, on a smaller chair, sat the Braskhiam eshtran, Harsq. The two children were hauled in front of the two men.

'What in the blazes ...?' Ludditch looked up at his clans-men. 'These two are Myunans. Where'd you get 'em?'

'Fell off the back of a truck,' one of them replied, to the sniggers of the others. 'Nearly got a whole lot more, but they got away. The boys is after 'em now.'

'A truck?' Ludditch snarled. 'Like the one Emos Harprag was in?'

There were blank looks from the clansmen. Taya nodded and Lorkrin scowled.

'I said go out and find anythin' that didn't belong!' the chieftain exclaimed. 'Harprag paid 'is tribute, ya fools. Now you've gone and taken his cubs? You're supposed to be on the lookout for ... for unseemly things. Forces of evil and the like. I mean, holy meat, Cleet, if'n you had two times more brains you'd be twice as stupid.'

'I didn't know about any Myunans!' Cleet retorted, the skin around his mass of freckles turning a deathly pale. He hunched his big shoulders and looked down at his feet. 'I was just doin' like I was asked.'

Ludditch ground his teeth to control his temper. Cleet was a close cousin, and so loyal as to be embarrassing. Too stupid to be scared of anything, he would fight wild dogs in a pit for his own entertainment. But the boy couldn't think worth a damn.

'The tribute system keeps the peace, Cleet. Harprag on 'is own is a menace, but you mess with a Myunan's cubs and you mess with their whole tribe. And the Noranians have already got 'em riled. You ever fought a war against Myunans, Cleet?'

'You know I haven't, Learup. But my pappy …'

'Yer old pappy was killed by Myunans, Cleet. But unlike you he was born with a cupful o' sense, and he knew what you don't, that fightin' Myunans is like fightin' ghosts. Now put these cubs back where you got 'em.'

'But the trucks've gone, Learup. We don't know where. It could take time to find 'em.'

Ludditch gritted his teeth and scratched the thick wrinkles on the back of his neck.

'All right, we keep 'em for now. Untie 'em!' He glared down at the two children. 'You're alive 'cause it'll keep the peace. Behave yourselves and you'll get back to your pappy …'

'He's our uncle,' Taya corrected him.

'... You'll get back to your uncle in one piece. Understand?'

'Yes,' the two children chirped in unison, as knives cut the spidersnakes from their wrists.

✦   ✦   ✦   ✦

The reflections of the five faces stared back out of the well's dark water, expressions of fear and curiosity etched upon them.

'You definitely didn't touch the water?' Nayalla asked again.

'For the third time, no!' Paternasse insisted. 'We didn't even breathe on it.'

'Could be a current,' Noogan suggested.

'Those were footsteps we heard,' Dalegin said tightly. 'Currents don't have feet and they don't come out of wells and wander around.'

'There's something else in here with us,' Noogan whispered. 'Maybe there are still some ghosts left down here.'

'Makes you wonder what happened to the folks who made the place,' Dalegin added.

Nayalla tried an experiment, dipping her torch into the water. It kept burning, the light dulled but still glowing. Then she took a pinch of the burning powder and rubbed it on her forehead. It stuck there, an improvised headlamp that would give her enough light to see by.

'I could go in and have a look,' she said, leaning over the rim.

'No.' Mirkrin shook his head. 'We don't know what's in there.'

'I'll get in,' Noogan said. 'Just to have a look under the water.'

'If anyone's going, it's me,' Nayalla said. 'Now keep your eyes peeled.'

Before anyone could argue, she slid over the side and into the water.

'Damn it!' Mirkrin clutched the stone rim so hard his knuckles went white.

He should have gone before she had a chance, but his fear held him back. The tiny black space terrified him and seeing his wife down there brought a cold sweat to his skin. He could see her pushing her way down the wall, working against her own buoyancy, looking to one side and then the other. She was far below the level of the floor when she stopped moving, her face looking towards her feet. Then suddenly she twisted up and kicked for the surface. She kicked, but did not move. Mirkrin leaned closer in. He could see her expression, panic as she struggled for the surface. Nayalla was being pulled down into the depths of the well. He turned, frantically searching for something to use to reach for her. There was nothing long enough. With a roar of desperation, he dived into the water.

He kicked downwards, reaching out for his wife, but she was dragged away from him, deep into the blackness. He could see the flame on her brow after he lost sight of her and he swam hard to catch up, his own terror forgotten in the fear for his wife. The pressure built up on his ears and he held his nose to clear it. Then he felt it; he was moving faster, caught in a current. It was strong, pulling him down faster and faster. There would be no way back to the surface. The light on his wife's forehead disappeared ahead of him, but suddenly, as if it had gone around a corner. The pressure of the water squeezed his chest and his lungs burned. He kept pushing out air to relieve the bursting feeling that he had to inhale. The water was crushing him with its weight, the walls closing in on him in the dark. Panic screamed at him to open his mouth and breathe. He could feel the walls either side now; they were closer, the current throwing him against one side and then the other. Twice, he brushed past side openings, but the current flowed in from them, driving him on. The walls narrowed until he was slunching to fit through the increasingly constricted channel. He was in complete darkness now, trapped in the water's grip. His lungs were going to burst. He had to open his mouth. He had to breathe, he had to open … Light ahead. He could see light. Holding his nose closed, he pushed some breath out and willed himself with all his might to hold the water out until he reached the light. His head spun. He saw pinpoints of light flash in front of his eyes and he started to pass out. If he passed out he was lost. He would drown as his unconscious body breathed in water. The light came towards him, closer … closer …

closer ... It seemed that it would never reach him. His vision blurred and he shook his head to try and clear it. He felt himself slowing down, rising out of the current's grasp. Then he saw ripples above him. The surface. He clawed up towards it.

His head broke the water with a gasp and he sucked in air. A few more coughing breaths later, he saw Nayalla floating motionless in front of him. She stirred, but her movements were weak and caused her head to sink beneath the surface. He swam to her and lifted her chin clear of the water. Mirkrin looked around. They were in a different kind of chamber; the pool was much larger than the mouth of the well and at floor level. He dragged his wife out and she vomited up water and coughed as she flopped down on the floor. They both lay there, shivering for some time.

8 THE CORPSE AND THE EARTHQUAKE

Draegar's hunt for the children was slowed in the dark. The mist was thick and the Reisenicks were cunning, cutting back and forth and sometimes travelling up in the trees. But they had made no real effort to hide their trail and Draegar was able to follow, slowly and methodically, by candlelight. His large frame was a hindrance in the thick brush and he often had to use his short sword to cut his way through. He had escaped from the road with relative ease and was now wary of being tracked himself by the remainder of the hunting party.

When he heard voices ahead, he snuffed out the candle and crept towards them, taking his time so as to allow his eyes to adjust to the darkness. It was a group of three Reisenicks.

'Well, what is it?' asked a tall, loose-limbed man.

'It's scrap, is what it is, Moorul,' a second one stated confidently, his jutting brow wrinkled up in thought. 'Plain as the nose on yer face.'

'Scrap don't up an' attack ya, Dourtch,' the third argued. He was a round barrel of a man with a thin bush of hair receding towards the back of his head. They were all standing on the edges of a net, caught up in the middle of which was a bundle of rusted wire, tools and various other bits of waste metal. Draegar was puzzled by the conversation until the bundle suddenly started thrashing around. The Reisenicks grabbed clubs that looked to have been cut recently to deal with the strange intruder and batted at the thing until it stopped moving again.

'Seems to me,' Dourtch announced. 'That this is just what that priest fella was talkin' about. Don't get much more "not belongin'" than this. We've got ourselves a ghost right here.'

'Damnedest ghost I ever saw,' Moorul grumbled.

'Ghosts come in all shapes and sizes,' Dourtch told him. 'Why, just last year, I saw a ghost out Timbermarsh way that was in the shape of a logger toad. But big as a house ...'

'That was that blindwater you were drinkin', Dourtch,' the balding man said. 'Now pipe down, so's I can figure out how we're goin' to get this thing back to Ainsdale.'

'Sure, Tupe.'

Draegar called out to them.

'Pardon me, sirs. Permission to come into the light?'

The three men were immediately on their guards, but kept their feet on the edges of the net.

'How many out there?' Tupe shouted back.

'Just me.'

'Come on out then.'

Draegar stepped out of the trees, and knew immediately that none of these men had ever seen a Parsinor before. They pulled long knives from their belts to supplement the clubs, staring at his twin pairs of legs, his armour and the sheer size of him.

'Holy meat, what manner o' creature are you, boy?' Dourtch asked.

'I'm a Parsinor, from the southern deserts.'

'You're a long way from the desert now, boy.' Tupe spat a gob of phlegm onto the ground. 'You're in Reisenick country.'

'The party I was travelling with paid tribute to be here,' Draegar told them. 'But there has been some kind of misunderstanding. Some of your clansmen took two of our people captive, mere children. I am just trying to ensure their safe return. I would like to speak to Ludditch. I have things I can trade.'

'If your people were taken, they'll stay taken, until Ludditch says otherwise,' Moorul sneered.

'Seems to me that your party has left you high and dry, Mr Parsnip.' Tupe rolled some more phlegm around his mouth. 'You're out here on your own, and anything we want from you we can take. Seems to me too, that you're just the kind of thing Ludditch is lookin' for, seein' as how you're unseemly and you don't belong in these here woods. So we'll be takin' you to see the chieftain all right, but first we're goin' to take that fine lookin' skin off of ya. It'll look right nice in ma kitchen.'

Draegar sighed. If the Reisenicks were more interested in trophy hunting than trading, then getting the children was going to be even harder than he had expected. He had been hoping that the attack on the trucks had been a mistake, that the clansmen would be open to a peace offering.

'I don't want a fight,' he tried again. 'Please, just let me speak to Ludditch.'

'Ludditch don't speak to animals,' Tupe growled and lunged at the Parsinor.

Draegar deflected the knife with the back of his hand and drove the heel of his palm into the Reisenick's chest so hard it broke ribs and hurled Tupe to the ground. Moorul was already leaping over him, swinging his club at Draegar's head. The Parsinor swivelled, the blow bouncing off his armoured shoulder and he slammed the edge of his hand backwards into the other man's groin. Moorul folded up and crumpled to the mud.

Dourtch threw himself on Draegar's shoulders, his blade seeking the Parsinor's throat. Draegar turned and smashed the smaller man against the trunk of a tree, his hinged shell crushing the spindly Reisenick against the wood. He stepped away and the limp body slid onto the gnarled roots. He turned to find Tupe standing up facing him, breathing painfully. The Reisenick slashed at him with his knife, drawing a line of blood across the Parsinor's arm. Draegar did not flinch, catching the hand with the knife and using its momentum to swing the arm back around and drive the tip of the blade into the man's thigh. Tupe screamed and fell to the ground clutching his leg.

'You should have traded,' Draegar grunted.

He hesitated, knowing that leaving them alive would ensure that the Reisenicks came out in force after him and might take out their grievances on the children. But killing in cold blood had never been in his nature and even with so much at stake, he could not bring himself to sink to it. Turning to see the mesh of metal struggling to free itself from the net, he decided on one more gamble. If this was the ghost Ludditch was looking for, then Draegar would bring it to him. Perhaps then they could work this out without more people getting hurt. Reisenicks mostly. He gathered the thrashing scrap up in the net, the whole bundle about the size and weight of a large pig, and swung it over his shoulder. Then he relit his candle and continued on after the hunting party that had taken the children. The first signs of dawn were probing through the trees. Soon he would have daylight, and then he would find them.

✦ ✦ ✦ ✦

Mirkrin and Nayalla huddled together, recovering from their ordeal. The room around them was low and rectangular. Corridors led off either end. There was no sign of false windows or the usual carvings of plants and trees, no sculptures of animals. It had a functional feel to it, as if it were here to serve a purpose, but that was all. The large pool took up one entire side of the chamber, with steps leading down into it and plinths around the edges for sitting on. But the light was the first thing they noticed. Oval sections of the walls themselves glowed a dull blue.

When he had rested for a while, Mirkrin got up and examined one of them, finding a fungus phosphorescing behind panes of aged and dusty glass. Water trickled down the wall inside the glass from somewhere above, obviously feeding the fungus the nutrients it needed. The fact that almost all the glass cabinets had surviving fungus showed that this was no accident, but, like all the other rooms, this one had that chilling, lifeless feel to it.

Another thing struck him about the room. There were no cobwebs. Dust, but no spiders' webs.

'Where are the spiders?' he wondered aloud.

Nayalla raised her head and looked around. She stood up, frowning. The flames on her head had gone out, the powder washed from her skin, and they had no torches to give them a better light. She peered down one of the corridors. It appeared to be a dead end; the light did not quite extend to the end wall, but she could see it was closed off. The other corridor was the same. She was about to explore further, when a skittering noise made them jump. There was no mistaking it. And this time it was at the bottom of the second corridor. They crept towards it, eyes straining in the poor light to catch sight of the source of the sound. Up near the ceiling, they saw four bunches of bulging eyes staring down at them.

Suddenly, the creature launched itself out of the shadows at them. It landed on Nayalla's head and shoulders – hard, pointed feet digging into her flesh and getting tangled in her hair. Nayalla shrieked and tore at it. Mirkrin seized its back legs and hurled it against the wall. It hit the floor with a thud, curled into a ball and started crying like a child. Despite themselves, both Myunans instinctively started hushing it and reassuring it softly. Then, feeling foolish that their parenting instincts had been brought out by a creature that had just attacked them, they stood back and studied it.

It was hairy, with at least a dozen legs, all sticking out at different angles from its body. In fact, its hairs appeared to be nothing more than legs that had not fully formed. It was small too, the size of a toddler, with four stunted arms that stuck out from around its head, a small hand extending from each. The four sets of eyes surrounded the four mouths, each pale, bulging orb a different size, each with a pale cornea and an X-shaped pupil. It was impossible to tell its colour in the blue light, but by its shape, it appeared as if the creature had no top or bottom. It could stand up just as easily on what was now its back; it could roll sideways and never fail to have at least four feet on the ground.

'What are you?' Nayalla asked, in obvious fascination.

'We are Scout of the Seneschal,' the thing answered, in what sounded like four voices. 'So you Barians have come at last? You're bigger than we expected. It does not matter. We will defeat your horde and drive you back to the Outside.'

Mirkrin and Nayalla exchanged looks.

'Are there more of you?' Nayalla asked.

'More than there are of you,' the creature said quickly, raising itself up slightly. 'We will pluck the hair from your heads and fill your mouths with dust!'

'And if you have your way, you'll lead us outside?' Mirkrin pressed it.

'We will throw you screaming into the daylight, no quarter asked and none given!'

'Then we surrender to your superior forces,' Mirkrin told it. 'And we'll surrender our "horde" too if you can help us get to them.'

'Tell us where they are. We shall watch them wither beneath our gaze!'

A sudden hammering resounded down the corridor. The creature dashed back into the shadows. The wall at the end of the corridor was in fact a solid metal door, the very door that the miners were now trying to break through. Mirkrin strode down to it, pressing his hands against it.

'Paternasse?'

'Is that you Myunans?' the old miner called back, his voice barely audible through the slab of metal. 'How'd you get out there? Can you open the door?'

Mirkrin found a counterbalance mechanism set into an alcove in the wall. It was ancient, but still in working order. He released the brake and cranked a winch that unwound a chain. A stone weight dropped through the floor, lifting the door straight up along greased rails – more signs of recent maintenance.

The miners stood poised and wary on the other side.

'We thought you'd drowned down there,' Paternasse said.

'Close as I'd like to get,' Mirkrin smiled wearily. 'Come on through. It seems we've found a native. It … they say they know the way out.'

+ + + +

Lorkrin and Taya were left in a small room off the main hall, with some gooseberry tea and a meal of potatoes and gristly meat in some kind of stew. They were both famished and they gobbled down the steaming hot grub, nearly burning their mouths in their haste. Once they had eaten, they went to the door and tried to listen in on what was being said outside. They could not hear much, the murmur of voices and the occasional exclamation, but nothing that told them what was going to happen to them.

'How long do you think it will be before Uncle Emos comes for us?' Lorkrin asked.

'I hope he hurries up,' his sister replied. 'The longer it takes, the worse it is for Ma and Pa.'

'And the miners.'

'Yeah.'

They sat glumly on the floor, their backs against the wall. It was a relief to know that the Reisenicks had kidnapped them by mistake. But time was not on their side and every delay could cost their parents their lives. And besides, sitting still did not come easy to them.

Lorkrin looked up at the ceiling. There was a hatch in it

that had to lead into the space below the roof. Taya read his mind.

'It wouldn't hurt to know what they're talking about,' she thought out loud.

'They didn't say we couldn't go up into the roof,' Lorkrin reasoned.

They took out the tools that Emos had made for them and began sculpting. The implements were crude and unfinished, but useable. They scooped the sides of their heads out into plate-like discs to form huge ears and then lengthened their fingers and toes, whittling the tips into claws. Lorkrin cupped his hands and Taya launched herself off them, caught the rafter beside the trapdoor and pushed it open. Then she swung up and into the attic space. She stretched out her legs to give her the extra length she needed to grip a nearby strut, and dangled down to catch her brother's hand when he jumped and helped him climb up.

The attic extended the full length of the hall. It was dark, lit only by light coming up through cracks in the floor. That made what they saw before them even eerier. The room was filled with objects covered with sheets of fabric. Whatever the objects were, they had the appearance of a large group of people draped in thin blankets. Lorkrin stepped carefully across the floor, checking for creaks in the floorboards and lifted the edge of one of the sheets. He gaped in shock and froze, a look of horror on his face. Taya thought her brother was trying to play a trick on her and went over to see what he was staring at. When she ducked her head under his arm and peeked in, she had to jam her fist into her mouth to stifle a shriek.

It was a Reisenick. A very old, very dead Reisenick – but

somehow preserved. Its skin was dry and leathery, brown and even black in places, but not rotten. The flesh had a thin, sunken quality, suggesting there was no muscle or fat beneath. The eyes were glass, clumsy copies of real eyeballs, with bubbles and imperfections in the cloudy glass itself and small coins set in as corneas, each with a hole drilled through the centre for a pupil. This was the body of an old man, strands of grey moustache hanging down each side of his mouth and sprouting thinly from his head. He was dressed in Reisenick splendour, a rich fur around his shoulders, fine leather jerkin and trousers and tall, well-heeled boots. Chains hung around his neck and there were bulky rings on his clawed fingers.

'By the gods,' Taya whispered. 'They stuff their dead.'

She had seen this done to animals, stuffed birds and wild beasts sold at markets in Sestina and Braskhia, but she had never heard of people doing it to their own. Lorkrin sneaked across the wooden floor, lifting one sheet after another. The attic was full of preserved bodies, some sitting, some positioned standing up, held in place with wooden frames. They were all well dressed; most looked as if they had reached old age, but there were some younger ones too, those who must have died through violence or disease. In all, there were nearly two dozen of these desiccated corpses.

'They're chieftains,' Lorkrin said quietly. 'It must be an honour to be preserved like this.'

'Look,' Taya pointed to a circle of chairs near the chimney flue in the centre of the room. 'They must hold gatherings here. They sit and talk with these things standing around them.'

'That reminds me,' Lorkrin pointed at the floor. 'Let's have a snoop.'

Peering through the cracks, they could see Ludditch and some other clansmen circled around the fire. Ludditch was speaking, his deep voice carrying over the crackling of the flames. The children pressed their enlarged ears to gaps in the floor and listened to what the Reisenick chieftain had to say.

'... and it's plain as a horse on a flat floor that the priest don't know what he's set in motion. He thinks the spirit of Absaleth is just some spirit, like in any old mountain. He don't know about the legend of Orgarth, or about the krundengrond. If he did, he wouldn't be doin' what he's doin'. Why, he even intends to go back along the road he came in when he's done. Like he thinks the road is goin' to be there.'

'Would it be that bad?' another man asked. 'I mean, it'll wipe out roads an' the like?'

'Spiroe, it'll change the damn map. If the legends are true, and Pappy says they been handed down faithful from father to son since the first clans settled here, then the krundengrond lies beneath everything south of Absaleth, as far as the Cloudscratchers and even up to the east of our land. That's half the Myunan territories and a fair hunk o' Sestina too. And the priest is gonna release the whole damn lot of it. That's what the quakes have been about. It's started already.'

'Damn, Learup. That's a whole lot o' people ...'

'A whole lot o' *other* people. Outsiders. And this thing is gonna wrap around us better than shell on a snail. Just about the only way onto our land after this'll be through the Gluegroves, and even the Noranians won't try crossin' that with their big fancy machines. I'm telling you, boys ...'

He stopped suddenly as the door opened. Lorkrin and Taya pressed their eyes to the cracks to see who had come in. It was the eshtran, Kalayal Harsq. He walked in as if he belonged, sitting down in the circle with the other men, seemingly unfazed by the Reisenicks' attitudes to strangers.

'I have been through what your men have brought in so far, sir,' he told Ludditch. 'A collection of diseased animals, stillbirths, oddly shaped vegetables and a bone totem that I'm sure one of them made himself. An impressive display of your tribe's resources.'

'I got them out of their beds to search for some mysterious, unknown nastiness in the dark,' Ludditch reminded him. 'One they have no means of identifyin'. I'd say it may take some time yet.'

'Well, let's hope daylight will bring some ...' The eshtran was interrupted by a tremble through the floor.

Taya felt the floorboards vibrate under her hands and looked to her brother. He was already on his feet, making for the trapdoor. Just as she got up to follow him, the tremor got stronger and knocked them both off their feet. The timber structure of the building creaked and rocked as the ground beneath it shuddered. Three of the preserved bodies fell over, breaking apart. Another toppled as Lorkrin crawled past, the head breaking off and rolling out from under the sheet. Before he could stop it, it bounced along the floor and tumbled through the open trapdoor.

'Aw bowels!' he swore softly, grabbing the edge and dropping down after it.

Taya followed him. He had grabbed up the head and she hung from the edge of the attic floor with the long clawed fingers of one hand, the other poised to close the hatch.

'I heard something upstairs!' They heard Ludditch shout. 'Check on those cubs!'

Lorkrin swung his arm to toss the head up, but the ground

swayed under his feet just as he let go and the head bounced off the ceiling, hit the wall and thudded against the floor. Taya gritted her teeth and swung back and forth, dangling precariously as the building shook. Feet clattered unsteadily up steps at the other end of the hall. Lorkrin picked up the head and threw it again. Taya caught it, flipped it into the attic, reached up and lowered the trapdoor. She dropped to the floor, both of them slunching into their normal forms just as the door swung open. Cleet poked his head in.

'You two up to anythin'?' he asked, suspiciously.

'No,' they answered together.

'Good,' he nodded; then added as an afterthought, 'Don't start bein' up to nothin' neither.'

'Aw, barnets!' a voice moaned above them. 'Some o' the forefathers is all broke up!'

Cleet turned and left, closing the door after him.

Taya heaved a sigh of relief. Lorkrin reached behind him and picked up three small, yellow objects from the floor, showing them to her. She put a hand to her face and shook her head. Lorkrin tugged at the edge of a loose piece of hide on the wall, and tucked the corpse's teeth out of sight behind it.

9 THE MAN WITH NO NAME

A tall, thin figure wandered through the forest. He did not know how long he had been walking. Perhaps days; perhaps longer. He felt achey and tired, as if he had come a long way, but he could not remember when and where he had started walking. The man became aware of his surroundings and wondered where he was. It was a dense, dark wood, the trees towering over him and blocking out most of the light from the sky. Shrouds of mist hung in the branches and lay in blankets over the undergrowth, making it hard to keep to the path. He did not know where the path was taking him and he wondered why he had started along it. A faint feeling of foreboding made him stare warily into the trees around him, as if he sensed some threatening presence out there in the darkness, but he could not put a face to it. He felt as if his mind, like the forest, was full of fog and the more he tried to remember, the less he could. The man was sure he was meant to have a name, but nothing came to him. He could remember words: tree, fog, sky ... the names of *things*. But nothing about himself. He was tall, the size of a fully grown man, and that meant he had to have a past of some kind.

He examined himself as he walked. Moving did not feel comfortable; he felt slow and awkward, making him wonder how old he was. There were gloves on his hands. He wore at least two pairs, and possibly three. He did not take the top ones off to check. His clothes were thick and heavy, as if he wore many layers. They had leaves and twigs sticking to them and thorns stuck out in places. His head and face were covered with cloth too. A hood and a thick scarf. Parts of his clothes were blackened and stiff in places. Burned. Fire did that. He wondered if he had been in a fire. He did not remember, but he knew what fire was. Bright, hot, energy. Fire. Taking some of these clothes off might tell him more about himself, but even as the thought occurred to him, he became frightened and panicky. For some reason, he was deathly afraid of what he would find. He left the clothes alone.

He heard voices ahead and he became curious. Others. Not him. These others might know where he was. They might even know who he was. He would ask. They appeared through the trees ahead of him, walking along the same trail. There were three of them, two of them supporting one who walked with a bad limp, blood soaking into one leg of his trousers. Red liquid that coursed around inside bodies. Blood. They stopped when they saw him and drew sharp metal objects. Knives. He stopped too.

'Who the heck is that?' one asked.

'How should I know?' another replied.

The third one, the injured one, lifted his pale face and glared.

'He's a stranger whoever he is,' he rasped. 'He don't belong.'

'The last one you said that about trounced us, Tupe.'

'This one don't look like the trouncin' type, Moorul. Bring 'im with us.'

Moorul sheathed his knife, pulled out a wooden club and strode up to the man with no memory, sizing him up. The man looked back at him. Moorul swung his club, connecting sharply with the man's head. The man nearly fell over, but regained his balance. Moorul hit him again. The man stayed standing. Moorul gave Tupe a doubtful look. Tupe nodded, egging him on. Moorul hit the man again. The man just kept looking at him, unsure of what he was supposed to do. Moorul frowned, lowered his club and pointed threateningly at him.

'You're comin' with us, boy,' he declared.

The man nodded. He had nowhere else to go. Moorul was at a loss for a moment. Then he took the man's arm and with Tupe and Dourtch following, he led the stranger toward their village.

+ + + +

Emos woke from a fitful sleep to see Khassiel sitting atop the cab of the truck, crossbow cradled in her arms. She nodded to him and turned her eyes back to the forest. The trucks were parked under the sheltering boughs of some beech trees. They were just out of sight of the banks of the river in the valley below them, where a Gabbit village lay, fishing nets trailing in the water and various workbenches set up to sort through and reconstruct the junk that the collectors brought back to the village. Houses made up of all kinds of materials were scattered along the near bank, and the Gabbits' dedication to the proliferation of their race was evident in the swarms of children playing in and around the houses.

There had been another tremor that morning, nearly forcing them off the road. Emos was still hoping that Draegar might get the children back and catch up with the party and had suggested that they eat and rest for a while. He sat up and considered for the hundredth time, since escaping the Reisenicks, going back and trying to make peace with Ludditch. But he knew that if the clansmen turned on them again, they might never get to Old Man's Cave. They had to press on. Ludditch would have some explaining to do later. Emos had followed the rules of tribute and been betrayed. Ludditch would have to be made to realise that there was a price to pay for that.

Forward-Batterer Cullum had recovered from the effects of the toxin on the dart with nothing more than a headache. Jube had drawn out the spine and seen to his wound and now he slept, snoring unevenly in the cab of the first wagon. Khassiel had slept earlier and seemed fresh and alert. Emos remembered the calmness with which she had shot Ceeanna from the air and, despite his distaste at having to work with her, part of him was glad of her cold blood. She looked fit and hard, her movements confident and he knew she would be useful if the Reisenicks fell upon them again.

He took out his tools and started working on himself. He wanted to take to the sky and scout the land. He normally chose the shape of an eagle because of its grace and the fact that it was closest to his size, but there were no eagles over Ainslidge Woods and the Reisenicks were expert marksmen with their blowpipes. They did not hunt the aukluk, however. It was the ugliest bird in the air; it was infested with parasites and its meat was poisonous, so it was good for neither trophies nor eating and it was this shape he chose to mimic for his flight.

One of the tools in his pack was a trowel with a wide, stainless steel blade that could be used as a mirror. Emos pictured the bird in his mind as he kneaded his face with his fingers. It had a knobbly, hooked beak, lumpy warts that stuck out of its face and large, red-rimmed eyes. It was a carrion eater, its head and neck bald; greasy feathers bristled from below its gawky throat, past the protruding potbelly to a clotted tail. Its legs were stumpy, ending in huge, boney feet.

The triangular brand that Emos wore on his face was lost among the warts in this form. He could neither sculpt the mark nor change its colour, for it was put there by Myunans as a mark of the plague and he was always wary that anyone who recognised it would see through any disguise he adopted. He enjoyed taking on this shape, always preferring the stranger forms that allowed him more room to play. He was nearly twice the size of a normal aukluk, but that would not matter as long as he stayed in the air.

Khassiel was staring at him when he turned around. He cocked his head at her and gave her his best attempt at an aukluk's ill-tempered squawk. She snorted and looked away, smiling despite herself.

'Suits you,' she said.

He beat his wings and lifted off, rising up from the bed of the truck and through the trees. Below him, he could see the Gabbit village, the river running down its rocky bed; further up there was a waterfall and some mushroom-shaped funjan trees. He resisted the urge to swing east, towards Ainsdale, aiming northwest instead for the forest at the foot of the hills that backed onto Absaleth. They had told the border guard where they were going when they'd crossed into Ainslidge Woods, so Ludditch might well already know.

If so, and the clansmen still meant them harm, it would be wise to stay off the main roads. He needed to find another route to Old Man's Cave. It would cost them time, but at least they might get there. What they would do if the Reisenicks decided to meet them at the cave entrance was something he did not want to think about. He wondered again about the Reisenicks' betrayal, praying that it was a mistake, that some hunting party had simply overstepped the mark, and that Taya and Lorkrin would be returned safely. He looked back to the east, but there was nothing to be seen but trees. If they were not released, then Draegar was the only chance they had.

+ + + +

Draegar was striding up a shallow stream when he heard birdcalls. The forest was full of the sounds of birds welcoming the morning, but there was a particular quality to these that caught his ear. They were made by men. He shrugged off the heavy netted bundle and held it up, raising the other hand to show it was empty.

'I bring tribute for Ludditch!' he bellowed. 'I am here for the Myunan children! I bring Ludditch his ghost!'

The scrap, as if woken by his shouts, thrashed around in the net. Draegar waited for an answer. He could hear no sounds in the trees, but knew the woodsmen were masters of stealth. They could be anywhere, creeping in the half-crouching position, which prevented their joints from giving off that telltale clicking. He could see flickers of movement in the shadows of the foliage. His keen senses told him there were Reisenicks all around him, at least a dozen, perhaps more. The Parsinor planted his feet further apart and waited. There were more birdcalls. Then a Reisenick appeared up on the bank upstream from him.

'What are yuh and what you got yourself, there?' the woodsman called out.

'Ludditch is looking for a ghost?' Draegar held up the net, walking forward in the knee-deep water. 'I think this ...'

Something caught his foot and he looked down and swore. A sinker crab. It had pounced out of its covered burrow and seized the front ankle of his right leg. Its powerful claws gripped like steel. Draegar threw the scrap away and pulled out his short sword and battleaxe. His tough hide protected him from injury and he was too big to be dragged into the massive crab's burrow, but none of that mattered, because Reisenicks used sinker crabs for trapping large animals in ambushes.

A hail of darts flew from the trees, most bouncing off harmlessly. Some stuck in, finding softer parts of his flesh and he knew he had to get into the trees before they shot enough into him for their toxins to have effect. He changed his grip on his sword and drove it through the back of the crab. The claws did not let go, holding on in a death grip. Draegar raised his axe and chopped off one shell-encased arm and then the other and started to stride towards the bank. A huge net fell from the boughs above him. He slashed at it with his sword, cutting a hole through it. Reisenicks dropped from the trees and leaped off the banks of the stream. Draegar roared a battle-cry and pulled his head and shoulders out of the net, his legs still tangled. The Reisenicks pounced.

The Parsinor cut the first one down in mid-air, impaling him on his sword. He pulled the blade free, his other hand already slamming his axe into the thigh of another clansman. More darts fell and he felt his head swim, but he was a long way from finished. He blocked the knife of a third attacker, slicing the man's hamstrings with a back-swing of his sword, and butted his head back into the face of a man coming up behind him, driving his axe back and up into the man's belly. But still they came, frenzied with the lust for a kill, each hunter eager to be the one who would take home this mighty creature's head. They were quick, and many of them were double-jointed and could twist and squirm like contortionists, making their strikes unpredictable. He fended off one assault after another. His vision blurred and he nearly lost his balance, but his hands stayed true, smashing away another knife, a blow from his sword taking the man's head right off his shoulders. Struggling to stay conscious, Draegar swayed on his feet, seeing more and more of the men appear around him. He raised his arms up and roared his defiance.

'Come on! Is that all you've got? You fight like little girls! Come and get some muuu–' His voice slurred and he shook his head and stumbled.

The Reisenicks closed in around him and he brought his weapons up into guard position once more. They shrieked and whooped, leaping into attack and he bellowed back, the clash of their weapons against his feeding power to his heavy limbs. The forest resounded with the ferocious fight, the tumult carrying down the hill to the village of Ainsdale, where people came out onto the muddy streets to listen to the distant sound of battle.

+ + + +

The Scout, as the creature called itself, refused to believe that the Myunans and their Sestinian friends were not a Barian

horde. It was, however, prepared to accept their uncon-
ditional surrender.

'We will take you to our Hubquarters,' it said, 'where the
Crux will determine your fate.'

The door at the end of the corridor on the other side of the
pool room had a similar counterweight mechanism, and
they opened it to find a low-ceilinged corridor with many
twists and bends in it, leading downwards. There was no
blue fungus in the walls here; the group, their heads bowed
to avoid hitting the ceiling, had to use their torches to see.
The Scout kept well ahead of their light, whinging any time it
got caught in its glare.

'The doors in that room both locked from the inside,'
Paternasse pondered aloud, 'as if the room was built to be
defended from either side. This corridor too, the way it
bends back and forth, with the low ceiling? That's another
defence feature. Barians would nearly have to bend double to
come through here, and every corner would provide cover
for defenders. It's a good design. But there is no way you
could last out in that one room. A siege would break you.'

'That's what the water tunnel was, then,' Mirkrin said. 'It
was too tight even for humans. No Barian would fit through.
It was a means of travelling through the mountain that their
enemies couldn't use. There are probably others connecting
to it too. I'm sure I felt junctions down there. Maybe the
undercurrent flows somewhere in particular, could even be
a way out.'

'I don't think even the Tuderem used them,' Nayalla said.
'By the size of the skull on that skeleton, they wouldn't fit.
You'd have to be an awfully good swimmer as well, to sur-
vive travelling in those things any further than we went. And

besides, I don't think they were much good as fighters. I think they built this place to be defended, all right, but they might have been relying on others to do the defending. And maybe to bring them supplies too, if they became trapped.'

She nodded towards their guide.

'Those things?' Dalegin chuckled dismissively. 'Against *Barians*?'

'Let's see where it's taking us,' Mirkrin shrugged. 'You never know, this might not be a typical one. There could be others that would rip your throat out and spit down your neck. Or breathe fire or something.'

The corridor branched in places, the Scout taking turns without any hesitation; it obviously knew where it was going. All along the walls, holes just large enough for the creature and its kind opened out, explaining why the things did not need to be able to work the doors. The Tuderem home was clearly laced with the small tunnels. The walls of the corridor also bore images, the drawings describing scenes that must have been from the Tuderems' history. Much of it had to do with science and politics. There was little sign of the usual historical upheavals, battles or revolutions. Mirkrin ran his fingers over them as he walked.

'It's one kind of stone set into another,' he murmured. 'Marble and obsidian and other types set into the granite. The finest workmanship I've ever seen.'

He looked closer. The stone hadn't been inlaid at all. He could see the grain of one kind of stone continue right through into another. Alchemy – they had changed the very nature of the stone itself and used it to draw their history.

The Scout stopped in one part of the corridor and pointed to a section of wall. The Myunans leaned closer to study the drawings, the miners waiting uninterested and impatient to move on. The scene the little creature was showing them was an image of the Tuderem gathering some kind of insect. Nayalla walked back along the wall, reading the story.

'They bred these things from insects that they found in the caves,' she said. 'The end result was a kind of creature that grew in clumps. This thing isn't just one animal; it's made up of lots of creatures joined together in one combined body. The Tuderem were trying to build an army to set against the Barians. These things were what they came up with.'

'So the pictures are ...' Mirkrin started.

'A legacy from their masters. To teach the servants about their origins,' Nayalla said quietly. 'To teach them about their past ... where they came from.'

'... now that their masters aren't here to tell the story themselves,' Paternasse finished. 'Probably because they were more interested in pictures on the walls than they were with getting out of this hole. Are we going or not?'

They were all hungry and exhausted and the cracks were starting to show. The miners were at the ends of their tethers, and had no time for history lessons. The Myunans swallowed their protests and waited for the Scout to lead them on. It scampered ahead of their lights, going faster now as it neared its home. They followed as quickly as their tired legs could carry them.

'Put out the lights!' the thing hissed back. 'No light in the Hubquarters!'

A dim, phosphorescent glow came from the round opening ahead, so the group snuffed out their torches and followed the creature through.

'Crux!' it shouted in its small voice. 'We have vanquished

the Barian horde and brought them to grovel and beg our forgiveness. The horde is defeated!'

'I think these things might have a slightly melodramatic view of life,' Mirkrin observed.

Nobody heard him. They were all too busy staring at what lay before them.

+ + + +

Taya and Lorkrin were perched on the steps of the meeting-house, under the watchful eye of a pair of Reisenick women who were sitting on the terrace, stringing skunkrin molars into necklaces. There had been a lot of other people out on the street, listening to the noise of battle that was taking place just over a nearby hill. Now some of them ran up the street, eager for news from the returning hunting party.

Down the hill that led into the village, the group of hunt-ers carried two prizes: one a net full of what seemed like scrap metal, the other a large body bound head to toe. Lud-ditch and Harsq came out to watch too. The hunters carted their catch up to where the chieftain stood and dropped both at his feet. Taya and Lorkrin stared aghast as they rec-ognised Draegar lying motionless before them, tightly bound, his body bearing numerous knife wounds and still carrying some of the darts that had managed to pierce his skin. They ran over and started to pull out the darts, but the hunters pushed them roughly away.

'What's that?' Ludditch pointed at the scrap first.

The tangle of metal moved and the chieftain's eyes wid-ened. Harsq stared hard at it.

'This thing was carryin' it,' Spiroe told him, pointing at Draegar.

'His name's Draegar!' Lorkrin shouted. 'He's not a thing, he's a Parsinor … and he's a friend of our uncle!'

Ludditch ignored him. He leaned over and peered into the mess of wire and metal junk.

'He said it was the ghost you were lookin' for,' Spiroe added. 'Sure is strange, whatever it is.'

Ludditch shot a glance at Harsq and then took a closer look at the Parsinor.

'This thing's a friend of Harprag?' he frowned. 'Parsinors. They're desert creatures, ain't they? 'S got a fine hide on it. Good, proud head. Look at that brow! Whose catch is it?'

'We all sort'a had a hand in it,' Spiroe shrugged. 'But I got to tell yuh, he didn't come easy. Tarne's dead. I'm real sorry, Learup. It got Bluno and a bunch o' others too. Some o' the boys is takin' the bodies back to the clans now.'

Ludditch's face darkened.

'Tarne's dead?' he moaned. 'You let this *thing* kill my baby brother?'

'Weren' nothin' I could do, Learup,' the woodsman cowered back. 'It fought like a skack and he was one of the first ones at it. Desert thing here cut his head right off.'

Ludditch's breathing grew hoarse and then he let out a massive roar of grief. He kicked Draegar's body over and over again, screaming hysterically with every blow.

'Stop!' Taya cried, the two children running forward. 'Leave him alone!'

They were pulled back and held in check by some of the clansmen.

The Reisenick chieftain continued to stamp his foot down on the inert body of the Parsinor. Taya burst into tears and Lorkrin trembled as he fought to control his sobs. Ludditch's rage eased and he laid in one last kick before moving away and brushing his hair back with his hand, heaving deep breaths.

'We flay it!' he snarled. 'Tomorrow morning. And we make sure it stays alive long enough to see its own skin on a stretchin' frame!'

He turned his attention to Harsq, who was examining the bundle of metal.

'Well?' he asked the priest impatiently.

'This is it,' Harsq smiled up at him. 'The last remnants of Absaleth's ghost.'

'Do what you have to do to finish it,' Ludditch told him, 'then settle up and get out of here.'

He looked at the children.

'Seems to me, if your uncle is ready to send animals like that up here to kill my kin, then he's wore out his welcome and used up his tribute. As of now, he's trespassin' on Reisenick land and that's a sin punishable by death in these parts. Might as well be addin' a Myunan hide to this here Parsinor's. Not that it'll be the first.' He spat at their feet, then gestured to Spiroe: 'Truss these whelps up and cage 'em. I'll decide what to do with them once I have their uncle. It may be that he'll want to see his cubs cooked up before he's skinned hisself.'

'What about keepin' the peace with the Myunans, Learup?' Cleet asked.

'Hang the peace. If this priest does what he claims he can do, there ain't gonna be no Myunans to worry about.'

He strode back into the meetinghouse, with Harsq's eyes following him in. The eshtran swivelled his head to look at the children, frowning. They scowled back and Lorkrin tried to spit at him, but they were pulled towards a row of hanging cages by the clansmen. Taya saw doubt on the Braskhiam's face and wondered what the Reisenicks knew that he didn't. Draegar was hauled across the street by six men to a building with various animal hides hung up on the walls and stretching frames propped up on its porch. They dragged him roughly inside and slammed the door shut.

The two shape-changers were locked up in a 'Myunan Cage'. Instead of bars, it was built of a steel mesh, the gaps too small even for a shape-shifter to squeeze through. The door did not have a lock, for Myunans had been known to pick locks with their fingers; the door was held closed instead by the simple method of hammering a pin into place. The pin could not be removed without a hammer and a punch, even if the Myunans could reach it. Their tools had been taken off them and after exploring all the possibilities of escape and failing to find a way out, they slumped to the floor in glum silence.

'What are we going to do?' Taya shuddered. 'They're going to … we have to stop them from doing that to Draegar. We have to do something.'

Lorkrin closed his eyes. He was as scared as he'd ever been in his life. He had never thought the Parsinor could be so completely beaten. It had shaken the boy to see the proud map-maker wounded, bound and drugged, rendered utterly helpless. He could not see how they could help him. What hope did any of them have now? If Draegar could not save them, did even Uncle Emos stand a chance? And if Draegar had come on his own, did that mean that Uncle Emos wasn't coming? And what about their mother and father, trapped beneath the mountain? By tagging along on this expedition, had he and Taya ruined any hope of their parents being rescued? He hugged his knees and looked around for something to take his mind off their situation.

Three Reisenicks came into view along the street, one limping and bearing a bandaged wound in his thigh, the second clansman supporting him. The third led a tall, gangly figure wrapped from head to toe in layers of shabby clothing. A hood covered its head and a scarf hid its face. Dull gleams from between the folds were all that could be seen of its eyes. Something about the figure bothered Lorkrin. As a shape-changer, he had a keen eye for form, but he could not place this creature. It was probably a man, but of what race, he could not tell. He thought from the walk that it might be Reisenick, but the clothes were Sestinian. He nudged Taya and she looked out. Frowning, she knelt up and leaned against the mesh.

'What is he?' she asked aloud.

'Don't know.'

The three woodsmen took the stranger up to a normal, barred cage alongside the Myunans' and opened the door.

'Get yourself in there,' one said to it.

The gangly figure did as it was told, folding itself up to fit into the cramped space in the cage. The door was closed, bolted and locked and the three Reisenicks made their way into the meetinghouse.

'What you in for?' Lorkrin asked it.

The creature turned to look at him and at first, he did not think it would answer.

'In … for?' it said, in a voice like dull, plucked harp strings. It sounded like a man, rather than a woman.

'Why have they locked you up?'

'I ... don't know.' The stranger spoke hesitantly, as if struggling to find the words.

'Probably 'cause you're strange. They don't go in much for strangers around here. Where are you from?'

'I don't know.'

'Right,' Lorkrin gave his sister a sideways glance. 'What's your name, then?'

'I don't know.'

'Do you know *anything* about yourself?' Taya asked.

'I know ... I have travelled a long way, but I don't know where I've come from. I can't remember ... anything else.'

'Nothing? That must be awful,' Taya said, sympathetically. 'Like having to start your life all over again.'

Lorkrin regarded the lanky figure folded up in the cramped cage and then looked around at the Reisenicks' sinister, stinking village.

'Probably could have picked a better place to start,' he said.

No one said anything for a while. The stranger failed to provide enough of a diversion to distract the children from their morbid thoughts and Lorkrin stood up and slipped his fingers though the gaps in the mesh. The building where they had taken Draegar was the tannery. They could smell the tannic acid from where they were, but could only guess at what was taking place inside.

Lorkrin stared over at the stranger in the cage next to them. He had long arms, this man. Long, thin arms. Lorkrin wondered how strong those arms were. Checking around to see there were no clansmen nearby, he tapped the mesh.

'Psst!' Hey! You! You in all the clothes!'

The stranger looked over at him.

'Can you reach our cage?' Lorkrin whispered. 'Can you reach the pin that holds the door closed?'

'Would you … like me to try?' the man asked.

'Yeah. That'd be great, if you could.'

The man tilted his head, peering at the locking pin. Then he reached his arm through the bars. He was just out of reach. He leaned further, twisting his body to push his shoulder through the gap. His fingers were just brushing the pin on the bottom of the Myunan Cage. The thin shoulder pressed hard against the iron bar and to Lorkrin's amazement, the bar started to bend.

'Stop!' Taya hissed. 'Someone's coming.'

The stranger looked up at them.

'Get your arm back in!' Lorkrin gestured at him. 'They'll see you.'

The man did not seem to understand why this would be a bad thing, but he pulled his arm back into the cage and turned to look unabashedly at the Reisenick coming up the steps to the meetinghouse.

'Psst!' Lorkrin called to him, after the clansman had gone. 'We'll wait 'til it gets dark. Then we'll try it.'

'Try what?' the man asked back.

Lorkrin leaned his head in close to his sister's.

'He's a nice fella,' he said softly, 'but I think he's a few birds short of a flock.'

+ + + +

Cullum stretched his leg out and winced. The wound sang when he extended his calf muscle, but the embarrassment at being injured in such a senseless way bothered him more than the pain. He leaned on his battle-hammer, using it as a crutch as he walked around to the back of the truck. He nudged Khassiel, who was dozing on a pile of sacks.

'Your watch,' he told her. 'Still no sign of the Myunan. I thought we were in a hurry?'

'We won't get there at all if we get caught like that again.' She rolled her head to ease a stiff neck and pulled her helmet over her short, cropped hair. 'He's only being careful. I don't think he expected them to be hostile.'

'Hostile is fine with me,' Cullum patted his battle-hammer.

Khassiel rolled her eyes and got to her feet. Jube was pacing back and forth between the two trucks.

'What's keeping him?' the miner said, through gritted teeth. 'They could be dying down there. This is taking too long.'

The crack of a broken twig caused them all to spin round. Khassiel raised her crossbow in the direction of the sound. There was a giggle and the sound of running feet. Jube parted some foliage and peered through.

'Gabbit young 'uns,' he said. 'Looks like we've been spotted.'

'Right, now we really need to go,' Cullum barked. 'I'm not waiting for them to squeal on us to the Reisenicks. Let's get out of here. The Myunan can come and find us.'

'We wait,' Khassiel insisted, staring down her superior, much to his dismay. 'He knows what he's doing. He'll be back.'

'You sound like you trust him,' Cullum sneered.

'He's got more to lose than us. I trust that.'

There was the beat of wings above them, and a startlingly ugly bird landed lightly in the back of the passenger wagon.

'The Reisenicks have got hunting parties out all over the forest,' Emos said as he shed the bird's form. 'But I don't think they're looking for us. They're on the hunt for something else. I'm convinced the attack on us was a mistake, but we can't take the chance. I've found a route that will take us out of the way of any Reisenick villages and their main hunting grounds. Even with the noise of the wagons, I think we'll be all right.'

'Well, let's get moving,' Jube grabbed the crank handle for his truck.

'There's one more thing,' Emos added. 'They know where we're going. I don't know what they're all out hunting for, but if they do want to catch us, all they have to do is get to Old Man's Cave ahead of us and wait. This isn't just a rescue any more.'

They all gazed at him in silence. The thought that they might walk right into an ambush at the cave had not occurred to them. Khassiel swore under her breath. Cullum grimaced and sat down to ease the pain in his leg. Jube leaned into the cab of his wagon and flipped the starter switch, and then walked around the front to crank the engine.

'You talk like we have a choice,' he said as he wound the motor into life. 'I'm not turning back until I've done everything I can to get my mates out of that bloody hole.'

He fitted the crank handle back into its brackets on the bonnet and glared at Cullum and Khassiel: 'What do you two say?'

The Noranians looked at each other.

'We say, let 'em come,' Cullum grinned. 'I was bored out of my mind back at that camp anyhow. Haven't killed anybody in *weeks*.'

+ + + +

The Seneschal was the collective name for the race that inhabited the Tuderem 'Nation' – the network of caves, tunnels and chambers beneath Absaleth and its neighbouring mountains, the Rudstones. Confusingly, the individual members of this race did not have names, as they did not put great store in individuality. Even the idea of an individual member was difficult to pin down, as each was made up of smaller component bodies that shared a common consciousness. 'Scout' was the title given to a particular breed, and could refer to any one of that breed. There were others, such as 'Chargers', 'Planners' and 'Carriers', each a different breed with its own characteristics, yet each similar to the others and each made up of more than one creature that shared a single consciousness.

This extended even further. For each consciousness was also shared with the Crux, which seemed to be nothing more than a very large gathering of the same kind of creatures, all bunched up tightly together in the centre of the spherical chamber that they called the Hubquarters. This chamber was the size of a large house, but with no flat floors, only its curved walls and struts of stone that arched across the space, branching and joining with others so that they acted as a network of routes across the chamber. The Crux was gathered at the central junction of the main beams, a quivering cluster of small, multi-legged bodies.

Irregularly shaped crystal panels held the now familiar blue fungus, casting a dim but constant light from every side. The Seneschal moved with precision throughout this huge room; some gathered in ranks, resembling soldiers on parade, others flowing to and fro like scouts and messengers. There were many different kinds of creature to be seen, although all variations of the one they knew, some longer, almost like millipedes, others more spherical. The place had been in uproar when the 'horde' had first walked in, but after some introductions, there had been a convening of the Crux; decisions had been made and order restored.

The group had named their guide 'Leggit', in an attempt to relate to at least one of the pieces of this collective mind. It appeared to be sneakily pleased with this illegitimate label, and whispered it to itself when it thought the Crux might not be paying attention. They sat in the bowl of this great room, eating the last of their food as they all waited restlessly for Leggit to lead them out of the caves, as promised. All of them, that was, except Mirkrin, who had accepted the delay, along with the bizarre surroundings, and fallen asleep. Nay-alla, in contrast, was trying to find out as much about the Seneschal as she could.

'Have you ever had visitors before?' she asked Leggit.

'You are the first Barians to invade the nation,' it replied, holding steadfastly to the conviction that they were a con-quering horde. 'We have waited for many lifetimes. Others have come from Outside, but they were merely animal deni-zens, easily despatched by our martial might.'

'Probably rats and mice and the like,' Paternasse guessed. 'What about us? When are we getting ... when are you going to throw us out?'

'You will be expelled when the portal's light has faded. Please be prepared to disassemble when the time comes,' Leggit told him.

'What does that mean?' Noogan asked.

'The portal to the Outside is very small. You must disas-semble in order to fit through.'

'Disassemble?' Dalegin bleated. 'You mean ...'

'Pull yourselves apart,' Leggit said.

10 THE BLIND BATTALION

Mirkrin had been woken up so that the whole group could discuss the latest turn in events. The Seneschal were serious about disassembling them. Leggit shut its eyes, clenched up, grunted and broke up into four equal segments, each part with one bunch of eyes, a single arm and several legs. The segments had raw, moist flesh and what looked like suction cups over the parts of their bodies that joined together.

'Like so,' they all said before promptly reassembling themselves.

'We can't do that,' Nayalla told it. She spread her arms in a helpless gesture. 'This is as small as we get.'

One look at the segments told her she and Mirkrin would have great difficulty squeezing down to that size. The humans would certainly have no hope of fitting through any hole that required these little creatures to break apart.

'We will brook no refusal,' Leggit retorted. 'You must disassemble or we will ... we will disassemble you on your behalf.'

'I've had enough of this,' Dalegin said. 'Let's get out of this anthill. If they have a way out, we can find it.'

'This place is a maze,' Nayalla argued. 'Getting them to take us there is still our best chance. Leggit? Where is this "portal"? If you lead us to it, we might be able to knock it through, make it bigger ourselves, so that we can get out without … disassembling.'

'Damage the portal?' the creature asked in horror. 'Open the Nation's borders to the Outside? Expose us to the savagery of the horde?'

'But you keep saying *we* are the horde.'

'And you say you are not. But we are not fools.'

'Have we attacked you?'

'You have invaded the Nation.'

'It was an accident; now we're trying to get back out again.'

'Perhaps you are spies, come to explore and report back to your commanders.'

Nayalla threw up her hands in exasperation and Leggit jumped back in fright.

'Enough is enough.' Paternasse got to his feet. 'As I see it, we're on our own here. I say either this thing helps us now, or we find this "portal" ourselves.'

'You are prisoners of the Nation!' Leggit squealed. 'You will submit to the will of the Seneschal!'

'Stow it.' Paternasse spat on the ground. 'It'll be a sunny day in Guthoque before I let a bundle of grubs tell me what I will and won't do.'

'Now, Paternasse,' Mirkrin made a settling motion with his hands. 'Maybe you shouldn't upset them.'

'Hang upsetting them.' Dalegin stood up beside the older miner. 'Let's get out of here and find this bloody door. Noogan? What do ya say?'

'I don't know if we should be getting them worked up,' the youngest miner said doubtfully. 'We're right in the middle of their place an' all – and there's an awful lot of 'em.'

'Ah, you never had any guts!' Dalegin sneered. 'Let's leave these hand-wringers here, Jussek. Let 'em rot. If we let this Myunan hag have her way, we'll be down here turnin' grey while she haggles with this vermin.'

'Mind your tone.' Mirkrin stood up and glared at the other man.

'Or what, waxwork? You have somethin' to say, say it. Stop your beatin' around the bush. Come on!'

'This isn't helping ...' Nayalla put in.

'You'd rather talk us to death, hag?' Dalegin snarled. 'Bloody Myunans, you're all the same. You won't get off your arses and do somethin' straight – it's always got to be sneakin' around and lyin' and cheatin' your way out of things ...'

'You keep a civil tongue in your head when you're speaking to my wife!' Mirkrin growled.

'... You can't deal with any problem that you can't lie or ... or sneak your way out of ...' Dalegin ranted.

'I've had all I can take of that sewer you call a mouth.' Mirkrin stepped towards him.

Dalegin lashed out, catching the Myunan across the cheek with his fist. Mirkrin grabbed the other man's wrist before the miner could draw it back again, his fingers melting and joining around it to hold it fast. Dalegin gasped, but Mirkrin was already stepping in and he brought his elbow up hard into the other man's jaw, flipping Dalegin onto his back.

'Will you stop this ...' Nayalla began, but was cut off as Paternasse charged her husband.

The two men went down, Paternasse getting a headlock on Mirkrin and squeezing. Mirkrin let him. The Myunan reached his arms back at an angle that would have dislocated a human's shoulders, clutched the back of Pater-nasse's head and pulled it towards him as he let the back of his own head go soft and envelop the old miner's face. Paternasse suddenly found himself blind and unable to breathe. He let go of Mirkrin's neck and heaved himself free of the Myunan's grip, laying in thumps with his big, hard hands instead. One struck the dented flesh of the shape-changer's shoulder and Mirkrin cried out in pain. Paternasse grunted with satisfaction, only to be caught on the bridge of the nose by a head-butt from the Myunan. They could make their flesh pretty solid too, when they wanted.

Nayalla sighed as she watched the two men lay into each other. She folded her arms and waited, keeping a weather eye on Dalegin, who lay stunned on the floor, in case he should recover enough to threaten her husband again. Noogan was not taking sides as yet, and she decided to take advantage of his indecision.

'We're trapped in a cave with no food, hardly any water, no way out and we're surrounded by creatures who want to dismember us,' she said to him. 'It's hardly the time to be turning on each other.'

'Aye,' Noogan nodded. 'But it might do them some good to let off a bit of steam. Let them go at it for a while longer. I'm not about to get in Jussek's way when he's got a rage on 'im, anyway.'

The two opponents fought furiously, grappling each other to the floor again. The punches, kicks, knees and elbows were getting less energetic, the breathing more laboured. Soon they pulled apart and sat, heaving in breaths and glar-ing at each other. Dalegin sat up, staring sourly at Mirkrin.

'That was a good scrap, lads,' Noogan congratulated them.

'Could o' sold tickets to that. All done now, are yuh?'

He looked to Nayalla to support his peacemaking efforts, but she was not paying attention to the two fighters. Instead, her eyes were trained on the masses of Chargers that had gathered above and around them. Hundreds of them stared unblinking at the five figures in the middle of the floor.

'Did we not say you were savages?' Leggit said quietly. 'You are powerful, but your violence is unrestrained, your troops without discipline. Your horde is no match for the elite cadres of the Seneschal. We have seen enough. The Crux has demanded your disassembling, to be effected immediately. If you will not carry it out of your own free will, the Seneschal have no choice but to expel you by force – piece by piece.'

The walls of the round chamber were crawling with the bizarre cave dwellers, the air alive with the sounds of hard sharp feet and multitudes of voices softly muttering drills to themselves as they took their positions. The Myunans and the three miners formed a circle, facing out towards the swarm of skittering creatures that surrounded them.

'If they're all like Leggit,' Mirkrin murmured. 'They've no real fight in 'em. As soon as you get rough they squeal like babies.'

'Even so,' Paternasse said back. 'There's got to be a few hundred of 'em. Get the powder out; if they don't like light, let's give 'em some.'

Dalegin took the jar from his satchel and poured some of the powder on the floor. They all rubbed the ends of their torches in it.

'They bear light! We must strike now!' Leggit shrieked and others took up the cry.

The Seneschal formed up in regimented lines, moving with a cohesion that would have made the Noranian army proud. Each company of Chargers shouted orders to itself as it moved, making the manoeuvres a noisy affair. The closest of these groups raised their hands in front of them in what looked suspiciously like an attempt at a fighting stance.

'Aaaaad … vance!' they all cried and started to march forwards.

'There's something not right about somebody ordering themselves into battle,' Mirkrin observed as he watched them approach.

Noogan struck a match and they all lit their torches. The effect was immediate. The Seneschal squealed, broke ranks and scattered, seeking shelter from the light. Only moments after the last torch had been lit, the huge chamber was cleared as the creatures hid behind the stone struts or in the mouths of tunnels.

'No wonder those bloody alchemists buried themselves in a cave,' Paternasse snorted. 'If this is the best defence they could manage with all their science, then they hadn't a clue. The Barians must have wiped the floor with them.'

'Bring out the Blinded!' They heard some of the creatures cry. 'Let them face the Blind Battalion!'

'Oh, this just gets better.' Dalegin grinned.

From one of the tunnels, a mass of new animals spilled out into the main chamber. Much like the others, they had a few crucial differences. Each one had scarred sockets where their eyes should have been; each one clung to the ones next to it and to those in front, as if one blind creature was being led by the next. The finer hairs on their bodies quivered, sensitive to the movements in the air around them.

They did not cry out like the others; they chattered quietly, communicating to their neighbours so that messages flowed across the mass like waves. The chattering made the Blindeds' teeth click together and the combined clicking of all these mouths created a shivering buzz that unnerved their intended victims.

'Well, the light's not going to work,' Paternasse said after some hesitation. He worked his false teeth around in his dry mouth. 'Let's try scarin' 'em.'

He roared and charged at the blind animals. The front line of the Blind Battalion shuffled back, but were pushed forward again as the lines behind them failed to react as quickly. The advance slowed as they all found their places again, then continued on at its slow, but steady pace.

The group of humans and Myunans backed away, making for the tunnel that they had originally come through to enter the chamber. Noogan and Nayalla held their torches before them, pushing back the grimacing little warriors that threatened to block their way. From the mouth of the tunnel, more Blinded appeared, spreading out as they entered, joining up on either side with the other swarm, completely surrounding the group. Their stumpy arms reached out, fingers questing for the first touch of their foes.

'Right,' Paternasse growled, passing the torch to his left hand and hefting his pickaxe with his right. 'A fight it is, then.'

'Bunch round me,' Nayalla said suddenly, kneeling down and pulling out her tools. 'Hide me from them. I have an idea.'

Gathering round her as she started to amorph, the men steeled themselves for a fight. Mirkrin drew his knife and the others lifted their picks. The circle of blinded animals closed around them and with a chattering buzz, the Blind Battalion set upon them with hard, clawing legs and clutching hands.

It was like fighting a swarm of bees. Individuals were killed with ease, the miners' pickaxes and the Myunans knives cutting down one after another, but they kept coming, each one scratching, or biting or stabbing with their sharp legs, frantically trying to grab hold of one of the cornered group. And little by little they were overwhelming their five enemies. These creatures did not cry like children; they did not hide away from violence. They fought with the hopelessness and fearlessness of the condemned, for the Blinded were the pariahs of the Seneschal's world. To die with honour was all they had left to them.

Dalegin cried out in frustration as his pick was torn from his hands and attackers flooded over him in a wave. Noogan had no more room to swing, so he dropped his pick, pulling out a chisel and driving it into one opponent after another. He kicked some of the bodies off Dalegin and helped him to his feet. Mirkrin stood with his back to his wife, slashing and jabbing with his knife, the fury of the fight sending fire through his veins. Paternasse fell and disappeared under a flurry of beasts. Mirkrin found the old man's hand and pulled him to his feet.

'Stop!' Nayalla screamed, and to their surprise, the men heard her cry repeated all around the space by the voices of the Seneschal.

Nayalla had amorphed, taking on a long-dead form. For the first time in centuries, one of the Tuderem stood in the Hubquarters, her four hands raised as she prepared to address their attackers.

'My loyal Seneschal!' she cried. 'You have been tested, and you have shone true! In all the centuries that we have left you alone, you have remained, brave and honourable warriors.'

The swarms of creatures looked at one another, trembling. Throughout the spherical room, whispers fizzed all around the trapped group.

'What is this?' a voice carried like a wave from a hundred mouths at once. 'Where have you been, our masters? How can you be alive once more?'

'Some of us took different forms,' Nayalla called back. 'To journey into the Outside and vanquish the horde. And now we are back, to lead you again.'

'Lead us where?' the voices asked. 'What have you come back to do?'

'We want you to take us to the portal. We will show you the horde is conquered.'

More effervescent whispering, as the Seneschal conferred amongst themselves. The Blind Battalion's feet clicked restlessly against the ground. They were slowly edging closer again. There was a long wait before the Seneschal spoke again.

'You left us alone,' the voices hissed. 'You all died and left us alone! For a hundred generations, we have been on our own. And now you want to do it again. But we won't let you! We will bring down the portal … close it forever, and you will stay down here with us – your loyal Seneschal!'

The Blind Battalion suddenly surged forward, and behind him, Mirkrin heard his wife cry out. He turned just in time to see her collapse under the weight of a dozen of the sightless wretches, who dropped from the ceiling above him. Roaring defiance, he threw himself at them.

Paternasse snatched a glance around the chamber, as he fought frantically against the wave of bodies clambering over him. The rest of the Seneschal forces were closing around them now. Every surface seemed covered by their dark bodies in the dim light.

'May the gods help us!' he gasped hoarsely.

There were so many of them that the ground was shuddering beneath their feet. The stone beams and struts shook and cracks appeared around the walls. The onslaught faltered as the shaking increased and Paternasse realised that it was not the mass of charging creatures, but another earth tremor. One of the bridges that crossed the chamber broke free of the walls with a massive crack and crashed to the ground, crushing dozens of the Seneschal beneath it. The Blinded stumbled about, their bearings lost in the tumult. Paternasse grabbed Nayalla and hauled her to her feet.

'They're confused by the quakes. This is our chance!' he bellowed. 'We have to get out of here now!'

She helped Mirkrin up and the old miner dragged the other two miners out from under a pile of bodies. Together, they all gathered up what gear they could find and staggered up the curve of the spherical room towards the nearest tunnel. They were forced to fall forwards and crawl on their bellies as the violent tremors made it impossible to walk. Slabs of stone crashed down around them. Noogan was struck on the arm by a piece of debris, but he kept going. They reached the mouth of the tunnel, where the ground levelled off and the earthquake started to ease. As soon as they could stand, they struggled to their feet and ran, unsteady at first as the last of the tremors rocked the floor, but then faster and more frantically as the ground became still beneath their feet. They knew the manic little beasts would be after them. They ran headlong into the darkness, holding up the last three torches to light the way ahead, not caring where the tunnels took them as long as it was away from the swarms of the Seneschal.

+ + + +

Kalayal Harsq undid the clips that connected the generator's cables to the bundle of wire and scrap. Around him, his disciples were looking on anxiously, and beyond them, the Reisenick villagers were standing and watching in some bewilderment. He had just performed the second exorcism of Absaleth's spirit and the earth tremor that had marked the departure of the ghost had left him shivering with fear and tension. He pushed at the tangled mess with his foot, but it did not react. The contact told him what he wanted to know, that the exorcism had been a success; the metal's spirit had been vanquished. But he did not feel any satisfaction. He licked his lips, wishing he could rid himself of the metallic taste in his mouth. There was something unsettling in Ludditch's interest in the spirit – more interest than his payment warranted. The Reisenick chieftain knew something that Harsq did not, and that was worrying. Ludditch's comment about the end of Absaleth signalling the end of the Myunans left Harsq wondering. What had he meant?

Kalayal Harsq was probably the foremost exorcist on this side of the world. But the truth he would never admit was that what he knew about the spirits of the land was dwarfed by what he did not know. Deep down, he was afraid that what he was doing would come back to haunt him one day, that there was a price to be paid for his practices. The lack of sleep, the nightmares and now the earthquake, it all spoke of ominous retribution. He took out his air canister and tried to draw a breath of the untainted air from it, but it was empty. The priest scowled. He would have none now until he saw his Braskhiam contacts again. He wished he'd never encountered that accursed mountain and all the twisted souls who lived around it.

+ + + +

Taya and Lorkrin watched through the mesh of their cage as the Braskhiam eshtran gave the bundle of metal another kick and then walked away, his head bowed and his shoulders slumped. One of the younger priests handed a bag of money to the clansman with the green-tinged skin, the one named Spiroe. The Reisenick poured the bronze coins on a table and counted them out, then bagged them and took them inside.

'How could the soul of Absaleth be caught in that metal?' Lorkrin wondered aloud.

'What I'd like to know is how it's supposed to get rid of Myunans, and the Noranians too,' Taya murmured. 'That Ludditch fella made it sound as if getting rid of Absaleth's ghost was the answer to all his problems. Uncle Emos would know what he was talking about.'

The priests packed up the paraphernalia of their trade and retired to the building they were using as lodgings. It was getting dark and one by one, the rest of the villagers returned to their homes. A light rain had started to fall and it cleared the mist that had gathered.

The Myunans waited until they were sure that the street

was clear. It was time to begin. The children had tried getting more information out of the stranger throughout the day, but had ended up doing most of the talking. They had, however, decided on a name for him. They called him Rug; because with the thick layers of clothes that he wore, he looked as if he had been put together from rolled-up rugs. He accepted the name gratefully, glad to have an identity of any kind.

'Hey, Rug!' Lorkrin called softly to him. 'Can you pull out that pin at the bottom of our cage?'

'I don't know,' Rug answered.

'Would you mind giving it a try? And keep your voice down. They'll hear you. We don't want them to hear us. We're going to try and escape and save our friend.'

'Why does he need to be saved?' Rug asked in an exaggerated whisper.

'Because they're going to … they're going to skin him alive,' Taya replied. 'We have to get him out of here. We think they're going to kill all of *us* too.'

Rug thought about this.

'I do not want to be killed.'

'Then you should pull out that pin,' Lorkrin said pointedly.

Rug nodded. He reached through the bars and his fingertips brushed against the bottom of their cage. He leaned further, pushing his narrow shoulder up against the bars and once again, they started to bend. He didn't seem to notice. He caught hold of the end of the pin between finger and thumb and pulled. The Myunans' cage just swung towards him; the pin was driven in too tightly. Rug got a better grip on it and twisted it one way and then the other. Lorkrin watched in awe as this tall, gangly man used his forefinger and thumb to work loose a metal rod that had been driven into place with a hammer. With a grating noise, the pin slipped out and Lorkrin and Taya were able to push up the door of their cage.

The two Myunans had already thought this through. If all three of them escaped now, the empty cages would be spotted by anyone coming out of the meetinghouse or passing along the street. If this happened, they would have no chance of rescuing Draegar or of making an escape. They needed to put something in the cages that would pass for prisoners in the dark.

Taya retrieved their bags, as well as their tools, which hung on a hook by the meetinghouse door. She pulled out a pinhook and used it to fashion one of her fingers into a lock-pick. Then she inserted the finger into the lock in Rug's cage. He watched, fascinated, as she felt around inside the tumbler until she found its shape. The tumbler effectively pressed her finger into the right shape as it turned and the lock clicked open. She took the lock off, slipped the bolt back and swung the door open.

Lorkrin had crossed the street to the large building that housed the tannery. Outside, on the boards in front of the building, furs were stretched out on frames. There were beaver, skunkrin, otter, cowhank and hillcat skins. Those being prepared as throws and rugs still had the skin of the animals' heads attached. Rug followed him over and helped him as he pulled down some of the hides. They arranged these liberated hides inside the cages in such a way that they looked from a distance as if they were sleeping figures. The rain was getting heavier now, and that would work in their favour, keeping the Reisenicks inside. The two children set the heads of some of the hillcat furs – tucking the pelts inside out, so that the fleshy part showed. With the holes where the eyes and nostrils had been, and the small mouth, it was a crude but effective way of mimicking a face. They replaced the padlock just as it had been before they had escaped, and got Rug to push the pin back into place in the door of the Myunan Cage. The three of them crept into the shadows down the side of the meetinghouse. Taya turned to their new friend.

'We have to rescue Draegar. You don't have to help – it could be dangerous.'

Rug suspected that she was only telling him about the danger to be polite. They fully expected him to help. He decided that they knew more about these things than he did and just nodded his agreement.

They told him to wait in hiding behind a stack of barrels, then let their colours fade to camouflage greys and browns as they crept around to the alley at the back of the tannery. There were three large vents close to the ground in the back wall. Foul fumes drifted out of them into the night air. A door could be seen at the far end of the wall, but they were not about to try opening that. They could hear voices, but could not make out what they were saying.

Lorkrin pointed at one of the wooden vents. He got the blade of his knife under the edge of one of the slats and quietly prised it out of its frame. He did the same with four more and made a gap big enough for them to squeeze through. They came in under a workbench that offered a shadowed hiding place from which they could survey the room.

Draegar was tied to a circular frame in the middle of the room. It was tilted back, and was turning in such a way that it kept at least half his body immersed in a deep vat of some kind of noxious liquid. At the bottom half of every turn, his head disappeared beneath the surface of the liquid and he was forced to hold his breath until he came up on the other side. He looked exhausted and semiconscious. Taya's mouth twisted in a sob, but she stayed silent.

'They're soaking him in lacharin,' Lorkrin whispered, 'to soften his skin, loosen it … make it easier to take off.'

The rest of the room was taken up with other vats, work-benches, rollers, stretching frames and shelves of tannin and other chemicals. Three women were hard at work there: one working the crank which turned the wheel that held Drae-gar, another scraping the dried flesh off a fresh pelt with a pumice stone, the third rubbing preservative into a cleaned hide. They chattered as they worked and it seemed Draegar was the latest gossip.

'… no, no, no,' the crank turner was saying, 'Tarne was killed after Bluno, got 'is head chopped off by this thing. Bluno was the first killed. I was talkin' to 'is sister in the after-noon.'

'And who else did the beast kill, Willeth?' the third woman put in. 'I heard that Yoggo and two of the Haytrop boys got it.'

'Yep, the twins, Jup and Bod Haytrop, Learup's cousins.' Willeth nodded. 'One's an uncle to Bluno's second cousin Sistrag too, through marriage. She lives the far side of Wil-drup now. One of the Haytrops had a daughter by her too, word has it. There was some argument over who was the father in that one, as I remember. That Sistrag never did learn her calendar.'

The other women cackled knowingly.

'You want to leave this thing right side up for a while, Ula?' Willeth asked the third woman, cocking her head towards the Parsinor. 'It's coughin' and chokin' some. Wouldn't want it to drown on us.'

'Best do that, Willeth,' the older woman replied. 'Learup Junior'd be awful angry if we killed it afore the skinnin'. He wants to do this one personal.'

Willeth stopped turning the crank and with a ratchet-like clicking of her vertebrae, she arched her back. She looked through the collection of bottled chemicals on the work-bench next to her, picked one out, uncorked it and drank some back. She gagged, shook her head and took some more. Ula stood back to look at how the preservative was soaking in, then poked at one of her nostrils with the tip of her tongue.

'Learup's eldest is almost at childbearin' age,' Bettith commented. 'She's goin' to be a catch and no mistake. Good knees. And nice, even features, too. Seen any suitors?'

'I think *Learup* might have somethin' to say about that,' Ula leered.

They all cackled again. Listening to them, the two Myunans seethed with hate for these women, who talked about Draegar as if he were an animal and laughed and chatted as he came close to drowning.

'We need to get them out of here,' Taya muttered.

'Leave that to me,' Lorkrin said, taking out the tools.

Willeth had taken down another hide from its frame to work some tannin in, when she saw something move under the workbench. An animal with long, tapered ears, orange, black and yellow striped fur and a prehensile tail scampered along under the benches. She ducked her head down to try and catch sight of it and her eyes went wide.

'You're not gonna believe this girls!' she exclaimed. 'There's a minkren under here!'

'The heck you say!'

'I'm tellin' yuh,' she pointed. 'There! Under the dyin' bench.'

'Holy meat,' Bettith gasped. 'I thought they were all dead and gone!'

'It's gotta be worth a fortune!' Willeth whispered. 'That coat'll trade for its weight in gold.'

'It's makin' for the door. Stop it!' Ula cried.

But they were too slow. The door was ajar and the creature took full advantage of it, racing out into the darkness.

'Get it!' Willeth shrieked, picking up a heavy piece of wood to use as a club. 'We split the trade on the coat, but the kidneys're mine. I got a recipe for pickled minkren kidneys.'

They rushed outside, leaving the tannery empty. Taya waited a few moments to be sure they were gone. Then she crawled out of her hiding place and hurried over to the unconscious Parsinor.

'Draegar!' she hissed. 'Hey! Wake up! It's me, Taya. I've come to get you out of here.'

Draegar's eyelids lifted as if they had weights attached and he looked up at her. There was no sign of recognition in his eyes. Then his face changed and he said something so weakly that she had to lean her head closer to hear.

'Get … out,' he croaked. 'They'll … kill you.'

'Well, you'll just have to stop them,' Taya told him, as she examined the frame he was tied to. There was a lever for tipping it back and she pulled on it, lifting his feet out of the lacharin. Then she unbolted the shackles holding his wrists and ankles and tried to help him off. He could barely move. His head rolled around his neck and his breathing was loud and strained. She looked anxiously towards the door. If he could not walk, they had no way of getting him out of the village. With great effort, he heaved himself over the side of the frame and got his feet under him. But he nearly collapsed when he tried to stand up. Every movement was laborious and seemed to take an age.

'Stand up!' she urged him. 'They'll be coming back. We have to go.'

'My gear,' he mumbled.

Taya saw his bags and weapons discarded in a corner and went to pick them up. They were heavy, and too big for her to carry comfortably. She helped him pull the various straps onto his shoulders, cursing the fact that these would slow him down even further.

Lorkrin appeared under the bench near the vent. Having led the women astray, he had returned to his normal shape and come back in through the rear wall. Seeing Draegar was up, he tried the door that led out into the alley at the back. It was unlocked. He opened it and peered out carefully. There was nobody to be seen.

'He can barely walk!' Taya muttered to him as he joined her at the Parsinor's side.

Between the two of them, they were able to give him enough support to make it to the door. But it was slow going and they knew they could not hold him up for long and there was certainly no chance they were going to be able to carry him.

'Draegar! You have to walk. If you don't, they're going to kill all of us!' Lorkrin said. 'Come on. Get your feet moving!'

The massive figure struggled against poisoning and exhaustion to stay on his feet and they walked out into the alley. Rug saw them come out and hurried over to help. His thin frame was dwarfed by the Parsinor, but he was able to take a lot of Draegar's weight. Not far away, they could hear that more voices had joined in the hunt for the minkren. Soon, the whole town would be out. But Lorkrin had been careful to leave tracks heading into the forest in the opposite direction, to lead their pursuers away.

'How did you finish the trail?' Taya asked.

'Changed my feet into horse hooves,' he told her. 'They'll have real problems tracking me back here.'

Taya nodded, but she was uneasy. The Reisenicks were renowned trackers, and even with the rain, they would find his trail sooner or later. The escapees had to be long gone by then. Draegar was going too slowly. She wondered how long they could evade the clansmen even if they managed to lose themselves in the forest. The whole village would be coming after them.

'We need to find a place to hide,' she said, 'or a quick way out of the area, a wagon or something.'

'They have some wagons in the village,' Lorkrin replied. 'Rug, can you drive?'

'What do you mean, "drive"?'

'Never mind.'

'Let's get Draegar out of here first,' Taya grunted. 'Then worry about shaking them off.'

It was a struggle. Without Rug, they would not have managed at all. But they willed Draegar on, coaxing and bullying and pushing and pulling him as he used all his strength to cling to consciousness. They made their way through the back alleys, from one building's shadow to another, avoiding the lights from windows and freezing when they heard footsteps or voices. It was tortuous going and more than once, the two children thought they were going to be caught. But the hunting fever was on the Reisenicks and in the gloom of the night, four very different figures were able to slip out of the village and climb the hill into the cover of the forest.

Draegar's strength was almost spent by the time they reached the top of the hill and only the rain kept him conscious long enough to get them there. But Rug was able to drag him the last stretch to the cover of the trees. Taya went ahead to scout. She was soon back with a plan.

'There's a river with a jetty further down the hill,' she told them. 'If we can find a boat down there, we might have a chance of putting some distance behind us.'

'Let's do that, then,' Lorkrin nodded.

When they reached the river, there was only a single skiff tied to the jetty. It would not even take Draegar's weight, let alone hold all four of them.

'We could paddle Draegar downriver,' Taya said.

'The boat is too small,' Lorkrin pointed out, in the slow exaggerated manner people reserve for simpletons.

'I didn't mean in the *boat*,' Taya retorted in the same tone. 'I meant we could paddle *him* downriver.'

Lorkrin looked at his sister with unaccustomed respect.

'You're right. We could.'

'What about his … armour?' Rug asked. 'Won't he sink in the water?'

'No,' Taya replied. 'The armour's light. We've seen him swim, even carrying all his gear. And there's a big layer of fat under his shell. He says it's for surviving in the desert. He definitely floats.'

The two Myunans already had their tools out and were starting to reshape their bodies. Rug watched in fascination. At first he could not make out what they were doing. Lorkrin had joined his legs together so that the bottom half of his body looked like the bow of a canoe, but he appeared to be missing the back of his boat. Taya, on the other hand, was fashioning her lower half into a form that could have been the stern of a boat, leaving her feet sticking out just below her waist. Then they asked Rug to take the map-maker's gear in the skiff and to slide Draegar into the water. The tall, thin man did as he was asked, and saw that the Parsinor did indeed float, although his feet dropped toward the bottom and his head sank beneath the surface until Taya caught it. The two children eased in after the Parsinor. The water was fetid and still, and coated with a film of green algae. Insects skated along its surface and gnats hung in clouds in the air above it.

Lorkrin took up a position at the front, using some cord to tie Draegar's feet around his waist. Taya bound the Parsinor's hands up out of the way, then took the back, supporting his head under her feet and tying herself up to his shoulders. Both the Myunans had taken shapes that allowed them to slot seamlessly into position so that together they made a kind of Parsinor boat. When they were in position, they both enlarged and flattened their hands into paddle-like blades. They could not resist some giggles at the spectacle – the proud warrior would have had a fit if he'd seen himself. They gave Rug some pointers on how to paddle, then they pushed off and started downriver. The two children were skilled paddlers and handled their 'boat' with ease despite

Draegar's unconscious bulk. Rug splashed about helplessly at first, the skiff spinning slowly as it drifted downstream.

'Come on!' Lorkrin called softly to him. 'Put your back into it!'

'It won't go where I want it to go,' Rug explained helplessly, trying to straighten the boat out.

'Paddle the other side to stop yourself spinning!' Lorkrin said in a hoarse whisper. 'Not that side ya dolt, *left!*'

'What is left?' Rug asked.

'Don't you know left from right? Look!' The boy held up one hand at a time. 'This is your left. This is your right. Got it? Now, you do the left, then right. Seeing as you can't do proper strokes, you'll just have to keep swapping.'

Rug did as he was told, switching his paddle to the other side. He understood that this was an escape, but he was not sure where they were escaping to. It was very exciting, whatever was going on. He was starting to get the hang of the paddling now too. At least, he was going in a reasonably straight line, which seemed to be the idea.

The river ahead and behind them was shrouded in mist, the rain having given up when they set off. They went forward cautiously, straining to see what lay in their path. The fog turned the darkness to a murky grey that fooled the eyes into believing there was more light. The constant signs of insect life around them made them twitch at imagined itches and maddening bites. But there was nothing to be done but bear it and put as much distance between themselves and their pursuers as possible.

+ + + +

Paternasse was the first to falter, stumbling to a halt and

leaning forward, his hands on his knees. He gasped for breath, his whole body trembling. Noogan looked back, and called to the others to wait. They were all drained anyway and, one by one, they collapsed to the floor and tried to get their breath back.

'I can't … run … any more,' Paternasse heaved. 'I'm done.'

'We're tuckered out,' Noogan nodded, clutching his bruised arm. 'I don't hear them comin' after us. I think we've lost 'em.'

'This is their territory,' Nayalla spoke up. 'We can't have lost them for long. We need to keep going.'

'I'm done, I tell you,' Paternasse wheezed. 'I can't go any further without a rest.'

'Then we'll rest,' Mirkrin said.

'Maybe they won't come after us,' Dalegin said hopefully.

'They're not finished with us by a long shot.' Noogan shook his head. 'They'll be comin' after us all right. And the next time they'll make sure of us.'

They were all bleeding from bites and scratches, and bruises were already starting to blossom on their bodies. As the effects of the adrenaline faded, the pains set in. Nayalla had some herbs and mosses in her pack and she dressed the worst of their wounds as well as she could.

'We need to find water,' she said. 'And we're out of food.'

'Right now,' Noogan muttered. 'What I need is some sleep.'

Paternasse was already slumped on the ground, snoring. Nayalla could feel herself wanting to nod off too, but she was afraid of the Seneschal finding them while they slept.

'Someone needs to keep watch,' Mirkrin said, echoing her thoughts.

'I won't sleep,' Dalegin said. 'There's no way I could sleep after that.'

'Wake me when you start getting drowsy,' Nayalla said. 'I'll take next watch.'

She huddled up close to her husband and was asleep in minutes. Mirkrin rested his chin on her head, stroking her hair. He wondered how long they could go on like this, running around in the dark, with no supplies and no idea where they were going, and enemies hunting them at every turn. But even as he thought about this, he remembered Taya and Lorkrin and hoped that they had been found safe and that they were now back with the tribe. All their troubles under this mountain would be bearable, if they could just be sure that their children were all right. Troubled by his thoughts, he drifted off into an uneasy sleep.

11 ARE THE GODS HAVING A LAUGH?

Ludditch was woken by the sound of his father's shuffling feet, accompanied by the old man's two canes, scraping across the floor outside his room. His father would not be dragging his crippled body out of bed for nothing. Ludditch's wife was still asleep beside him as he sat up, threw back the heavy fur and pulled on his soft, rawhide shoes. Ludditch Senior opened the door.

'The clans're out on the hunt. Someone's seen a minkren in the village,' the crippled old man said. 'Best get down there and show yur face, less'n you want someone else claimin' the head fer theirselves.'

'A minkren?' the younger man frowned. 'They were all hunted out. Even if they weren't, there's no gobden trees round here.'

Realisation dawned.

'Skullucks!' he swore. 'The damned Myunans!' He jumped to his feet and pushed past his father. 'Cleet! Get the hunnuds out. We got Myunans on the loose!'

The rest of his immediate clan were up and armed in no time, and Cleet opened the hunnud cages and went inside to put on their leashes. His appearance was greeted with shrill chatters and howls and the sound of clawed feet running back and forth in excitement.

The village was nearly deserted when the chieftain and his party arrived. The first thing Ludditch did was to hold a light up to the cages hanging up outside the meetinghouse. He snarled at what he saw. In the darkness, it would have been easy to mistake the arranged hides as sleeping bodies.

'Canny little wretches,' he said, baring his teeth.

'The Parsinor's gone, Learup,' Spiroe called, coming out of the tannery. 'Someone let him loose.'

'Set the hunnuds on 'em,' the chieftain growled. 'Get the scent off the cages. Send word to the lookouts on all the roads. And someone go and check the river. Find those skullsuckers! The Parsinor's mine. Whoever catches the others can have their skins. And bring me whatever bowel-brains were supposed to be on watch tonight. Someone's gonna lose some fingers over this.'

+ + + +

Lorkrin swore bitterly as another gnat flew up his nose. He snorted it out angrily, unable to scratch the itch because he was using both his hands as paddles.

'I've just about had it with these bloody insects!' he growled.

'Me too,' Taya said from behind him. 'What's up ahead?'

'Fog,' her brother replied.

'The ground looks a little more open over to the right,' she said, ignoring him. 'Maybe we should try walking from here on. They're going to come down the river after us sooner or later, and we won't be able to outrun them.'

'Right,' Lorkrin agreed. 'We'll have to scuttle the skiff.'

They pulled up into the mud of the bank and the two Myunans shed their canoe forms as they dragged Draegar's head and shoulders up out of the water. The ground was more open here, the trees thinning out to give way to tufts of bush and grass. Taya followed it away from the river until she was almost out of sight in the damp mist.

'There's a steep slope down into a valley,' she said, coming back. 'I can't see any more than that.'

Rug paddled to the shore, but got stuck in the mud. Lorkrin rolled his eyes and dragged the little boat further up so that the man could get out. Then he went to have a look at the slope for himself.

'It's as good a way as any,' he said.

'We should head north and west until we hit the mountains,' Taya added. 'At least that way we'll be able to figure out where we are.'

'Here, help me sink this thing,' Lorkrin said to Rug as he walked back towards the boat.

'Why are we sinking it?' Rug asked.

'Think, Rug. If they find the *boat*, they'll know where we got *out*, won't they? So we're sinking it so they won't find it. Now get your mits on that end and hold it while I put some holes in it.'

They noticed a soft rumble through their bodies. They all froze. Rug felt a sickening feeling come over him.

'What is tha–?' he began, but then he saw ripples run across the still surface of the river and a shudder ran up through his feet from the ground.

They were knocked off their feet by the violence of the next tremor. It struck with a suddenness that stunned them, the ground jolting under them and stopping them from getting back on their feet. The fact that they could not see what was going on around them made it all the more frightening and Rug cried out in fear. Another shockwave followed and they felt it to their bones. Trees could be heard toppling nearby, and animals awoke, screeching in panic. Birds burst out of the trees and into the air, flying blind in the dark.

Then it was gone, as suddenly as it had started. Lorkrin picked himself out of the mud and stood up on shaking legs.

'What is going on?' he shouted.

'Lorkrin, hush!' Taya urged him. 'Someone might hear!'

'Who gives a flying fart!' he snapped. 'Our luck couldn't get any worse if we prayed for it. I mean, earthquakes? On top of everything else? Are the gods having a laugh, or what?'

'Quiet!' his sister hissed.

'Why should I …?'

'Listen!'

They all fell silent. There was something, a dull, slipping, rumbling sound. It was coming from the hill that towered, half-hidden, above them on the far side of the river.

'What's that?' Taya asked.

Rug was frozen to the spot as he listened, as if trying to recall a lost memory. Then he held up his hand to point towards the opposite side of the river.

'I know this sound,' he said. 'Mud and rock slipping down the hill. Lots of it.'

'Landslide,' Lorkrin said, matter-of-factly.

'It could take the whole hillside with it!' Taya exclaimed. 'Lorkrin, the boat …'

The two Myunans pulled the boat up out of the river and dragged it with them towards the edge of the slope. The rumbling grew louder.

'Come on!' she called to Rug. 'You can ride this down the hill. It's the quickest way!'

'But what about you?' he asked.

'You go on,' she told him. 'We'll take Draegar.'

Rug shook his head and ran back to them. Something massive was coming down the hill, pushing air ahead of it. A faint breeze blew through the mist.

'Maybe the river will stop it,' Taya said hopefully as they all grabbed hold of Draegar and pulled him through the mud, away from the water to where the ground dropped away.

'And maybe it'll take the river with it,' Lorkrin grunted. 'Look, we can't carry him …'

'We won't have to,' she told him. 'He's going to carry us. Rug, get back in your boat and go, we've got him.'

Rug nodded and hurried over to the skiff. With one look back, he climbed in and Lorkrin shoved the boat forwards. The boat's bottom scraped over the ground, the bow stuck out into empty space for a moment, then dropped and Rug slid down into the fog, quickly gathering speed and disappearing into the grey.

Draegar's feet were still bound and the two children pointed them downhill, Lorkrin holding the ends of the rope so that he could lift the feet if he needed to. Then they sat atop the Parsinor, Lorkrin on his belly and Taya on his chest. With one foot either side of his torso, and his arms tucked under theirs, they eased his unconscious body over the edge. Even as they did, a wall of black muck hit the far side of the river hard enough to send a wave ploughing across it and over the near bank. A flood of mud and water surged towards them.

'We're not moving!' Lorkrin cried, as his feet slipped against the wet ground.

'Push harder!' Taya shouted, digging her own heels in as hard as she could.

'I *am* pushing harder!'

With that, the first wash of the flood hit them, lifting Draegar's body enough to slide it over the edge and they were gone. Their makeshift sled bucked and rocked as he picked up speed, the wet ground carrying them on downwards. Steering was out of the question; they could only hope that they would not run into a tree or other obstacle. They veered into the path of a shallow stream and found themselves channelled down its course, Draegar's back and legs crashing over stones and driftwood as they swept faster and faster downhill.

'Hee … e's going to be a wreck, wh … en he wakes up!' Lorkrin bellowed as they bounced and slipped along.

'If the … re's anything left to wake … up, I'll be ha … appy!' Taya grunted.

The mud was rushing past with a roar around them, and they were only just keeping up with it. Taya risked a glance back and saw fallen trees and rocks being carried along behind them. They were running a race with the mudslide and they could not get out before it ended. They would be crushed by everything behind them if they stopped before the mud did. A boulder loomed up in their path and Lorkrin used the rope tied to Draegar's feet to try and steer them clear, but it was no use. Taya shut her eyes. The mud swept by on their right, washing up against the bank and slopping back down, pushing them sideways and around the boulder. Taya opened her eyes and looked back at the boulder in amazement, but then fixed her gaze on the course ahead. They couldn't expect that kind of luck to last.

Off to one side and slightly ahead of them, they saw Rug careering down the slope, the avalanche of muck and debris closing swiftly on him. With the bank rising and falling past them, the two children could only get fleeting glances of their new friend, but they saw the little skiff buck sideways as it hit a tree and then it tumbled over and over, rolling on top of the tall, thin man. The bank of the stream blocked the Myunans' view as the mudslide crashed down over him.

The slope was easing off and Draegar's descent was slowing now. But the momentum of the landslide carried them on and the surge built up behind them, lifting them up on its leading wave. Draegar's head and shoulders tilted higher and higher and then Taya and Lorkrin felt themselves being pitched forward. They plunged into the stream, its water deeper as it was pushed ahead of the landslide, and they found themselves carried headlong down a narrowing channel. There, ahead of them, they saw a mill-house, its large wooden wheel turning under the force of the water. They were going to be carried right under it.

With a scream, Lorkrin slunched just as the water swept him under and he felt the pressure of the wooden wheel's paddles crushing him against the bottom. He lost what breath he had in his lungs and nearly blacked out from the pain. When the wheel spat him out the other side, his body was marked from head to toe with a ladder-like pattern of grooves. He could feel every one of them. Taya's serrated body was ejected from under the paddles after him and she shunted up against him as they both floated with the slower current into a wider stream.

There was a crunch of splitting wood and Draegar's unconscious form was spewed out from under the wheel, bringing some of the broken paddles with it. Lorkrin winced at the sight. That was going to hurt when the Parsinor woke up. Then the roar of slipping earth bore down on them and they saw the mudslide tear the large wheel from its mountings and bring it crashing towards them. Taya and Lorkrin threw themselves against the bank of the stream and covered their heads as the world came down around them.

+ + + +

Rug came to and found that opening his eyes had little effect on the darkness. Apprehension came over him as he remembered the landslide and he knew he had been caught beneath it. But there was air around him, and he could move the top half of his body. He felt above him; there were wooden boards over his head. Was it a … he struggled to remember. A box that people were buried in. A coffin. A chill went through him. Had someone actually buried him, thinking him dead? He pushed up against the boards. They were slippery with mud. With his fingertips, he followed them and found they angled downwards and pressed into his thighs. If it was a coffin, he was only halfway in. He felt further up and realised he knew this shape. This wasn't a coffin – it was the skiff; upturned and acting like a roof over him against the mud, it had probably saved his life.

He pushed with all his might against the boat, but it did not budge. He shouted for help, but no one answered. He lay embedded in the mud, the overturned skiff protecting the upper half of his body. His legs were caught in muck up to his thighs, but a crack of light up under the other end of the skiff told him that he was not completely buried. He wondered how long he had been unconscious.

Rug realised he should be more scared. Being buried beneath a landslide was a frightening thing. But there was something about the darkness that he found comforting. He had a sense that the home he could not remember had been a dark place, a cave perhaps. Yes. He could imagine feeling at home in some deep cave. He heard sounds of movement nearby.

'Hello? Taya? Lorkrin?' he called. 'Is there anybody to help me get out of the mud, please? I can't seem to move! I'm over here ... under the boat. Can anybody hear me?'

Nobody could. He waited and listened. Nothing. It was raining outside; he could hear it. And water was seeping down into his little hole beneath the boat. He wondered how long it would take to fill up completely. He pushed against the boards to try and lift the boat, but it did not budge.

'Can somebody help me, please?' he shouted. 'I'm very stuck here. Completely stuck, actually.'

He heard urgent footfalls. There came the sound of digging and soon the boat was lifted away, exposing him to the full force of the sunlight. Draegar stood over him, a dark shape against the sunlight.

'Hello,' Rug said, hesitantly.

Draegar regarded him for a moment.

'Who are you – and where are the children?'

+ + + +

Dalegin's head rolled to one side where he was leaning against the wall and he jolted awake. He looked around anxiously. The remaining torches were going out. Had he fallen asleep? How long had he been dozing? He had been awake when everyone had been roused by another earth tremor, but it had been distant and had passed quickly, so they had all just gone back to sleep. He fervently hoped that it was the last they would see of the earthquakes. Picking up his torch, he replenished it from the jar of silver powder and stood up. They were at a branch in the tunnel. He felt vulnerable, exposed to anything that might come at them. The Seneschal could come from anywhere and catch them by surprise. Utterly exhausted Dalegin's body craved sleep. Nayalla had told him to wake her, but he was loath to give her the satisfaction of relieving him and he simply did not trust the Myunans.

Just as he was about to wake up Noogan, he thought he heard something further down the tunnel. He held up his light, but could see nothing. Dalegin was not a cowardly man, but he had no stomach for taking unnecessary risks either. He listened for a while longer, but did not venture any further down the passageway. Eventually he decided that he had imagined it and went back to where the others were slumped, asleep in the passageway. Shaking Noogan's shoulder until the younger man came groggily to his senses, Dalegin told him to take next watch. The young man got to his feet to rouse his cold, numb limbs, and the other miner settled down to sleep on the warm spot on the stone that Noogan had left behind.

Mirkrin woke up not long after, nodding to the young miner and huddling up closer to his wife as he gazed into the darkness.

'I'm cold,' Noogan muttered, hugging himself and shivering. 'Just can't seem to get warm.'

'It's the stone,' Mirkrin said softly. 'Sucks the warmth right out of you. Should never sleep on bare stone. And we're hungry too. We need to get some food in us.'

'I could eat a horse …' Noogan stamped his feet and flapped his arms. 'No, a bexemot! Or a pile of good steaks, fried in butter, with new potatoes and some cabbage, done the way my ma does it, cut up with some onion and fried up lovely.'

'I could murder some sausages in gravy,' Mirkrin closed his eyes. 'With mashed potatoes and beans and some bread and butter on the side. Nayalla here does this great nutty bread. You can wrap the sausages up in it …'

'Neither of you know nothin' about food,' Paternasse's voice chided them, his false teeth loose in his mouth. 'What you want at a time like this is a good pie. My wife does a chicken and mushroom pie as'd make you drool like a dog. And an apple tart to follow, with cream and sugar an' all on it.'

'That's my daughter's favourite,' Mirkrin said quietly. 'A nice apple pie. Or blackberry. She loves them.'

He had been trying not to think about his children. It only made things worse, knowing they could be in danger themselves. Paternasse saw the expression on his face and recognised it for what it was.

'You just got the two?' he asked.

'Yes. Lorkrin and Taya. Trouble since they were born.'

'Hah!' Paternasse chortled. 'I know what you mean. I've got six myself, with the old lady haulin' around number seven as we speak, due to drop in the autumn. They don't give you a moment's peace, do they?'

'No,' Mirkrin smiled to himself. 'And I wouldn't have it any other way.'

'Aye,' the old miner nodded solemnly.

Nayalla had woken, but did not join in the conversation, content to stay curled up against her husband and listen to the men talk. It had always fascinated her how men could be at each other's throats, trading blows like mortal enemies one moment and then talking genially like close friends the next.

'What about you, Noogan?' Mirkrin asked. 'You married? Any little ones?'

'No, no,' the young man put his hands in his pockets and stamped his feet some more. 'Still sowing me oats, you know?'

'Pay him no mind,' Paternasse snorted. 'He's got eyes for that Ellene Magiden, 'aven't you lad? Always had!'

'No I 'aven't,' Noogan retorted, with a blush that went all the way to the tips of his ears.

'Lad, she's the only one as doesn't know, yuh fool! When you goin' ta show your hand? They won't wait around for-ever, you know.'

'I was waitin' for the right time!' Noogan protested.

'The right time's when yuh ask her yuh dolt, not the other way round! When we get out of here, I'm marchin' you right back to her door and standin' you in front of her.'

'Ah, Jussek …'

'It's got to be done, lad, or she'll end up with some clod-hoppin' farmer lookin' for someone to tend his herd.'

Noogan looked shocked and pleased in equal measure, but did not say any more. He gazed down one of the passageways to avoid looking at the others.

'Lads,' he whispered, 'I think I see a light. And it's movin'.'

12 THE KRUNDENGROND

Afternoon light was seeping through the trees when Lorkrin opened his eyes. He lifted his head and found that he was half-buried in the ground, and covered in mud. Taya was nearby, already sitting up, but still rubbing her eyes as if she had just woken from a long sleep. She was equally coated in the muck.

'Where are we?' he asked.

'Don't know.'

He sat up and groaned as his body viciously reminded him of the previous night's events. He was aching all over. The lines of bruises from the millwheel hurt the most. He concentrated for a moment and the bruises faded almost to nothing, hidden by his ability to change the colour of his skin.

Looking around him, he could see they were in a quiet glen; one that must once have been quite picturesque … before the landslide had piled in on top of it. The shattered remains of the millwheel that had crushed him were off to one side, lying on the mound of rubble that – until recently – had been the mill itself. And standing beside the pile of earth-strewn wreckage was a dejected-looking Reisenick. Lorkrin gave a start, but the man just glanced over at him, and then went back to looking at the wheel.

'Hello,' Taya greeted him hesitantly, as she stood up.

'How y'all,' he replied without looking up.

'Are you a … are you one of Ludditch's clan?' she asked.

'No, I'm a Pluggitch – the last o' my line.' He shook his head miserably. 'Don't have no clan no more since my old maw died. Just had me this mill and this here wheel. Had a dog for a time. Dog died too.'

'I'm sorry,' Taya said, sympathetically.

''S all right – waren't your doin'.'

'Taya! Lorkrin!' Draegar staggered down the broken earth of the hill towards them. 'By the gods, I thought you were dead! We've been searching all morning. Are you hurt?'

'A bit battered,' Taya told him. 'But we're okay. We were sort of buried, I think. That's why you didn't see us.'

Taya and Lorkrin waded out of the mud and threw their arms around Draegar.

'Oof!' he exclaimed. 'Go easy. I feel like I've been run over by a stampede of bexemots. I won't walk right for a week. What happened to me?'

'You got caught in an avalanche, but we saved you,' Taya told him, throwing a pointed look at Lorkrin. The Parsinor beamed at them.

'You did marvellously. And that avalanche should put Ludditch off our trail for a while too. It seems luck is on our side for a change. My thanks to you, children, for saving my life.'

'That's all right,' Lorkrin chirped. 'Springing you from the Reisenicks was harder though.'

'I remember some of it,' Draegar nodded. 'You showed nerves of steel. But how did we get here? I seem to remember being in a boat or something.'

'That's right,' Taya said, uneasily. 'We put you in … a boat and went downriver.'

'Then another earthquake happened,' Lorkrin put in. 'We got you out of the water … eh, boat and … well, it was all downhill from there.'

'I woke up with my hands and feet bound up with rope,' Draegar grunted. 'That was the Reisenicks, I presume?'

'Absolutely,' Lorkrin nodded.

'I met your new friend, by the way,' the Parsinor said. 'He says you gave him his name. Rug, eh? You could have come up with something more dignified.'

'It suits him,' Lorkrin shrugged.

Rug shuffled forward, raising his hand in a hesitant wave.

'You made it!' Lorkrin exclaimed. 'We thought you'd copped it when we saw the boat turn over.'

'No, I didn't … cop it,' Rug said happily, as he wondered what to do about the two children whose arms were now wrapped around him. In the end he patted them tentatively on the heads and waited for them to finish their hugging. Taya stood back and looked at him.

'You feel cold, and you look a state,' she said in a heartening voice, looking towards the large pool that was all that remained of the river running through the centre of the glen. 'We all do. We need a good bath.' She turned to the Reisenick, and called: 'Do you mind if we swim in your pool?'

'Can't do no harm,' the Reisenick called back, still staring at his wheel. 'River's gone now anyhow. You go on and swim there – enjoy yourselves. Got to take what little pleasure there is in this life, that's what my maw always used to say. 'Fore she died.'

'Fancy a swim?' Taya tilted her head towards Rug.

'I don't think I can swim,' he replied.

'You can wade,' Lorkrin took his arm. 'Come on. Get some of those clothes off you before all that mud dries on.'

'No!' Rug barked, pulling his arm away and making Lorkrin jump. 'I … I'm not taking anything off. I'm staying the way I am.'

'That's okay,' Lorkrin stepped back warily. 'Well … we're going for a swim to have a wash. You can come along if you like.'

He made a face at Taya as he turned around and they waded into the pool.

'He's a bit touchy, isn't he?'

'Maybe he's just shy,' she said. 'He still doesn't remember anything about who he was; he's probably really uptight about everything. And see the burns on his clothes?'

'Yeah, so?'

'I think he was in a fire, maybe a forest fire or something.' She looked back to check that Rug was out of earshot, then leaned closer to her brother. 'I think he might have been badly burned.'

Lorkrin's eyes widened.

'You reckon? That'd be mad. I wonder what it looks like?'

'Don't be sick.'

'Don't act like Ma, I know you're wondering yourself.'

They both went quiet at the mention of their mother and said nothing more until they reached the water. The day was warm and the water looked dark, but inviting. They plunged in and paddled around for a while, washing the mud from their bodies and talking about what had happened over the last few days.

Rug came down to the riverbank later and lowered himself into the water with all his clothes on. He stood there, shoulder deep, moving his arms around and rubbing dirt from his clothes absent-mindedly. He did not even pull down his hood or the scarf that hid his face. Taya watched him with concern, but did not say anything.

'Imagine getting burned on the face,' Lorkrin whispered. 'It must be horrible.'

'Shut up,' his sister muttered.

They were about to start arguing, when Draegar strode up to the bank and called to them.

'Come on out of there. This clansman knows of a story-house not far from here. He says we can get transport there to catch up with your uncle.'

+ + + +

Noogan and Mirkrin undertook to investigate the light, while the others waited behind in case they should run into trouble. The two men walked cautiously down the tunnel. On one side, there was a flight of steps leading up to another level, while down the passage on the other side, another flight led even further into the depths of the mountain. The light had flitted just at the limit of their vision for an instant before disappearing and they reasoned that it had gone around a corner. They would walk down as far as that corner, but would not go out of sight of the others behind them.

'Could've sworn it was like someone carryin' a lantern,' Noogan said quietly. 'The way the light moved, sort of swayin', like.'

'If there is someone else down here,' Mirkrin replied. 'Chances are, they're not friendly. Or they think we're not. Either way, it might be best if we didn't run into them.'

'But what if they know a way out?'

'Well, that's why I'm following a strange light down a dark tunnel in the middle of mountain that's tryin' to kill us. 'Cause being careful hasn't really worked out for us so far.'

They reached a junction; their tunnel ended where it met another going at an acute angle to it. The floor was sloping downwards.

'I'm only guessing here,' Mirkrin said, feeling uneasy about the new passage. 'But I don't think we want to be going any further downwards. If that light wants to steer clear of us, then let it. I reckon we should take those stairs we saw back there and head upwards, once everyone's ready to move.'

'I'll second that,' Noogan breathed. 'Doesn't smell too invitin' down there, anyhow. Let's head back.'

'Right you are.'

They walked backwards for the first few steps, wary of the sloping tunnel, but unable to say why. Then they turned and retraced their steps back to the rest of the group.

+ + + +

Draegar was talking to the Reisenick, Pluggitch, about what had happened to them. Pluggitch nodded slowly as he listened, never losing his expression of perpetual dejection.

'Ludditch does well out of the tribute system,' he said, finally. 'It keeps the peace in Ainslidge Woods – helps him put up with all the strangers who pass through. He hates strangers, but you can't fight the whole world. On the other hand, we don't get many of … of … of your sort round here. Some of the more … sheltered of the clansmen might see you as just another animal to be hunted. Their blood lust is an unfortunate hindrance to clear thinkin', if you ask me. Myunans, now, they're a different matter. They're neighbours to our woods and any Reisenick would be careful in their dealings with them. If what you're sayin' is true, then Learup Ludditch has started somethin' that would bring the Myunan tribes into our woods in search of vengeance. I know Ludditch some, and he is not what I'd call a rash man. He wouldn't go startin' somethin' like this unless he was sure to profit by it. But I can't see how he could escape the consequences of killin' Myunan children. Myunans are not warmongering, but they are relentless in the protection of their own.'

'Maybe the exorcist has something to do with all this,' Taya piped up.

'Kalayal Harsq's presence in these woods is certainly a cause for concern,' Draegar mused. 'Where he goes, great loss follows. He and Ludditch are a bad mix.'

'Ludditch said they wouldn't have to worry about the Myunans any more,' Lorkrin interrupted. 'What did he mean?'

'Really?' Draegar growled. 'I wonder how he reckons on that?'

'And what's krundengrond?' Taya asked. 'He said there'd be krundengrond.'

'Krundengrond means "ferocious earth",' Draegar told them. 'I saw a stretch of it once, far southwest of the Kartharic Peaks. The earth churns and chews on itself like a sea in a storm. But the violence comes from within the earth itself, rather than from the wind.'

'Like an earthquake?' Lorkrin put in.

'No, this is different. An earthquake is a shaking

movement that starts in one place and passes through the ground. It happens once and it is over. Like these ones we've been having. You feel a vibration through the ground, but the ground itself is only moving because something else is having an effect on it. Krundengrond is almost like a swarm of creatures. Every piece of it is equally dangerous. The soil itself grinds up anything that falls upon it. It is not like swamp, for it can lie over hills and is as dangerous dry as it is in the wet. Only the most skilled and daring men ever try to cross the krundengrond plain that I visited and many of them are killed in the attempt.'

'The Reisenicks think there is some in the Myunan territories,' Taya said. 'They were talking about it while we were there. They thought we were living on top of it.'

Draegar snorted.

'If there were krundengrond there, you would know all about it. And as for living on it, nothing lives on that accursed earth; it would be like living in the jaws of a skack.'

'What would it have to do with Orgarth?' Lorkrin asked. 'That's the god of Absaleth, isn't it?'

'It was said that Orgarth was the size of a mountain and had a body of iron,' Draegar told them. 'He was cast down from the stars and his fall laid waste to the land. Your uncle would probably know more about this. He collects such stories for amusement. You can ask him when you see him. But you have to understand, the Reisenicks know little of the world beyond their own territories. They do not travel ...' He glanced at Pluggitch: 'No offence meant.'

'No, you have a point there, all right,' Pluggitch shrugged. 'We're all home birds at heart, and that's the truth.'

'Many of them are suspicious of strangers,' Draegar went

on. 'They are especially afraid of the Noranians, because they know that the northerners have turned their attention to this land. The Reisenicks can hunt and kill most things in these forests, but in the end they would be no match for the Noranian armies. They make up stories about what goes on beyond their borders because fear of the outside keeps the clans united. And because they don't listen to much news from the outside, there is nothing to contradict the stories they concoct. You should not take their tales too seriously.'

'They sounded pretty serious to us,' Taya insisted. 'And they said other people didn't know about it, not even that Braskhiam, Harsq. They said all the Myunans would disappear and all the maps would change.'

'Take it from me, child,' Draegar reassured her, 'maps do not change overnight; they change over decades ... centuries. I have drawn more than most, and it would take more than a Reisenick's flight of fancy to change a landscape.'

Taya looked at her brother, who was keeping quiet. Lorkrin idolised Draegar and she knew he would want to believe him, but they had heard Ludditch talking and the Reisenick chieftain did not seem the kind of man given to flights of fancy. He seemed the kind of man who knew what he was doing. Draegar arched his back and groaned.

'By the gods, I'm stiff!' he said, at last. 'I suppose we could all do with a rest, but we need to keep moving. Mr Pluggitch, you were telling us about a storyhouse?'

+ + + +

Taya, Lorkrin and Rug followed Draegar along the trail the morose Reisenick had shown them. The two Myunans wanted to transform themselves and fly ahead, but Draegar would not allow it. The Reisenicks hunted birds in the air, as well as beasts on the ground. The Parsinor was walking stiffly, as if his back were hurting him. The mist wisped through the trees around them, strands of it seeming to catch in the branches. Carkhams croaked to each other, and the children remembered that the Reisenicks used trained birds as messengers and trackers as well as for hunting. Strange animal sounds carried through the trees. It brought Taya back to the eerie room in the roof of the Reisenick meeting-house and she mentioned it to the Parsinor.

'The Reisenicks put great store in ancestry,' he told them. 'Most of their dead are laid to rest in burial grounds, sacred places where even the Reisenicks are not allowed to hunt or build. But the most respected chieftains are preserved so that their spirit will remain to share their wisdom with their descendants. Ludditch will no doubt have all his most important ancestors from the last century in that room.'

'That's sick,' Lorkrin wrinkled his nose.

'It is their way, Lorkrin. Myunan ways can seem strange to other races.'

'We don't stuff our dead, though.'

'I didn't say I didn't agree with you, lad,' the Parsinor arched his back and grunted, reaching behind and scratching at his armour as if something irritated him.

'The Reisenicks love the past,' he went on. 'They live for telling stories of ancient days. A clansman's status is decided before he is born, by the actions of his forefathers. The dead are easily explained and hold no surprises. They are suspicious of anything new or different, so the living mould themselves in the image of their dead.'

'Aw, they're just sounding weirder every time somebody

talks about 'em,' Lorkrin grunted. 'I'm amazed Uncl
ever managed to get through this place in one piece. A
wanted to do was try and reach Ma and Pa and we end up
kidnapped, caged, crushed and lost and we've only been
here two days …'

He was interrupted as Draegar dropped into a crouch and
gestured to them to get under the cover of some low-
hanging foliage. They scurried into the shadows and looked
up at where he was pointing. In the gloom of the trees above
them, something leapt from a branch, throwing itself in a
sprawling glide to a tree on the other side of the trail. It was
the shape of a weasel, but the size of a tall man, with striped
brown and blue-grey fur, a flat tail and powerful, hooked
claws on its feet. It glided on two flaps of skin, which
stretched down on each side of its body from its elbows to
its knees. Even in the quick glimpse they had caught of it,
they could see that it wore a collar.

'It's a hunnud,' Draegar told them. 'The Reisenicks use
them for running down quarry. They are formidable trackers
and savage predators, and they are pack animals. Where
there is one, there will be more. I don't think it saw us, but
we were lucky to spot it. We might not be so lucky the next
time. We need to move on, quickly.'

+ + + +

Kalayal Harsq glared at the clansman who blocked the road.

'What do you mean, "we can't leave"?'

'Orders from the chieftain. He says you got ta stay fer a
while.'

'But he told us to go!'

'He's gone and changed his mind, then, hasn't he?'

'And what's made him change his mind, exactly?'

'Says you haven't finished with your part of the deal.'

'I paid the man! That *was* my part of the deal!'

'Well,' the Reisenick shrugged. 'Learup says you don't leave, then you don't leave and that's the end of it.'

'Where is he?' the Braskhiam demanded. 'I want to have this out with him. By Brask, I'll not be treated like one of his vassals.'

'He's off huntin' some fugitives, so "vassals" is all you got to have this out with. An' I'd mind your tone, if you ever want ta see the outside o' Ainslidge.'

Harsq motioned angrily to the wagon behind him and the two vehicles reversed awkwardly back up the narrow road to a place wide enough to turn around. From there, they drove back towards the village. The exorcist was careful to hide his concern from his followers. He had slept badly again during the night and the strain of his fears was wearing him down. And now this. If Ludditch was changing the terms of their agreement it could mean anything. Harsq was growing increasingly suspicious about the Reisenick's motives – there was something else afoot, something he had unwittingly started with his ceremony at Absaleth. Seething with frustration, he glared into the trees. He could feel it out there somewhere, the ghost of the mountain. Somehow, it had escaped him again. He had never known such an elusive spirit, and he could not help but feel respect for a soul that could withstand not just one, but two withering assaults. And that respect was mingled with fear. His best efforts had not defeated the spirit, and he knew that despite the damage he had done it, the thing would be coming for him, looking for retribution. The earthquakes were part of it, but they were only the beginning; there would be worse to come.

He had to escape this land before the spirit claimed him, but Ludditch meant to get further use out of him and he knew that if he crossed the chieftain, it could cost him his life and the lives of his disciples. He needed to give the clansmen a reason to let them leave, and for that, he needed to know why Ludditch wanted him to stay.

He climbed down from the wagon as it drew up outside their cabin once more and jumped to the ground.

'I'm going to the tavern,' he told his driver. 'Wait for me here. And stay together. I don't trust these Braskforsaken inbreeds.'

'The tavern, Kalayal? But …'

'But what?'

'But you don't drink.'

'No, but *they* all do.'

Whipping his robes around him, he strode down to the ramshackle, wood-and-hide building that served as a tavern for the village and swung the door open. The chatter of conversation inside died the instant he walked in, and he found himself being stared at by a dozen pairs of eyes. He walked to the counter and slapped some drokes on the stained, wooden surface.

'Drinks all round,' he told the proprietor. Then he turned to face the room. 'And there'll be more if I get to hear a good story or two.'

✦   ✦   ✦   ✦

Cullum was in a bad way. The wound in his leg was filled with pus and the leg itself was nearly twice its normal size. The Forward-Batterer's face was drenched in sweat and screwed up in pain. Emos shook his head and covered up the wound again with the dressing he had prepared.

'This needs to be treated, and by a real healer. I've done what I can, but if you don't get some help soon, you're going to lose the leg. And if we don't take the leg off in time, you'll die.'

'Don't pussyfoot about. Give it to me straight,' Cullum scowled.

'My guess is the trap was dirty, probably used over and over again without changing the spikes. The rot is spreading fast. You need proper treatment and there is only one place within reach where you will get it.'

'And let me guess,' Jube grunted. 'It's not on our way.'

The dark look on Emos's tattooed face was all the answer he needed. It seemed that everything was working against them. The cave entrance seemed as far away as ever.

'We need to head east,' the Myunan said. 'It will take us out of our way, but from there, we can get on another road that will take us in the direction of the cave. There is an old Reisenick woman who knows the healing ways as well as anyone, and she's not from Ludditch's clan. She will help for a price.'

Without another word, they all climbed aboard the wagons. Cullum lay in the back of Jube's truck, his wounded leg stretched out on a soft, folded blanket. The vehicles started up and he winced with pain as the flatbed shook with the motion over the rough track. They were in a gully that followed the course of a stream down through a narrow valley. The banks on either side hid the vehicles well and would help muffle their sound.

Emos sat with the Noranian, his eyes on the layers of clay

and stone that had been cut away by centuries of water, his mind out in the wilderness, desperately willing the safe return of his niece and nephew. He wondered if Draegar had found them. If so, the wise move for them would be to make their way home, but he knew they would come after him. It was all going so wrong. Instead of saving his sister and brother-in-law, he had led others deeper and deeper into trouble. He was beginning to doubt that Nayalla and Mirkrin were alive at all, or that the fissure they had found had any connection with the tunnels beneath Old Man's Cave. All their efforts could be for nothing.

He was gazing up at the bank of earth above him, when he spotted a bright bunch of pink and yellow flowers. He called to Jube to stop and jumped down, climbing the bank and gently parting the flowers to see what lay beneath. There, as he'd hoped, were a number of small snails with copper-coloured shells. He picked up a few and brought them back down to truck.

'What are they for?' Cullum grunted.

'They're for you,' the Myunan replied.

He picked up the Noranian's canteen and opened it. The snails had retreated into their shells, but that did not matter. What Emos needed was the slime they used to seal themselves in. He rubbed his little finger in the opening of each shell and then smeared the mucus on the inside of the cap of the canteen.

'Hey!' Cullum barked. 'What are you playing at? I have to drink out of that!'

'That's the idea,' Emos replied, putting the cap on the container and shaking it, so that the water mixed with the snail's slime.

He held the canteen out to the injured man.

'The mucus is a palliative,' he told the Noranian. 'Try not to think about where it came from, but even mixed with water, this is powerful stuff. It'll numb the pain, but it'll numb everything else as well. Just take a bit at a time as you need it, all right?'

He leaned over and tossed the snails into the grass at the top of the bank.

'Right,' Cullum took the canteen from him and screwing up his face, he gulped some down.

'Now, you see, that was probably a bit too much.'

Cullum managed a dismissive sneer before his eyes rolled back into his head and his face went slack. Khassiel, who was using the stop to strip down her crossbow, looked over and chuckled.

'I'll have to get some of that stuff for when we head back. There's a few more of the lads could do with having their brains disconnected for a while.'

It was strange, hearing this implacable woman laugh, and Emos gave her a quizzical glance.

'What's it like, being a woman in the army?'

'There are no women in the army,' she said, a hint of sarcasm in her voice. 'A soldier is a soldier. We're all the same.'

'That's how it is, is it? Sounds very fair … very disciplined.'

'Yes,' she nodded, the sarcasm heavy and bitter now. 'It's very disciplined. Your family gives you up when you're barely old enough to walk, because they've one too many mouths to feed and from there on in the officers can do what they like with you. And they keep breaking you down until they've beaten the child out of you and you just can't break any more, so that they can build you up to be an obedient

servant. And so you become disciplined, because it's what
they want. And because you're a woman, you have to train
harder and work more and kick the teeth out of any man
who tries to prove you're weaker than he is – and I mean
really hurt him, because if you don't they'll all try it on and
then you'd just be meat for them to beat up on and there'd
be no way out for you, because you can't leave once you're
in and that's what it's like being a woman in the army. So,
what's it like being a Myunan?'

'Easier.'

They stood smiling slightly at each other. Emos checked
Cullum's breathing and put the top back on the canteen,
before looking to Jube, who had grabbed the chance to eat
and refuel the wagons while they were stopped.

'Time to be getting on, I think.'

'Aye.'

They set off again,

Cullum's breaths were slow and laboured from the drug;
he had a fever and the leg was looking worse. The sick man
reminded Emos of the days he had spent nursing his dying
wife. He had been helpless then, unable to save her. Now he
felt the same frustration as he steered the trucks away from
the cave where he hoped to be able to make his way in
under Absaleth and find Nayalla and Mirkrin.

To the north and west, the Rudstone mountains were just
visible through the mist, their tops lost in the clouds. Emos
gazed bitterly at them for a while, before turning his mind to
the more immediate task of keeping Cullum alive.

+ + + +

When Noogan saw the shaft of bright light, he started

running. There was no mistaking that gorgeous, blue-white light; it was daylight, beautiful, beautiful daylight. Twice, he nearly tripped and fell over unseen obstacles in the passage-way, but he did not stop. Behind him, the others hurried after him, crying out with joy and relief. He slowed as he got closer, for the beam of light was narrower than he had first thought and as he approached it, he saw that it was small, the hole through which it shone was barely large enough to squeeze his forearm into. Nearly blinded by the strength of the light, he shielded his eyes with his hand and squinted as he studied the square hole.

The others ran up behind him, panting with the exertion of their run. As their eyes slowly adjusted to the brightness, they were all puzzled by what they saw. The hole was just the end of a long, thin, square shaft that stretched far up to the surface. They could even smell the fresh air on the other side.

'I don't believe it,' Dalegin moaned. 'I don't believe it. There's got to be something else here.'

'There's bound to be,' Paternasse patted his back. 'We're almost there. Come on, everybody split up and start looking for a door or something.'

They all started searching for other signs of a way out, walking further down the tunnel, checking the passages that branched off it, shining their torches on every wall in the hope of finding the outline of a doorway, but there was nothing. No other hint of daylight could be found. One by one, they all returned to the beam of light. They tried screaming up the shaft, but no answer came.

Dalegin reached up to the lip of the opening, pushing his fingers up into the glow.

'Solid stone,' he said. 'There's no way we could dig our way up.'

'What about you?' Paternasse asked the Myunans. 'Couldn't you squeeze up there, go and get help?'

'No, it's too narrow and too long,' Nayalla replied, miserably. 'We can only crush our torsos and heads down so far. We could never fit up through there.'

They all stood, staring up at the light.

'This is the portal the Seneschal were talking about,' Mirkrin muttered. 'The one they had to break themselves up to get through. It was this hole, or one like it. They must go outside sometimes themselves, but nothing bigger than a rat can get in.'

'We have to go on, then,' Paternasse told them. 'We can't stay here.'

'But there must be something around here,' Dalegin whimpered in desperation. 'Maybe we should try digging. Anything would be better than wandering around in the bloody dark until we die of thirst or … or worse.'

'This is no good,' the old miner said to him. 'We can stand here wishin' ourselves up that hole all we like; it's not going to happen. We have to find another way. I've seen this before, where men can't let go of some ghost of a chance and end up doomin' themselves when they could have saved their bacon some other way. It's false hope and it'll kill yuh, sure as a knife through the heart. We have to move on.'

Dalegin looked ready to break down. He glared at one face after another, but everybody else agreed with Paternasse. Each of them cast one last, longing look at the daylight and then they walked away. Dalegin was the last to leave, his face turned up to the light, unwilling to let go of its tantalising glow. But the footsteps of the others were getting further away, and the fear of being left alone forced him to turn his back on the shaft of light and follow them into the darkness.

✦ ✦ ✦ ✦

The argument in the tavern was getting heated and Kalayal Harsq nervously wondered if things were going to turn nasty. The two clansmen who had offered to tell him some of the local folklore were disagreeing on some of the finer points of the story of the Tuderem, the alchemists who had lived in the shadow of Absaleth.

'... I'm tellin' ya, it wuz Orgarth what got rid of the krundengrond,' one was saying, the sparse hair on his balding head damp with the sweat of passionate debate. 'He reached out from the mountain and stamped the life out o' that wild ground. It's been told that way since my clan was first seeded.'

'And I'm telling ya, it were the Tuderem,' the other insisted, his large, single ear glowing pink with ire at his friend's stubborn ignorance. Where the other ear had been, there was an old, puckered white scar pierced with an earring. 'They used their powers and whatnot to lay it to rest. Why else would it have kept goin' until they got there. They laid it to rest and started their farmin' and minin' and such and that's the end of it.'

'The heck it is!'

'Damn straight!'

'Maybe you want to discuss this outside!'

'Maybe I want to discuss this right here, where everyone one can see the beatin' that's comin' to ya!'

'Oh? And who's gonna give it to me?'

'I am, that's who. Gonna beat you like your pappy used to …'

Harsq excused himself and left them to it. Behind him there was the sound of stools being pushed back and the occupants of the tavern rising to their feet as men took sides in the dispute. The priest had no doubt he had just helped start a feud that would last two or three generations, but he was more concerned with mulling over what he had heard.

Krundengrond. The very thought of it chilled him to the bone. He had seen some once, a small area in a valley that had lived with its curse for centuries. He had been summoned by a village there to carry out an exorcism in the hope of quelling its violence. One of his disciples had foolishly got too close while setting up the generator and had been pulled in. He had been chewed up like grain under a grindstone, his body broken and crushed by the kneading of the earth and stones. It took a long time for the pieces to disappear completely into the ground. The exorcism had failed, of course, but then krundengrond was not caused by some landlocked spirit that could be driven out.

Ludditch seemed to believe there was some of this deadly ground around the edge of Ainslidge, that the soul of Absaleth had held it in check and that the exorcism had freed it. But no one had seen any yet and Ludditch was not going to let the priest and his disciples go until he was sure he had no more use for them. Harsq suspected that they might never leave at all. He knew the krundengrond story was a myth – the tales of Orgarth and the alchemists might have a foundation in fact; most legends had a kernel of truth in their heart. But the Reisenicks were using folklore to explain what was happening to their land. He knew better.

The earthquakes had started after his visit to Absaleth. He could only guess at what else was happening to this territory, but the tremors would not be the end of it. Dead rivers, certainly, diseases in the trees, animals suffering stillbirths, he had seen it all happen before. A vengeful spirit was a terrifying thing to behold. If Ludditch was going to hold the priests until he saw the outskirts of his territory erupt into krundengrond, they would be waiting a very long time. But if the chieftain realised that the earthquakes were just one weapon in the arsenal of a ghost that Harsq's ministrations had driven to the Reisenicks' land, then the Braskhiam and his followers could look forward to slow, ugly deaths and to various parts of their bodies being used to adorn the walls of the clansmen's meetinghouse. They had to get out of Ainslidge.

As he walked up the muddy street he saw Jennas, one of his disciples, coming towards him. She was a tall, fair-haired young woman with an innocent manner and an airy grace. There was a look of anxiety on her face as she hurried up to him.

'Kalayal, Ludditch has returned. He does not look happy. He has called some kind of special council and he wants you to join them.'

'That's fine, Jennas. I need to have words with our gracious host and his cohorts. There's some straightening out to be done.'

'Kalayal, is everything all right? I mean … they're not going to hurt us, are they?'

'No, my child. They cannot hurt us while we are under Brask's watchful eye. Keep the good Lord in your heart and cherish your faith. There is sanctuary in His love.'

'Of course, Kalayal. Praise be to Brask.'

'Praise be to Brask, child,' he called as he walked towards the meetinghouse. 'He will watch over us.'

Though it wouldn't hurt to stack the odds a bit more in our favour either, he thought to himself. If Ludditch was going to let folklore govern his thinking, then Harsq would provide some mythical elements of his own.

The council was not being held in the main hall of the meetinghouse. Instead, the priest was led upstairs, where he was faced with one of the most horrific sights he had ever seen – dead Reisenick bodies preserved and posed in all their tribal splendour. In the centre of the room near the flue for the chimney sat Ludditch with his most important, living relatives, already deep in discussion. So this was what the Reisenicks called a Forefathers' Council. Trying to hide his revulsion at the scene, the Braskhiam made his way over to the group and was pointed towards an empty chair.

'Thank you for joinin' us, Kalayal,' Ludditch said, with the slightest hint of sarcasm in his voice. 'Glad you could stay with us a while longer.'

'I'm grateful for the opportunity,' Harsq replied. 'Seeing as my work is not yet done here.'

'Glad you think so,' the chieftain lit his bone pipe and tugged on it a couple of times. 'See, we was kind o' expectin' more of a … upheaval, if you like, followin' your exorcism. We were expectin' things to change somewhat.'

'You were expecting krundengrond, perhaps? You thought the ground around your territory would erupt and cut you off from the rest of the world. Is that what you were expecting?'

Ludditch sat forwards, taking his pipe from his mouth.

'You been hearin' things, priest?'

'I've heard enough to know that I've been misled. That I've been tricked by the Noranians and by you into starting something that you don't know how to finish. You should have told me that Absaleth was inhabited by a god. You've endangered everyone by hiding it from me. The Noranians obviously did not have a clue what they were dealing with, and the Myunans could not be expected to warn me, given their hostility, but once the threat had come to your land, you should have told me everything. You should have told me about Orgarth, for now you have a god contaminating your territory and he will be a threat to your people for as long as he remains free.'

'What are you talkin' about?' Ludditch scowled. 'You exorcised him. We all saw it. Heck, we all felt the damn thing.'

'I thought I was dealing with a mere spirit,' Harsq leaned towards him. 'Not a god! Do you think a god can be bettered so easily? I drove the spirit from the body, but we did not find his heart! To vanquish a god, I must deliver his heart to the esh, where it can be consumed by the almighty Brask himself.'

Ludditch leaned back in his chair and stuck his pipe in his mouth, his hard, narrow eyes regarding the priest thoughtfully. He was quiet for some time and nobody interrupted his thoughts.

'Is that why there's been no krundengrond?' he asked finally. 'Because Orgarth's heart is still out there somewhere?'

'Exactly,' Harsq lied. 'A god can manifest himself in more than one place. We need to find the core of his spirit. And what's more, no exorcism will drive him from it, the god-heart must be taken to the coast, where we can bring it out into the esh and throw it into its depths. Only the might of Brask can vanquish the power of this lesser god.'

'So where's this damned heart, then, priest? How do we find it?'

'It's right where it always was,' the priest explained patiently. 'Deep in Absaleth. Let me return to the mining camp with my disciples and we will draw it out and transport it to Braskhia, where we can employ the services of an esh-boat and plunge the heart of Orgarth into the chilly depths of the esh.'

Harsq settled back in his chair, a light sheen of sweat on his forehead. There was no Orgarth, no god-heart, but Absaleth's soul was still loose in Ainslidge, and it could be anywhere. Every material had its own essence, and it was this essence that made up the spirit. Unlike Brask, the one true god, other 'gods' were merely the life-force of a particular land or material. Harsq had razed enough of them to know. But a disembodied spirit could find purchase in materials of the same kind. Absaleth's ghost could have found a host in any iron-rich piece of earth, any lump of ore or the smallest shard of iron or steel. If the eshtran sought it out, he was sure he could find it, but all the signs were that the ghost was taking root in this land and with every day that passed, its power over it would increase.

It would be better to flee and leave the Reisenicks to their fate. If he could persuade Ludditch to let him leave for Absaleth, he could be out of their territory within a day. Once beyond their borders, he would make for Sestina, for if he actually went anywhere near Absaleth, the Myunans would find him and kill him. He was in an extraordinary bind.

It was a frightening thing, to lie through your teeth to a man who would gut you and skin you if he even suspected what you were doing, but he had no choice. He had to stay calm and play this through to the end if he was to get out of Ainslidge.

'Doesn't feel right,' Ludditch grunted, as if reading his thoughts. 'What wuz Orgarth doin' here, if his heart wuz still back in Absaleth? No the heart's here somewheres. We just got to find it.'

'No, no,' Harsq replied anxiously. 'I only performed an exorcism at Absaleth. It would not have affected the god-heart ...'

'Drove him out, though, didn't it? And what about that scrap that the Parsinor brought in? He was tryin' to trade for the cubs. Maybe he found it and was gonna give it up 'cos we took their cubs. He could have had the heart an' all! I mean how big is it? He could've hid it on his person some-wheres or swallowed it or somethin' and the boys trounced him before he could trade! Holy meat, Harsq. He could've had it on him all along and we didn't know and then he escaped and took the damned thing with 'im!'

Harsq struggled to follow the chieftain's line of reasoning. He could feel his plan beginning to unravel. He remembered the massive creature that had been brought into the village. The Parsinor had been carrying the scrap that was the old host on his back, and even after the exorcism, there had been a metal tinge to his aura. Ludditch might be closer to the truth than he realised. Dangerously close.

'No, I assure you, sir. Absaleth is the key. I have to go back there.'

'Damn, boy, you're right! That's what it's all about!'

Ludditch exclaimed, standing up suddenly and stabbing the air in front of Harsq's face with the stem of his pipe. 'Half--right, anyways. The Myunans've been on to this all along. We've been played for fools, you an' I. Don't you get it?'

'I'm not sure I do.'

'Harprag and his crew show up on the border, sayin' they're makin' for Old Man's Cave. Say they've got some res-cuin' to do down there. But it's just a cover, see? They're really here to find their precious Orgarth and return him to Absaleth. That mountain's like a … a mother to 'em. Now, the Parsinor's out in the forest searching' for the cubs, finds some o' my boys tusslin' with this possessed metal, and takes it off 'em. But we've got those cubs and he has to trade to get them back. So he brings it along, but he hides the most important bit of junk and we miss it when we truss 'im up. You did your thing, but you couldn't finish the job because the brute didn't give us the whole hog. The Parsinor's still got Orgarth's heart!'

Harsq listened helplessly. A few moments ago, Orgarth's heart had been something he'd made up to escape from Ainsdale. Now Ludditch had managed to use it to explain everything that had happened over the last day and night. The man was truly mad.

'The god-heart is still in Absaleth,' Harsq tried again. 'If you let me …'

'No.' The Reisenick shook his head, looking around at his clansmen. 'It's right here in Ainslidge, and we're going to track it down. I can smell it. I'm gettin' a feel for how you operate, priest. You got instincts; well, I think I've got 'em too. And mine're tellin' me to give chase to that Parsinor and his Myunan toads and where we find them, we'll find the heart. You want to know about the krundengrond? Give me a couple o' days and I'll show it to yuh.'

Harsq sank lower in his chair, the metallic taste strong in his mouth, his arms folded to hide his trembling hands. At the mercy of the Reisenicks, haunted by Absaleth's ghost and under threat of death from the Myunans, the eshtran felt as if his sanity was sliding away from him on smooth, hard ice. All he'd ever wanted to do was carry out Brask's good work. But now everything was going wrong, as if all that power had slipped out of his control and turned against him. He managed a reassuring smile at Ludditch and excused himself, hurrying from the room.

13 DALEGIN CHASES THE LIGHT

Draegar stopped the group when he spotted something further down the track. Motioning them to stay back, he advanced cautiously. There, in the branches of a tree above the path, was a cobweb made of bones. The spiralling net was about an arm's length across and swayed gently in the hint of breeze that passed through the trees. The bones were strung together with wire and seemed to be from the feet of some small animal. They could smell the faint bite of bleach from the macabre web.

'It's a Reisenick sign,' Draegar called back to them as he studied the web. 'We're in a trapping area. The way ahead is going to be laced with animal traps, all set up so that one catches what another misses. They leave signs so that other clans don't go wandering into them.'

'That's a nutty way to make a sign,' Lorkrin said from right behind him.

Draegar turned to him.

'You were supposed to stay back,' he scolded the boy. 'Why don't you ever do what you're told?'

Lorkrin shrugged.

As they walked, Draegar described the array of methods the Reisenicks had of catching their quarries. He would find one trap and point out how escape from it would lead an animal straight into another. Often, they found dead or maimed animals caught in snares, or pits, or hanging from ropes. There were spring-loaded wooden spikes, nets, nooses, tripwires, cages, swinging battering rams and poisoned darts. The group walked painstakingly slowly as Draegar guided them through the array of hazards, avoiding what they could, disarming some and setting off others to clear the way.

Eventually they came upon another bone cobweb hanging over the path and the Parsinor told them they had reached the other side of the trapping area.

'Now it's just the normal snares and things we need to watch out for,' he said lightly.

He grimaced and leaned over, first to one side and then the other.

'Here, one of you have a look at my back,' he said to the Myunans, pulling his bag aside. 'There's something caught in my armour.'

Lorkrin ran his hands over the knobbly, hinged armour plates that covered the Parsinor's back.

'Can't see anything,' he said.

'Try higher up, under the top joint.'

Draegar kneeled down so that the boy could reach and Lorkrin ran his fingers under the joint in the carapace. His fingertips came up against something and he pulled out his knife.

'Yeah, there's something here, all right,' he said, digging at the obstruction with the tip of the blade.

It popped out and fell to the ground. Taya picked it up.

'Rusty old nail,' she said. 'You could have picked it up when we were caught in the landslide.'

'Or maybe from that pile of scrap I carried up to the Reisenicks,' Draegar guessed, shrugging his bag back into place.

Taya tossed the nail away, but Rug, who had been watching with interest, went after it and bent down to fish through the grass for it.

'What are you doing?' Lorkrin asked. 'It's useless. It's not even straight.'

'I'd like to keep it anyway,' Rug replied, as he found it and put it safely in a buttoned pocket. 'Just in case.'

'In case you need a bent, rusty nail?'

'Yes, I suppose so.'

'You're a strange one and no mistake.'

Evening was setting in and the light was failing. The wind picked up and brought rain with it, a lazy fall of hazy damp that slowly but surely wet them through. Taya and Lorkrin were starting to feel the cold, worn out by the last couple of days. They shivered as they trudged through the wet, the grey clouds visible through the trees turning their moods sombre and their thoughts to their parents. Rug had said little all day, content to be led along, but disturbed by a growing unease. The talk of Old Man's Cave had stirred something in him. He was sure that if he had ever possessed memories of that place, then not all of them had been pleasant ones.

The trail brought them to the foot of a rocky hill. It was a steep climb, and they had to use their hands to clamber up in places. The rocks were slippery with the rain and their fingers cold and numb. Draegar reached the top first and grunted with satisfaction. The rest of them struggled up the last stretch of levelling ground and came up beside him.

There below them, in a sheltered glade, surrounded by apple trees, was a wood-and-hide building with warm, glowing windows and a chimney that gave off the welcome smell of wood smoke and baking bread. There were three wagons parked around the side, as well as a row of stables that no doubt housed horses and other mounts.

'Is it safe?' Taya asked uncertainly.

'Only one way to find out,' Draegar told them. 'That Reisenick at the mill said the Maggitch clan have no love for the Ludditches; they have been feuding for years. There could be others there who might give us away, but this is our best chance of hitching a ride to catch up with Emos.'

'We could disguise ourselves,' Lorkrin offered, looking up at Draegar. 'But there's no way to hide what you are. You're going to stand out like a third ear. Maybe you should stay outside.'

'Not likely,' Draegar snorted, and started striding down the slope. 'Let us make the Maggitchs' acquaintance and see what kind of storyhouse they're running here. We take this risk now or wander through this forest for days, maybe weeks. We have a cave to get to.'

They each descended with that tentative scramble that steep slopes force on two-legged creatures and reached the bottom in a last, shuffling run. Draegar strode up the road to the terrace and swung open the double doors of the storyhouse. Everyone in that rough, dark, smoky room looked up as he entered.

'My name is Draegar, of the Aknaradh Tribe,' he announced. 'And I have travelled further than any man here and seen more strange things then most men will see in ten lifetimes. I have stories to tell to a kind host with a tankard of mead and some hot food for myself and my friends. Lend me your ears, friends, and I promise you tales that will warm your hearts, chill your blood and stand your hair on end!'

+ + + +

The colour of the walls of the passageway seemed to have changed; they were paler, more mottled and there was a dampness in the air. Paternasse ran his finger down the stone and put the tip of it in his mouth, and then spat out the dust.

'Limestone,' he said. 'I don't think we're under the mountain any more.'

'What makes you say that?' Nayalla asked.

'That mountain's laced with iron. I've never seen anything like it myself. It's the richest source of iron I've ever heard of. You can't tell me you didn't know?'

'We've always known there was iron in Absaleth,' Mirkrin told him. 'Amorite, the metal we use for our tools, comes from the ground high up on the mountain. You can't get it anywhere else in this land. But we've never mined the mountain for iron.'

'Oh, right. I forgot,' Paternasse sniffed. 'You're all against mining. Except for making your *tools*, of course.'

'We're not against mining. Just *your* kind of mining. The kind that leaves great holes in our territory and poisons the ground,' Nayalla retorted. 'And we don't mine iron on Absaleth, because any fool can see that it's important to the land around it. You can feel it when you stand in its shadow. Absaleth's iron is special. Or at least it was.'

Paternasse would have laughed at the idea a few months before, but he just nodded now. Even without the strange world they had found beneath its skin, there was something special about the mountain.

'Well, anyway,' he said. 'You just don't find pure iron in large quantities. You find patches of the metal around, but only in small deposits. Some say it falls from the sky, but I've no time for such fables myself. Normally, if you want to find iron, you have to dig it out of the ground as ore, hematite or magnetite or the like. Then you smelt it – you heat it all with charcoal in a furnace to separate the metal from the slag.'

Dalegin and Noogan listened quietly with the Myunans. Unlike the old miner, they knew little about the ground they worked; they just dug where they were told to dig.

'Now, that mountain, it's mainly hematite on the outside,' Paternasse continued. 'With some magnetite and that red jasper. But the lads who did the surveys a couple of years ago said that the core of the mountain could be pure iron. And that's unheard of. That's why the Noranians are so keen to mine it, 'cause their armies use iron like it's goin' out of fashion, for everything from weapons to medals.'

'And the fact that the mountain doesn't belong to them doesn't bother them in the slightest,' Nayalla said bitterly.

'Not a chance,' Paternasse shrugged. 'The way they look at it, their iron's stuck under your mountain, and tough luck to anyone who thinks different.'

'Why do you work for the Noranians,' Nayalla asked, 'if you think so little of them?'

'Because I'm a miner; I've got seven mouths to feed and I have to put food on the table. The mines near our town closed down a couple of years back. Now I go where the work is.'

They emerged from the even, chiselled walls of the passageway into a cavern whose walls glistened with moisture, the ceiling and floor lined with stalagmites and stalactites.

'You were right,' Mirkrin said. 'Limestone. I wonder where we are?'

'I lost my sense of direction long ago,' Nayalla admitted.

'Still headed north of the mountain,' Paternasse grunted.

'How do you know?' Nayalla frowned.

'He just does,' Noogan answered her. 'He's like a mole, old Jussek.'

Mirkrin was kneeling down, studying the floor.

'It might be the end of the passageway, but this floor is well travelled. It's worn smooth, and there's recent wear on this step here.'

'Those little terrors, probably,' Dalegin sniffed.

'No, they climbed walls as easily as walking along the floor, and this is a scuff, from a hard, heavy foot …'

'Does anybody else hear a noise?' Nayalla interrupted him.

They all went quiet.

'I hear it,' Mirkrin nodded. 'A rumbling, or grinding or something.'

'Don't hear a thing,' Paternasse said. 'Your kind must have good ears. Is it a tremor?'

'No, it's constant,' said Nayalla. 'Like a machine, or a waterfall. I can't place it.'

'Water would be a good thing about now.'

'Can we get a move on?' Dalegin urged them, switching his torch to his other hand and putting the free one in his pocket. 'I'm getting cold. And I'm bloody starving.'

'I'm thirsty too,' Noogan spoke up. 'Has anybody got any water left?'

Mirkrin handed him his canteen.

'I'll have some too, if you don't mind,' Dalegin said, moving up beside Noogan.

'That'll be the end of it, then,' Mirkrin told them.

'Aye, the same for the rest of us, I think,' Paternasse added. 'We need to find water soon. Maybe that sound you're hearing?'

'Let's see if we can follow it. It's as good a chance as any,' Nayalla suggested.

'What was that?' Dalegin whispered, squinting into the darkness ahead of them.

'What?' Noogan asked.

'Don't you see it? There!'

'By the gods, yes!'

Far back in the gloom, the swaying light of a lantern could be seen. Dalegin suddenly took off, scrambling up the path through the stalagmites after it.

'Wait, lad!' Paternasse yelled.

They rushed after him, getting in each other's way, the limestone spikes forcing them to file one by one along the path. The shadows from their torches played on the limestone pillars, casting sharp-toothed shapes on the walls of the cave. In their hurry to catch Dalegin, they failed to notice that the path branched and were confounded when they lost sight of his torch in the labyrinth of stone columns. Noogan was out in front. He stumbled to a halt as he came to a place where the path petered out and could have led in any direction.

'Where did he go?' he snarled in frustration.

'The damned fool!' Paternasse swore. 'The damned, blind fool!'

'Well, we'd better just wait here for him to come back and

find us,' Mirkrin breathed. 'No point running off all over the place. We'd just end up getting split up.'

'I think there's another path back here,' Nayalla called from behind them. 'He might have gone this way.'

'We stay together. Wait where he can find us,' Paternasse told them. 'But if he's not back soon, we'll go looking for him.'

'What was that light? Did you see it? It was a lantern, wasn't it?' Noogan panted, leaning on his knees.

'I thought it looked like an old woman,' Nayalla said. 'They ran for it, whoever they were.'

'Aye, well, you would too if some stranger came rushing at you, shouting and waving a torch,' Paternasse grimaced. 'If it is an old woman, he's probably scared her halfway to Noran.'

He sat down and propped up his torch.

'I'm tired, tired as a hard-worked dog.'

They all sat down to rest, miserably wishing they had some food and water and the means to make a fire. Nayalla shivered, huddling up to Mirkrin, and Paternasse gazed at them and brooded about how much he missed his own wife.

'We've got to find some food,' Mirkrin thought aloud. 'I wonder if those Seneschal are edible.'

'Anything's edible if you're hungry enough,' the old miner assured him.

'Well, at this point I'd eat sand if it smelled good.'

'You'd probably manage some roasted Seneschal then, so …'

A ragged scream froze their blood. It echoed around the cave and slowly died away.

'Gods,' Noogan croaked. 'That was Dal.'

'It came from down that way,' Paternasse pointed, his voice tight in his throat.

They hurried back down the path and took the branch that they had passed, wanting to rush, but wary of running headlong into the darkness and whatever it held. Their breathing came fast and shallow, and each was sure the beat of their heart must be resounding through the cave. A blue-white glow came into sight and they crept towards it. It was Dalegin's torch, resting against the slope of the wall. On the very edge of its light, they could see a boot lying on its side, the laces torn open.

'Oh no,' Paternasse rasped. 'Oh no, what's happened to him?'

He edged further forwards, the torch in his hand stretched out ahead of him as far as he could reach. He was panting and the sweat was cold on his skin. In the stillness he felt a drop run down his back. The light picked out a piece of torn trouser leg and then Dalegin's satchel. Wedged between the glistening columns of two stalagmites was what remained of Dalegin.

+ + + +

Being on the run from the Ludditch clan had given the four fugitives a certain celebrity status in the storyhouse. Two outlandish stories from Draegar had cemented the Mag-gitchs' good will and now Draegar and the Myunans were entertaining their hosts even further. Taya added the finishing touches to Lorkrin's face, his head and shoulders now a striking resemblance to Learup Ludditch III, if slightly smaller than the original. Draegar, who had never seen the Reisenick chieftain, started to draw the likeness onto a sheet of vellum provided by the proprietor. The drawing was taken and pinned up on the wall, and used for a blowpipe contest. Any man who could land a dart in each of Ludditch's eyes, with the allotted three shots, received a free pitcher of mead. Draegar had the honour of being the first to deface his own drawing, and the room cheered heartily.

Lorkrin slunched and let his face settle back so as to avoid any of the hostility that was being aimed at the picture. He and Taya sat back, feeling bloated and sleepy after their huge meal of wild hog and rice stew. Taya saw Rug stand up, make his way to the door and slip quietly outside.

'Tell us another yarn, there, feller!' a Sestinian with an acne-ravaged face called out to Draegar. 'And make it a chiller!'

'I have just the tale,' the Parsinor announced. 'And it'll make you think twice about walking out on a dark night such as this! I'm going to tell you the story of the Lantern Lady!'

'I've heard this one,' Taya murmured to her brother. 'I think I'll go outside, I could do with some air.'

'Me too,' he replied. 'But we're bringing the doughnuts.'

He grabbed the plate of doughnuts and they squeezed out through the mass of bodies, keen for the clear forest air after the hot, smoky atmosphere of the storyhouse. Outside, they found Rug sitting in a chair on the terrace, looking out into the night.

'You all right, Rug?' Taya asked. 'You didn't eat anything.'

'I don't feel hungry,' he answered, without taking his eyes of the gloom. 'I don't feel well at all, actually. I have a … pain, inside me. And sometimes I hurt all over.'

'Uncle Emos knows a thing or two about healing,' Lorkrin

said to him. 'When we catch up with him, he should be able to tell you what's wrong. With all you've been through lately, it's not surprising you're feeling out of sorts.'

Rug didn't answer, so the two Myunans decided to leave him to his thoughts, idly wondering what a person thought about when they didn't remember anything about themselves. They probably thought about getting their memories back. Lorkrin swatted the gnats away from the doughnuts and they both sat down under the orange glow of one of the windows with their backs to the wall.

'When are we going to get moving?' Taya complained. 'I mean, I'm glad for the meal and the rest, but we're wasting time.'

'Draegar knows what he's doing – this is his thing,' Lorkrin reassured her. 'We don't have any money to pay for a ride, so he says we need to make some friends and find someone who's going our way.'

'Well, I wish he'd hurry up. Here, stop hoggin' those doughnuts.'

+   +   +   +

Draegar knocked back some mead and belched, holding his hands up for silence. When the noise had died down, he began his story in a low, soft voice.

'I was one of three travellers; the others a Noranian mercenary and a Braskhiam trader, and we had two Karthar guides.

'We were making for the valleys deep in the Kartharic Peaks, where most of the Karthars live. We had to pass through the Axmantle, a stone jungle of latticed spars that is as complex as the growth of the cobrush trees here. The sun shines through in thin spears during the day, and at night, it is pitch black and the sounds of the animals that inhabit the place reverberate around the stone. Only a fool would try to travel through this maze without an experienced guide.

'We had two oxen as pack animals, for the Karthars do not allow vehicles to pass through to their valleys. We stopped on the first night and made camp. It was as black as a cave, but the wind blew through that web of stone as through a mountain pass and it chilled us to the bone. The guides lit a bule-oil stove and set about making some supper, while the rest of us stood looking up through the network of stone in the hope of spotting a star or two.

'I confess, I wanted to explore and I am not one to shy away from a wander when I'm curious, but the guides insisted that we not leave the trail and that we stay in easy sight of the camp lanterns.

'It was the Braskhiam who spotted it first – a light flitting through the shadows just within sight of us. He called out to the person holding the light, and strode out to see who they were. He was an ambitious man, always looking for a chance to sell his wares. The guides called him back, and the urgency in their voices persuaded him that he should do as he was told. We settled down to eat and saw no more of the light before we went to sleep.

'I woke later to find the Braskhiam was gone. I looked up in time to see him carrying one of our lanterns into the darkness of the stone web. Cursing his stubbornness, I called after him and the others woke up. The Noranian and I wanted to go after him, but the guides would not have it. They jabbered something about a "Lantern Lady", and their faces barely hid their fear. In the end, the Noranian and I took a lantern each and went by ourselves. Careful to keep the camp in sight, we crept out into the maze, calling the Braskhiam's name. There was no answer. We heard a tearing sound out in the blackness and hurried after it. Surrounded by a mesh of rock that looked the same whichever way you turned, it was all too easy to imagine ourselves getting lost and we looked back constantly to check we could still see the lights of the camp.

'We found the Braskhiam – or what was left of him – in a hollow out of sight of our guides' light. The Noranian stayed where he could see the camp, and I walked down to examine the body. What I saw there will stay with me the rest of my life. The man's body had been peeled like a piece of fruit and the bones removed. The meat lay where it had fallen, but there was no sign of a single bone – not one. To do such a thing would take a measure of power and ferocity that struck fear even into my stout heart. Drawing my sword and battleaxe, I backed out of that hollow and told the Noranian what I had seen. He loaded his crossbow and pulled down the visor on his helmet.

'We were loath to leave the body unburied, but we were vulnerable out there in the darkness with a terrible predator nearby. The remains were in such a state as to make collecting them a difficult and messy business, so we decided to forego the task and make our way back to the camp as quickly as we could. It was then I looked to where the light of the camp was and something struck me as odd.

'I am a map-maker, and I am blessed with an accurate sense of direction. I was sure the light was in the wrong place. The Noranian assured me it wasn't and started off in that direction. I followed, against my better judgement. As we got closer, I realised that the quality of light was different from a bule-oil lantern and I said so. The Noranian was suspicious too, but, unwilling to admit that he might be wrong, he kept on going.

'We drew near enough to see that it wasn't our camp at all, but a lone figure holding up a light. She was moving, and we could see what appeared to be an old woman. The Noranian called out and ran up to her and then stopped in his tracks. He turned and started running back towards me, shouting at me to flee. The old lady's lantern went out and suddenly there came the sound of heavy, drumming feet. The Noranian spun to fire his crossbow – there was a cry, but the creature kept charging. Unable to see what was coming at us, I yelled at him to get out of the way and threw my lantern into the animal's path. The glass smashed against something and the oil sprayed out and ignited, setting fire to the thing. Whatever it was, it was certainly no old lady and it was at least my size, probably larger. The Noranian fired another crossbow bolt into it and I scored a blow with my battleaxe across its neck as it passed me. But it kept going. It charged on into the night, the flames engulfing its body. It stumbled on, dying noisily and eventually we lost sight of it.

'We had no doubt that it was dead, but we were not about to go looking for the body and trust our lives to our remaining lamp, so we started looking for our camp. I was confident of the direction, and before long, we saw the light again. In our relief at finding our way back, we forgot the crucial rule: always announce yourself when approaching a camp from out in the dark. There was the muffled blast of compressed air and something smashed through the lantern, punching straight into the Noranian's chest. I shouted at the Karthars to hold their fire, but it was too late for my companion. They had shot at the light in his hand, fearing he was the very beast we had just killed. The harpoon had killed him outright. I stamped out the burning oil and cursed their names. The guides watched me warily as I approached, their harpoon guns reloaded.

'The rest of the night and the following day passed without further adventure, but the guides assured me that there were many more "Lantern Ladies" out there in the Axmantle. They prey on the gullible and the lost, feeding on their bones and leaving the flesh like discarded rind. I don't know how this one fooled us as it did, but never again will I go hunting strange lights in the dark.'

+ + + +

Something sailed down out of the trees and landed lightly on the ground. Taya and Lorkrin stopped talking, looking out into the dark yard, ringed with apple trees that lay at the front of storyhouse, trying to make out what it was. Another glided down and this time they caught sight of it while it was silhouetted against the sky. The animal had jumped from high up in the tangle of trees on the hill and controlled its fall with the flaps of skin, which ran down the sides of its body from its elbows to its knees. The two creatures snuffled their way along the ground, approaching the building.

'Hunnuds,' Lorkrin whispered. 'They must have found our trail.'

'We have to tell Draegar,' Taya replied softly. 'If these things get back to the Reisenicks ... I mean, the other Reisenicks, then we're in trouble.'

'We're downwind of them, and they haven't seen us yet. Maybe we can sneak inside.'

They both let their colours fade to match the worn, oiled hide of the wall behind them. Looking up, Lorkrin saw that

Rug was lost in his thoughts and tried to get his attention by hissing softly at him. Rug heard him and looked down.

'What is it?' he asked in a normal tone of voice.

The hunnuds both looked up at them.

'That's torn it,' Taya sighed and grabbed Rug's arm, pointing. 'We need to get inside, quickly.'

The first one growled and squatted, baring its teeth. It launched itself forward with incredible speed, covering the distance to the terrace in moments, aiming straight at Rug. Taya tried to push him aside, but failed to budge his awkward frame. Rug reached out over her head instinctively and even as Taya felt claws dig into her back, there was a stifled yelp and the claws let go. She ducked down and rolled away, and saw that the hunnud's throat was held firmly in Rug's hands. The animal clawed desperately at the tall man's arms, but he did not seem to feel a thing. The second hunnud let out a hoarse, shrill bark, much like that of a fox, and the two Myunans knew it was calling to others in its pack. They had to shut it up.

'Over here!' Lorkrin shouted suddenly, jumping up onto one of the windowsills so that he was silhouetted against the light. 'Come on, you big louse! Come on!'

The hunnud snarled and charged forwards, pushing off the ground and spreading its arms and legs so that it swooped up towards the boy on its stunted wings. It came in with the speed of a cat, and although he went to drop down out of its way, Lorkrin was caught in its jaws and their two bodies crashed through the window and onto a table inside. The table tumbled over and Lorkrin screamed as the creature got a better grip with its jaws. But then half a dozen weapons descended in a savage blur of stabbing and cutting, and eager hands seized the dying animal and dragged it off him. He stood up with some help and winced as someone pressed a cloth against his bleeding shoulder.

'You need to get that seen to,' the landlady said, getting him to hold the cloth in place himself. 'Their bites can get infected. Are you all right?'

'Taya … outside,' he managed as he panted for breath.

Men were already crowding out the door to investigate the throttled yelps outside. Lorkrin followed the crush out to find Rug still standing, holding the thrashing hunnud by the throat. The gangly figure seemed at a loss as to what to do with it. The Reisenicks from the storyhouse had no such problems and fell on it with their knives, pushing Rug aside in their haste to despatch the beast. They were a little too enthusiastic for Lorkrin's tastes and once he'd seen that Taya was all right, he turned aside rather than watch. Draegar ruffled the boy's hair and led him back inside.

'Let them do what they will, lad,' he said. 'They've made this their business now. Come on, let's get you fixed up.'

Taya checked Rug over for wounds as he got back on his feet.

'It's a good job you wear all those layers of clothes,' she told him. 'I don't think it got you. Do you feel okay?'

'Yes. It was quite exciting, actually. But I didn't know what to do with it once I had hold of it.'

'You were brilliant. Come on, we'd better go and check on that daft brother of mine.'

Lorkrin was having his wound washed and an ointment applied by the landlord's wife. He flinched as she dabbed some of the stinging liniment to the bite. Draegar was standing nearby, talking with a small, grey-skinned, greasy-looking man in furs and rawhide. Despite his style of dress, however, it was clear he was not a Reisenick; he looked like a Gutsnape, from the Gluegrove Swamps.

'… and that swamp-gas slurpin' toad of a Reisenick, Ludditch, can sniff the steam off of my sweat if he thinks he can ruin a perfectly good evenin' at my favourite tavern with his rot-ridden, mangy, nit-bitten hunnuds and get away with it!' He punctuated his litany by accurately expelling some hajam-stained saliva into a nearby spittoon.

The woman treating Lorkrin smiled reassuringly at Draegar. 'Don't mind his foul mouth, sir,' she said. 'Ol' Trankelfrith is a sweetie, really. You have to mind he doesn't overdo the hajam weed while he's travellin', but he'll get you where you need to go.'

'I'm headed back to the Gluegroves. Where you wanna go and how many of you are there?' Trankelfrith asked Draegar.

'There are four of us, two children, the thin man there and myself. We're making for Old Man's Cave, and we're trying to catch up with two trucks headed in the same direction. We'd like to avoid any contact with Ludditch's people if it could be helped.'

'I wouldn't mind some contact with that fart-mouthed, frog-faced, fly-swallowin' crab, myself, but if you don't, I can take my sweet time getting round to it,' Trankelfrith retorted. 'Be ready to travel at daybreak.'

+ + + +

Harsq woke from a nightmare in a cold sweat and sat up, swinging his legs off the bed. The taste of metal in his mouth was strong enough to make him grimace. His hands were trembling and he clasped them together to still them. He knew the earthquake was coming before he felt it. The bed began to shake and the wooden frame of the building creaked and groaned. The tremor steadily increased in strength and Harsq threw open the door of his room and ran outside in a panic. It was not enough that Absaleth's spirit was pulling apart the fabric of the land to reach him. When the Reisenicks realised what he had brought down upon them, their vengeance would be vicious and terrible – vengeance he had already tasted in his tortured dreams.

His disciples stumbled out of the building after him, shouting and crying, looking for somewhere safe to stand and not finding anywhere. He watched them from his hands and knees, feeling sick to the stomach with the motion of the ground. Behind him, he heard the cracking of wood and the building that housed the mechanic's workshop buckled and folded in on itself. People screamed from inside.

'They're all out to kill me,' he sobbed. 'Dear Brask in the esh, what have I done to deserve this? What did I do wrong?'

Another building collapsed, and then another. People ran out onto the street and animals cried out in terror. Fires broke out as lamps fell and smashed. Men and women rushed to grab buckets of water, but no one could do any-thing while the tremors continued to rock the town. Harsq laid his head on his forearms and cried.

When their world stopped trembling, the people of the clans tackled the fires. Harsq's followers joined in, doing what they could to help.

Ludditch appeared not long after, just as the first rays of dawn were brightening the sky. He found Harsq in the cab of the generator truck, clutching his empty gas canister and

staring into space. The priest jumped when th
opened the door.

'This is it,' the chieftain declared to him, 'I can
comin' … it's almost here. We just need to do this one la.
thing, find that damned heart and finish it like you said and
we're done. The ground's just tryin' to pull free, that's all this
is. And we're goin' to cut its chains. You with me, priest?'

'Brask be praised,' Harsq coughed. 'Let His will be done.'

'*That's* the spirit, boy. Now, when they first showed up,
Emos and his cronies said they were headed for Old Man's
Cave. Could be that was just to put us off, but I reckon their
story was straight. So, we're going to head that way. My boys
have been staking out all the main trails up to the north and
we got some on their way up to wait at the cave itself. You
see, those caves are the only way into the mountain itself.
Used to be an old hermit who lived up there who knew
every inch of the place – straggly old bird who figured hisself as some great alchemist, and he told me all about that
mountain, though not without some persuasion! And I know
that there's one tunnel that leads right into the heart of
Absaleth itself. Now, where do you think they'd be takin'
Orgarth, if they wanted to get him back in his boots?'

'Mr Ludditch, I still believe you're wrong about this,' Harsq
protested. 'The god-heart is back at the *mines* …'

'Aw, now, don't you worry about runnin' Orgarth down,
Kalayal, that's our job. You just have to help us catch hold o'
him and bundle him out o' here. Now, get your people in
order and be ready to roll. We're goin' huntin'.'

The chieftain strode away, bellowing instructions to his
clansmen. Harsq put his head in his hands. Ludditch was out
of control. He was insane. The exorcist sniffed and wiped

running nose. The land was coming apart. He had to flee Ainslidge before the Reisenicks realised what he had done to them. There would be no escape when Ludditch discovered the truth. Harsq looked sourly out through the windscreen at the ruined street, seeing only the mud road and the hungry soil he knew lay beneath. A sickened resolve settled in his heart. He had always been a faithful instrument of his god. If it was Brask's will that he should die, then so be it. Praise be to Brask.

✦ ✦ ✦ ✦

Lorkrin awoke groggily. Somebody was shaking his arm and the movement shot a dart of pain through his injured shoulder. He opened his eyes to see Taya looking down at him. He was lying in a bunk in a small, room, the only light coming from the grey dawn glow through a small, latticed window.

'Up you get – it's time to go,' she said, in that annoyingly bright tone their mother used in the mornings. 'How's that shoulder?'

'Sore,' he mumbled, wishing he could sleep longer.

'That was some quake last night. I nearly fell out of the bunk.'

'There was an earthquake?' Lorkrin gaped. 'Did I miss anything good?'

'Nothing broke, if that's what you mean.'

He sat up and groaned; it felt as if he had only just laid himself down. He saw that Rug was already standing by the door, waiting patiently for him and his sister. With a last regretful look at his bed, Lorkrin quietly followed his sister out and closed the door behind him.

The air was cold and damp, the morning still dark as the sun had risen high enough to light the sky, but had not yet reached down into the glade. Still feeling sleepy and hunching their shoulders against the cold, the Myunans followed Rug around the storyhouse to the stables. Trankelfrith, the Gutsnape from the Gluegroves, was there with Draegar, helping the Parsinor draw up a map of Ainslidge.

'Morning!' Draegar greeted them, as if he had enjoyed a long, deep sleep, rather than a night of drinking and telling tales. 'How's that wound, lad?'

''S okay,' Lorkrin yawned, stretching to try and loosen up his stiff body and wincing slightly as it caused a twinge in his shoulder. 'So are we taking horses, or what?'

'Not quite,' Draegar winked at them. 'You're in for a bit of a treat.'

'Ah, young 'uns.' Trankelfrith grinned at them, revealing teeth stained green by hajam weed. He pinched their cheeks and they winced as he shook the pinched flesh in some kind of show of friendliness. 'Why don't you two help me saddle up my little beauties here? But mind their mouths, they'll give yah a nasty bruise if they get a hold o' your flesh.'

'And not just *them*, either,' Taya muttered, rubbing her cheek as he turned away.

The two Myunans came forward, faces lifting in curiosity as the Gutsnape unlatched the door of the stable and stepped inside. There came the sound of mewing, as if from a pair of huge kittens. Trankelfrith made some comforting noises, and there was the rattle of a bridle being strapped on and buckled up. Then he led the first animal out.

The head was at about chest height, but was the size of a large hog's. It had a triangular mouth set in a flat face, with three jaws lined with blunt, flat teeth. Its two shiny, black eyes were huge, set in raised sockets that moved independently of each other, so the animal could look two different ways at once. Along each of its sides, two sets of spines were folded in close to its body. Its green skin was dry and knobbly with turquoise blotches that suggested the dappled shadows of foliage.

'A gruncheg.' Taya smiled, approaching it carefully and running her hand through the coarse hair on the back of its neck.

Trankelfrith led the animal forwards and seeing it come out of the stall was not unlike watching a magic trick. The stall could only have been seven or eight paces deep, but the gruncheg just kept coming, walking on row after row of stumpy legs, its body revealing itself to be at least twenty-five paces long. The creature had been coiled up inside the stall like a snake. With its rotund, green body and rows of legs, it resembled a giant caterpillar, but it moved more like a centipede. When Trankelfrith had led the first one out, Draegar took the reins and the Gutsnape went inside for the second. Lorkrin and Taya fussed over the creature, scratching the top if its head and stroking its neck. It mewed sleepily and pushed its head up against their hands.

'This is going to be a laugh,' Lorkrin said, grinning from ear to ear.

'I don't understand,' Rug muttered. 'How are we going to catch up with engined wagons on these creatures? They don't look very fast to me.'

Trankelfrith, who was affectionately plucking lice from the skin of the second one, looked over at Rug and cackled hoarsely. He licked his fingers and wiped them on his jerkin.

Then he lifted the first of five saddles from inside the stall and hauled it onto the gruncheg's back. The saddle had sturdy leather straps for stopping the rider from falling off.

'They can trot along fast enough,' he said, and gave another short cackle.

The animals were loaded with saddlebags filled with Trankelfrith's wares and then the riders climbed on and Trankelfrith strapped them in. Draegar and the two children were mounted on one and Rug climbed on behind Trankelfrith's saddle. Before the Gutsnape got on himself, Draegar had a quiet word with Rug about their new companion.

'You probably don't remember anything about hajam weed,' he muttered, 'but it's best that you know. Those that eat the weed experience the world as a brighter, sharper, more exciting place, but it has some nasty downsides. They can become a little too fearless and take unnecessary risks and there are times when they become so absorbed in what they are experiencing that they can forget important little things. Like breathing, for instance. If you see him starting to turn blue, just give him a shout and remind him to breathe. Apart from that, you should be just fine. Enjoy the ride.'

'That's not going to be very likely now,' Rug said anxiously.

Trankelfrith climbed on, pulling a fur cap with leather ear-flaps onto his head, turned back to wink at his passenger and then flicked his reins.

'On, Plessebel, ya ol' hag, there!' he called to his mount. 'Hup, girl!'

Plessebel moved with a smooth, winding motion, crossing the yard to the wall of cobrush trees that lined the hillside. Rug wondered how they were going to penetrate the tangled mass. But as they reached the tree-line, the gruncheg suddenly lifted the front half of her body and Rug found himself being hoisted up into the air. The creature's front legs found a gap high up in the mesh of branches and caught hold with the claw-like toes on the ends of her feet. Then Rug was tipped back, held in only by his straps, as the gruncheg pulled the front half of her body up into this gap and lifted the back half up off the ground. Through the gap was what appeared to be a path beaten through the tangle, the branches so interwoven that they created a rigid track which the gruncheg now followed upwards. Rug tipped himself forwards as the animal levelled out and grabbed the pommel of the saddle when Plessebel suddenly lurched forward, quickly picking up speed.

They came out on the roof of the forest and all around them Rug could see signs of more of these tracks, spreading in a network across the top of the forest. The spines along Plessebel's sides extended and Rug was startled to see flaps of skin unfolding between them. These sheets of skin were held aloft and angled to catch the wind. The word escaped him at first, and then he remembered. Sails. The grunchegs had sails.

He stared in amazement. It made perfect sense if you had the body to do it. Instead of struggling through the thick forest, you could run right across the top of it. He heard Lorkrin and Taya whoop as their mount eased into a run behind him and he held on tighter as Trankelfrith whipped the reins and let Plessebel have her head. The sails were angled to not only push her forwards, but also to lift her slightly, taking some of the weight of her body. The sensation was like running downhill.

There was little of the constant fog up at this height and

Rug could see further than he could ever remember seeing before. On all sides, the trees stretched away over rolling hills. Then it all disappeared as Plessebel swept down into a dip in the path and he was surrounded by the long-leaved treetops again. They were moving at great speed, faster than any man could run and perhaps as fast as a horse, though the only horses he could remember had been back in the Reisenick town.

He clung on, trying to quell the sickening sense of constantly being off balance as the gruncheg dipped and climbed, swerved and banked, her long body following the contours of the path. He was thrown one way and then the other into the straps, tipping from side to side, trying to take his weight in the stirrups and gripping the pommel, feeling as if he was about to be flung off the gruncheg's back by a tight turn or a steep climb. Taya and Lorkrin's voices laughed and screamed behind him, relishing the ride until Draegar told them to quieten down for fear of alerting any Reisenicks below them. The drumming of Plessebel's feet caused a constant quiver through her body and added to the ill feeling in Rug's head and belly. Trying to take a leaf from Lorkrin and Taya's book, he let out a laugh and discovered that he immediately felt better. He laughed again and realised that he did not even recognise the sound. It felt good, he decided and let out a whoop as they descended into another precipitous hollow. Trankelfrith looked back at him and guffawed, then spat a green lump of hajam weed out over the trees and bit a new chunk off a wad from his pocket.

'Hang on in there, ya angular gank,' he shouted around the mouthful of weed. 'We'll make a leather-cheeked grunchegger out of you yet!'

14 BLINDWATER, BREAD MOULD AND MAGGOTS

Paternasse tripped and fell forwards, hitting the ground with a pained grunt.

'I'm all walked out,' he groaned. 'I have to stop.'

'We don't even know where we're going,' Noogan whined. 'We could end up right back where we started.'

'We're still headed north,' the old miner assured him. 'But we're windin' back and forth for sure. We've probably walked twice the distance we could've covered in a straight line.'

'My feet are killing me,' Nayalla added, her voice distorted by the fangs that filled her mouth, her eyes hidden in the folded contours of her face and forehead.

She and Mirkrin had adopted the appearance of skacks in an effort to ward off attacks by the new predator that was stalking them. No one wanted to talk about Dalegin and what had happened to him, as if to talk about it would bring it on themselves. They had fled from the sight, running until they were so tired that they could only stumble on, still driven by their dread. Paternasse and Noogan had been particularly distraught and even now their faces wore expressions of hopelessness and defeat, as if seeing their friend's mutilated body had finally broken their spirits.

The onset of another earthquake had sent the four of them cowering into each other's arms and it had taken them a long time to find the will to start walking again once it stopped. Paternasse assured them that he was leading them northwards, but the others were dubious. They felt hopelessly lost. Their nerves on edge, they stared fearfully into the darkness, waiting for the attack of some unseen monster, or the first shudder of the next quake – the one they were sure would bring the weakened rock down on top of them. They were all suffering the effects of thirst and were aching with hunger. Noogan had even tried licking the moisture from the walls, but found it only made the unbearable, gagging dryness even worse. They had no idea how long they had been wandering through the caves, but it felt like weeks. The fear and fatigue had taken their toll and for the first time the four survivors were losing hope of ever seeing daylight again.

The two Myunans sank down beside the miners and let their tired bodies shed their fearsome shapes. Nayalla was shivering and Mirkrin held her close to try and warm her up, but he had little warmth to offer.

'I don't think it's followed us,' Nayalla said hopefully.

'How do we know?' Mirkrin shook his head. 'Whoever or whatever it is, this is its hunting ground. It could just be stalking us, biding its time.'

'We're going to be all right,' she insisted in a determined tone.

'That's easy for you to say,' Noogan shivered. 'It only takes the bones. You don't have any bones.'

'It still has to open us up to find out!' Nayalla snapped back at him.

'I'd really like to change the subject,' Mirkrin interjected.

'We need to bunch up when we stop,' Paternasse croaked. 'Try and conserve our heat. The cold could get us even before the thirst does.'

'I don't know if I can keep goin',' Noogan mumbled. 'I feel dizzy, and my head's sore.'

'That's the thirst. Hang on in there, lad. You're strong. There's plenty of life left in yuh yet.'

Mirkrin said nothing, but he kept his eyes closed against the stone walls that threatened to close in and crush him. He forced himself to breath normally, opening his tightened chest and taking slow, deep breaths.

'There's that sound again,' Nayalla said suddenly, lifting her head. 'Do you hear it?'

Eager for a distraction, Mirkrin listened intently.

'Yeah,' he nodded finally. 'Yeah, a rumbling noise.'

'Water.' Paternasse lifted himself up on his elbows. 'It's got to be water. An underground river or something.'

Forgetting their exhaustion, they clambered up onto their feet.

'Sounds like it's coming from down there,' Paternasse pointed towards a fissure in the wall.

'Come on then,' Nayalla stepped towards it.

'Wait! Hold on there!' Noogan exclaimed. 'The last time we heard this, something killed Dal. How do we know that bloody thing's not the one making the noise?'

'It's not an animal sound,' Nayalla replied. 'It's water all right. But you've got a point. If it's the only water around, it would make sense for the thing to stay close by.'

'We don't have a choice,' Paternasse sighed. 'We have to find out.'

The Myunans took their tools from their bags and set to work resurrecting their skack-like forms. Noogan watched, no longer embarrassed or disturbed, but comforted by the sight of the shape-changers distorting their flesh. If the Myunans could use their talents to fend off the creature hunting them, then he was glad to have them around and grateful for their strange ways.

The fissure looked new, as if it might have been created by one of the recent tremors. The rumbling echoed up from its depths and even Paternasse could hear it now.

'It's big,' he said. 'A river, I think.'

The jar with the silvery powder was running low, but no one commented on it. They had lost the lantern somewhere back in the Seneschal's tunnels and their only other source of light was the little spirit lamp in Noogan's helmet. Nobody wanted to think about what would happen when their torches ran out. Mirkrin insisted on leading the way, despite Nayalla's protests, and he found himself trembling as he worked his way forward down the narrow tunnel. The fissure was only just wider than his shoulders and at times he had to turn sideways to get through. With the torch tied to his forearm, his long, serrated claws were useful for gripping the wet rock as he went, but the extended shins of a skack were not cut out for walking through narrow, awkward spaces.

The walls of the crack tilted over to the right and he was forced to sidle along the right wall, the skack's claws becoming too much of a hindrance to sustain, so he let his hands regain their shapes. He slunched his legs back into their natural forms while he was at it. Soon, he was crawling along on his belly and the memories of being trapped beneath the cave-in made themselves felt with merciless clarity. He panted for breath, fighting the urge to claw his way back up the narrow tunnel, or simply to curl up and give in to the panic.

The sound grew steadily louder and he stopped every now and then to listen and make sense of it. The water seemed to be rushing over gravel; the tumult had a hard, gritty quality. He sniffed the air, but could not detect any of the usual smells he associated with underground streams, no fungus or mildew, or crisp, cold dampness. He came upon a slab of broken rock and then beyond it, another. It was clear that the ceiling of the fissure had collapsed and Mirkrin imagined that he felt the pressure increase in the air as if the roof above his head was about to come crashing down. He gritted his teeth and dragged himself up over the pile of debris and held up his torch. The rumbling sound was all he could hear, drowning out the movements of the others behind him, but the empty space around him revealed no sign of water anywhere. And the sound was wrong; it was hard and grating, like spilling gravel. A trickle of dust falling on the back of his neck made him roll over and look up. He screamed and threw his arms across his face, knowing that this time, there would be no one left to dig him out of his grave.

+ + + +

For Emos, changing his appearance to that of a Reisenick was the easy part. He cleared the markings from his skin, altered the look of his clothes, gave his elbows and knees a swollen stiffness and increased the size of his hands and feet, squeezing his fingers out thinner and emphasising the knuckles. But the main problem was his face, and the triangular brand that marked it. That could not be wiped off, for it was the mark of the plague and had been put there by Myunans as a warning to others of their kind. Some Reisenicks knew enough about Myunans to recognise the brand for what it was.

He slunched the skin of his face and then pulled back hard on his hair, dragging the flesh of his face right up onto the top of his head and crefting it in place. His eyes, nose and mouth stayed where they were, but he had to use his tools to reduce the stretched look. He used a blending comb to create more hair on the top of his head, sweeping some more from the back to cover the brand. Then he used a scapulet to add the finishing touches to his suitably misshapen Reisenick face. The brand was already starting to itch and he knew that before long, it would begin creeping back down onto his face. But he had time enough to do what he needed to do. He had already checked out the small settlement from the air. Now he had to show his face. Or somebody's face, at least.

He packed his tools away and scrambled down to the road, which he followed to the gate of the healer's house. A sign on the gatepost read: 'Shindles Vidditch, Healer, Apothecary & Bonesetter'. There were three grunchegs coiled up in a corral to one side of the main cabin, and some kind of workshop on the other. He strode right up to the front door of the house and knocked loudly. A young man answered. He was thin and gaunt, with red-rimmed eyes and large gaps between his teeth.

'Yuh?'

'I'm looking for Shindles.'

'Are yuh now? And who might you be?'

'Tell her it's the man who brought her the bexemot bone a few years back.'

'All right then, stay right there,' the youth instructed him. He went to the top of the stairs down to the cellar and yelled: 'Aunt Shindles? There's a fella here says he brought you some bexemot bone some years back, says you know him. Got the look of the Tunditch clan about him.'

'The Tunditch clan?' a crackly voice replied and a middle-aged woman with a wizened nose and turned-in foot hobbled up the stairs. She was wearing a look of puzzlement on her face and she glared at Emos in suspicion.

'Only fella that ever managed to get me bexemot bone was a Myun–' Her face brightened in realisation. 'Emos Harprag! That look don't suit you, boy! What brings you back to these parts?'

'I have a friend who needs your talents,' Emos replied. 'And we'll need your discretion. Learup Ludditch has decided he doesn't want us in Ainslidge.'

'Overblown fart-whistle,' Shindles snorted. 'You got the money, I got the discretion.'

'We can pay. I'll go and get them. It's an infected leg, badly rotted but I think it can be saved.'

'Let me do the diagnosin', you just fetch 'im in.' She waved her hand, then turning to her nephew, added her orders: 'Pobe, go get me a flagon o' blindwater, some of my bread mould and some fresh maggots.'

'Yes, Aunt Shindles.'

Emos was about to ask about the maggots, but Shindles had already disappeared into one of the rooms. He grimaced at the thought of what was to come. Shindles Vidditch was a gifted healer, but her techniques were … well, eccentric. He hurried back across the yard to the road, shedding his disguise as he made his way as quickly as he could to where the trucks were hidden.

+ + + +

'Mirkrin! Mirkrin, love! It's all right!'

He did not know how long his wife had been calling to him, but slowly the terror subsided and he looked up from behind his arms. She was hugging him and stroking his hair.

'Look up,' she said. 'It's not coming down on us. I don't know what it is, but it's staying where it is.'

He looked up and cowered back at first, but then his curiosity overcame his fear and he stared up at the ceiling in the torchlight. It was earth, not stone, and it was moving. It was as if something was stirring it, the soil turning in on itself like boiling water. Dust and particles of soil sprinkled down from time to time, but the roof seemed to be staying where it was.

'It's krundengrond,' Paternasse told them over the noise. 'I've only ever heard of it before, but that's what it has to be. And we're underneath it.'

'How can it stay suspended up there like that?' Nayalla asked. 'Normal earth would have fallen right in on us if it were that loose.'

'It's unholy stuff,' the old miner replied. 'Figures, finding it under here with all this other madness. It's a living thing. It holds together because the soil is its body. I don't know why it hasn't filled this space. It's odd that.'

He looked around, then ran his finger over one of the slabs of stone they were kneeling on and tasted it and then spat it out.

'Iron,' he told them. 'We're back under iron. Something about it the krundengrond doesn't like.'

'I know the feeling,' Noogan snorted. 'I thought we were out from under the mountain?'

'We are. The ore must extend further out than anyone thought. That'll be an eye-opener for the Noranians.'

Paternasse caught a sharp look from Nayalla.

'That would be if anybody told them, of course,' he added, hurriedly.

'Well, there's no water.' Mirkrin sat up. 'Let's get out of here and back to the passage. That stuff might not like iron, but it might well like Myunan and I don't really want to find out.'

They all agreed. Being in such a low, tight space was unnerving enough without the ceiling grinding itself up over their heads. They crawled back up through the fissure until they could walk and then hurried back to the main section of cave. It was a relief to return to the quiet. Their ears were still ringing with the sound of the krundengrond.

As they set off up the tunnel again, they failed to notice the swaying light behind them. It winked out after they emerged from the fissure, but not before the creature that carried it had started moving closer to its quarry. It did not need the light. The four animals ahead made enough noise and disturbed enough air and gave off enough heat to make following them pitifully easy. But it was patient. They were aware of it now, and would be on their guard. It would wait until they went to sleep again and then it would take its next victim. There was no rush; the bones of its last kill were slowly dissolving away in its stomach. It would not need to eat again for some time. And they had nowhere to go.

+ + + +

Shindles Vidditch gazed down at Cullum's wound and took a thoughtful gulp from the flagon of blindwater.

'Hold 'im down,' she told them.

Khassiel, Jube and Emos grabbed the Forward-Batterer's shoulders, arms and legs and held him firmly as she poured some of the alcohol over the pus-filled wound. Cullum jerked upwards and screamed. Shindles, unmoved by his obvious agony, studied the area she had just cleaned out and nodded to herself.

'I can save it,' she affirmed. 'It'll take some work, but the leg's still good. Keep him still.'

She took a long thin knife and parted the edges of the wound. Cullum roared again. He slumped back onto the table and gave her a baleful glare.

'Could you possibly make it hurt any worse?' he hissed through gritted teeth.

'Yes, darlin', if that's what you want,' she replied in clipped tones. 'Though at the moment I'm intent on savin' you from havin' to hop around for the rest of your life. Here, eat this.'

She handed him a piece of bread covered in a blue mould.

'You're joking.'

'Eat it or I pour on some more of this fine blindwater.'

He hastily chewed down the mouldy bread, his face twisted in disgust. Pobe, her nephew, brought in a jar of live maggots and Cullum jolted upright again, wrestling against the grip of his friends.

'What are they for?'

'I'm just goin' to pop a few in the wound, darlin'.'

'Over my dead body! What kind of quack are you? Maggots?! Not bloody likely ...'

Shindles reached behind his neck as he protested, feeling around his spine with her fingertips. She apparently found what she was looking for and pinched his flesh just above his shoulders. His voice wound down and he collapsed back onto the table, unconscious.

'I'll have to get you to show me how to do that,' Emos quipped.

'Bring me some more of that bexemot bone and I'll trade yuh.' She arched her straggly eyebrows at him. 'This is goin' ta take a while. You all might as well wait outside.'

'What are you going to do with the maggots?' Khassiel asked suspiciously. 'It doesn't sound right to me.'

'That's 'cause you're a learnin'-starved footsoldier with no education,' Shindles retorted. 'The maggots eat the dead flesh in the wound, but don't eat the livin'. They can clean a wound out better than any hand ever could. Now get out o' my operatin' room and let me work.'

Emos gestured to the others and they filed out, collecting outside where they sat down in the shade on the steps of the house. Jube filled and lit his pipe and puffed contemplatively on it, while Khassiel opened a tin of corned beef. They heard a soft singing float out from the back room and Emos saw the other two peer into the house.

'She sings to the injury,' he told them. 'The same way that some people talk to plants. She thinks it encourages the flesh to heal itself.'

'I think she's a few warts short of a toad,' Khassiel declared, around a mouthful of beef.

'Maybe so, but I'll wager that Cullum will walk out of this house.'

They sat in silence, each alone with their own thoughts. They were uneasy, stopping and exposing themselves like this, but there was no way around it. Emos was tired, but his impatience eventually got the better of him and he pulled his pack in front of him and unrolled his tools to shape himself into an aukluk again. Just as he did, two burly Reisenicks walked through the gate. Jube and Khassiel were about to stand up, when Emos told them that these two were not from Ludditch's clan. It would be better to wait and see where they stood before doing anything that might start a fight.

The two men saw the trucks parked in the shadows of the trees on one side of the yard and looked at them suspiciously. Then they saw the three strangers on the steps. Their stance changed, hands dropping to the long knives sheathed on their belts. They strode up to the house.

'Afternoon, folks,' the bigger one said. 'You got business with Mrs Vidditch?'

'We do,' Emos replied. 'She kin of yours?'

'Cousin's aunt,' the other answered, sniffing back a runny nose. 'You're a Myunan, aren't you?'

Emos had hidden his tribal markings, but the young man had obviously recognised the brand on his face.

'Yeah, you're right there, Vuntz,' the first one nodded. 'That's their plague sign. You got the Myunan plague, boy?'

'No,' Emos replied. 'I was just in the wrong place at the wrong time.'

'Likely story. That's why you're here, no doubt. Lookin' for a cure off of Mrs Vidditch. Damned Myunan scum should keep your diseases to yourselves.' He spat on the ground at Emos's feet. 'Vuntz, go get Pobe and let's do us some huntin'.'

Vuntz trod up the steps and went inside, while his friend Macob walked over to the corral where the grunchegs were sleeping out the humid heat of the afternoon.

'By the gods,' Jube commented, rolling his acorn necklace between his fingers. 'Don't you ever just want to pile into people like that?'

'I've better ways to spend my time,' Emos replied.

+ + + +

Taya gasped as Crissabel, their gruncheg, plunged down a steep drop in the path and bathed them in fog. The excitement of the ride had left her breathless and she cried out in delight when the animal arched back up again and climbed another slope with hardly any change in speed. Behind her, Lorkrin hooted as he was thrown back into the straps of his saddle, the pain in his shoulder forgotten.

'I ... I ... could do with a ... rest!' she called back to her brother. 'This is wearing me out!'

'I'm hungry too,' he replied. 'Maybe we could stop for a break.'

'How can you be thinking of food?' Taya grimaced. 'My stomach's all over the place.'

'I didn't get any breakfast!' her brother protested.

'What have we got, anyway?'

Lorkrin reached back into a pouch on his pack and pulled out one of the packages wrapped in leaves that the storyhouse's landlady had given them. He unfolded it and frowned.

'Dried fish,' he said. 'Smells like you wouldn't believe, but it looks all right.'

'It'll have to do,' Taya sighed. 'I'll have to wait until we stop, though.'

Her brother took a bite and nearly choked on it as they were tipped back into another climb.

They were seated near the middle of the gruncheg's back. Draegar was up the front, visible between the first pair of sails, sitting just behind Crissabel's head. Taya was about to shout to him when she saw a movement out to their left and slightly ahead. It caught her eye because it was bigger than the birds they had been disturbing all morning and larger even than the other creatures which occupied the strange world above the forest. It was a gruncheg. Then she saw another, and another – three of the long, winding mounts, each with its own rider. She frowned. The three figures were headed in their direction.

Rug was holding onto the pommel for dear life. Trankelfrith was yelling encouragement, beating the side of the animal with a riding crop as they hurtled over the treetops. Rug heard Draegar shouting behind him and looked back. The Parsinor was pointing, and Rug looked over his other side to see what he was pointing at. There were three figures on grunchegs, approaching fast from the west.

'Mr Trankelfrith!' he called to the Gutsnape. 'Mr Trankelfrith! Grunchegs! I mean, other grunchegs! With men on them!'

At first he didn't think the Gutsnape had heard him, but then Trankelfrith dropped down into his saddle and bent hard over the pommel. A piece of the chewed weed was propelled out of his throat and into the trees below. He sat up and coughed, then looked out to where the other riders could be seen, rising up and down over the slopes of a path that was going to intersect with theirs.

'Highwaymen!' he shouted, and pulled a blowpipe from a sheath in his saddle. He put a dart in his mouth, raised the blowpipe and took aim. He fired just as the nearest rider disappeared into a dip. Rug thought the Gutsnape had misjudged the shot, but then the rider appeared again at the top of the rise and the dart struck him in the thigh. He cried out and plucked the projectile from his leg. Trankelfrith loaded another dart into his mouth and raised the blowpipe again, but a dart embedded itself in Plessebel's neck and the gruncheg flinched, causing the Gutsnape to pull the weapon away or risk breaking his teeth. Another dart hit his arm and the pipe dropped from his nerveless fingers. Trankelfrith yanked the dart out as quickly as he could, but Rug could see the toxin was already taking effect. The Gutsnape countered one drug with another, biting off some more of his hajam weed and shouting a battle-cry. He turned Plessebel towards the attackers and hung down on her side to avoid the flying darts. Rug tried to follow his example. Unable to dangle off the side like the Gutsnape, he hugged the back of the gruncheg and kept as low as possible. Darts flew past him and more than one struck the side of the gruncheg. He wondered how many it took to knock out an animal this size.

Draegar had drawn his sword and was goading Crissabel into the fight. The other three grunchegs were males, bigger than the two females and more fearsome. The first to reach them squirmed into a knot around Plessebel. Lorkrin and Taya watched in dread as Trankelfrith pulled out his knife and climbed onto the attacking beast. Crissabel reared as one of the males crashed in towards her and gave a high squeal, before being muffled by the weight of its body crushing her head down into the branches of the tree beneath them. Draegar was rolled underneath, still held in his saddle by his straps.

Lorkrin had pulled out his knife, but couldn't decide what to do. The larger gruncheg carried on wrapping its bulk around Crissabel and suddenly the two Myunans found themselves caught between the two writhing bodies. Taya unbuckled herself and slipped down between them, hanging from a stirrup. One of Lorkrin's buckles snagged on the pack on his back and he was caught. He cut the safety strap with his blade and rolled sideways off the gruncheg's back. The branches beneath were two sparse to support him and he fell through, losing his grip on one limb, then another, but finally catching hold with an arm and a leg on the third branch he hit.

Though Taya had managed to dismount quickly, she was still on the narrow path of interwoven branches and she felt the tenuous track begin to give way beneath the weight of the two massive animals. She dived out into the thinner branches even as the track gave way and the two animals crashed down through the trees.

'Draegar!'

It was Lorkrin's voice. Taya looked down in despair; she had not seen her brother get off, and the Parsinor had still been strapped into his saddle when Crissabel had fallen. The two animals were visible further down, still thrashing against each other in a savage struggle. Neither Lorkrin, nor Draegar, nor the rider of the attacking gruncheg, were anywhere to be seen. She watched the fight, but it was hard to tell what was happening down in the foggy darkness. Eventually, she climbed out along the branches, looking for her brother and calling out to him. From somewhere below, she could just hear him shouting to her. He was barely visible in the shadows of the cobrush trees to one side of the new hole in the forest roof. He was dangling precariously over the void, his weight only just supported by the branch he had grabbed.

'Are you all right?' she called.

'Oh, you're there,' he said casually. 'Yeah, fine. Don't worry yourself.'

'Yeah, but you do have the *tools*. Anyway, you don't have to be snotty. I was afraid you'd fallen with Crissabel. Hang on. I'll find something to pull you up. I'm fine too, in case you were wondering.'

'Great,' Lorkrin's grip slipped slightly on the smooth wood and he looked down nervously. There was nothing close enough to catch hold of and it looked like a long fall to the bottom, interrupted by the occasional, hard tree limb.

A vine snaked down to him and he seized it, testing his weight on it before letting go of the branch and pulling himself up to where his sister had tied the end of the vine to another, more sturdy limb.

'Did you see what happened to Draegar?' he asked her.

'He was still strapped in. He's down there somewhere.'

They both peered down. The two animals had fallen further, the sounds of struggle growing weaker. The two Myunans were at a loss as to what to do. If they went down looking for Draegar, there was a good chance he might be climbing back up and they would miss him on the way down. They could wander around for ages trying to find each other. If, on the other hand, he was badly hurt, they were his only chance. But Rug was still up on the forest roof somewhere, and he could be in trouble too.

'We have to climb down and try and find Draegar,' Lorkrin decided finally. 'Maybe he didn't fall all the way. He could be caught in the trees somewhere.'

'But what if he's all right and he's already climbing up, looking for us?'

'What choice have we got?'

'What if he's already dead?'

Lorkrin didn't answer.

'What about Rug?' she asked.

'He's with Trankelfrith. Or at least he was. Anyway, Draegar's got to come first. We saw him fall. We know he could be hurt.'

Taya did not want to desert Rug, but she had to agree with her brother. Draegar could not have fallen so far without being injured. They had to find him. The trunk of the tree offered plenty of hand and footholds on the way down and the thick, tangled foliage was as much a support as an obstacle.

As they began their descent, a noise from above made them freeze and they saw something coming down past them. It was the one of the other grunchegs that had attacked them, its rider, a young Reisenick, egging it on downwards. They disappeared into the mist and the Myunans heard the mewing of two of the creatures beneath them. Then the new gruncheg appeared again, with the other male. Between them, they carried Crissabel's inert form using leather harnesses. The Myunans could not tell if she was alive or dead. Draegar and his saddle were gone. The gruncheg's body was spirited up to the roof of the forest and hauled out of sight. Even more despondent than they had been before, Taya and Lorkrin continued their descent.

+ + + +

The gruncheg's tremendous weight held Rug down firmly against the branches beneath him, the straps of the saddle preventing him from trying to slide out either side. The darts fired by the three hunters had taken effect and Plessebel had surrendered to the greater strength of the male gruncheg, rolling over onto her back. Trankelfrith had not surrendered. The other rider was already groggy with the effects of the dart and the Gutsnape clambered up behind him to finish the job. He took the knife he was holding between his teeth and drove it up under the other man's ribs. Then he grabbed the reins and took control of the mount.

Rug felt queasy at the sight of the dead man being pushed off the saddle and into the green depths and he looked away. He patted his pocket for comfort and discovered with a start that his nail was missing. He did not know why it was so important, but ever since he had picked it up, he had not been able to keep his mind off it, and had felt the need to constantly check on it. Now it was gone. It must have fallen out when Plessebel had rolled onto him. Rug panicked. It had to be close by. He twisted his head to try and peer down into the foliage beneath him, but could not see it. If it had fallen through there, he had lost if forever.

He did find the tail of a dart protruding from his shoulder. He pulled it out and looked at it. Draegar had told him about these. The tips were normally dipped in either poison or sleeping draft. Rug went still, waiting for any signs of drowsiness or oncoming death. But he felt fine. Someone must have forgotten to dip their dart. He wriggled to try and get free of the saddle, straining to reach the buckles that were pressed between his body and the gruncheg's back. As he did so, he felt something sharp stick into him and, expecting to find another dart, he pushed his hand in to get at it. It was his nail. Heaving a sigh of relief, he held it up, looking longingly at its beautiful, rust-coloured shape. On a whim, he held it out above his head where he could get his other hand to it and gently straightened the nail with his fingers. It was easier than he expected. He put it back in its pocket and buttoned the flap down carefully.

Trankelfrith appeared suddenly beside him, giving him a fright.

'We'll be havin' no more trouble from that filthy, gas-bloated pond-scum!' he assured his passenger. 'Let's get you out from under there until ol' Plessebel can right herself, eh?'

The Gutsnape used the captured animal to roll the unconscious gruncheg over enough for him to reach the buckles on the straps and free Rug. Then they sat on her belly and got their breath back.

'Other one went after the one that fell down there with Crissabel,' Trankelfrith told him sleepily, the toxin from the dart still doing battle with the hajam in his system. 'Pox-riddled sons of a crack rash made off with her somewhere. We'll have to go after 'em when Plessebel wakes up.'

'What about Draegar and the children?'

'They're down in the underside somewhere.'

'Shouldn't we go and help?' Rug asked.

'Take too long to climb down, and longer to look for anybody. I got a gruncheg to fetch back,' the Gutsnape replied simply, taking out his lump of weed. 'Still, Plessebel's got some sleepin' to do. Let's see who comes up in the mean-time. Want some?'

'No, thank you.' Rug gazed at the ragged hole in the forest roof, feeling a dull pain in his chest as he thought about the friends who were lost down there.

He patted his pocket and made a decision.

'I'm going to see if I can find them,' he said.

'Have it your own way.' Trankelfrith spat out some green saliva. 'But when Plessebel wakes up, I'm gone.'

Rug nodded and slid off the belly of the sleeping grun-cheg, treading carefully on the path that meandered over the top of the foliage.

'You'd better crawl,' the Gutsnape told him. 'Path's not strong enough unless you spread your weight some. And mind how yuh go. There's plenty down in those woods that'll hurt yuh, or kill yuh, or just plain eat yuh whole.'

Rug raised a hand in a wave, got down on his hands and knees and crawled towards the hole in the forest.

✦   ✦   ✦   ✦

The forest floor was a long way below them and the climb down was slow and complicated. By the time the Myunans had reached the bottom, there was little daylight filtering through the mist and foliage and the grey gloom closed in on them with damp and quiet menace.

'We need to mark the trees, so we don't get lost,' Taya whispered.

Lorkrin nodded. They both took out their knives and, as they walked, they made cuts to mark their passage. They could just see the broken limbs above them where the grunchegs had fallen through, and they walked back and forth across the area looking for the Parsinor. The way was blocked with fallen debris and knotted foliage and searching was a tortuous process. Sometimes they were sure they heard somebody calling, but the sound was distant and lost in the trees. When they had made their way from one end of the area to the other and still not found anything, they began to get scared.

'What if he's still up in the branches somewhere?' Lorkrin wondered aloud.

'It would take forever to find him,' Taya shook her head and sat down on a moss-covered stone. 'What do we do now? Climb back up again?'

'I suppose we'll have to. Rug and Trankelfrith are still up there somewhere.'

'If they're alive. Who were those men? Were they with Ludditch, do you think?'

'I don't know,' Lorkrin sniffed. 'They might just have been out hunting. You can't tell with these Reisenicks. That's going to be a long climb.'

Taya stifled a sob and Lorkrin looked at her in surprise. He sat down next to her and she turned away from him and burst out crying.

'What are we going to do?' she sobbed. 'Draegar could be dead. We don't know where we are. Everybody's after us. And Ma and Pa are still stuck under that bloody mountain! I can't take this. I want to go home.'

Lorkrin put his arm around her and tried to comfort her, but he could feel himself giving in to his own fears. Seeing Taya like this shook him more than he wanted to admit. He could always be brazen about things as long as she was there beside him. But now she was giving in and leaving him on his own.

'Hey, come on. It's okay,' he said hesitantly, knowing it was a poor attempt at reassurance. He never knew how to deal with emotional people; he normally left that to Taya.

He wrapped his arms around her and she hugged him back, each of them drawing strength from the other.

'We'll be all right,' he said. 'But we can't stay here. Draegar could have landed up among the trees somewhere. We'll climb up and work our way around as we go.'

She nodded and wiped her face. Knowing her eyes would be red from the crying, she willed the colour away, and patted her brother's shoulder as if to assure him that she was better now. It was amazing how a good cry could clear the air sometimes.

'Let's get changed,' she said.

Lorkrin nodded and took off his pack. It would be impossible to search every tree from top to bottom, but they would cover as much area as they could on the way up. It would be harder than their climb down and they would need every advantage they could get, so there were a few improvements they had to make. Unrolling the tools, they started reshaping their bodies. They had to improvise at times, as the kit Emos had started making was not complete, but they managed, even in the sparse light that shone through the thin mist. It felt good to be amorphing again; the familiarity of it was comforting and exercising their skills helped restore their confidence.

Every now and again, one of them thought they heard something and looked up, but the woods were still except for the movements of birds and the small animals in the undergrowth. Their new forms soon took shape and before long, they were ready to climb.

Their legs were shortened and their arms beefed up, their

toes and fingers longer and ending in claws. They had given themselves prehensile tails, which were clumsy, because adding a limb was always difficult, but useful nonetheless. In a moment of inspiration, Lorkrin had suggested giving themselves climbing fangs, like the rockrats in the Kartharic Peaks. He tried it first and Taya could not help but giggle.

'What?' he asked, his voice slightly distorted by the four huge, hooked teeth jutting from his top jaw. 'How does it look?'

'Like you've got a bear's foot in your mouth. You'd better strengthen your neck if you're going to use those. I'd hate to see you get a grip and then rip the top of your head off trying to pull yourself up.'

Lorkrin smirked. That was the Taya he knew.

The final touch to their new forms was mottled green, brown and ochre camouflage, to hide them as they climbed. They rubbed moss and soil into their packs to help the effect. They were packing up the tools when a new sound made them raise their heads. A shrill, hoarse barking. One voice cried out, and then more answered the call.

'Hunnuds,' Taya gasped.

'They're still quite far away,' Lorkrin said. 'They might not be after us.'

'Let's not hang around anyway.'

Slinging their packs onto their backs, they ran to the nearest trunk and started climbing.

+ + + +

Emos did not even know what he expected to find. In his aukluk form, he circled the forest around Shindles' homestead, wishing there was some way his eyes could penetrate the layers of foliage that hid the ground below him. The delay was maddening. They could have reached the cave by now if things had not gone so badly wrong. He was still baffled by the behaviour of Ludditch and the Reisenicks. Something had set them off and he did not know what it could be. Weariness was starting to set in. He had gone days without proper sleep, but he could not rest until he had done all he could to save Nayalla and Mirkrin. He could only hope that Draegar had found Taya and Lorkrin; he was going out of his mind with worry for them. He had to believe that his friend had got to them.

Swooping lower, he scouted the road ahead – the one that would get them back on to a heading for the cave. Something in the brush by the side of the track caught his eye and he wheeled for a better look. Reisenicks, a group of four crouching in the undergrowth, hidden from sight of the road. The clansmen did not hunt on the roads; they must be watching for something. Emos swept over them and flew back to a branch in the road. Could the four men be looking out for the two trucks? Did Ludditch want to catch them so badly? He glided down over the fork in the road and out along it. Not far up the trail, he saw another group, once again hidden from the road, but visible from the air.

Emos gained some height and looked around him. There was another road off to the west, the main one leading along the foot of the Rudstones towards the Gluegrove Swamps. It would have been his chosen route to the cave if they had not run afoul of the clansmen. He turned towards it, already knowing what he would find.

+ + + +

Climbing was tricky, Rug discovered. The bark was slippery

from the damp mist and the tops of the trees were thin and flimsy. Several times he nearly fell when a limb broke or his feet slipped. Further down, the branches were stronger, but the foliage was thicker and hard to penetrate. He had made it halfway down the first tree he had tried and was now at a loss as to how to carry out any kind of a search. Just getting down this far had seemed to take forever. He could see why Trankelfrith had dismissed the idea. It was getting dark too, and the gloom finished off the job the foliage had started, hiding everything around him that wasn't within arm's reach.

'Lorkrin! Taya! Draegar!' he called again. But once again, there was no answer.

At times, he heard other animals moving through the trees and more than once he was startled by birds bursting out of the leaves and taking flight as he disturbed them.

He tried calling again, almost ready to give up and climb back to the forest roof, hoping that Trankelfrith had not already left. Somebody called back, and he went still to listen.

'Down here!' the voice came again. It was Draegar.

With a fair amount of struggle, Rug followed the sound of the Parsinor's voice through the maze of branches, twigs and leaves. He found Draegar's huge feet. The Parsinor was hanging upside down, still strapped into his saddle, which was tangled up in some branches. He looked thoroughly frustrated.

'How are you?' Rug asked.

'What kind of question is that?' the map-maker snapped, his dignity already badly strained. 'Get me up out of this.'

Rug took hold of his feet and pulled. Draegar let out a great roar, causing the would-be rescuer to jump back.

'My back right leg's broken below the knee,' Draegar told him. 'Get below me and cut one of the straps, so I can hold on and climb out. I can't reach my sword. You'll have to do it.'

Rug did as he was told, clambering down to where he could reach the sword that was sheathed on Draegar's back. He drew it out and slid the tip under one of the straps that were supporting the Parsinor's shoulders. The razor-sharp edge cut through the tough leather like paper. The other strap gave with a snap and Draegar suddenly dropped like a stone, crashing through the foliage beneath and disappearing from sight with a loud gasp. There was a crunching thud further down and Rug clutched the sword to him in alarm, staring down into the foggy gloom.

'Get me out of here, you great clod!' a voice bellowed up. 'And don't drop my sword!'

He was jammed in the fork of a large branch and was still upside down. Rug made his way down and took his hand, heaving him upright. The Parsinor was pale and drenched in sweat. The shin of his back right leg was badly swollen and misshapen. Draegar snatched his sword back and cut a vine free from a nearby branch. Tying it around the ankle of his injured leg, he threw the other end through the fork and pulled it back to him. Shuffling around behind the trunk of the tree, he balanced on his left leg, leaving his right sticking out around the trunk. Then he pulled slowly and firmly on the vine. A growl grew in his throat, building into a roar and Rug actually heard the grating of bone as Draegar forcefully reset the leg. The Parsinor let go of the vine and leaned forwards to rest against the tree trunk with his eyes closed.

'Where are the children?' he asked.

'I don't know,' Rug replied, looking at the Parsinor in awe. 'I was looking for them, but I haven't seen any sign of them. Can you move with that leg?'

'The front ones take more weight when I'm climbing,' Draegar told him, opening his eyes. 'I need to bind it up. Can you spare some material? A sleeve torn into strips will do.'

Rug hesitated. He did not want to remove even a part of his clothes. He could not say why, but he felt protected by the layers of cloth. There was no doubt in his mind that if he saw the body that lay beneath those clothes, it would tell him something about what had happened to him to make him lose his memory. And for some reason, the thought of it terrified him.

But how could he refuse the Parsinor? Taking hold of his left sleeve at the shoulder, he tore a layer free and pulled it off, handing it to Draegar, who nodded gratefully.

'Thank you, Rug. And thank you for your help. Only the gods know how long I could have been dangling there.'

Rug watched him break off a thin branch and bind up the injured leg with splints to support the broken bones. It looked painful, but there was no sign of it to be detected on the Parsinor's face.

'Are we going to look for them?' he asked.

'No,' Draegar replied. 'They got off before the gruncheg fell. If they're not topside, they're out in the trees somewhere. Those two can get around down here like monkeys; we'd be crawling around in the dark. If they have to, they can fly too. We'll get back up topside and wait for them there. They'll find us.'

'If you think that's best,' Rug said. 'What's a monkey?'

✦   ✦   ✦   ✦

Khassiel looked up at the sound of beating wings in the darkening sky above her. She was sitting in the shadows of the porch, her crossbow cradled in her lap. Emos spiralled slowly to the ground and landed with a stumble. He slunched out of his birdlike shape and stretched his arms wearily. His shoulders were slumped and he looked drained.

'You were gone a long time,' she said. 'We were starting to wonder.'

'The Reisenicks have men posted along all the roads to the cave. They're waiting for us.'

'That must take a lot of men.' She stood up and leaned on the railing as he came up the steps. 'Why are we so important?'

'I don't know,' he replied, flopping into a rocking chair. 'This whole thing has been strange from the start. We've done nothing to offend them. At first, I was sure it was just a mistake – a hunting party trying their luck. I thought if Draegar could just reach Ludditch, he could sort things out and Ludditch would pull the rogues into line. But putting lookouts along our route, that's a different matter. Only the chieftain could be organising that and I don't know what we've done to earn that kind of attention.'

'Maybe it *is* all for someone else.'

'Can we take the chance of being wrong?'

Jube looked out from the doorway.

'Cullum's up and about. Well, up anyway. Shindles has cooked us some food too. Anybody hungry?'

Cullum was already in the kitchen when they walked in, gazing down at his plate of stew but obviously still feeling too sickly to make the most of it. He glanced up when they came in, but just nodded when they greeted him. Once they had assured themselves that he was on the road to recovery, they turned their attention to the inviting smell. It came from a huge pot that sat over the fire and looked like it was never moved from its position. Shindles was ladling some kind of stew onto plates and handing them out. The guests sat down at the long wooden table and breathed in the aroma. It smelled rich and meaty … if a little strange.

'What is it?' Khassiel asked, sniffing her plate cautiously.

'Constant stew,' the healer replied.

'What's that?'

'Taste it and tell me if you like it,' Shindles insisted.

Khassiel took a spoonful, swilled it around her mouth and then shrugged.

'It's nice enough. What's in it?'

'Different kinds of meat, rice, vegetables, some spices and a few years of simmerin'.'

'What do you mean?'

'It's constant stew. You never take the pot off the fire, just keep adding the ingredients as you use it up. The older the stew, the better the taste. Helps keep the flies out o' the kitchen too. This stew has been goin' since my grandmama's time and it only stopped then 'cause o' the Great Autumn Flood. Put out the fire, y' understand.'

Khassiel and Jube looked down at their plates in distaste, but their taste buds overruled them and they dug in anyway. Emos was already wolfing it down. Vintage constant stew was a rare treat for a Myunan. There was little talk while they ate – everyone too hungry to chat. But once they had all had a second and third helping, they each pushed their plates back and slumped back in their chairs, bellies stuffed to capacity. Shindles took out a pipe, filled it and lit it up and Jube soon followed her lead. Talk turned to the rescue mission and the reasons the Reisenicks might have for stopping them. Shindles could offer little information. She avoided contact with Ludditch's clansmen as much as she could. She considered them a coarse lot with no schoolin'.

'My nephew, Pobe,' she declared. 'Now he hangs around with the Juddatch boys. They mix with the Ludditch clan some. They're out huntin', but when they come back you could ask them. Should be back soon, now it's got dark.'

'Time's not on our side,' Jube said around the stem of his pipe. 'We need to be getting on. Those folks are down there in the dark and the cold with no food, no water and little in the way of hope. We have to get to them quickly.'

'We need to know what we're getting into, as well,' Emos countered. 'Something's going on with Ludditch and we don't know what ...'

He was interrupted by the sound of a piercing cry, like the ragged bark of a fox.

'Hunnuds,' he muttered. 'Someone's on the trail tonight. Is that your boys?'

'No, they don't use hunnuds,' Shindles told him. 'They're on grunchegs – they hunt topside. Which means someone else's huntin' on my patch without my consent. Where the heck are those boys when I need 'em? If they're not takin' care o' this, I'm likely to be addin' kin to my pot.'

15 THE HUNNUD'S BREATH

The scrabbling of claws on bark was the only warning Lorkrin and Taya had before the hunnud pounced. It was only barely enough. The lithe animal sailed through the air at them, landing on the same branch and bolting in towards them. Lorkrin, who was further out, threw himself backwards and into empty space, gripping only with his tail, but it got him out of the way of the hunnud. The beast, carried on by its own momentum, switched its sights to Taya instead. She dived off completely, only just catching Lorkrin's outstretched hand as she fell. His tail lost its grip, but Taya was now within reach of a lower branch and she caught hold of it, pulling them both to safety. The hunnud bounded back off the trunk and paced out along the limb again, snarling down at them as it lunged off, spreading its legs to catch the air and slow its fall with its crude wings.

'They can't fly – they can only jump,' Taya breathed.

'It's still a good trick,' Lorkrin muttered. 'Move!'

The hunnud gave out a shrieking bark, and the Myunans' blood turned cold when they heard at least three others answer the call. They dropped through a hole in the matted twigs and pulled themselves through a tangle of tree limbs. It was so dark they could hardly see. The hunnud barrelled into the opening, but was too big to fit through the knotted branches. It growled at them and sought another way around.

'We're going down,' Lorkrin panted. 'We need to go up!'

'Right, thanks!' Taya snapped. 'How, exactly?'

Lorkrin had no answer. The hunnud was above them somewhere; climbing up was out of the question. They heard claws in the blackness above them and swung around a tree trunk just as the hunnud dropped into view. It cast its eyes around, nose raised to find their scent. They huddled up against the trunk, wishing they could run, but afraid to move. The creature's breathing was quiet, but they could smell the stink of its breath from where they stood. Taya sniffed; that meant they must be downwind. It could not smell them from where it was. The beast leapt over to another tree, still sniffing the air. Taya waited until it was a little further away, then she whispered to her brother.

'We need that fish you were going to eat,' she said.

'*Now* she gets hungry.'

'No, for the *smell*, you idiot!'

His eyes widened and he slipped the leaf package from his pack. They each took a piece of the fish and rubbed the stinking flesh all over themselves.

'It's bound to work,' Lorkrin grimaced. 'You could fart right now and I wouldn't smell it.'

'Don't ever, ever tell anyone back home about this,' Taya said, with her nose wrinkled in disgust as she rubbed the fish over her face.

The hunnud was working its way around in a circle, searching around the last place it had seen its quarry. The two Myunans waited until it was far enough out that they couldn't hear it moving, and then they started climbing again. If the hunnud were anything like a dog or a wolf, it would depend mainly on its sense of smell to find its prey. They were counting on the fact that the fish would hide their scent long enough to put some distance between them and their hunter, and that their camouflage would hide them from its sight.

Taya and Lorkrin continued their climb, hauling themselves up quietly towards the roof of the forest. Lorkrin suddenly froze and put a hand on Taya's arm. She went still and listened. There was something breathing close by. They were stretched out on a bushy limb, Taya reaching for the next branch up. Slowly, she got down low and hugged the branch she had been standing on.

Lorkrin was about to look up when he felt the branch sink slightly beneath him as something landed further out along it. He heard the breathing of another animal. Taya, who was closer, felt something creep towards her and the bough giving under its weight told her it was big. A wet nose snuffled near her ear, then made its way over to her neck, then the small of her back. A heavy foot stood on her back and pushed the air out of her, then another stood on her and it was all she could do not to cry out. The heavy, four-legged animal walked over her and back onto the branch beyond her feet. With her head turned down, she was now able to get a look at it and her heart went into her throat. It was a hunnud – a huge one.

It sniffed around Lorkrin's head. Taya clenched her teeth together to stop them chattering. It didn't recognise their scent. It was just curious about the fish smell. She hoped Lorkrin kept calm. If he moved, it might mistake him for prey, and then the creature would tear him apart.

Lorkrin was trying not to breathe. He hugged the branch, his hands locked tight to each other on its underside. His face was pressed hard against the bark, his eyes squeezed shut. He felt the moist nose on the bare skin of his neck, drawing in his scent to try and identify it. A warm, rough, wet surface ran up the back of his head and he felt sharp teeth brush his scalp. It was tasting him with its tongue. Its breath was hot on his skin and it smelled of rotten meat and bile. Lorkrin stifled a shudder that threatened to run through his body.

The animal took one more sniff and then planted its feet on Lorkrin's back and bounded over him and on to the trunk, where it started to climb. But its weight had dislodged Lorkrin's legs and the Myunan felt himself slipping sideways. He tried to get a grip with his prehensile toes, but the bark was damp and smooth. He let out a gasp as the lower half of his body slipped off the branch. The hunnud looked back sharply and growled. Lorkrin hung where he was, still with his arms wrapped around the branch. The predator dropped back down and made its way out to where Lorkrin's hands were clasped over the top of the branch. Taya watched in terror as it bent its head down close to her brother's fingers and opened its mouth to sink its teeth into them to get a proper taste.

'No!' she screamed.

The hunnud looked up and bared its teeth at her with a ragged snarl. It crept towards her, haunches lowered in readiness to pounce. With the beast distracted, Lorkrin got his foot back up over the bough and pulled himself up. Swallowing his fear, he edged forward after the creature, unsure what he was going to do to help his sister, but determined to try. Taya got up on her hands and knees and crawled backwards, looking down either side of the branch to see if there was anywhere to drop to. The hunnud was advancing faster than she could go backwards and she found herself looking out into misty darkness. The branch was protruding out over the hole in the foliage caused by the falling grunchegs.

The tree limb was very thin towards the end, and it started to bend under her weight. She was running out of branch. The hunnud kept coming, more cautiously now, its claws gripping the slender bough. Its weight was making it bend even further and Taya could hear the fibres of wood tearing at the middle of the bend. She yelped as the hunnud leaned forward and gnashed its teeth at her, but it seemed reluctant to come any closer. The branch dipped even further down-wards and a split appeared at the centre of the bend. Taya gripped tightly with fingers, toes and tail. The split grew, the end of the branch dropping steadily lower. Taya looked around desperately for a means of escape, but there was nothing. She looked back again into the grey chasm below her. Lorkrin was squatting behind the hunnud, watching helplessly.

'Lorkrin,' she gasped. 'I can't get ...'

The branch snapped at the split, her weight pulling the last piece loose. The hunnud hurled itself at her. Lorkrin sprang after the hunnud, seizing its tail. Taya let go of the branch with her hands, reaching up to fend off the animal. She caught hold of its ears and its own momentum pushed her body clear of its teeth. They were all falling together and the beast spread its legs to catch the air under its wings, but the extra weight was too much for it and they landed hard on the ground below. Taya and Lorkrin slunched and absorbed most of the impact through their soft bodies. The animal came down harder and was winded; it wheezed out a pained whine, and struggled to its feet. Lorkrin stood up first, adrenaline coursing through his body and infecting him with a fighting rage. He lifted the creature's tail and delivered a kick to its groin with all his might. The beast yelped and leapt away, limping into the dark forest as quickly as its injuries would allow.

'That's it!' Lorkrin bellowed. 'That's it ya louse. Run! And tell your friends!'

He collapsed in a shaking heap on the carpet of leaves and twigs.

'Well,' Taya panted. 'We're back … at the bottom … again.'

'I'm sick of trees,' Lorkrin mumbled.

They lay there, resting as long as they dared, utterly exhausted.

'We have to go,' Taya said eventually.

'I'm not doing any more bloody climbing.'

'I don't think we would have found Draegar anyway. I think we need to fly.'

Lorkrin nodded, but he could barely muster the energy to walk, let alone sculpt himself wings and take to the air. But it was the only thing they could do.

Draegar had not let them fly before, because they could be seen in the open sky and Reisenicks were skilled at hunting birds, but that did not matter now – not with the hunnuds after them. If those hunters were still up on the forest roof, the two Myunans would just have to take their chances. With the adrenaline gone, fear started to seep back in again. What had happened to Draegar? Would they ever see him again? And what about Rug? Cold began to seep into their weary limbs.

Moving sluggishly, they slunched out of their climbing shapes and reworked their bodies, increasing the bulk around their chests and backs, shortening their legs and helping each other sculpt the flesh of their arms, backs and shoulders into wings.

'Draegar's probably up there looking for us,' Taya said, trying to convince herself.

'Right,' Lorkrin nodded.

They worked gingerly around their respective wounds, wincing as they moulded injured flesh. They gave themselves bat's wings. The ability to sculpt feathers that actually worked was still a little beyond them. To go with the wings, each worked their face and head into the likeness of a bat too.

'And Rug will be safe with Trankelfrith; he's as tough as old boots,' Taya added.

'Right.'

'Let's go,' said his sister.

Beating their wings stiffly, they managed to lift themselves off the ground. Flying was an advanced skill in the Myunan art of amorphing, and Lorkrin and Taya had taught themselves, but they were still far from experts. Circling unsteadily, they rose up through the trees and out into the night. There was no sign of the hunters, the grunchegs, of Rug or Draegar or Trankelfrith. The forest roof stretched out of sight into the gloom in every direction. They were all alone.

+ + + +

The hunnud struck in a flash of fur and teeth, landing on Rug's back and knocking him off the branch where he had been waiting to follow Draegar over to another tree. He fell hard, bouncing off one tree limb, then another, his neck held firmly in the hunnud's jaws. The creature controlled the fall and then dragged him in towards the trunk, pinning him against the bole. Rug cried out, reaching behind and slapping at the animal's head. It was not trying to kill him, just hold him, and Rug heard the cries of more of the predators getting closer. He felt panic rising in him and thrashed harder. The jaws closed tighter and pain lanced up into the back of his head, making him wail.

'Hold still,' Draegar said from behind him and Rug felt the Parsinor wrap an arm around the creature's neck, closing its throat. The hunnud opened its mouth to gag and Rug was free. Draegar broke the animal's neck with a sharp twist and tossed the corpse into the fog below.

'There's more on the way,' the Parsinor told him. 'We can't fight them all. Let's pick up the pace.'

They continued climbing. Time after time, they were forced to stop as they heard the hunnuds scuttle past nearby in the darkness. Scaling the trunk of the tree with renewed vigour, they soon saw starlight and, not long after, were above the mist and crouching in the thin boughs near the top of the tree. They could not go any higher, neither of them light enough to get safely to the top.

'By the gods!' Draegar swore. 'We're too late!'

Off to the northwest, two winged shapes circled in the bright, night sky.

'I know what they are,' Rug said, distantly. 'Bats. Those are bats.'

'No,' Draegar muttered through gritted teeth. 'Those are Myunans.'

Rug and Draegar watched them for as long as they could, but the two children soon disappeared from sight.

'How are you so sure?' Rug asked. 'They looked like bats.'

'They had backpacks, and they weren't flying very well,' Draegar said bluntly. 'At least they're out of the woods. Seeing as they haven't found me, they'll go looking for Emos. Where did Trankelfrith get to?'

'He's gone to rescue his gruncheg,' Rug replied.

'If I ever get my hands on that Gutsnape, I'll wring his scruffy neck. Right, well, we're up here now. We need to find a path that'll take our weight. Preferably before the hunnuds find our trail and come after us in a pack.'

Finding a safe path in the darkness was not easy and when they did finally manage to pull themselves back onto the roof of the forest, they had to stay on their hands and knees to avoid putting too much weight on one spot and falling through. They were back near the edge of the hole through the trees, which helped them get their bearings.

'We need to head northwest,' Draegar told his companion.

Even as he looked up in that direction, they heard the drumming rustle of feet and soon a shape rose out of the blackness of the horizon and approached them. Rug and Draegar threw themselves flat, the Parsinor drawing his sword.

Two grunchegs drew up to them, one behind the other, the second animal without a rider, its bridle tied to the one in front. The lead one sniffed carefully and the silhouette of the man in the saddle leaned forward over the animal's head, chewing noisily and then spitting a lump of well-used hajam weed out into the trees.

'If you boys could use a ride, I could use some

reinforcements. These puss-filled, mangy, dog-eaten bladder mouths've got theirselves some friends.'

+ + + +

Emos woke slowly, opening his eyes and staring up at the
night sky. He was under a blanket on the flatbed of Jube's
wagon. There was some kind of commotion over at the
house and he sat up to look out over the side and see what it
was. In the lantern light from the porch, he could see that the
three grunchegs were back. He looked again; there were
three animals, but one of them was different, a female. Shindles was up on the porch, arguing with Pobe and his friend
Macob. Vuntz was nowhere to be seen. Emos got stiffly to
his feet and stretched, trying to rouse his senses – he was still
feeling very tired.

Jube was asleep on the other side of the truck, snoring
softly; Khassiel was sitting on the tailgate, her legs dangling
over the end, her ever-present crossbow nestled in her arms.
She glanced back at Emos, but seemed intent on listening to
the dispute. Cullum was up on the porch, dozing in the rocking chair, oblivious to the whole affair. Emos looked up at
the sky, judging the time.

'You should have woken me earlier,' he told her.

'You looked like you needed the sleep,' she replied. 'Our
friends here have lost their mate, and they say the woods are
full of hunnuds, but they don't know whose.'

Emos jumped down off the truck and walked over to the
porch.

'You can't just've lost 'im,' Shindles was saying. 'Where did
you last see 'im?'

'He'd caught that other gruncheg,' Pobe explained. 'We

had this one so we came on back. We thought he was followin' us.'

'Well clearly he wasn't!' the healer snapped. 'And if you
two half-wits had been born with more intellect than the
gods saw fit to give an aukluk, you'd 'ave had a look behind
yuh and seen that for yourselves. Now you go on back out
there and you find your cousin. And when you find 'im, you
go and find out who's huntin' on my land without my say so.
What you standin' dawdlin' for? Get!'

The two humiliated young men led the female gruncheg
they had captured into the corral and were about to get on
their own mounts when a voice called down to them from
high in the trees overlooking the yard.

'Hello there at the house! We mean no harm, we're
coming down!'

Emos's face burst into an uncharacteristic smile. There
came the sound of dozens of feet and two grunchegs wound
down through the trees and into the yard. Draegar was
riding the first, and behind him were two strangers. Emos's
smile slipped as he realised Taya and Lorkrin were not with
the Parsinor. He strode up to his friend, taking his hand as
Draegar dismounted, the two touching foreheads in the
Parsinor manner of greeting.

'I found them. We got away from the Reisenicks,' Draegar
told him. 'But we got separated when we were attacked.'

He aimed a hard stare at Pobe and Macob. Emos's eyes
turned cold as he looked towards them.

'They've taken to the wing,' Draegar continued, the pain
written on his face. 'They're up there somewhere now.
Trankelfrith here was helping us catch up with you when
those two and another one jumped us. I'm sorry Emos,'

'That's my animal,' Trankelfrith was saying to Macob and Pobe. 'And I'll be takin' her back.'

'I don't know what you're talkin' about,' Macob sneered. 'I've owned that gruncheg for years. But I recognise that other one you've got there. Belongs to my kin.'

'Your kin left it to me when he died,' the Gutsnape told him.

Macob's face went purple and he pulled his knife from its scabbard. Trankelfrith drew his and held it loosely by his side. He was weedy and old compared to the stout Reisenick, but looked completely undaunted by the younger man.

'Macob!' Shindles shouted. 'There'll be no knife-fightin' in the yard. The Gutsnape's got a fair grievance and if Vuntz is dead, then there's a body to be found and brought home.'

She came down the steps and faced Trankelfrith. Cullum woke as she passed him. He stood up and limped to the top of the steps to see what was happening.

'You killed him to protect yourself an' your property an' that's life,' the healer said. 'If Macob wants to even the score, then that's life too. But the boy you killed is kin and I want to find that body, so I say you can take your gruncheg away from here if you'll lead us to where you left Vuntz. After that, you and Macob can go at it all yuh like. But not in my yard. I demand peace and quiet around my home. So, are you agreeable?'

Trankelfrith returned her even gaze.

'I am.'

'I'm not!' Macob snarled. 'I'm droppin' this runt right here. No one kills my kin and bargains with his remains.'

'Macob,' Shindles hissed, keeping her eyes fixed on the

Gutsnape. 'If you don't put that knife away, I'm goin' to take it off yuh and trim your ears with it myself.'

The big Reisenick ground his teeth, but one steely glance from the old woman wiped the defiance from his face and he sullenly sheathed his knife. Trankelfrith did the same, and then made his way over to the corral, clicking his tongue at his beloved gruncheg, who squealed with delight at seeing him again. Muttering under his breath, Macob stamped up the steps and as he came up onto the porch, he accidentally stood on Cullum's swollen foot. The Noranian let out a bellow and swung a fist into the woodsman's jaw. Macob's head was rocked back and he flipped backwards over the porch railing. He landed in a heap by the side of the steps, a stunned groan drifting from his lips.

'Boy always had a hard mouth and a glass jaw.' Shindles shook her head in disappointment.

Emos was leaning against the posts of the porch, the blue brand on his face standing out strongly against his now pale skin. While he had believed Taya and Lorkrin were with Draegar, he had been able to focus on getting to the cave and helping his sister and brother-in-law. But with his nephew and niece lost over Ainslidge, he was torn between looking for them and continuing on. And with the roads being watched, their chances of reaching the cave safely seemed all the more remote.

'They're smart, and they're tough little urchins,' Draegar said, putting a hand on his shoulder. 'The trucks will be visible from the air. They know which direction we're going. They'll find us.'

'Not if Ludditch finds us first,' the Myunan replied. 'And they're exposed in the air. If the Reisenicks see them …'

'Have some faith in them,' Draegar told him. 'They'll be driving you demented for years yet.'

Rug was standing out in the yard, having dismounted from the saddle and was now at a loss as to what to do. He wasn't feeling very well. His insides were aching and his head felt slightly numb. Jube had woken up and after watching the exchange between the Reisenicks and the Gutsnape, he strolled over to where the tall, gangly figure was hovering.

'I'm Halerus Jube,' he said, holding out his hand. 'What's your story?'

Rug looked at the hand, unsure what he was supposed to do with it.

'My name is Rug,' he responded, looking at the hand, then up at the miner's face. 'I don't remember what my story was. Now I'm just following Draegar and Taya and Lorkrin, until I start remembering again.'

'A few days ago, I'd've thought that odd,' Jube quipped, taking up Rug's right hand and shaking it gently. 'We're on our way to Old Man's Cave to rescue some folks who are trapped down there. We could use another strong pair of hands.'

'I would be grateful if I could come. I … I don't have any-where to go. I would like to help, too.'

'Glad to have you aboard.'

Emos was having a few words with Shindles. He thanked her and strode over to the others. Cullum was limping along behind him.

'We're leaving,' Emos told them all. 'We need to get back on the road to the cave as soon as possible.'

'What about the lookouts on the roads?' Khassiel asked.

'Let me worry about them.'

The look on Emos's face discouraged any further

argument. They all got the wagons packed up and the engines started. Rug joined Draegar and Emos on the flatbed of the lead wagon, Cullum climbed into the cab of the equipment wagon with Khassiel. They waved goodbye to Shindles and Trankelfrith and then the trucks rumbled out of the yard and started down the dark, foggy road.

Rug took the nail from his pocket and gazed at it. He caught Emos looking curiously at the rusted bit of metal and furtively returned it to his pocket. They were going to a cave, the man had said. That had triggered something in his mind. Somewhere, way down deep, a memory stirred. Darkness and stone and agonising pain. There were no images, just sensations, and it left him even more confused. But the more he thought about it, the less he could hold on to the vague memory. A sudden need came over him. He wanted to see this cave; he was sure it had a story to tell him. He stood up to look over the roof of the cab, eagerly watching the road pass beneath them in the light of the headlamps.

+ + + +

Taya shifted her bottom to make it more comfortable on the hard wood. She and Lorkrin were in the tallest tree they could find, ensconced in a cradle of forking branches high up on the trunk. Lorkrin was dozing and Taya had to keep her eyes on him to make sure he didn't slunch in his sleep. They had kept their bat-like shapes when they landed, knowing that if the hunnuds found them here, they would have to take off quickly. But it was difficult for Myunans to creft their shape-shifts while asleep.

They were overlooking a road. It was going in the right direction, so they had decided to follow it as far as they could. It was a reassuring feature on an otherwise unbroken plain of treetops and fog that stretched into the darkness. It would be a while yet before it was her turn to sleep, and Taya kept herself alert by listening to the sounds of the forest and trying to identify them.

There were the bats, of course, flying past with their incessant clicking. The occasional owl, too, would hoot in the distance. But there were also more unusual sounds – ones she had rarely heard, if at all. There was some kind of nocturnal woodpecker that she was sure was communicating with others further away with its pecking. There was the mewling of grunchegs, either wild or domesticated. But most of the noises were furtive and soft: hunting animals on the prowl, and grazers trying not to attract attention to themselves. At the limit of her hearing, another sound attracted Taya's attention. As it grew nearer, it developed a rhythm and several distinct strains. It was music. She turned towards the southeast, searching for the source and saw a glow on the horizon. There was something on the road, and it was coming their way. She shook Lorkrin awake.

'… I didn't eat it!' he blurted out, blinking and looking around in bewilderment.

He gradually remembered where he was and groaned as he stretched his wings.

'There's someone coming,' she told him, pointing at the light.

Turning to look, he cocked his head at the sound of the music.

'Reisenicks,' he said. 'Playing the twangoes and those rattles of theirs. Sounds like they're off to a party or something. Making enough noise.'

'What do they have to be quiet about?' Taya muttered. 'Nobody's hunting *them.*'

The Reisenicks were on five well-lit wagons, one covered, one with a cage on the back for their hunnuds and two flat-beds. The fifth was Kalayal Harsq's generator truck. Behind the vehicles, six woodsmen on horses brought up the rear. The flatbed wagons were filled with singing, laughing clans-men of all ages. Sitting in the lead vehicle was Learup Lud-ditch III, singing along with the rest of them. The wagons passed beneath the Myunans' tree and carried on up the road.

'Oh, something's definitely up,' Lorkrin said. 'Why are they heading that way? They can't be going to the cave?'

'Let's find out,' Taya suggested.

'You're on.'

Launching from a height still made them a bit nervous. If they took off from the ground, they would be quite low if they made a mistake in the first few shaky beats of their wings. There was no such luxury jumping out of a tree. But the thrill was well worth it. Lorkrin spread his wings, ran out along a sturdy bough and leapt into the air. He dropped at first, then caught his weight on his wings and swooped away. Taya followed him, throwing herself into the damp night air and relishing the feeling of swimming in the sky. Careful to keep low and over the trees, they kept as close to the wagons as they dared, reinvigorated by their new challenge. The sight of Ludditch and Harsq still working together told them that the problems were not over for the lands around Absaleth, or for those trapped beneath.

✦ ✦ ✦ ✦

The three clansmen were playing knucklebones on a bare patch of earth out of sight of the road. Beyond their hiding place, the road came to a bridge spanning a surging river; it was one of the few places that a vehicle could cross the river in this area. Tupe had already won all the money the others had on them, so Moorul and Dourtch were now using their jewellery as a stake to try and make back their losses. It wasn't working.

'Aw, for the love o' mother!' Moorul moaned as Tupe rolled another six and scooped up a brass pendant.

'It was that damned aukluk,' Dourtch whined as he watched Tupe try on the pendant. 'Spoiled our luck good.'

They had seen the aukluk fly over before the sun had set. The birds brought bad luck like corpses brought flies. Tupe scratched under the bandage on his injured leg and winced as his broken ribs sent pain shooting through his chest. They were all still suffering from the trouncing that desert creature had given them, back when it had stolen the scrap metal from them. Tupe should have been at home in bed with his mother tending to him, but Ludditch had insisted every man jack of them get out and watch the roads to Old Man's Cave. And Ludditch had not been in an arguin' mood. Taking Moorul and Dourtch's money was only a small consolation for hauling himself out here to sit in the woods in the dark.

'Stop moanin',' he snapped at them. 'You're like a pair o' kittens in a bag …'

He stopped in mid-sentence, his attention drawn towards the bridge. He was sure he'd heard a creak from its wooden frame.

'Anybody hear that?' he asked.

Without waiting for an answer, he got up and walked out onto the boards of the bridge. The other two followed him, knives drawn. Warily, they prowled its length, peering over the heavy railings into the misty darkness of the river far below. Moorul straightened up and looked up the road.

'There's nothin' here, Tupe ...'

The wood gave under his feet, and he let out a cry as he started to sink into it as if it were mud. He tried to step forwards, but his feet were caught. Tupe and Dourtch reached out for his flailing hands, but Moorul could only give a panicked squeal as he fell through the stout wooden boards of the bridge and disappeared, screaming into the fast-flowing river below.

'Holy cheese,' Dourtch gasped, staring at the boards, which now seemed perfectly solid again, except for the gaping hole left by Moorul's body. 'What in sufferin' blazes is ...'

A pair of hands slid up through the boards beneath him, as if rising from water, and seized his ankles. He shrieked in terror as he was pulled down through the watery wood and hit the river below with a mighty splash. Tupe risked a quick glance over the railings to see his cousin being washed away, and then hobbled hurriedly on his injured leg towards the end of the bridge. It was the Myunans – it had to be. This was the kind of low-down, unholy trick that they would pull.

His breaths came in pants as he reached the solid ground of the road. The dark forest, so often his ally in the hunt, was now an ominous threat. You could hide a horde of shapeshifters in those shadows. Backing up against one of the stone pillars that anchored the bridge to the bank, he braced his feet against the hard ground beneath him, raised both his knives before him, and tried to control his frantic breathing. Let them come; he'd a cut a good few of them up before they got him.

Behind his neck, fingers emerged from the stonework of the pillar. A hand suddenly grabbed his collar, shoved him forwards, and then slammed his head back against the stone. He dropped to the ground, senseless.

On the other side of the pillar, Emos carefully drew his arm out of the stonework, his lips moving to mouth the incantations that helped keep him in his transmorphing trance. The hole left by his arm collapsed as he withdrew, then went solid again, the pillar left permanently scarred by the Myunan's unnatural assault.

He breathed deeply as he looked around. Then he quickly bound the unconscious Reisenick with strips of rawhide from the clansman's own pockets. Somebody would come looking for these men eventually, but not for some time yet. For good measure, he untied the tethers of the carkhams, which were perched in the tree over their camp and took them with him. Nobody was going to be sending messages with those birds. He took a tinderbox from his pocket, lit it, and walked out onto the road to hold it up. He waved it back and forth and far down the road, another waved back. Then the two wagons drove up with their headlamps extinguished. He made his way back in to where the Reisenicks had been concealed, picked up a couple of the blowpipes and a roll of darts and then dragged Tupe onto the road.

'Put this one in the back. We're taking him with us,' Emos told the others. 'It's clear now as far as the main road to the west. There'll be more lookouts there, but it's not far after that. And we'll be able to make good time once the sun rises. Anyone feel like plucking some carkhams? They're tough, but they make good eating.'

+ + + +

Ludditch was travelling with most of his clan. Word had got around that he was going to be making history – and not the safe, old kind either, but some of the dangerous new variety. Everyone wanted to be there to see it happen, or go wrong, whichever it might be. It would be a good story to tell their grandchildren either way.

The chieftain himself was in an effusive mood. He led several folk songs and then told a tale or two from the rich store of Reisenick legends. He was loving all the attention and, despite some futile attempts at false modesty, was achingly proud of what he was about to achieve. When they were setting out, he had been against all the older members of the clan coming along, but now he was glad that they had. They would be there to see his dreams come true. Total isolation for his land. Nobody would be able to set foot in Ainslidge Woods soon without a guide provided by his family, and most importantly, no more worrying about the Noranians invading. Or any trouble from the Myunans for that matter. Getting rid of most of their number would be a fine bonus. He would gain complete control of Ainslidge and eliminate his most hated neighbours in one fell swoop.

Ludditch's musings were interrupted by a sudden change in the chugging of the wagon's engine and the squeal of brakes as steam gushed up from under the bonnet. Spiroe got down from the cab and opened one side of the bonnet. Steam billowed out.

'What's wrong with it?' Ludditch demanded.

'Overheated is all,' Spiroe grunted. 'We were drivin' her a mite hard. Just need to let her sit a spell, then give her some water. Nothin' serious.'

The trucks, like most vehicles, were from Braskhia and the bule-oil-powered internal-combustion engine was a mystery to most Reisenicks. Spiroe had actually been to Braskhia once and as such was considered 'Well Travelled'. He also had the greatest understanding of engineering among Ludditch's clan. So Ludditch didn't argue; he simply shook his head, muttering under his breath, and then beamed to the clan and called on his pappy to give them a tune. Once nimble, but now arthritic, fingers strummed a lively intro and then the rest of the instruments took up the tune, knocking out a rowdy number from the olden days.

While the relatives sang and stamped their feet in time, Ludditch sauntered back to the wagons waiting behind and called Harsq to him. With all his clan tagging along, he had some concerns. The exorcist got down from the cab of the generator truck and walked up.

'Just had a bird from one of the hunting parties, out not far from here,' he told the priest. 'They saw some grunchegs off to the east, and they think one of the riders was that Parsinor fella. I'm wagerin' the prey's not far off, and makin' for the cave like we thought. The Myunan, Harprag, an' his trucks haven't turned up yet either, but it wouldn't surprise me if they're all right about here some place. Now, this thing, the god-heart or whatever you want to call it, it's in dangerous company. That Parsinor's a handful and if they hook up with Harprag, then we could be talkin' all sorts o' headaches. Those Myunans are a curse to deal with, and there's

Noranian soldiers with 'im too. I'm just goin' to have the whole plum lot of 'em killed outright. We can worry about the skinnin' an' all that later on. We'll set the women on 'em when we've got the bodies back to Ainsdale.

'But the heart, now that's a different matter. What are your plans for catchin' hold o' that?'

'You'll see,' Harsq replied, not having the faintest idea.

'You religious types!' Ludditch grinned. 'All the same, with your mysteries and your secrets! Just don't let it slip away again. That thing breaks loose, an' I'll personally cut out *your* heart. But you do a good job, I might even let you take home that Parsinor's skull. How's that?'

'You're a very fair man, Mr Ludditch. Very fair. Orgarth will not escape again. You have my word.'

As there was no god to capture, Harsq was reasonably confident that it would not slip out of his grasp. There would be nothing to grasp in the first place.

'That's what I like to hear.' Ludditch put his hands on the priest's shoulders. 'And I know you're a man of his word, Brother Harsq. So let's go catch us a god.'

Harsq nodded and watched the chieftain walk away. All the ceremonies he had carried out over the years had been flashing through his mind in dazzling detail during the drive from Ainsdale. He wondered now if any of them had achieved what he had claimed. His only chance of getting out of Ainslidge alive seemed to lie in capturing Orgarth's heart and being allowed to take it back to Braskhia. But it did not exist. Or did it? Ludditch seemed to think it did. Perhaps, if you believed enough, anything could exist.

The eshtran's mind was filled with possibilities. He knew Brask could do amazing things – astounding things. He saw that if he truly had faith, then he could achieve anything. Reality was simply a state of mind. He ambled back to the generator truck, bathing in his new-found enlightenment.

Up in the branches above him, two oversized bats crouched out of sight. They waited until the wagon had been started up again and the wagons had moved on. Then they unfolded their wings and took flight.

The sun was starting to shine from below the horizon and the sky brightened steadily. A dull rumbling carried up to them, sounding at first like the passing of the trucks, but growing rapidly in depth and magnitude. Below them, a shudder ran through the land, and through the gaps in the trees they could see animals fleeing eastwards, as if terrified by some voracious predator. Frightened squeals and cries could be heard and birds were erupting from the foliage. Taya and Lorkrin watched the spectacle uneasily. They flew low over the forest, wary of being spotted by the Reisenicks against the sky, continuing to follow the convoy. What they had heard between Ludditch and Harsq made them all the more desperate to find their uncle and save their parents before the Reisenick chieftain could carry out his threats.

+ + + +

The trickle of water was barely enough to wet their mouths, but they knelt before it as if in worship. It didn't smell good, and Paternasse told them that water seeping from the soil above could carry minerals from the ground, poisonous minerals, but nobody cared. It was water, cool, wet, beautiful water.

It dribbled from a crack in the rock, one that appeared to have split open miraculously in the midst of the most recent earth tremor. The men insisted that Nayalla drink first and she swallowed her pride with the first refreshing drops. They each waited their turn with restrained impatience. The water trickled painfully slowly and made them even more conscious of their thirst. When they were done, they filled their canteens, and decided to bed down for some sleep.

Nayalla and Noogan took first watch, keeping close to the others to conserve their warmth. Mirkrin's skack shape slowly slunched away as he fell into a deep sleep, but Nayalla let him be. Her stomach ached with hunger and she folded her skack's claws over her belly. Noogan cupped his hands and blew into them.

'I'm cold to the bone,' he shivered. 'Can't remember ever being this cold before.'

'Tell me about your home,' Nayalla said to him.

'Why?'

'Because I probably haven't been there, and I'm curious. And it'll give you something else to think about.'

'I'm from Brodfan, in Sestina,' he told her. 'It's full of farmers and fishermen, mostly. It's just a small town with little going on.'

'What's your favourite bit of it?' she prompted.

He shrugged, struggling to find something interesting to say about his home, but it was all so ordinary to him. There was nothing there to compare with the lives of the Myunans.

'There's a spot under the bridge where you can stand so that there are no reflections on the water because of the bridge's shadow, and you can see clear to the bottom of the river. On the bottom there's this head from a statue of a Noranian war hero. The statue stands in the middle of town, and some lads broke the head off it and threw it in the river a few years back. The Noranians never found it. That's my favourite bit.'

Nayalla smiled.

'Tell me about the bit of home you *hate* most.'

'That'd be the statue.'

They laughed quietly together. Nayalla's laughter was cut short by a sudden feeling that something else was listening. Like all Myunans, she had keen instincts and put great faith in them. She stood up and looked down the tunnel in the direction they had come. They were only burning two of their torches to conserve the powder, but she did not need them to tell her that there was something waiting back there in the darkness.

'We can't stay here,' she said softly. 'It's followed us. It's waiting for us to fall asleep. We need to get to a place we can defend.'

Noogan looked in the direction that she was staring, but could see nothing.

'That means leaving the water.'

'We can't stay here anyway,' she insisted. 'Come on, wake the others. We have to go.'

Mirkrin's flesh was still bruised from the cave-in that had crushed him and he gritted his teeth as he crafted his body into that of a skack. Gazing down at his claws, memories came back to him of the battle at the generator truck at the foot of Absaleth. It seemed so long ago now, and yet only a few days had passed. The tribe would be on its way back now, having left the children and elderly in a haven deep in the mountains. Those of fighting age, he was certain, would be preparing to resist the Noranians' attempts to mine the mountain. He and Nayalla should have been with them. He could only guess where their children were, but he prayed that they were safe. At least they were not trapped down here.

'You ready?' Paternasse asked.

He nodded. The two miners picked up all the bags, the Myunans taking up the front and rear of their little group. They all knew they were weak with hunger and thirst and lack of sleep, but with a powerful predator stalking them, they couldn't rest until they found a safe place to hole up. They trudged on, Mirkrin keeping his eyes on the passageway behind them.

'Some of this has been carved out,' Noogan said, as he looked around.

'Aye,' Paternasse mumbled. 'And by the same hands. But no pictures ... and no care taken to civilise it. Looks like a rush job compared to the other tunnels.'

'Maybe this is the limit of their territory,' Nayalla speculated.

'Aye, maybe.' Paternasse was too cold and tired to be very interested.

They came to a junction. The passageway split off into three separate tunnels.

'Which way now?' Noogan exclaimed in frustration.

'Does it matter?' Paternasse grunted. 'It's not like we're going anywhere in partic–'

He halted in mid-sentence and sniffed the air.

'Do you smell anything?' he asked them.

'Yes,' Nayalla drew in a breath. 'By the gods! That's ... it's fresh air!'

'Find the draught,' Paternasse grinned. 'It's fresh air all right. Just a whiff, but it's there! Find where it's a coming from!'

It was the centre tunnel. As they walked further down, they could feel the faintest draught on their faces and their pace quickened. There was a dull glow ahead, indistinct but unmistakable. Daylight. They ran towards the light and the tunnel turned a sharp corner and opened into a larger cave. Nayalla, who was in the lead, slowed to a stumble when she saw the source of the light.

'No!' she screamed. 'Not again!'

The others caught up and let out roars of frustration. It was another of the Seneschal's portals, a narrow, rectangular duct bored horizontally through the stone wall, barely wide enough for a fist. Walking closer, they saw that it was more than just a wall. It was a doorway, but it was sealed from the outside by a massive slab of stone. Judging by the length of the channel, it was three paces thick. Nayalla beat her fists against it, tears streaming down her face.

'We're going to die here,' Noogan whimpered, putting his back to the wall and sliding down to the floor.

'This is worse than the darkness,' Paternasse groaned. 'It's like it was put here to torment us. Look at that, the outside is right there! This was a doorway once and someone's blocked it up. We can't move it, we can't dig through it. They've killed us as sure as if they'd driven a sword through each of us.'

'Help!' Nayalla shrieked through the opening. 'Can anybody hear me? Somebody help us!'

Noogan stood up beside her and joined in, shouting out through the duct. Mirkrin watched them, anxiously casting his eyes back into the darkness of the cave.

'We sound like we're in trouble,' he muttered.

'What are you talking about?' Paternasse squinted at him.

'We *are* in bloody trouble.'

'No, I mean to the thing following us. We sound like animals in distress.'

Paternasse looked long and hard at him.

'Quiet down,' he said to the others.

They didn't hear him over the sound of their own voices.

'Quiet down!' he barked at them and they looked back at him in surprise.

'It's like Mirkrin says. We sound like panicked animals. If that monster back there is like any normal predator, it's going to be attracted to that noise. We sound weak.'

They all gazed at each other in weary desperation.

'This hole's not as long as the last one,' Nayalla said at last. 'I think I could get a hand out to the other side. Somebody might see it.'

'It's worth a try,' Paternasse agreed.

'Maybe we should try it later,' Noogan rasped.

'Why's that then?' Paternasse asked.

'Because there's something else in here with us.'

They all fell quiet and in the silence, a skittering sound could be heard. One they recognised immediately. The Seneschal had followed them after all.

16 PAPPY DIDN'T RAISE NO STINKIN' SONGBIRDS

Emos listened as Draegar recounted the story that began with his hunt for Lorkrin and Taya after the Reisenicks had kidnapped them and ended with how he and Rug had come to find themselves at the healer's house. For an anxious uncle, it was a disturbing tale.

'I should have known better than to let them come along. They have a gift for finding trouble. But I thought it would just be a trip to the cave. What could it hurt to have them with us? '

He looked over at Rug. He had already heard the stranger's story, but was curious about the Reisenicks' interest in him.

'So what's your part in all this? Why did the Reisenicks pick you up?'

'I didn't belong,' Rug replied. 'That's all I know.'

He self-consciously put his hand on the waist pocket where his nail was nestled. Emos noticed the gesture, but said nothing. The Myunan had been watching Rug since he had joined them, and had seen that the thin man moved stiffly and sometimes looked as if he were uncomfortable, or in pain. The way he held himself was slightly awkward too, and Emos was suspicious of the way he never uncovered his face or hands. That could only mean one of two things:

either Rug was deformed in some way that made him ashamed of his appearance, or he was afraid of being recognised, or perhaps even both. His voice was odd too, twangy and brittle, and his smell was unusual. It was part human, but there was something damp and rotten and cold about him. Emos eyed him as the wagon trundled along the muddy track.

'They could be hunting you as much as they are Draegar and the children,' he told the stranger. 'Do you know Kalayal Harsq, the exorcist? Have you any idea what's causing the earth tremors?'

'I don't know anything,' Rug insisted, uneasily. 'I can't remember who I am, let alone who or what I used to know. I … I think I want to see this cave you were talking about. I couldn't say why; it's just a feeling I have.'

'Well, you'll see the cave,' Emos said. 'I don't know yet what it will cost us. Let's hope it brings back some memories, eh?'

'It's a strange affair, altogether,' Draegar observed. 'The Reisenicks seem to have lost the run of themselves.'

'Ludditch is no fool.' Emos shook his head. 'Whatever he's planning, he'll have thought it out. I may be an outcast, but he must know that if the rest of our tribe hear what's happened to Taya and Lorkrin, they'll be out for a reckoning. They won't stand for the children being harmed. Ludditch must be sure that whatever he's cooking up is going to be worth trouble with the Myunans.'

Ahead, they saw the junction where their track joined up with the main road to the west. Tall cobrush trees towered either side, forming a dark corridor, which threw a shadow over the road in the dawn light.

'Perhaps Ludditch thinks they'll be too busy with the Noranians back at Absaleth.'

'I don't know. I think we're just a thorn in his side. There's something bigger going on here, and if Harsq is tied up in it somehow, it can only be bad for everyone else living on this land. Something about this whole situation has got my teeth on edge. The earth tremors are part of it, and they're definitely Harsq's doing. He's hurt the land's soul.'

'Aye, he's a blight, that one,' Draegar muttered. 'That unholy cur's going to get his comeuppance one day, and I wouldn't mind having a hand in it …'

A groan made them turn to see Tupe opening his eyes and discovering he was bound. He winced as if his head hurt and then looked around. His face twisted into a scowl as he recognised Draegar. It did not take him long to assess his situation.

'Ludditch is going ta have your skins for this!' he leered.

'Tell us what we need to know and we'll let you go,' Emos assured him.

'I'm not tellin' yuh nothin'.'

'Why is Ludditch after us? What's it got to do with Absaleth?' Emos squatted down in front of him.

'You *deaf* as well as ugly, yuh diseased freak? You'll get nothin' from me.'

Emos took the man's jaw in his hand.

'We've met before, haven't we?'

'Yeah, I know you. You're Harprag. You can melt wood and metal an' stuff with your fingers. Saw you do some work in Ainsdale once.'

'I can do the same to the bones in your face.'

'Fancy that. I ain't talkin'. If you're goin' to torture me, get on an' do it. Otherwise, get out o' my hair. Like I say, I know you. You Myunans are all the same. Your wills're as soft as your flesh. You want to show me pain? You want to cut me up? Go on ahead. My pappy didn't raise no stinkin' songbirds. Ludditch is my second and third cousin and my eldest son's uncle. Anything you do to me, he'll visit on you and yours. And I'd say he'll give those *cubs* of yours some special treatment.'

Emos's face turned to stone and he grabbed the Reisenick by the scruff of his jerkin, hauling him to his feet.

'I'm telling you now,' he growled into the clansman's face. 'Ludditch has already earned your tribe more grief than you'd believe, grief I'll be happy to deliver. And I promise you that what he's started here, I'm going to finish. You tell that to your second and third cousin when you see him.'

Lifting the Reisenick onto his toes, Emos shoved him backwards over the side of the truck, his bound body hitting the ground with a heavy thud and rolling, the clansman crying out in pain as he tumbled into the undergrowth.

'Probably should've kept hold of him,' Draegar commented.

'He wasn't going to give us anything. And I've no stomach for torture.'

'Might have been useful all the same,' the Parsinor shrugged.

'Let's just get to the cave. We can worry about Ludditch and his lot once we've found Nayalla and Mirkrin. '

'That reminds me,' Draegar frowned. 'The children were telling me something about Ludditch while we were walking to the storyhouse ...'

He was distracted by the sudden appearance of two large

bats over the treetops. They were wearing backpacks.

'Emos!'

The two men stood up and gaped. Taya and Lorkrin banked and came in from behind.

'Turn around!' Lorkrin shouted. 'You have to turn back!'

'Come down out of there right now!' Emos called to them. 'I've been going out of my mind worrying about you two. Are you all right?'

'Ludditch is coming!' Taya yelled at them. 'He's right down the road!'

Emos's face dropped and he swivelled to face forwards as Jube pulled the wagon out of the forest track and onto the well-worn mud of the westbound road. Down the road to their left, other trucks were visible through the thin morning mist.

'Jube!' Emos barked.

'I see them,' the miner replied, and brought the wagon to a skidding halt.

'No! Don't stop!' Emos shouted. 'They've seen us now. Put your foot down!'

Even as Jube stamped on the accelerator, Khassiel's wagon pulled out behind them and she and Cullum reacted immediately. With the Forward-Batterer taking the controls, she swung out the door and up onto the back of the truck, taking cover behind a crate and loading her crossbow. Cullum gunned the engine and took off after Jube. Emos swore and looked back up at Taya and Lorkrin, waving them down.

'Keep your shapes!' he told them as they landed on the flatbed, and he hugged them both tightly. He held them at arm's length and examined them for any signs of injury.

Apart from some bruises, they seemed fine. They started to talk excitedly, but he held up his hand to silence them.

'You can tell me all about it later,' he said. 'We're in trouble here. Be ready to fly again if I tell you. Until then, stay down.'

Draegar picked them both up and embraced them with a growl.

'I swear, you take years off my life, the pair of you!'

He put them down and Rug greeted them shyly, patting them both on the heads. Draegar drew his sword and Emos picked up one of the blowpipes he had taken. Engined wagons had many advantages over horses and other animals: they didn't tire, they didn't need feeding when you weren't using them, they carried more and made less mess. But there wasn't a truck in existence that could outpace a horse and the Reisenicks had come prepared. The six clansmen on horseback raced towards them.

They didn't see Khassiel until it was too late. A crossbow bolt caught the first one in the chest and he toppled backwards off his mount. Before they had passed the equipment truck, she had reloaded and put a bolt through the head of a second man. Two of the others lifted their blowpipes, but she ducked in time to dodge the darts. Cullum swerved suddenly and collided with one of the attackers, knocking the horse onto its side and throwing the rider. Two others were driven off the road and into the trees.

The last one galloped towards Jube's wagon, his blowpipe raised to his mouth. Rug, who had dropped to the boards when the rider approached, looked up to find himself staring straight into the horse's face. He yelped in fright and lashed out with his fist, catching the horse on the side of the head. The animal staggered sideways, stunned by the blow, and Emos, taken aback by the thin man's strength, seized the chance to shoot a dart into the rider's leg. But it landed harmlessly in the man's knife sheath. The Myunan ducked down behind Draegar, who was using his armour-plated forearms to cover his own face and chest. The clansman took aim again, blasting a breath through the pipe, but the dart bounced harmlessly off the Parsinor's shoulder. The Reisenick drew alongside, quickly reloading his weapon. The remaining two burst out of the trees to one side and goaded their horses on, taking turns to fire darts at Khassiel and keep her from aiming her crossbow. Cullum weaved from side to side to hold them at bay.

The Reisenick alongside the front wagon tried to take aim at Draegar's upper arms, which had no armour. But as he levelled the pipe, Draegar turned his back and crouched down, showing only his hinged shell. The rider cursed and pulled back for a clearer shot. Jube veered suddenly, forcing the Reisenick to fall back behind the truck. As he did, Emos stood up from behind the Parsinor and fired a dart that struck the rider square in the chest. The man pulled the dart free, but was already losing consciousness. Emos slipped another dart into his mouth, raised the tube and landed the second projectile right next to the last one, finishing the job. The Reisenick toppled from his saddle and crashed to the ground, only narrowly escaping being run over by Cullum.

One of the remaining riders galloped forward, blowpipe raised, but his comrade made the mistake of giving Khassiel time to take aim over the top of the cab. She fired a bolt into the small of the advancing rider's back. He fell from his horse and tumbled into the trees. The last horseman hung down the side of his horse, using his mount's body as a shield. From under the animal's neck, he fired a shot at Emos, who dived for cover. Draegar picked up one of the planks of wood in the back of the truck and hurled it like a javelin between the horse's front legs. The beast's legs caught on it and it crashed to the ground, crushing its rider beneath it.

Two of the Reisenick wagons were gaining on their quarry. The heavily laden equipment truck could not get up enough speed to lose them. Cullum glanced in his mirror and saw the front of the leading clansman's truck quickly closing the gap. The men in the cab were keeping their heads low and out of Khassiel's line of fire. From behind the cab, others kept a steady hail of darts raining in on her, to deter her from any further attack.

Cullum looked in his mirror again and noticed the arm of the hoist that protruded off the back of his vehicle. He rapped on the glass at the back of the cab, getting Khassiel's attention.

'Hang on!' he yelled back at her and then, gripping the steering wheel tightly, he slammed his foot on the brake.

The wagon skidded to a halt, giving no warning to the truck behind it. The Reisenicks' vehicle crashed into the back of it, the hoist's arm ramming through its radiator. Water and steam poured forth through the punctured metal. Cullum changed down gears, hit the accelerator again and tore loose, revving the engine to try and catch up with their friends ahead. The clansmen got moving again, but did not get very far before their engine overheated and cut out completely.

Cullum looked back in his mirror and laughed. He was

having a good time. The second Reisenick vehicle overtook the first and quickly closed the gap. Jube's wagon was slowing down. They moved out to the side and let Cullum draw level with them.

'There's a hard left turn coming up!' Emos shouted to him. 'Be ready for it!'

They steamed ahead again and no sooner had they taken up position in front then Jube was swerving down a track barely wide enough for the wagons. Just visible in the tangled trees, it was signposted with a horned goat's skull hung with flowers. Cullum hauled the steering wheel round and followed them down the steep, dark, muddy trail. There were painted bone sculptures hanging from the trees along each side and they clacked and rattled against the sides of the cab.

Jube shook his head as he steered the wagon down the trail. It did not look like it led anywhere. If the Reisenicks got them cornered, they were done for. The track dipped and then rose again. There was a gate ahead, bearing a sign written in Reisenick. Jube gripped the wheel and drove right through it, careering out into daylight. They were in a green meadow dotted with mounds, each with its own bone sculpture atop it. In the middle of the field, at its highest point, stood a wood-and-hide hut that appeared to be some kind of shrine. Jube drove around in a circle, looking for a way out. There was none. They were trapped.

Emos slapped the top of the cab.

'We can stop here,' he called in to the miner.

'What are you talking about? They've got us now. We've had it!'

'No, we'll be all right for the moment.'

Cullum and Khassiel were just coming through the gate.

The first Reisenick wagon wasn't far behind. Emos turned to Taya and Lorkrin.

'Right, before the clansmen catch up and see you. I've got a job for you.'

He murmured a few words to them and they took to the air, flying off towards the shrine at the top of the meadow.

'Where are we?' Rug asked, looking up from the floor of the flatbed. 'Won't they catch us here?'

'This is a burial ground,' Emos told him. 'And it's going to give us a chance to clear the air.'

+ + + +

A swarm of blind creatures herded Nayalla, Mirkrin, Paternasse and Noogan away from the light and back down the passage to the junction. The four fugitives backed away from the mass of small bodies, reluctant to make any move that might trigger an attack.

'I've no more fight left in me,' Noogan whispered.

'I'm all tuckered out myself,' Paternasse hissed. 'But they won't take me easy, all the same.'

They were steered up one of the branches, along a steadily narrowing tunnel that cornered left, then right, then left again in the way they had seen under Absaleth. The ceiling got lower and soon they were scraping their heads against it. This was even more unnerving, for the Seneschal crawled along the walls and ceiling as easily as they did the floor and some of the advancing creatures were right at face height.

'I thought they wanted us out,' Nayalla wondered out loud. 'Why are they leading us away from the portal?'

'Might be that their plans have changed a touch,' Paternasse grunted.

He and Noogan were carrying the torches, but they were no deterrent against the Blind Battalion. Behind the sightless troops, other breeds were following in the gloom beyond the glow of the burning powder.

'This is one of the defensive passages,' Nayalla said. 'I think I know what they're doing. They're going to push us in so far that we've no room to fight.'

'We'd best stop here, so,' Mirkrin replied, and did exactly that.

The others halted too, the four of them planting their feet and standing their ground. A quiver went through the mass of the Seneschal and a voice called out from behind the blinded.

'You will keep walking, please, or you will be disassembled where you stand.'

It was Leggit – or one of his fellow Scouts.

'Come on then, if you're want to try it!' Paternasse yelled, wearily.

'Keep walking, please.'

The four of them looked at each other.

'This is too much, altogether,' Noogan whined. 'I'm not budgin'. I'm not going to be herded like a sheep to the slaughter.'

Nayalla cocked her head to one side and gazed at the Seneschal bristling around them.

'They're not pushing us towards something,' she said at last. 'They're pushing us *away*. They want us for themselves. I think …'

A buzz of clicking teeth carried like a wave across the bristling bodies and the Seneschal turned as one to look back down the corridor. A light grew from around the corner and the main force of Seneschal filtered through from the back, shoving the Blinded forward to face this new adversary. A figure carrying what appeared to be a lantern came around the corner. The light swayed from side to side, moving with the gait of the bearer. The Seneschal were growing frantic and some started pushing the four fugitives further down the tunnel. But the way was blocked by still more of the little animals, some of which were scurrying away in terror.

Nayalla and Mirkrin placed themselves between the two miners and the approaching light. In the moving shadows, it seemed to be an old woman, with a jutting brow, hidden eyes and a long face that peered through curtains of straggly hair. Then the Blind Battalion attacked and the light went out. There was a deep, guttural snarl and the noise of skittering feet and clicking teeth filled the air. But these were drowned out by shrieks and the sound of tearing flesh.

'By the gods!' Noogan sobbed. 'What is it?'

With the light gone, the Seneschal positioned behind the Blinded threw themselves into the fray. Paternasse and Noogan held up their torches, trying to see what was happening, but all that could be seen was a wave of small, quivering bodies swarming down the tunnel into the dark. More wet, ripping sounds erupted, and the stink of freshly opened insides filled the passageway. The Seneschal suddenly turned tail and fled past them.

'Run!' Paternasse wailed.

But there was nowhere to run to; the tunnel behind them was crammed with the bodies of the Seneschal, fighting to get past one another. Clawed, padded feet bounded towards them, and Mirkrin and Nayalla turned back to face the oncoming predator, baring their teeth and raising their claws as it clambered over a heap of mutilated Seneschal corpses. A light flashed on suddenly, dazzling them and then a heavy body crashed into them. They were both smashed off their feet, Nayalla thrown against the wall, Mirkrin falling beneath the attacker. He ripped at the insides of the creature's legs with his long claws, and buried his fangs in its belly. The skin was sour and smelled rotten. He opened his mouth and bit in again. The beast seized his shoulders with powerful talons and hauled him forward, tearing his teeth free. Nayalla was jammed against the tunnel wall by its bulk. She fought back, raking her claws across its shoulders and neck.

It was as large as both of them put together, and far more powerful. It had six legs, two of which extended forward like arms. The 'lantern' was a glowing, bulbous sac of some kind of chemical that hung from a single antenna, protruding from the top of its head. It went out again as they tackled it, leaving them with only the light from the torches. Its jaws were mounted on each side of its huge head, closing horizontally rather than vertically, with some of its teeth facing outwards, obviously for pulling the flesh away from the bones that were its food. Its hide was tough and leathery.

A Myunan could mimic the appearance of a skack, but not its talent for killing. The beast shook the shape-changers loose and crushed Nayalla against the wall, its massive jaws closing to grip the sides of her head. She slunched with a scream and slipped her head free, much to the creature's surprise. Mirkrin picked himself off the ground and slashed their attacker across the eyes. The animal's bony brow protected it from being blinded, and it swivelled to face him, moving awkwardly in the tight confines of the passageway.

As it turned in the torchlight, he saw that lumps of bone

stuck out from its brow, forming a rough impression of a face, the 'old woman's' hair simulated by a rough mane that hung down from the narrow ridge atop its skull. It clacked its teeth together and lunged at him. He sidestepped it, but there was nowhere to go in the small tunnel and it caught hold of him, slamming him against the ground. Nayalla lashed out, hitting the stalk that held the creature's lamp. It hissed and flinched, then moved with lightning speed, jamming its claws up against her body, pushing her against the wall. This time it seized her too suddenly for her to escape and she gasped as its teeth dug into her.

Paternasse and Noogan ran at it, shouting and waving their torches in an attempt to draw it away from her. It snarled at them, but did not release her. Paternasse tried to drive his knife into the creature's side, but the beast twisted sideways and the blade was deflected by its tough hide. Paternasse caught a clawed foot in his chest and was thrown back down the passageway, his knife falling near Mirkrin's feet. Noogan thrust his torch in its face, but it knocked the cold flame away. Mirkrin jumped up, shedding his skack form as he did so. He had seen how the thing had reacted when Nayalla slashed at its antenna. He picked up Paternasse's knife and slashed the blade through the bladder that formed the animal's lantern, cutting a long gash through its skin. An acrid-smelling liquid sprayed out and Mirkrin felt something burning his eyes and nose. He staggered backwards, but even as he did, he heard the beast howling in pain. The howls carried away down the tunnel and then he felt hands helping him up.

He rubbed frantically at his eyes and somebody poured water over his face. Eventually, he was able to open his eyes and look blearily around. Noogan was standing holding an empty canteen and Paternasse was tending to Nayalla, who was bleeding from wounds to her chest and belly. There was no sign of the Seneschal. He scrambled over to his wife and knelt by her side.

'I'm all right,' she told him. 'I'll be fine.'

But her voice was shaking and he could see it hurt her to breathe. His sight was still blurry and he rubbed his sore eyes.

'Is it gone?' she asked.

'It's gone. We got it,' he told her. 'Lie still, don't talk, love. We need to patch up these wounds and then you'll be right as rain.'

'I can still hear it.'

The distant howls were echoing down the tunnel. Mirkrin threw an anxious glance at Paternasse. The old miner shrugged. There was no way to be sure if they had driven it off for good.

'Don't worry about it. It's gone,' Mirkrin insisted. 'We're safe.'

Nayalla patted his hand.

'You never could lie worth a damn, dear.'

17 GREAT AUNT ELDRITH

The Reisenick wagons rolled into the burial ground, but unlike Jube and Cullum, they did not drive in among the mounds, stopping just inside the gate. Ludditch climbed down from the back of his vehicle, the expression on his face a mask of hate. He strode over to where Emos stood waiting with his arms folded.

'You've crossed the line now, Myunan!' Ludditch exploded. 'You hurt my kin, you kill my brother and now you're trespassin' on hallowed ground. That's going to get yuh an ugly, painful trip into the earth!'

Emos regarded him with equanimity.

'You're still wearing my tribute, Ludditch.'

The Reisenick pulled the pendant from his neck and threw it at the Myunan's feet.

'Take it back then!' he snapped. 'I'll strangle yuh with it when yuh leave here. You think you're safe just 'cause you've got yourself onto sacred ground? You can't stay here forever.'

'I've been travelling through these lands for years, since your father's time,' Emos continued. 'You've always respected the tribute system. Now you turn your back on centuries of tradition. For what? What's got into you, Learup?'

'You'll find out soon enough.'

'Well, if you won't talk to me, maybe your father will,' Emos said, seeing Ludditch Senior climbing stiffly down from the back of the wagon.

He also noticed Kalayal Harsq, standing behind the rest of Ludditch's clan. Harsq looked scared, and he was keeping his distance from the Reisenicks. Ludditch Junior glanced back and scowled at the sight of his father hobbling towards them on his canes.

'You stay there, pappy!' he called. 'I'm dealin' with this! There's no need to bother yourself there.'

He rounded on Emos.

'I'm chieftain, you talk to me or nobody, got it?'

'I want safe passage to Old Man's Cave, and then from there back to the border.'

'Do you now?' Ludditch snorted. 'How's about I get my mama to rustle you up some constant stew and a tray of her fine flapjacks to help yuh on your way? The only way you and your friends are going to make it back across the border is as part of my wife's winter wardrobe. We'll see how her new Myunan-skin skirt goes with her Parsinor-hide boots.'

'What in the blazes is goin' on here, Junior?' his father came up behind him.

'I'm handlin' this, Pappy.'

'That'll be why there's cousins out lyin' dead on the road an' outsiders walkin' on your kin's graves then. Handlin' it indeed.' He turned to Emos. 'You got yourself a deathwish, Harprag?'

'Just trying to find out why we've been hunted ever since we crossed your border, Mr Ludditch. All we want is for your son here to abide by the tribute system, as it has always been in the past.'

'My boy's got little respect for the past,' the old man wheezed. 'But he's got big plans for the future. You've just gone an' got in the way. Now, you've had your little chin-wag. Get yourselves back on your wagons and leave our burial ground before you taint it any further. We'll be waitin' for yuh outside. The boys're keen to get their knives into yuh an' I've promised my daughter-in-law I'd be home in time for supper. She's cookin' up a sinker crab special like, so I'd thank you not to delay me any further. The longer you make me wait, the longer young Learup here's goin' to take des-patchin' yuh. He's a genuine artiste with a skinnin' knife.'

'I want safe passage to Old Man's Cave,' Emos repeated. 'Some of my family are trapped in the catacombs down there. It could take us several days to search for them. After we get them out, I want an escort to the border.'

'Why are you tryin' to bargain?' Ludditch Junior frowned, looking suspiciously at the other members of the would-be rescue party. 'You ain't got nothin' to bargain *with*.'

'I'm just trying to appeal to your generous nature,' Emos said, spreading his hands in a placating gesture.

✦   ✦   ✦   ✦

Taya and Lorkrin stood inside the shrine at the top of the mound, the door of which was out of sight of those involved in the negotiations. Still in their batlike shapes, they were both feeling a little queasy about what they were going to do.

'Do you think it'll fall apart when we pick it up?' Lorkrin whispered.

'I don't know,' Taya replied. 'I've never stolen a dead body before.'

In a tall chair in the middle of the tiny building sat the

preserved corpse of an old woman. Just as the Reisenick chieftain's male ancestors were valued for their presence in council, so too were the females, who watched over the other dead. Every major Reisenick burial site in the Ludditch territory was protected by one of the clan's former matri-archs. This old lady was dressed in long, old-fashioned robes, heavily laden in jewellery and scented with stifling perfume to hide the smell of the preservatives. The two Myunans screwed up their faces at the stench.

'We need a bag or something,' Lorkrin said.

'Let's wrap her up in her cloak.'

'Right, then.'

It was a tricky business. They did not want to waste time having to resculpt themselves, so they made do with their wings as they were. Pulling the dead woman's cloak from her shoulders, they laid it out on the floor and then pushed her body out of her chair, letting it fall onto the cloak. Then they wrapped her up in it as best they could, pinning the bundle with the same sturdy broaches that had held the cloak to her shoulders.

'We should have taken off the jewellery,' Taya tutted. 'That's going to make her heavier.'

'There's only so much of this sickness that I can take,' Lorkrin muttered. 'She can keep her bloody jewellery.'

+ + + +

The younger Reisenicks were growing restless. The clans-men would not violate the sanctity of the burial ground, but they were keen to finish off the outsiders. Emos watched them impassively, with Draegar standing like a pillar of stone by his side. Behind them, Cullum and Khassiel leaned against the front of their wagon, weapons at the ready. Only Rug and Jube looked anxious – facing death at the hands of bloodthirsty killers still being a relatively new experience for them. They could not see any way out of this. Ludditch was right; they couldn't stay here forever.

'If your kin are down in those caves,' the chieftain was saying, 'then they're done for. You don't know what's down there. Those tunnels are a maze, and they ain't empty. Yuh hear what I'm sayin'?'

'I can't give up on my family,' Emos told him. 'And there are signs that can be read down there, if you know what to look for. Caftelous showed me how.'

'The hermit? Didn't tell me about no signs.'

'He hated you. Why would he tell you anything?'

'I got wondrous powers of persuasion, particularly when I'm tryin' to learn some history.'

Emos stared hard at him.

'He disappeared a few years ago. Did you have anything to do with it?'

Ludditch chuckled.

'Damn, Harprag, I'd everything to do with it. It was me who killed 'im! After I was done with 'im that is. Dumped what was left of 'is body in the woods for the animals.'

The Myunan's face was expressionless, but his eyes burned with hate.

'All this is going to come back on you, Ludditch.'

'I don't think it will, somehow,' Ludditch laughed. 'And certainly not at your hands, Myunan. If it wasn't for my respect for our dead, we'd fall on yuh right here. But you go on and stay here, we can wait you out. Sometimes huntin' is all about waitin' …'

His voice faltered as two winged figures appeared over the roof of the shrine, carrying a long bundle between them. Their wings beat the air urgently, the two creatures gaining height and flying away over the trees.

'What the blazes is that?' Ludditch rasped.

'If I read the sign on the gate correctly,' Emos replied, 'it's your Great Aunt Eldrith.'

Ludditch and his father looked in horror at each other and then started to spit curses at Emos, but the Myunan held up his hands.

'You've been threatening us with torture and death since we crossed your border, so save your breath. We'll assume that this means you'll kill us even slower now, if you get the chance. But know this, Learup. If you ever want to retrieve your great aunt's corpse, you'll give us safe passage to the cave, you'll wait while we search for our people, and then see us from there to the southern border. Then, when we're back in Myunan territory, we'll return old Eldrith in the same perfectly preserved state that we found her. Make any move against us, or even get in our way or try to slow us down, and my nephew and niece there will start dropping pieces of her all over the forest.

'I'd suggest you send some birds out and make sure none of your hunters try shooting the young ones down. You wouldn't want them to drop the old girl from such a great height.'

'Harprag,' Ludditch snarled. 'I'm goin' ta …'

'Spare me,' Emos cut him off. 'We're leaving. Don't get in our way.'

He walked back to the wagon and climbed in beside Jube, who was sweating profusely and uttering prayers to Everness under his breath.

'I was scared before,' he said. 'I'm ready to soil myself now. They're going to go insane over this.'

'They can only kill us the once,' Emos reassured him. 'This way we have them over a barrel. Not even Ludditch will brook risking the body of a dead relative. They had it in for us anyway. I've just raised the stakes. He'll have to let every hunting party and lookout from here to the cave know that we're not to be touched. We're safer now than we were before they found us.'

'That may be so, but just the way they're lookin' at us is loosenin' my bowels. Where to now?'

'Back onto the road, the same way we were heading,' the Myunan replied. 'We'll be there by the afternoon.'

Jube shifted into gear and drove down towards the Reisenick horde. They slowly parted in front of the vehicle, but not before each one looked the intruders in the eyes. Some of the oldest were by the gate, determined to be on the expedition despite being barely able to walk without canes or staffs. Every one of them had murder written on their face.

'Everness protect us,' Jube muttered.

'And Eldrith too,' Emos added.

+ + + +

Lorkrin adjusted the grip his prehensile toes had on the bundle and pushed down against the air with his wings.

'I'm getting tired,' he gasped, at last, embarrassed that he had said it before his sister.

Taya nodded, already too out of breath to answer, but relieved her brother had spoken up first.

'He said we could come back to the wagons once they were on the road,' Lorkrin panted. 'He said we just had to give Ludditch time to give his orders. Let's catch up with them.'

'Okay,' Taya replied.

They both looked down in surprise as the expanse of trees gave way below them and they found themselves flying over what looked like a freshly ploughed stretch of land. It looked so out of place that they kept looking at it and noticed that the ground appeared to be moving, as if it were alive, clumps of it kneading together and breaking apart in perpetual motion. It was not unlike watching a mass of maggots writhing together. The noise was a constant rumble, like white water, but with a gritty edge to it. They flew lower to get a closer look. Every now and then, a spout of soil burst into the air, and while they watched, some trees at the edge of the clearing had their roots eaten away and with tormented groans they toppled to the ground. Each was swallowed up with frightening speed, the weaker branches and twigs broken and crushed in the malevolent earth's grip, the trunks engulfed with a sound of straining, tearing wood.

'Krundengrond,' Taya breathed.

They spiralled upwards over it, higher and higher so that they could look out over the land. It was not the only stretch of fresh earth in sight. The closer to the mountains the expanse of forest got, the more they could see it was broken by gaps in the trees.

'It's spreading,' Lorkrin shouted between heaving breaths. 'Draegar was wrong, it *is* here. This is what Ludditch was waiting for. But what's it got to do with Absaleth?'

'Don't know … but he sounded pretty sure of himself,' Taya replied, wearily. 'He thinks we've got this god-heart … must mean Orgarth's heart. Wonder what that is.'

'Remember Harsq did that thing on the stuff, the second time, I mean?' her brother wheezed.

'Yeah,' she panted, knowing he was referring to the exorcism on the scrap.

'Well, if that nail was stuck in Draegar's back ...' he heaved in a breath, '... then it didn't get exorcised, did it? Maybe the heart ... is the bit left after all ... the rest is gone.'

'Can a god fit in a nail?'

'Maybe he's a very small god ... who knows what size any of 'em are ... when you get right down to it.'

'Uncle Emos'll know,' Taya called back. 'What I want to know then, is ... what's it got to do with Rug? He was the one ... who kept the nail.'

With the dead body in its robe dangling from their feet, they sought out the road and soared along it until they came upon the wagons, the rescue party leading, followed closely by Reisenicks. The two Myunans glided down towards Jube's wagon. Dropping their hostage into Draegar's upstretched arms, they flopped to the floor of the flatbed and squatted wearily, trying to get their breaths back.

'Well done, the pair of you,' Emos said warmly, putting his arms around them. 'You saved our lives back there.'

'Uncle Emos,' Taya puffed. 'There's krundengrond breaking out east of here ... It's spreading towards the mountains ... We're going to run right into it.'

'Krundengrond?' Emos frowned. 'Here? I don't think ...'

'It's here,' Lorkrin said, firmly. 'We've seen it. That's what Ludditch has been trying to start. He's after a "god-heart", we think he means Orgarth's heart. He thinks we have it and if he takes it from us, he's going to let the krundengrond out all over the place. '

'Could a god fit in a nail?' Taya asked, slowly regaining her wind. 'We think Rug's nail might be what they're looking for. Like it's the last bit left of Orgarth.'

She explained where the nail had come from.

'Rug thought it was important too, but he didn't know why. Do you think it could be … controlling him, or something like that?'

Rug stood up in alarm.

'I've been possessed?' he exclaimed. 'Is that what's wrong with me?'

'Everybody calm down,' Draegar said. 'Children, your imaginations are running away with you. Either yours or Ludditch's anyway. There is no krundengrond here. It doesn't break out, because nothing can hold it still in the first place …'

'Will you just *listen*, instead of treating us like babies!' Lorkrin snapped.

'Don't you take that tone with me, lad.'

'Uncle Emos!' Taya pleaded. 'It's real – we've seen it!'

Emos wasn't listening. He was looking out at the mountains, lost in his own thoughts.

A shudder ran through the ground beneath the truck's wheels. They heard a deep, ripping sound ahead. A tree pulled its tangled branches free from its neighbours at the side of the road and crashed to the ground, falling diagonally so that it nearly blocked the way through. Everyone turned to look towards it.

'It's an ambush!' Draegar shouted.

'No. It's *not*,' Lorkrin retorted, rolling his eyes. 'If you'd just listen …'

Jube swerved around the top of the tree, nearly sliding

into the ditch at the side of the road as he avoide
cle. The men all looked warily up into the trees
attack they thought must come, but Taya and Lo
watching the ground. The wagon suddenly jolted to a ha
throwing them all off their feet. Jube pressed down on the
accelerator, but the vehicle was caught fast. All around them,
the road was breaking up. Cullum pulled past them, the
heavier equipment truck still caught in the ditch after
making it past the tree. There was a point where the side of
the trough had collapsed and the Noranian used it to scramble up and onto an intact section of road. He stopped and
the Noranians looked back, Khassiel already jumping down
with a roll of chain to tow the other wagon free.

'Don't come any closer!' Emos shouted to her, then turned
to the others. 'Forget the wagon. Everybody get out!'

'By the gods,' Draegar muttered, staring at the erupting
road. 'It's true.'

Lorkrin beat his tired wings and took off, with Taya following a moment later. Draegar picked up Ludditch's great
aunt, grabbed Rug and hauled him over the side. The two of
them staggered across the splitting clay to where the Noranians were watching in disbelief. Jube was still at the wheel,
trying to reverse out of the quagmire. Emos rapped on the
small glass window on the back.

'Jube! Get out of the truck!'

The miner waved his hand at him, then changed into first
gear again and tried the accelerator once more. Draegar
started across to them, but the ground pulled at his feet and
he had to stumble back. The wagon shook and shunted forwards and at first it seemed as if it was starting to move, but
then the front sank suddenly and something crunched

ainst the undercarriage. With a violent shudder, the front
wheels and nose of the vehicle were pulled into the ground.
Jube clutched the steering wheel in terror.

'Get out!' Emos yelled at him.

There was the creak of buckling metal and a jolt went
through the chassis. Jube tried to open his door, but the
earth was already up to the bottom edge, jamming it shut.
The door's window had a crossbar; only the top half of the
glass could be opened, too small a gap for the burly miner.
The truck tipped further forward. The ground was already
halfway up the windscreen. Emos watched in dread. The
back window was tiny, it offered no way out. He swung over
the side and pulled frantically at the window's crossbar. Jube
fell back from it and raised his feet. Emos pulled his hand
aside and the miner began slamming his heavy boots against
the thin bar. It bent, the glass shattering. The krundengrond
was nearly to the sill. Emos kicked at it from the other side,
trying to bend it down enough for the miner to get through.
The earth was over the sill and probing in through the
broken glass. The cab's doors creaked under the pressure.
The windscreen cracked by the Reisenick's rocks burst
inwards. Jube screamed and then his cry was cut off. Emos
was forced to climb onto the back of the cab. He looked
down through the tiny window, but all he saw was writhing
earth, pressed against the glass. He beat his fist against the
solid wood panelling.

The krundengrond was coming up over the cab, the
wagon tipping further and further over. Emos looked urgently
around. The vehicle was surrounded on all sides. He clambered up the flatbed and perched on the tailgate. Holding up
his hands, he cast his eyes around above him … and there

they were. Taya and Lorkrin swooped down, Taya grabbing his hands and Lorkrin catching his feet, the two of them lifting him from the sinking wagon and carrying him to safety.

They landed heavily at the side of the equipment wagon. It was still on a solid stretch of road, but the fringe of the krundengrond was edging steadily closer. The tree that had blocked the road was already being eaten up. On the far side, the Reisenicks watched in fear and amazement. All except Ludditch. He was wearing an expression of satisfaction.

'Let's get out of here,' Draegar said. 'Jube's gone. There's nothing we can do for him now. We need to make it up into the mountains before we all follow him. At least that mess'll get Ludditch off our backs for a while.'

Lorkrin and Taya watching in grieving silence as the ground swallowed the remains of the wagon, the sound of rending metal and splintering wood filling their ears. And then there was only the grating rumble of the churning earth itself, its edges creeping outwards with slow, unrelenting force. The others climbed aboard the equipment wagon, Cullum taking the wheel once more.

'Taya, Lorkrin!' Emos called. 'We have to go.'

They turned at the sound of their uncle's voice and jumped up onto the back of the truck. Leaving the Reisenicks stranded on the far side of the krundengrond, the wagon drove off, making for the relative safety of the thin, rocky soil of the mountains.

✦   ✦   ✦   ✦

Ludditch gazed at the krundengrond like a man in rapture.

'Look at that,' he choked. 'Harsq? Harsq!'

'I'm here.'

The chieftain looked round at him.

'Didn't I tell yuh? It's started now,' he said to the exorcist. 'And all we have to do to make sure it spreads right around the territory is get our hands on those outsiders. Damn it, boy. It's the most beautiful thing I've ever seen.'

'How do we catch them now?' Harsq asked. 'Your dream come true is blocking the road before us, and even if we get past, they still have your aunt.'

Ludditch waved his hand dismissively.

'There's other roads, and we've men all along the trail. And as for Great Aunt Eldrith, she's a tough old bird. She'll come through this all right.'

Harsq could not take his eyes off the krundengrond. The myths had been true. But how could they be true? What could have held the earth still all this time? His gaze was fixed on the violently tossing ground. He was certain that it was looking back at him. His faith was shaken by what he saw, and he did not know what it meant for his promise to rid Ludditch of the god of Absaleth. But there was no god, he reasoned. After all, his exorcism had driven the spirit of Absaleth out. It had been a potent ceremony, but had he really unseated a god? Was he really that powerful?

The priest looked down at his hands, and then back at his generator truck. Perhaps it had nothing to do with the spirit of Absaleth. Perhaps the krundengrond had not been there before. Perhaps he had created it, an accident caused by his new, unfettered state of mind. He had always known his ceremonies had massive effects on the land. Could it be that, empowered by Brask's might, he had unwittingly infused this earth with *life*?

A fevered light came into his eyes. If he had given it life, then he could control it. He stared out across what had once been the section of roadway in front of them. Kneeling and putting his hands on the ground in front of him, he felt the krundengrond's vibrations through the clay. And he knew that it felt him too.

'Harsq!' Ludditch shouted.

The priest looked up. Everybody else was already back aboard the vehicles. They were waiting for him.

'Stop prayin' and get your backside up on your wagon,' Ludditch barked at him. 'We got to take a detour, but we'll be back on their tails faster'n a skunkrin up a drainpipe. Get aboard, now.'

Harsq took one last longing look at his creation and climbed back into the cab of the generator wagon. There would be plenty of time yet for them to get to know each other.

18 RUG'S HANDS

Taya and Lorkrin sat quietly on a crate with their backs against the wall of the cab, watching the road behind them. Everybody had lapsed into silence after their escape. Emos was staring into the distance, deep in thought.

'I'm sorry, children,' Draegar said at last. 'I'm sorry I didn't believe you. Perhaps if I had, we might have been able to …'

'Ludditch knew,' Emos cut in abruptly. 'He came here himself and he had his whole family with him. He's here personally to hunt us, and he's brought Harsq with him.'

'He thinks we have what's left of Orgarth,' Lorkrin said. 'Rug has this nail that we got out of Draegar's back after that second exorcism – we were thinking it might be that. Ludditch figures if he gets rid of Orgarth, the krundengrond keeps growing and when it's finished, it'll cut off the Reisenick land from everywhere else. What I don't get is where the stuff came from.'

'It's always been here,' Emos said softly. 'It's an old, old legend and I didn't believe it myself. I have only heard of it once, in connection with the stories of the Tuderem, the alchemists who once lived here. Thousands of years ago, the land around Absaleth is said to have been a swathe of krundengrond, stretching over half of what is now the Myunan Territories, and covering the flat country southeast of Absaleth as far as Sestina. Which coincidentally, would form an impenetrable boundary around the south and east of the Reisenicks' territory. It tormented Orgarth, the spirit of Absaleth, constantly eroding the iron and stone that was his body. He was being eaten away, painfully slowly.

'Then the Tuderem came from over the mountains. They had been driven from their homeland by the Barians, whose empire stretched from the esh in the east, to the great sea in the west. Their rule was barbaric and the Tuderem had suffered much at their hands.

'Now the Tuderem had nowhere else to go. They had no home. So they resolved to make one. They prayed to Orgarth and he answered. Their skills in the science of alchemy would provide both with what they needed. They knew of Orgarth's power over iron – it is the source of his essence and he can work his will on it. For nearly a century, the Tuderem worked on the krundengrond. They changed the elements of its earth, lacing it with iron, and as the concentration of iron rose, Orgarth was able to exercise his power over it and still the earth's constant raging. Eventually, the entire stretch of land was tamed, though they left enough on their borders to keep the Barians at bay.

'And it was rich, fertile land, for it had never been farmed; nothing had ever been able to grow on it before. The Tuderem made a new life for themselves, and Orgarth was saved from the torments of the krundengrond. After scores of years had passed, the Barians disappeared from the neighbouring lands and the Tuderem began to feel safe once more. With their numbers growing as they thrived in their new home, they gradually did away with the last of the krundengrond to give themselves more land. It was a fatal mistake.

'The Barians did come back, more powerful and savage

then ever and they laid waste to the new land. Rather than serve these cruel masters, it is said that the Tuderem sought refuge in the caves beneath Absaleth. They sealed themselves in, not knowing when they would ever be able to return to the outside world.

'No one has heard of them since, but Caftelous, the old man who lived up here, claimed that he had found markings in the tunnels that told their story. He showed me some once, deep in the caves. He learned much of his alchemy from studying these markings. But even he never mentioned krundengrond.'

'But what made you keep the nail?' Taya asked Rug. 'How did you know it was so important?'

'We still don't know if it is,' Emos pointed out.

'It makes sense to me,' Lorkrin persisted. 'Harsq drove Orgarth out of the mountain. Orgarth lost control over the krundengrond. Ludditch thinks Orgarth is on his way back to the mountain, or at least his last remaining nail has hitched a ride with Rug ...'

'I don't feel possessed,' Rug put in. 'I'm sure I'd know, somehow.'

'... and Ludditch wants to stop him, so that he can keep his krundengrond,' Lorkrin concluded. 'Sounds simple to me.'

'But Orgarth was born of iron and stone,' Emos explained. 'He would have no power over flesh and blood, but he could have found purchase in metal. And Harsq knew it too. He must have sensed the spirit, and followed it to the forest. But he needed the Reisenicks' help to find it. And now he's sent them after us. So, why is he still searching, after two exorcisms? And what's it got to do with you?'

He turned to look over at Rug. The gangly figure lifted his head. Thoughts were racing through his mind. Flashes, fragments of what could be memories were tantalisingly close and yet just beyond reach. Emos's story was triggering all kinds of images in his head.

'I don't know,' he answered, looking over at the Myunan. 'But I am connected to this, somehow. I ...'

He stopped, putting his hand to his pocket. He unbuttoned the flap and took out his nail.

'The Reisenicks are trying to kill us because of a nail?' Khassiel snorted.

Emos took it and held it up. He smelled the metal, and rubbed it between his fingers.

'It got stuck in your back before the ceremony?' he asked the Parsinor.

'If that's where it came from, then yes,' Draegar replied.

'So Orgarth could fit into that?' Lorkrin smiled uncertainly. 'Little fella, is he?'

'Spirit has no size,' Emos told them. 'Orgarth could live as a particle of rust if he escaped Harsq's ritual. Rug, why did you hold onto this?'

'I just felt it was important to me,' the thin man shrugged. 'I don't know why.'

Emos squatted down in front of him.

'We need to know who you are. Take off the scarf.'

'No,' Rug shook his head fearfully. 'I can't. I just can't.'

'Jube is dead,' Emos said sternly. 'We could still follow him, and that would mean those in the caves would die too. I don't give a damn if you're shy about how you look. Take off the scarf.'

'No!' Rug retorted firmly.

Emos suddenly grabbed his hands and dug his fingers into the musty fabric of Rug's gloves. He pulled hard, before the other man had time to react, and yanked the material away. It tangled on something at first, then the top pair of gloves came away cleanly, the second pair tore. There was even a third pair underneath. Rug clutched his hands protectively to his chest, but Draegar stepped behind him and grabbed his wrists, forcing them out so that Emos could get a grip on the backs of the last pair of gloves.

'By the gods, he's strong!' the Parsinor grunted.

'Let me go!' Rug screamed. 'Leave me alone!'

His fingers stayed clenched tightly closed. Emos ripped the wool open, dragging the last shreds of material off Rug's exposed hands. But these were like no hands anyone had ever seen. Taya and Lorkrin scrambled closer for a better look, even Khassiel's cynical expression disappeared in utter amazement. Rug let out a long wail of horror.

The palms were the rusty blades of trowels, the fingers pieces of corroded chain and steel cable. Rusty wire wound around and through all of this like veins, sinews and ligaments in a macabre, metal imitation of human hands. They curled into fists and opened again as Rug screamed once more.

'This can't be me!' he sobbed. 'What's happened to me? What's happened to my body?'

'You were driven from your true body,' Emos told him, gazing into his face. 'So you made another. It's an honour to meet you, Orgarth.'

+ + + +

Nayalla clutched her chest as her husband adjusted his grip under her legs. Her wounds had been dressed with makeshift bandages torn from the miners' shirts. Myunans could will their flesh to stop bleeding and knit their skin together when the injury was not too grievous, but she was too weak from hunger and lack of rest to go far. Mirkrin was carrying her on his back now. She draped her arm over his shoulder again and rested the side of her head against the back of his, closing her eyes.

'We're going away from the door,' she muttered.

'The creature's back that way,' he replied. 'We can't go back.'

'Ah, we had it beaten.'

'You're nothing if not positive. I'll give you that.'

Noogan trudged warily ahead, the torch stretched ahead of him as far as he could hold it. The Seneschal were still up there somewhere, but facing them was marginally less frightening than tackling the lantern beast again. Behind them, Paternasse guarded the rear. Soon, the passageway became too low for them to walk upright and Mirkrin put Nayalla down and unrolled his tools. With slow, tired movements, he shaped himself into a more suitable form, shortening his legs and lengthening his body, making it wider and flatter too, until he resembled a stretcher with legs. Nayalla laughed weakly, but laid herself gratefully on his back. The group carried on up the tunnel.

'Let's stop here and have a think,' Paternasse said, finally.

He and Noogan were almost on their hands and knees. It was incredibly tiring. The two miners sat down and Mirkrin just settled where he was, with his wife still on his back. The steadily shrinking space was fraying his nerves and the temptation to close his eyes and back down the tunnel was growing ever stronger.

'The little buggers probably think we're dead,' the old man reasoned. 'But if we keep going this way, we're bound to run into them again. The thing with the lamp is hurt. It might be running scared, or it might have it in for us. We don't know. But we know it'll be more wary of us now. That doorway is the best chance we've had of getting out of here. I say we wait for a bit to see if there's any more sign of the beast and then try and get back to the door.'

'I'm up for it,' Nayalla mumbled.

'I don't know,' Noogan shook his head. 'It almost had us that time. I think we've just ticked it off. If we run into it again, it'll make mincemeat of us.'

They all looked at Mirkrin. He was quiet for a while. He did want to go back, as much to escape this shrinking tunnel as to reach the doorway again. But he thought of his wife, already injured and unable to fight and he remembered the ferocity of the animal.

'Who knows where this passage goes?' Paternasse said. 'It might be taking us right back to that monster anyway! And that beast can't be the only one down here. There must be others if the thing's to breed. We should take our chances back at the door. What choice have we got?'

Mirkrin sighed. The old man was right. There was no choice.

'All right,' he nodded.

He felt a trembling beneath his hands and looked down. The vibrations grew and in moments the whole passage was shaking violently. Cracks appeared, snaking their way down from the ceiling and up from the floor. Mirkrin rolled Nayalla onto the ground and threw himself on top of her, trying to shield her with his body. The two miners covered their heads and screamed. Pieces of stone fell from the ceiling and slabs split away from the walls, collapsing to the floor. Dust showered down over them, dousing the torches and plunging them into darkness. Around them, they heard the sound of breaking stone and then a deafening crash brought their hopes of escape to an end.

+ + + +

As the earth tremor shuddered up through the wagon's chassis, they all anxiously watched the ground ahead. Rug wrapped his arms around his body and groaned. His hands were gloved once more and he had not said a word since Emos had shown him his true nature. He had fiercely denied Emos's claim of who and what he was and would not listen to anything further. Now he curled up and cried out in pain.

'What's wrong, Rug?' Taya asked softly.

'Something hurts,' he moaned.

'Where, can I have a look?'

'It's not in any place,' he muttered. 'I just hurt all over. It started yesterday, I think. But it's getting worse.'

Emos crouched beside him.

'The problem's not here,' the Myunan told him. 'It's in your true body.'

He pointed towards Absaleth, its peak visible over the ridge of mountains that lay to the southwest.

'Think about it,' he said. 'The krundengrond's been held in your grip for thousands of years. Now all that pressure is being released all around you in a matter of days. Imagine what that must be doing to the land. And to the mountain. We can get you back there, but I have no idea how to restore your spirit. That's something you have to do yourself.'

'I don't know what you're talking about,' Rug hissed at him. 'I'm not a spirit. I'm not a mountain. I'm a man.'

'With a body of rusted metal?' Emos asked. 'Where did it come from? The mine, I'd wager. Somehow you got out into the forest, and Harsq knew it and he followed you.'

'And he thought he'd finally got rid of you when he did the second exorcism,' Taya added. 'But he only found part of you. You'd already made yourself a new body. And now they're after you again, and us with you.'

'You're out of your minds!' Rug snapped.

'You've got metal hands, for goodness' sake!' Lorkrin pointed out. 'Wake up and smell the porridge!'

'Leave me alone!'

They all fell quiet, none of them having the will to carry on the argument. In the woods around them they could feel the eyes of the clansmen watching them, waiting for permission to strike, and ahead of them the mountains rose up, their sheer sides like a wall barring the way west. To the north lay the Gluegrove Swamps. When the wind blew from that direction they could even catch the faintest whiff of swamp gas in the air. The truck wound up the hill, Cullum shifting up and down through the low gears to keep the engine from stalling. Emos looked ahead and leaned around the side of the cab to talk to the Forward-Batterer.

'The next left. Careful, it's a narrow track and not made for wagons.'

'Typical,' the Noranian sniffed.

It was a tight fit. Low boughs scraped across the top of the cab and the wheels slipped constantly to one side and the other, forcing Cullum to weave back and forth to stay on the track. With the trees crowding in so close, they all watched

uneasily for a Reisenick attack or a sudden onset of krundengrond. Very little of the afternoon sun filtered through
the thick foliage.

When they rolled out into bright daylight again, it was to
climb the last section of steep trail to a small, flat clearing
that lay before a low cave entrance in a limestone cliff face.
Taya and Lorkrin stood up excitedly. It was time to find their
parents.

As soon as Cullum had brought the vehicle to a halt,
Draegar and Khassiel jumped down and began unloading
the gear. The rock they would have to move appeared to
have been made specifically for blocking the carved-out
entrance. Like the doorway itself, it was rectangular, with
clean-cut lines, and a single, rectangular hole about the size
of a man's fist bored right through it at chest level. It was the
height of two men, at least half that across, and three paces
deep. It was cut from some kind of marbled material, which
looked like a swirling blend of metal and stone, and Emos
took little time to confirm that whatever it was, he could not
transmorph it. It must have weighed nearly as much as the
truck. It was set in grooves in the cliff face, which ran nearly
to the top of the stone and ensured that the obstruction
could not just be pulled over. It had to be drawn straight
upwards. Taya and Lorkrin watched impatiently as the others
set to work.

Jube's expertise was sorely missed. They had to work out
how to assemble the frame for the hoist by trial and error.
But Cullum and Khassiel had done enough engineering
training to recognise all the necessary parts and put them
together. For once, the Myunans were grateful for the Noranian army's thorough approach to military operations.

'This stone was held above the doorway when I stayed here,' Emos told them as they worked. 'Iron posts beneath it kept it in place. Caftelous lived in the cave inside. He used to pray to Orgarth. He said that the Tuderem had built the entrance and that Orgarth could have locked us in any time he pleased.'

'I think I can guess how,' Khassiel muttered, glancing down at the rust-stained stone at the base of the rock. She told them about what had happened to the tools used in the mines beneath Absaleth. They all looked over at Rug, who sat curled up in the rear of the wagon.

'Rust the posts to powder and down comes the door,' Draegar said. 'So even out here, you had power over iron.'

They were nearly finished assembling the hoist on the back of the truck when Draegar lifted his head and sniffed the air. Even as he did, a group of four well-armed Reisenicks emerged from the trees without a sound and walked over. Lorkrin and Taya lowered the bundle that was Great Aunt Eldrith over the tailgate and onto the ground, then sat above it with their feet dangling, ready to drop their combined weight onto it at a moment's notice.

'You know the deal, here?' Emos asked the clansmen.

'Sure do,' one answered. 'We're just spectatin' 'til Ludditch arrives. Just pretend like we're not even here.'

They spread out, each standing uncomfortably close to the rescuers without actually being in the way. Draegar glowered at them but then joined the others in finishing the hoist. When it was up, its arm high above the slab of stone, they bored holes into the rock and hammered in heavy steel pins. Khassiel climbed into the cab and reversed the wagon into position. Chains were attached to the pins and then to a

heavier chain that ran through the hoist's set of pulleys. Taya
and Lorkrin watched impatiently. It was all taking so long.
Cullum checked the whole rig over and then nodded to
Khassiel, who was now crouched by the winch controls
behind the cab.

'Go!' he shouted.

The winch was powered by the wagon's engine; Khassiel
eased it into gear. The barrel slowly rotated, taking up the
slack, the chain making a straining sound as it became tense.
The men waited, each holding a guide rope as the rock
resisted moving at first, then, achingly slowly, it grated up
along the grooves in the wall.

'Pull it all the way out!' Emos called. 'Let's not take any
chances!'

As the rock slipped out of its grooves, it swung towards
the hoist slightly. Khassiel locked the winch, disengaged it
from the engine and climbed around into the cab. Then she
shifted into gear and took off the brake, gently rolling the
vehicle forwards and pulling the stone away from the
entrance. As the Noranian took control of the winch again
and lowered the stone to the ground, Taya and Lorkrin let
out a cheer, which the Reisenicks echoed sarcastically.

'You don't want to go in there!' one exclaimed. 'There's all
sorts o' nastiness down that hole!'

Ignoring them, Emos stepped inside the cave with a lantern and had a look around. He came back out and looked at
the sky. Evening was falling, the sun already in its descent
towards the mountains.

'Draegar, you, Khassiel and Cullum stay here and set up
camp. Taya, Lorkrin and I will go in first. We'll be back
before sundown. I'll mark each section of tunnel as we

search it so that we don't double up.'

He looked over towards Rug, who was staring into the darkness of the cave from the back of the truck.

'Are you coming or not?'

'All right, now you hold up right there,' one of the clansmen said, hand on the hilt of his knife. 'Nobody's goin' down that hole without Luddtich's say so. Why don't we all sit tight and wait for him an' I'm sure he'll show you around in there hisself.'

Draegar strode over to Eldrith's dead body and kicked it, making the Reisenicks jump.

'Go away,' he growled.

They didn't move. He kicked the corpse again. Something inside gave with a dry crack.

'I can do this all night,' he said. 'And I'm going to want something soft to sit on when we get a fire going.'

The Reisenicks looked fearfully at each other. This was against everything they believed in. Nobody should mistreat the dead. At least, not the Reisenick dead. Draegar kicked the body once more.

'We might even need an arm or a leg to get the fire started,' he added.

'You're goin' ta die like the animal you are!' the nearest clansman yelled plaintively.

But the Reisenicks slowly backed away and with a few more curses and threats, they melted into the trees. Emos nodded approvingly and turned back to Rug.

'Well?'

'I'm not going in,' the gangly man replied sullenly. 'This is all some kind of ... of sick plan. You're telling me these lies so you can use me, somehow.'

Taya came up beside him and took his hand.

'It's only a mountain,' she said softly. 'You can try it out, and if you don't like it, you can always come back out again. You can come back to the village with us, if you want.'

Rug slowly climbed down and walked warily towards the entrance. He was trembling slightly.

'We'll be with you,' she said to him. 'Come on, let's go.'

They each took a lantern, Emos leading the way into the black cave. He studied the floor as they made their way in, hoping against hope that he would find tracks there, but it was a painstakingly slow business to track over solid rock and they did not have time.

The cavern inside gave way to a tunnel at the end, where a sharp corner turned down towards a junction, off which lay three branches. Mumbling an incantation, Emos pressed his finger into the wall, marking it with an arrow pointing back towards the entrance and started down the left-hand branch.

'Why are you going that way?' Rug asked.

'Because it's as good as any,' Emos replied. 'We'll check them all in turn.'

'But your family is down *here*,' Rug said, pointing at the right-hand branch.

The three Myunans looked at him.

'And how do you know that, Rug?' Emos inquired.

Rug looked uneasily at the floor. He shrugged.

'Is it 'cause you're Orgarth?' Lorkrin chirped, raising his eyebrows.

Rug shook his head, but then started up the right-hand branch without them. They shared a look and followed behind, their hopes raised by the discovery that they had the spirit of the mountain as their guide.

19 BONE STEW

Cullum changed the dressing on his leg, noting with satisfaction that the wound was healing well. Draegar too, changed his splints and bandage. He was tired and his injured leg throbbed painfully. They all kept a watch out for the Reisenicks and Draegar was careful to keep Eldrith's corpse close to hand. A fire was lit and Cullum started preparing some food as Khassiel positioned herself with her crossbow on the back of the truck, where she had the best view of the clearing. Draegar used the time to fill Cullum in on Rug's story, as he had been in the cab the whole time. Cullum snorted at the tale and, having decided that everyone had clearly gone mad, dished out the beef, rice and beans he had cooked up.

They were in the middle of their meal when they heard the sound of engines. Cullum got up to look. Draegar stayed seated and finished his food.

'I think we'd best get inside,' he told the Noranians. 'No point giving them a target, now they're here in force.'

He and Khassiel moved into the cave, bringing Great Aunt Eldrith and the most important gear with them. Cullum quickly disabled the hoist before following.

The four remaining vehicles of the Reisenick convoy came into sight, emerging from the trees and driving up the hill to pull into the clearing, surrounding the rescuers' camp. The horde of young men jumped down and took up positions around the clearing, the old relatives staying on the back of the largest truck in their comfortable chairs. A large pot was lowered down and a fire quickly set under it. The smell of reheated stew filled the air, the breeze carrying it into the cave. Two middle-aged women stirred it slowly. The Reisenicks were settling in. Ludditch jumped down from the back of the lead truck and waved at Draegar and the Noranians, but did not come any closer.

'Smells good,' Cullum commented. 'What's that meat I'm getting?'

'Bone marrow,' Draegar replied, relishing the scent. 'It's bone stew. Nobody makes it like the Reisenicks.'

+ + + +

Harsq walked up beside the chieftain.

'They're already in the cave, Ludditch. What are you going to do now?'

'We're already doin' it, Kalayal. All we have to do is wait and soon we'll be able to send all the boys in to finish the job.'

'What do you mean? What about your great aunt?'

'That's to keep *us* at bay. But *we're* not going to do any attackin', it'll all be done for us. Won't be our fault if those trespassers fall afoul of the lampheads, now will it?'

Harsq looked towards the cave.

'What's a lamphead?' he asked.

'You'll see, soon enough.'

'What makes you think your great aunt's going to be safe?'

Ludditch grinned.

''Cause the lampheads only eat freshly dead bones. They

like the marrow in 'em. And the smell of that stew is goin' to bring 'em runnin' like flies to a dung-pile!'

+ + + +

Emos stopped and sniffed the musty, still air of the cave.

'The Reisenicks are here,' he said.

'How can you tell?' Lorkrin asked.

'I smell stew,' his uncle replied. He paused and took a deep breath through his nose. 'Bone stew. Didn't take them long to start cooking.'

His expression changed; suddenly he was on his guard, casting his eyes back the way they had come.

'That cunning swine,' he muttered. 'Stay close to me. Rug, mind how you go. We might run into …'

A sound ahead of them made him stop. It was a soft, deep moan, like an animal in pain. He went quiet and they all listened carefully, but heard nothing more.

'Rug, do you know what that was?' Taya whispered.

Rug did not answer, his attention fixed on the tunnel ahead.

'It's an animal known as a Lantern Lady,' Emos told her, drawing his knife with his free hand. 'A nasty piece of work. They live in these caves, dangling a light to attract prey. We should avoid meeting it if at all possible.'

Taya and Lorkrin exchanged looks. They remembered Draegar's encounter with one of the creatures. Emos took a pouch from his pack and opened it, sprinkling some dust on each of them.

'What's this?' Taya asked.

'Bone dust,' replied her uncle. 'The smell of dead bone will put it off.'

'I can feel it,' Rug rasped. 'It's not in this tunnel. It's off to one side. We can go on.'

The passage was growing lower and every few dozen paces, it turned a corner. It would be all too easy to walk into an ambush. At one point, they came to a fork. Rug pointed up the left-hand branch.

'It's up there,' he said. 'Your family are the other way.'

Lorkrin was crouching down, his hand pressed against the ground.

'Does anybody else feel that?' he asked.

Now that he had mentioned it, they all felt it. A slight trembling carrying up through the soles of their feet. Rug put his hand to his chest and grunted.

'It's getting stronger,' he wheezed. 'It's like something's crushing me.'

'We have to hurry!' Emos exclaimed. 'Come on, man. Find them, for pity's sake. If this gets worse, the whole place could come down.'

+ + + +

Outside the cave, the Reisenicks were looking worriedly down at the ground shuddering beneath their feet. Further down the hill, they heard the sound of a tree falling, and then another one. Birds were taking to the air and animals fled through the brush.

'How we goin' ta get back home, if this stuff blocks off the way, Learup?' Spiroe asked uneasily. 'Are you sure we're safe here? I mean, you do know where it's goin' to come up, don't yuh?'

'Don't go gettin' yourself all worked up, Spiroe,' his chieftain replied. 'This is our time. If we have to go back through the Gluegroves after, we will. But we've got to see this done.'

'Don't worry, my son,' Harsq placed his hand on Spiroe's shoulder. 'As long as you are with me, you are quite safe from the krundengrond.'

Spiroe gave him a faltering smile and then threw a wary glance back at Ludditch. The last thing they needed now was for the priest to go soft in the head.

More trees fell behind them and soon they could hear the telltale rumbling of the ground at the bottom of the hill starting to pull itself apart.

'Let's have a song, Pappy!' Ludditch called. 'Somethin' with a bit o' kick in it!'

+ + + +

Cullum swore to himself as he looked out the doorway.

'Now they're bloody singin',' he said. 'The earth's comin' apart and they're having a party.'

'Will that … that krundengrond come up the hill?' Khassiel asked.

'Hard to tell,' Draegar replied. 'I've never seen it come to life like this. The soil is thin here, lying on solid rock. I would have thought it safe, but this is beyond my experience.'

'That's a comfort.'

Draegar was looking back into the cave behind them. Outside the carpet of light thrown by the rectangular entrance, he had the sense of something moving in the darkness. He did not know these caves, but his instincts told him not to trust the empty blackness. A glow appeared around the corner at the end of the cavern. He drew further inside, trying to let his eyes adjust to the gloom. At the far end, somebody turned the corner carrying a lantern, its light swaying to and fro. Cullum turned to look.

'They're back already,' he said. 'Maybe they've found them.'

'The light's wrong,' Draegar said suspiciously. He drew his sword.

Cullum nodded and raised his battle-hammer. Khassiel stared through the sights on her crossbow. The light came closer, swinging gently with the motion of the person carrying it. Behind it, they could see another one following. The glow from the nearest one illuminated what looked like the face of an old woman.

'Shoot it,' Draegar growled.

Khassiel did not hesitate. She fired a bolt straight into the old lady's forehead. There was a throaty shriek and the light went out. Something charged at them. Khassiel reloaded calmly and took aim, levelling her sights at the darkness above the sound of running feet. She fired again. The bolt struck home, but the creature kept coming. She stepped aside and Cullum moved into its path. Turning his hammer so that its spike faced forwards, he raised it and waited as the animal burst into the light. It rushed towards him and at the last moment, he sidestepped and swung his weapon with all his force at its head. The beast staggered sideways, but was still standing, despite the fact that Cullum's hammer was embedded in its brow. Draegar drove his sword into its side and twisted it back and forth. The animal gave a strangled gasp and collapsed on to the floor.

Khassiel had already put a shot into the head of the second one, but these monsters had thick skulls – it was still coming fast across the cave at them. Placing her foot in the crossbow's stirrup to hold the nose against the floor, she pulled the string back and set another bolt in place. Lifting it to her shoulder, she took aim again and this time sent a bolt through the lamp itself. The animal roared in pain, and slowed down, but then charged forwards once more, blind with rage and splashing acrid fluid from its injured sac. Cullum was on the far side of the beast which lay dying on the floor and could not get across in time. Draegar leapt forward and swung his sword low, chopping through one of the creature's legs. It shrieked and lashed out at him, knocking him backwards.

Cullum and Khassiel fell upon it with their short swords, hacking at its back and flanks. It turned awkwardly on its three remaining legs and got hold of Cullum with its powerful arms. It tried to sink its teeth into his chest, but his armour saved him. Corrosive alkali sprayed from its lamp and he shut his eyes against it. Khassiel nearly cut another of its legs clean through and it released Cullum and turned towards her, wild with pain and desperation, but badly maimed. Khassiel, faced with the animal's nearly impregnable head and shoulders, swung her sword and cut through the stalk jutting from its skull, the remains of the lamp smacking against the wall and falling to the floor. The beast let out another shriek and lunged at her. But it was stopped short. Draegar had caught hold of one of its rear legs. Khassiel cut its arms aside and stabbed her blade up into its throat. It crumpled to the ground, nearly pulling her arm with it.

'It was the stew,' Draegar panted. 'Ludditch drew them out with the smell of the bone stew. He's going to pay for that. Where's that damned aunt of his?'

Cullum grabbed the handle of his battle-hammer, putting his foot on the creature's head, and wrenched the weapon free.

Suddenly, a hail of darts came flying through the doorway.

+ + + +

Kalayal Harsq watched as one tree after another toppled, forming ever-larger gaps in the forest on the hillside. The ground shook with increasing violence, causing some of the old people's chairs to bounce alarmingly. They climbed down and sat on the bed of the wagons instead. Harsq smiled warmly at them and waved like a visiting dignitary. He looked forward to seeing his creation again, and prayed to Brask to grant it strength and speed. His disciples did not share his prayers, watching the signs of the oncoming krundengrond in terror.

'That stuff's comin' almighty close,' Spiroe moaned.

'It'll be fine,' Ludditch reassured him, looking out at the trees. But he seemed less certain now. 'Have some of the boys move the old folk around and up the side of the mountain just in case, though.'

Spiroe's eyes widened, but he did not question his chieftain. He started off to obey his order, when suddenly, the sound of some wild animal burst forth from the mouth of the cave. There came the noise of frantic battle and Ludditch whooped with triumph.

'That's it!' he bellowed. 'Now, while they're shook up! In yuh go, boys!'

Some of the clansmen had already powdered themselves with bone dust. The smell of the dead bone would deter the lampheads from attacking long enough for the hunters to net and kill them. A swarm of darts was sent shooting in the entrance of the cave and then the Reisenicks stormed inside.

The first clansman in was struck across the face with something dry, leathery and stinking of perfume. He fell back and gasped in shock as the man after him was beaten to the ground by the same weapon, Great Aunt Eldrith's disembodied arm.

The third clansman caught a hammer across the head and fell dead on the spot. They still had not made it inside, the defenders out of sight on either side of the entrance. When a fourth clansman had a sword driven into his belly, the others scrambled back and the corpse's arm was thrown out after them.

'There's plenty more left of her!' Draegar roared. 'Keep on coming, we'll give her back to you piece by piece!'

'You've gone too far!' Ludditch screamed back at them in a frenzy. 'We're comin' in, and we're goin' ta put yuh in the ground!'

'Come and get us, ya ugly, inbred, rotten-boned bunch o' mother's boys!' Cullum yelled at them. 'We're goin' ta pile you up!'

'I'm deeply sorry, Aunt Eldrith,' Ludditch muttered in trembling voice. Then, to his men: 'Boys, this hasn't worked out. If we're going to triumph today, we're goin' to have to pay a terrible price. That Orgarth's still in there and we have to get him out o' there before he finds his way home. Now, if we're goin' to serve 'im up for the priest here, we're goin' to have to catch him right quick. Are yuh with me, boys?!'

There was a chorus of raucous yells.

'Then let's get in there an' take some hides!'

In a massive rush, the Reisenicks charged the entrance of the cave. Behind them, they left their aged and crippled relatives, still cowering in the backs of the trucks.

20 A VEIN OF IRON ORE

The Myunans dug with feverish haste, pulling at the stone debris until their fingers were bruised and bleeding. Rug had led them up the steadily shrinking passage, only to find it blocked by a cave-in. Their family and the miners were trapped beneath it. Even as he had said it, another earth tremor had run through the rock and he had fallen to the ground, huddled up in agony.

Taya and Lorkrin were close to tears as they dug. To have come all this way and survived so much, only to find their parents buried like this was more than they could bear.

'Can't … can't you do something?' Taya looked at Rug, her voice broken by sobs.

Rug did not answer. He rolled onto his side and groaned.

'It's limestone,' Emos told her as he hauled a large rock aside. 'He can't affect limestone. Come on, keep going. They could still be alive.'

They found a space at the top of the pile and made it bigger. Taya crawled up into it and slunched, squeezing in.

'Ma? Pa?' she cried. 'Can you hear me?'

There was no reply. She dragged herself further in.

'Ma! Pa!'

From ahead of her came a muffled reply. Rocks were pulled away and a hand reached out of the darkness. It was her father's.

'We're here, love,' a distant voice said. 'We're all right.'

She burst out crying and kissed his hand, holding it to her face.

'They're here!' she called back, torn between laughing and sobbing.

There was a good way still to dig. The four of them had been trapped in a tiny air pocket under a slab that had fallen in from one wall and wedged against the other. Mirkrin had stretched his arm out to several paces in length in order to reach his daughter. But with both parties digging from their ends, they soon cleared a crawlspace large enough for the miners to fit through. Dusty and dirty, they all hugged and laughed and cried when Mirkrin, the last one, finally crawled through. Even Rug was able to stand well enough to join in the joyous occasion.

'We're not out of the woods yet,' Emos said wearily. 'And I mean that literally. Let's start walking and we'll tell you all about it.'

He gave Rug a concerned look.

'This is as far in as we can go for now,' the Myunan told him. 'But you should find a clear tunnel and keep going. This is where you belong.'

'I'll come back with you, if that's all right,' Rug murmured.

Emos was visibly disappointed. He picked up his lantern and the whole group started down the passage, having to bend over to keep their heads from hitting the ceiling. Nay-alla was able to walk with Mirkrin's support, but Noogan was reduced to hopping on a freshly broken ankle, leaning on Paternasse's shoulder for balance. Before long, the tunnel became high enough for them to stand upright and their walking became more comfortable. Echoes of a tumultuous fight carried to their ears. They were approaching another corner, when an acrid smell pervaded the air and Rug stiffened.

'That animal. It's right there,' he said hoarsely.

'I can smell it,' Nayalla said. 'We've run into this thing before.'

'We injured it,' Mirkrin added. 'But it's far from beaten. We might just have made it angry.'

There was a low, hackle-raising growl and Mirkrin pulled out his knife, letting Nayalla lean against the wall. Emos and Paternasse also put up their guards, blades at the ready.

'Lorkrin, Taya,' Nayalla said. 'Get behind me, now.'

'We're not babies, Ma …' Lorkrin began, but then there was a roar and the beast came around the corner at a furious charge.

It swept Emos aside and piled into Mirkrin, closing its jaws around his shoulder and driving him backwards. Paternasse was caught behind him in the narrow tunnel and staggered back against the wall. Emos's lantern dropped and smashed, spreading burning oil across the floor. Mirkrin screamed as the animal's teeth sank in. The creature tossed him to the floor, puzzled by the lack of solid bone in his body. The Myunan cried out in pain as it tried his foot instead, but again it found no bones. Nayalla and Emos attacked its sides with their knives, but it violently crushed one and then the other against the wall with the sheer weight of its body. Taya and Lorkrin only narrowly managed to drop to the floor out of its way. It advanced on Paternasse, who scrambled backwards. Mirkrin grabbed his shoulders and pulled, but it was no use. The beast seized the old miner's leg and bit into it, dragging him down the passage, thrashing to free him from the Myunan's grip. It shoved past Taya and Lorkrin and they tried to hold on to the old man's hands, but they could not stop the creature's retreat. Paternasse screamed.

Lorkrin looked at his sister.

'Draegar used ...'

'... his lantern,' she finished for him.

Lorkrin swung his lamp underarm and threw it past the beast. It shattered behind it, against the wall at the corner and exploded in flames. The animal shied away from the fire, frightened by the sudden heat. It dropped Paternasse with a frustrated snarl and turned on them instead. Taya hurled her lantern at its head and the beast knocked it out of the air with one clawed hand, but the lamp still broke, spilling burning oil over it. It bellowed with pain but did not stop. It was almost upon them when a long pair of thin arms reached out and seized its flaming head.

'Run!' Rug shouted at them. 'Run, all of you!'

The flames were starting to go out as the creature crashed against one wall and then the other, trying to break Rug's grip. Nayalla and Mirkrin grabbed Noogan, and Emos stumbled forward, pushing Taya and Lorkrin past the pair of struggling bodies. Together, they helped Paternasse up.

'We can't leave Rug!' Taya cried.

'His body doesn't matter!' Emos gasped, still trying to get his breath back after being crushed against the wall. 'It can't hurt him, but it can kill you! Now go!'

She looked back in distress, but Rug stared back at her.

'Run!' he yelled.

And they did, rushing through the dying flames that flickered over the wall and floor and stumbling down the passage as fast as their injuries would allow. They lost sight of

Rug when they turned the corner, but the beast's snarls followed them far into the darkness. With only one lantern left, they were soon forced to slow down. The ground shook, constantly knocking them off balance. Over the rumbles and dull cracks of the rock around them, the noise of battle reached them.

'Something's gone wrong,' Emos said, grimly. 'Wait here.'

Leaving the lantern with them, he ran ahead, reaching the three branching tunnels and treading carefully down the last tunnel to the cave entrance. As he went, he changed his colours to meld in with the surroundings. There, just before the corner where the passage turned in to the cavern, Draegar, Khassiel and Cullum were making a last stand against the Reisenicks.

The clansmen were having to climb over their own dead and injured to reach the defenders. The fight was close and brutal, with Draegar standing in the centre, dealing death in quick, accurate strokes of his sword and the two Noranians covering his sides. The corner in the passage meant the Reisenicks had to get close before they saw their opponents, so they could not use their blowpipes. Khassiel had swapped her crossbow for her short sword and was proving she was equally skilled with both. Cullum, too, had switched to the close-quarters weapon and was wielding his blade with battle-crazed fury.

'Wow,' Lorkrin gasped.

Emos turned in annoyance and saw both the children and their parents standing behind him, also in camouflage, all with their knives drawn.

'When I said wait there …'

'It's our fight too,' Nayalla cut him short. 'We're not getting stuck back in those caves again. The children can stay back here, but we're keeping them close.'

Emos nodded.

Taya and Lorkrin watched their father, mother and uncle shed their camouflage and march down the tunnel to join the fight.

'I'm not staying here,' Lorkrin said defiantly.

'Yes, you bloody are,' his sister retorted.

Lorkrin looked up at the cave roof, which was making alarming, grinding noises.

'The miners,' Taya said urgently.

They sprinted back to where Noogan and Paternasse were lying beyond the junction. Noogan was trying to get to his feet, looking anxiously at the ceiling as dust and fragments of rock showered down around him. Paternasse had passed out.

'Things are a bit mad up at the entrance,' Taya told the young miner. 'But I don't think we can wait around. Can you walk?'

'I can bloody well hop if I have to. Can you help me with Jussek?'

'You hop along,' Lorkrin replied. 'We'll take him.'

Noogan watched with weary amusement as the two children hoisted Paternasse up into a sitting position, then each sucked their stomach right in to create a cradle to support an upper arm, which they then slunched down around. With the weight of his upper body hung on their hips, they proceeded to haul the old man down the passageway. Noogan chuckled and hobbled along after them.

+ + + +

The beast had won. Rug was thrown to the ground and he

grunted with the impact as the creature tore his thick layers of clothes open. He was surprised to find that it did not hurt when it plunged its jaws into his chest and tried to pull his insides out. Instead, the monster squealed in pain and stumbled backwards, spitting blood. Rug looked down at what the creature had uncovered.

His insides were a tangled mass of rusted metal. Old mining tools, barbed wire, steel cable, even nuts, bolts and nails were woven together to form his gangly body. The beast had dragged some of it out, but it did not hurt in the least. Not like the pain he was feeling from the land going insane outside the mountain. The scarf fell away and he put his hands to his face. Two pieces of broken glass sat where his eyes should have been. His nose was a folded hinge, his jaws made from rusted riding stirrups. He sat up and gathered in his metal guts as best he could, tucking them into his torn clothes and fastening what was left of the buttons.

Standing up, he stared at the creature, which glared balefully back at him. He noticed it had some nails caught in its gums and teeth.

'I'm going to make sure those really hurt,' he told it.

The monster backed away, then turned and ran. Rug watched it go, in the last light of the flames. When the light went out, he realised he could still see. He corrected himself, he did not need to see. The world shook around him and he steadied himself against the wall. The release of the krundengrond was tearing the land apart. It was time for him to go home.

He strode back up the tunnel to where the cave-in had trapped the Myunans and their friends. There he climbed up the pile of debris and crawled through to the flat slab of limestone that had protected the survivors. In the cavity it had left in the wall, he reached in and found what he knew would be there. A vein of iron ore. This was where, millions of years ago, when Absaleth lay at the bottom of the sea, the ridge of limestone mountains had formed against its side. He remembered it well. This was where the limestone ended and the iron began. He felt its hard, cold texture under his fingers. Rug's body slumped onto the rocky debris, the rusted metal beneath his clothes suddenly lifeless and still.

+ + + +

The Reisenicks had withdrawn to rethink their plan of attack. More than a score of their number were dead, and nearly two dozen others badly wounded. Draegar leaned wearily against the wall and closed his eyes. Cullum flopped to the floor, exhausted. The Myunans, their eyes extended like a snail's, peered around the corner to keep watch.

'Something's got to give,' Cullum wheezed, pulling off his helmet and wiping his brow. 'We can't keep this up forever.'

He looked towards Khassiel and saw that she was trying to unbuckle her armour. Her face was deathly pale and blood was pooling on the ground by her side.

'Khass?'

'Damned, double-jointed freak got a blade into me,' she gasped.

Cullum scrambled forward and helped her take off the ornacrid shell, pulling up her tunic to look at the wound. His expression told her all she needed to know.

'Ah, bowels,' she moaned.

Emos knelt by her side. The flow of blood was already slowing, but he pressed his hand against the wound.

'You'll make it,' he said to her, urgently. 'You'll be all right.'

'He's right,' Cullum reassured her. 'It's not too bad.'

'Don't be so bloody soft,' she grunted. And then she died, her last breath a hollow gurgle.

They all stared at her limp body in morbid silence.

Lorkrin and Taya crouched further down the tunnel, at a safe distance from the fighting, but close enough to watch the Noranian die. For the first time, they wondered if they would get out of the cave alive. The rock was continuing to tremble around them and in the darkness beyond the light of their lantern, they heard masses of stone collapsing into the tunnels.

'We have to get outside,' Nayalla breathed.

'Right,' Cullum muttered, as he used Khassiel's helmet to cover her face. 'Let us know when they surrender.'

Suddenly, a jolt passed through the ground and moments later, a section of the roof crashed in, sending a cloud of dust over them. They all stared upwards in desperation. Cracks snaked out across the stone ceiling, dust raining down in light sprinkles like the first leaks in a dam about to burst.

'Oh, no,' Nayalla whispered.

'Go!' Draegar bellowed, picking up Paternasse's inert body and charging out of the tunnel. The Noranians followed close behind.

Taya and Lorkrin grabbed Noogan and half-led, half-dragged him over the Reisenick bodies and around the corner. Mirkrin and Nayalla stumbled out after them, frantically trying to get ahead of their children. Behind them, the tunnel collapsed with a tremendous roar of breaking stone.

The Reisenicks were waiting. Draegar was ensnared in a

net, ropes winding around him to bind it closed, the clansmen falling on him and beating him with rocks. Cullum was
caught too, and thrown to the floor, struggling violently to
cut through the mesh before their blades finished him off.
Mirkrin and Nayalla were knocked off their feet by three
snarling men, falling under their attackers, and fighting back
wildly as they tried to reach their children.

Lorkrin and Taya scrambled forwards, still trying to support Noogan. They stopped short when Ludditch stepped in
front of them. He smiled grimly and raised his knife.

'Your uncle's goin' tuh see your insides before I take his
skin!'

The Myunans' fear turned to disbelief when they saw the
blade. Rust was crawling up the steel like a swarm of ants.
Ludditch saw their faces and glanced down at his weapon.
He dropped it in shock and as it hit the floor, it shattered into
pieces, corroded right through.

Around them, the Reisenicks were finding their knives disintegrating in their hands and they cried out in fright.

'Ludditch,' someone near the door shouted. 'The old folk
are caught!'

He grabbed the two Myunans by the necks, pulling them
away from Noogan, and dragged them with him to the doorway. They punched and kicked, scratched and bit him, but
he paid them no mind. When they reached the entrance,
they were stunned by what they saw.

The land was erupting outside the cave. The last light of
evening was fading, but even so, they could see that most of
the trees on the slope had disappeared, the ground where
they had stood churning like a stormy sea. The clay of the
clearing was breaking apart. Harsq's disciples were backing

towards the cave, staring in abject terror as the edge of the krundengrond crept closer and closer, the clay pulling asunder and writhing with a force that cracked stones and swallowed everything that stood upon it. The wagons were being dragged down into the ground and torn apart.

On the back of the largest truck, Harsq stood with the old Reisenicks, his hands raised in the air. They had been cut off, the krundengrond coming up from beneath them; there was nowhere to run, even if their stiff, arthritic legs could have carried them.

'The blessed ground will not harm us!' he intoned. 'We need only pray to the almighty Brask and he will protect us. The land is our ally, our friend. There is nothing to fear if we all pray together!'

The wagon sank lower in the earth, its wheels buckled and disappeared with the tortured sound of rending metal. A lantern fell from the side, but instead of smashing, it disappeared into the ground with barely a burst of flame. Ludditch's aged relatives screamed and held each other as the vehicle tipped to one side.

'Have no fear!' Harsq shouted to them. 'We must all pray and Brask will deliver salvation. Pray to Brask for your lives!'

His voice was faltering, his face drenched in sweat. Ludditch ran out as far as the edge of the krundengrond, hauling the two struggling Myunans with him, a despairing moan escaping from his lips. His father was on that wagon.

'Pappy!' he wailed. 'Pappy, hold on!'

But the wagon's back broke, the chassis was ripped apart and the two halves tilted into the air. Harsq tumbled over the side and hit the ground. It came up to embrace him and with a shriek he was gone. Two more men fell in and were swallowed whole by the churning earth. Ludditch watched as his father slipped down the upturned flatbed and rolled, flailing into the krundengrond. The last lantern on the truck went out and the vehicle was plunged into shadow. They could hear the others on board calling desperately for help. Ludditch let out a sob and shoved Taya and Lorkrin aside, launching himself out over the seething ground. He managed one step, then another. By the third, he was caught and was being pulled in. He reached out for where his father had fallen and howled into the evening sky with grief.

And then the earth around him went still. He heaved sobbing breaths, putting his hands down to push against the ground, which was up to his waist, solid and motionless. The krundengrond was losing its force. The violence of the earth receded into the darkness, stillness settling over the ground and the noise gradually dropping away to silence. In the eerie quiet that followed, Taya and Lorkrin walked out past where the Reisenick chieftain stood, his legs embedded in the ground. They gazed around them. Lorkrin jumped up and down as Taya looked at her feet, twisting her toes in the clay. The krundengrond was gone.

Many of the old folk were still alive on the wood-and-metal island that was all that remained of the wagon. They called out fearfully for their kin. Seeing the two Myunans walking safely on the earth, the Reisenicks rushed out to their family, helping them down and hugging and kissing them passionately.

'He made it, then,' Taya said.

Lorkrin nodded. Rug had found his way home.

EPILOGUE

The Reisenicks made no more trouble for the Myunans and their friends, leaving them alone to tend their wounds. Cullum was able to retrieve Khassiel's body from beneath the rubble and insisted on burying her alone. He marked the grave with her crossbow. They all paid their respects and then turned their attention to making camp, none of them fit for anything but sleep.

It was some time before any of the Reisenicks bothered to dig Ludditch out. He stood there, staring at the ground, not saying a word, until Spiroe came over with a shovel and sourly freed his legs. The Reisenicks set out for home on foot as the moon·came up, the younger men supporting or carrying their aged relatives, others bearing their dead and injured on makeshift stretchers. Ludditch followed behind, unable to endure the bitter, hateful stares of his clan.

Lorkrin and Taya were the last to fall asleep. They lay gazing up at the cliff face, exhausted but eager now to return to the Myunan Territories, both wanting to look up at the face of Absaleth again. Eventually, they too drifted off into a deep, healing sleep.

They all slept late into the following morning. Draegar was the first to wake. He salvaged what was left of their supplies from the cave and the rest woke to the welcome smells of breakfast being fried up. There was a chorus of groans and grunts as all their injuries made themselves felt, but seeing what a sorry sight they were gave them all something to laugh at.

'It's a long walk home,' Emos said, as they tucked into their food. 'And I think a visit to old Shindles wouldn't go amiss. We're a right state, altogether.'

'Look at that,' Noogan gestured with his head, his mouth full of bacon. 'I've never seen the like.'

On the hillside below them, what looked like freshly ploughed land stretched out, littered with the remains of rocks, trees and grass.

'Wonder what's happened back at the mining camp?' Paternasse mused. 'If it's anything like this, I think I might be heading back home to the wife and kids.'

'I think there's going to be lot of grief coming out of this,' Emos said, solemnly.

'At least the view's changed,' Lorkrin commented. 'I was getting sick and tired of trees.'

'It's the ugliest landscape I've ever seen,' Nayalla said. 'But I love the sight of it. Anything's better than being stuck down in that cave.'

'We owe our lives to you all,' Mirkrin said, looking at their rescuers, and smiling proudly at his children. 'And I think you two are going to get spoiled rotten when we get home.'

'Does this mean we can have our tools back?' Taya asked.

'Absolutely,' Nayalla grinned.

'And will you teach us how to sculpt feathers?' Lorkrin put in.

'I think we might be able to do something about that.'

'And a dog. Can we get a *dog*?' Taya added, excitedly.

'Don't push your luck, young lady.'

As their children put their heads together to plan how to make the most of this new opportunity, Mirkrin and Nayalla touched hands and smiled in happiness and relief. Draegar looked out over the devastated land, wondering how long it would take to heal and what maps would have to change. Cullum spared a glance for his dead comrade's grave. The miners were lost in thoughts about the friends who hadn't made it and their own victories over death. Emos stood up, stretching his stiff legs, his eyes fixed on the dark entrance to the cave.

'Will you tell us more about Orgarth some time, Uncle Emos?' Taya asked, seeing the distant expression on his face.

'I'll tell you all I know about the legends,' he replied, giving her a subdued smile. 'But you two probably know the real Orgarth better than anyone now – you've become part of his history. Some day somebody will tell stories about you.'

'Damned straight,' Draegar exclaimed. 'That'd be worth a good tankard of mead in anyone's storyhouse! Pass the last of that sausage, if nobody's having it.'

They finished their breakfast and relaxed for the rest of that day, eating and drinking and talking. If felt good to be safe, with full stomachs and true friends and to know that they had played a part – if only for a short time – in a great mountain's history.

Vol. 1 The Archisan Tales

The harvest tide project
Oisín McGann

Taya and Lorkrin are Myunans –
shape-changers who can sculpt
their flesh like modelling clay.
They accidentally release Shessil
Groach, a timid botanist working in captivity on the top-secret
Harvest Tide Project. A massive
manhunt is launched by the sinister Noranian Empire, which

will stop at nothing to protect its Project. With the
help of a scent-seller, a barbarian map-maker and
their Uncle Emos, the teenagers and Groach keep
one step ahead of the Noranians, while they try to
find a way to sabotage the Harvest Tide Project
and avert the disaster it will unleash …

Paperback €7.95/STG£5.99